REIGN OF FOUR

BOOKS III & IV

JAKE BIBLE

A PERMUTED PRESS BOOK

ISBN: 978-1-61868-538-4

Reign of Four:
Book III and Book IV
© 2016 by Jake Bible
All Rights Reserved

Cover art by Dean Samed, Conzpiracy Digital Arts

PERMUTED
PRESS

Permuted Press, LLC
permutedpress.com

Published in the United States of America

REIGN OF FOUR

BOOK III

ACT I

A GIRL, A WOMAN, A MISTRESS

"*There had never been a monarch the likes of Alexis the Third of Station Aelon.*"
    —Dr. D. Reven, Eighty-Third Archivist of The Way

"*Woman shall be under the protection of Man for woman is the weaker of the species and must be shielded from the harshness of life. While Helios protects all, the Dear Parent has granted the job of true protection over woman to the Fathers, the Husbands, the Brothers.*"
    —Book of Telling 14:6, The Ledger

"*If they do not see me as fit then I cannot guess as to what they define as fit. Even ripe with child I could best half the Royal Guard by myself. In fact, I shall look at my calendar and see when I can arrange that.*"
    —Journals of Alexis the Third, Mistress of Station Aelon and its Primes

CHAPTER ONE

The pain of the landscape gnawed at Alexis's heart.

It wasn't the ever present Vape clouds that hung over Aelon Prime like a shroud of impenetrable despair. It wasn't the churning gas sea that she'd had to cross to get to the lands of her birthright. It wasn't the winds that tore at the environmental suit she wore like the grasping, desperate fingers of lepers looking for a messiah to heal them. It wasn't even the fact that the breen harvest had already happened and the land before her looked even more barren than usual, despite the healthy clumps of scrim grass that moved in to take the crops' place.

It was that what had once been a beautiful, if rustic, royal estate house for Family Teirmont, had been reduced to nothing but ash with some teetering scorched walls and airlock entrances. The place had been her home once, but then it became her prison, and finally it became her father's grave.

She stood in front of the royal skids and their deep shadows covered her, but they held no more darkness than what was already in Alexis's soul. Her eyes betrayed her by allowing the scene to penetrate her mind and she hated them for it. If she hadn't been a girl of immense self-control she would have ripped her traitorous eyes from their sockets without a second thought.

"It will have to be completely razed," Bella said as she placed her hand on her daughter's environmental suit-covered shoulder. "We'll rebuild from the dirt up, Alexis. The tragedy that befell this place will no longer be. A fresh start is what we'll have, my daughter. A fresh start."

Alexis—blonde, fair skinned, and already taller than her mother even at the young age of fourteen—turned her attention away from the burned out husk of the old Aelon Prime royal estate house and studied her mother, the Mistress Bella Herlict Teirmont Beumont of Station Aelon and Minoress of Station Thraen. Their eyes were separated by two helmets and the poisonous air of Planet Helios, yet there was an almost physical spark of connection between the two. Mother and daughter, daughter and mother, forever bound by more than just genetics, but by a primal, ancient understanding of what it meant to be a woman in a system controlled by men. Yet, even with that understanding, Alexis held nothing but contempt in her gaze.

"Why has it been a year?" Alexis asked her mother while a contingent of Aelish royal guards set out from the skids to secure the area from any threats. "Father died here a year ago, Mother. Why wait this long to bring me down here?"

"Because of your grief," Bella stated, her hand moving from her daughter's shoulder, down her arm and into Alexis's hand. She gave it a quick squeeze, but when the gesture wasn't reciprocated she let go and tried to smile. "You needed time to grieve the horrible passing of your father and also to get used to your new duties as Mistress of Station Aelon."

"I am hardly the mistress," Alexis replied as she stepped from the skids' shadows, her environmental suit rustling in the steady wind that blew across Aelon Prime. "Your greedy husband has seen to that."

"He is not just my husband, Alexis; he is your step-father and Regent of Station Aelon," Bella replied as she hurried to keep up with her long-legged daughter. "You will show him respect even when it is only you and me talking."

Alexis sighed as she walked through the barely standing main airlock entrance at the front of the ruins. Her hand ran across the threshold and she didn't even flinch as the archway nearly toppled, but miraculously managed to keep its balance and stay upright.

"Your Highness!" a guard called out as he rushed forward from his place deep in the scorched husk. "You should not be in here! The engineers have not signed off on its safety!"

"I lived here," Alexis said. "For three years, I lived here. Even when it stood solid and whole there was no safety, so why should I care about it now?"

The guard stopped and looked past Alexis to Bella as the older woman finally caught up.

"Mistress, please explain to Her Highness the dangers—" the guard began.

"I have, guard," Bella said. "But she is the Mistress of Station Aelon and this is her prime. I could no more hold her back than I could stop a Vape storm from spreading its malice across Helios."

"Don't be melodramatic," Alexis said as she turned and frowned at her mother. "You speak of me as if I am a force of nature when I am not."

"You are a fourteen year old girl who holds the crown of one of the most powerful stations in the System of Helios," Bella laughed. "If you were to look in The Way's directory under 'force of nature' there would be a picture of you, my daughter."

Alexis rolled her eyes and turned back to the guard. "What's your name?"

"Jex, Your Highness," the guard replied. "Jex Lemnt."

"Lemnt?" Bella asked. "Is that not Flaenian?"

"It is, my lady," Jex replied. "My parents were Flaenian, but came over to Station Aelon before I was born. I am Aelish by birth, if not fully by blood."

"Are your parents still alive?" Alexis asked.

"Alexis, don't be rude," Bella said. "Leave the young man be. You don't need to pry into his personal life."

"I asked; I want to know," Alexis replied, her focus still on the young guard. "Your parents?"

"No, Your Highness," Jex replied. "My father died during the troubles between Alexis II and the meeting of stewards. My mother passed just last year."

"Last year," Alexis nodded. "It was not a good year for me either."

"No, Your Highness, it was not," Jex said.

"She does not need your agreement on that, guard," Bella stated and waved her hand at the young man. "Go about your duty and secure the area with the others. Leave us in private so we may talk without interruption. Alexis, change your com channel to Royal Private, please."

"No," Alexis said as she walked up to Jex and grabbed his arm as he was turning away. He flinched and looked down at the mistress's hand. "I am sorry for your loss, Jex. Both of them. Please know that I understand the pain."

"Alexis!" Bella snapped. "Do not touch a guard that way! It is well outside the rules of decorum!"

Alexis turned her head, but still held Jex, and laughed. "Decorum, Mother? Is that really your argument?" Her eyes trailed about the burnt ruins. "This is a place where you should never use that word. Or have you forgotten how I found you and step-daddy the night I was almost assassinated?"

"Hush, child," Bella exclaimed. "And change your com channel this instant."

"I won't," Alexis said as she looked back at Jex. "I prefer my guards to hear my voice and know my thoughts. They'll be better able to protect me that way. I will keep my com on Royal Open. . .for my protection."

Alexis looked down at her hand on Jex's environmental suit and gave his arm a firm squeeze before letting go. Jex bowed low and turned to leave.

"How old are you, Jex?" Alexis asked.

"Twenty-one, Your Highness," Jex nodded.

"Twenty-one? That's forever away for me," Alexis laughed. "I'm only fourteen. Can you believe it? Fourteen. I feel forty, though. I'm afraid I skipped my youth somewhere between taking the crown from my father and learning of his death. But, I'll be fifteen next month and perhaps my youth will be returned as a birthday gift. Do you think that is possible, Jex? That Helios, our Dear Parent, will see fit to give me some joy and youthful fun for my birthday?"

"I could never speak for Helios," Jex said as he bowed his head. "I am only a royal guard, not a gatekeeper. They would be better suited to speak on that, Your Highness."

He put his hand on Alexis's and gently removed her grip from his arm.

"If you will allow me, my lady, I must continue my duty and search the area for threats," Jex said, the fear on his face evident as he took the bold move to touch a royal. He held her hand until she nodded, then he let it go. "Thank you, Your Highness."

"Don't go far, Jex," Alexis said as the guard turned and started to walk away. "I'd prefer it if you kept an eye on me. One orphan looking out for another."

Jex slowed and looked back over his shoulder. "I will stay close, Your Highness."

"Mistress Alexis," Alexis said. "I prefer to hear my name when addressed, please. It reminds me of where I came from."

"Of course, Mistress Alexis," Jex replied and bowed deeply. "It is my honor to say your name."

"Oh, please," Bella said. "Go, guard. This whole scene is making me ill. Do your duty and let me be with my daughter."

Jex bowed again and then hurried from their presence.

"That was rude," Alexis said.

"Your treating him like he is more than your servant is rude," Bella replied. "You are too familiar with our subjects, Alexis. You speak to your handmaidens as if they were your cousins, the cook as if he was your oldest friend, and the guards as if you were their sister. Please stop. It shows your immaturity and youth. If you are to take full control of the crown when you are eighteen then you must act like a ruler and monarch now or you will not be respected then."

"Eighteen," Alexis scoffed. "A lifetime away. And two years past my legal right to take the crown."

"Yes, well, do not bring that up tonight when we dine with the High Guardian," Bella said as she stepped between the refuse of the ruins, her feet carefully placed so she did not trip and fall into the ashes and long dead coals. "Jackull has worked hard to keep the High Guardian happy with a woman being mistress of station. If you anger the man then he will more than likely withdraw his support, which could nullify your right to the crown."

"He can try," Alexis said. "But I don't think the man has the nuts for it."

"Alexis!" Bella snapped. "You blaspheme!"

Alexis sighed, rolled her eyes, scrunched her shoulders and then stuck out her tongue. "Blah, blah, blahspheme, Mother. The High Guardian wouldn't risk losing the kickbacks and bribes that step-daddy pays him. How else would he pay for his gelberry wine colonics and commoner whores?"

"Oh, dear Helios, I have borne a monster unto this plane," Bella grumbled. "Where did you hear those horrible things from?"

"The royal guards," Alexis smiled. "And my handmaidens and the cook. It's funny what people will admit they have heard and are thinking when they believe you to be their friend. Even more amazing is what they tell you when you actually are their friend."

Alexis walked off without another word and made her way deeper into the ruins while her mother was left to stand there, jaw hanging open and eyes wide.

*

The pile of melted glass was hard to miss. Alexis knelt down to study it as it caught the dim light from the Vape clouded sky above. Gelberry wine bottles. There had to be several dozen of them all fused together from the heat.

"Oh, Papa," Alexis whispered. "Was this what your last days were like?"

"They were worse," a voice sighed from behind her.

Alexis jumped up and spun about, her eyes went wide with fear as she stared at her late father. He stood before her, without an environmental suit, and held out his arms.

"Hello, sweet little one," he said. "I have waited for you."

"Papa?" Alexis asked, her legs shaking and close to collapse. "But. . .you're dead."

"Yes, my love, I am," the apparition of her father said. "But this planet has a way of bringing us back. You are very much like your grandfather, my father, but you are also very much like me. I didn't know my true self until the day before I died."

"Papa, who killed—" Alexis began to ask.

"That is not what I am here to talk about, not now," the apparition said. "I am here so that you will always trust in your instincts, always trust in your destiny, and always trust in fate."

"In fate?" Alexis asked.

"That guard, the one you spoke to earlier," the apparition continued. "What was his name?"

"Jex," Alexis answered.

"Yes, him," the apparition nodded. "He is part of your fate. Intertwined in ways you cannot begin to see. Keep him close, Alexis. Keep him by your side. He will never let you down."

"I. . .I. . . ." Alexis stuttered.

"No matter what your mother tries to tell you, your instincts are what matter," the apparition continued. "They will keep you on your path, keep you connected to fate."

"Papa, I don't understand," Alexis said.

"There is no need to," the apparition laughed. "Understanding is just an excuse to disagree with fate. Don't think too hard about it all. Be aware, be constantly awake and aware, but never let understanding get in the way of doing what fate wants. I know more than anyone how that ends."

Alexis stood there and stared at her father's ghost, studied every line on his face, they way he stood, the way he watched her.

"I have gone mad, haven't I?" Alexis asked. Finally.

The apparition grinned so wide that his face was taken over entirely by the beaming smile.

"Dear one, you are a Teirmont," the apparition laughed. "You were born mad! It is our curse. Some say the Teirmont rage, that legendary temper, is our burden, but it is not. Pure, unadulterated, unfettered madness is our burden. So, embrace it, sweetheart. Make it yours and rule from a throne of madness that is filled with joy, and emotion, and love, and compassion, and a never swaying belief that fate knows what is best."

"I don't think Mother would like me to rule that way," Alexis sighed.

"Yes, well, you are not your mother, are you?" the apparition replied. "And you never will be. Watch her, Alexis. She thinks she has power, but she only has what the meeting allows. The same can be said for you. The meeting is not your ally, whether of the stewards or the passengers. You must find your own allies. Trust in fate."

He started to turn and walk off.

"Oh, and no matter what your mother says, I am very real," the apparition grinned.

"Papa, I'd like to—" Alexis started but stopped as she realized the vision of her father was suddenly no longer there, only empty air.

"Your Highness?" a guard asked as he stepped around the ruins and came upon her. "Are you alright?"

"Yes, I am fine," Alexis said, feeling like it was the truth for the first time in her short life. "That guard. . .Jex? Yes, Jex. Do you know where he is?"

"I do not, Your Highness," the guard replied. "Shall I find him for you?"

"Yes, please," Alexis nodded. "I believe I need to speak to him as soon as possible."

*

"There they are! My beautiful ladies!" Regent Jackull Beumont exclaimed as he watched Alexis and Bella enter the wide banquet room. "I was beginning to worry that you'd fallen ill on your excursion to Aelon Prime."

"We are fair and fine, my love," Bella said as she hurried to her husband and gave him a solid kiss on the cheek then a quick one on the lips. "But we doddled longer than I would have liked, so I apologize we are late for dinner."

"It is not I you should apologize to," Beumont said as he turned and bowed to their host. "Your Grace, may I present my wife, Mistress Bella Herlict Teirmont Beumont of Station Aelon. And, of course, this is the true Mistress of Station Aelon, my step-daughter Alexis Teirmont the Third."

The High Guardian stood from his massive chair at the head of the dining table and held out his hand. Bella curtsied and hurried over to him, took his hand, kissed it six times, then backed away six steps before standing upright.

"It is my honor, High Guardian, and I apologize we have not met face to face before this," Bella said as she took her place next to her husband.

"You have been busy, my lady," the High Guardian replied, his eyes lingering on Bella for only a second before he turned his attention to Alexis.

The man was tall, thin, and fairly young for his position as the pontiff and leader of The Way. The Way was not only the spiritual and religious order that guided the inhabitants of System Helios, but it controlled all ingress and egress onto planet Helios, so that only by The Way's permission could stations remove their harvested breen and mined Vape gas to the stations for use and trade.

The High Guardian was considered the most powerful man in the System and it was that man that locked eyes with Alexis. Then he turned his attention to what hung from a wide bejeweled belt cinched around the mistress's waist and over her elaborate gown. He shook his head and smiled.

"Is there really a need for weapons at dinner, Mistress Alexis?" the High Guardian asked. "Surely you do not think me a threat or potential assassin?"

"I think everyone a threat and potential assassin," Alexis replied as she curtsied and then placed a hand each on the hilts of her two short blades. "It is why I am alive to be the kept monarch that I am."

"Oh, my!" the High Guardian laughed as he sat down and gestured for the rest to do so as well. "She is as cheeky as you said she would be, Jackull! How refreshing not to have a master, or mistress in this case, suck up to me like a sycophantic bog toady. I can't stand those that think flattery is how you win my favor."

The pontiff's eyes hardened as he looked at Beumont, and no one at the dining table missed the dig.

"Alexis, we have spoken about you wearing blades to official functions," Beumont growled, his teeth gritted and lips nearly pressed together. "Our royal guards are more than capable of keeping you safe."

"Not to mention my Burdened," the High Guardian added. "The most highly trained fighting force in the System. They have been chosen and ordained by Helios, the Dear Parent, to serve The Way and all that we in turn serve. No harm can come to you as long as you are under my protection, child."

"First, not a child," Alexis said. "Second—"

"Alexis!" Bella snapped. "Not here, not now. Sit and be polite."

Alexis started to reply then just nodded to her mother. She pulled the blades from their sheaths and the blood-red armor clad men of the Burdened that lined the walls of the banquet hall did the same and hurried forward.

"Relax," Alexis said casually, not impressed with the show of force. "I can't sit with these things still on me, now can I? Not in this costume, at least."

The Burdened stopped as the High Guardian snapped his fingers. The man snapped his fingers once again and they returned to their posts along the walls.

Alexis set her blades on either side of her dinner plate, like two massive pieces of cutlery then looked down the long table at the High Guardian.

"You don't mind if I set these here, do you Your Holiness? I like to have them on hand in case the meat is tough and I need to carve it quickly," Alexis smiled.

"My Helios," Bella whispered as she lowered her head, her eyes cast askew at her daughter. "You will have us executed before dessert."

"No, please, please," the High Guardian laughed. "If my chef overcooks the shaow shank I have requested then I may borrow one of those blades myself and teach him a lesson in culinary technique."

This received a sincere grin from Alexis and she bowed her head towards the amused pontiff. "Thank you, Your Holiness. I appreciate the hospitality and the kindness."

"Of course," the High Guardian replied. "It is not every day, or any day really, that I get to dine with the first ruling Mistress in System Helios's history. I believe hospitality and kindness is the least I can do."

There was a small cry and a clatter from the wall and Alexis looked over to see one of the Burdened bending down to retrieve the sharp pike he had let fall. He looked to be no more than Alexis's age, but there was a sturdiness and confidence in him that seemed to radiate beyond his red armor. He stood back up and kept his eyes averted from the dining table as he took his place once again.

"You," the High Guardian said. "Are you unwell?"

"No, Your Holiness," the Burdened soldier replied. "My grip was loosened and I let my pike drop. My apologies, Your Holiness. It will never happen again." He glanced quickly at the man next to him then looked straight ahead.

"Your grip loosened?" the High Guardian asked, his voice turning cold. "You are one of the Burdened, boy. I know you are freshly inducted into the ranks as a full time soldier, but that is no excuse for sloppiness. Remove yourself from the banquet hall and report to the latrine master. Your duty is now to guard my toilet. Prove you can do that, and maybe in a year or so I will forget this transgression."

The young man nodded and stepped out from the wall, turned crisply, and started to March away.

"Hold up," Alexis said as she stood and hurried over to the young man. "You're injured. How did that happen?"

"Alexis, be seated at once!" Beumont nearly roared. "This is beyond contempt!"

"Hush, Step-Daddy," Alexis said as she placed a hand on the young man's chest and kept him from taking another step. She looked into his eyes and saw he was truly about her age, a teenager in armor, forced to act and live as a man. "May I look at your armor, sir?"

"Your Highness, I cannot permit that," the young man said. "To allow you to touch me would be to blaspheme against your ordination as Mistress of Station Aelon and one of Helios's chosen rulers."

"Well, doesn't he have a way with words?" Bella whispered to her husband.

"Hush," Beumont said as he stood and rushed to Alexis's side.

"Oh, be quiet," Alexis said to the young man then held up a hand just as Beumont was going to speak. "I'm talking to you as well, Step-Daddy."

She moved from in front of the young soldier and to his side, her hand running up and down the thick polybreen armor. She pulled her hand away and held it up for all to see.

"I know the armor of the Burdened are supposed to represent the blood of our Dear Parent Helios, but I am fairly certain the armor is not meant to literally bleed," she announced then turned back to the young soldier. "What is your name?"

"I am of the Burdened, Your Highness, my name does not matter," he replied. He looked over his shoulder at the High Guardian, but only received a brutal look of malice in return, not one of assistance. "Again, I must ask that you—"

"Tell me your name," Alexis ordered, but not unkindly.

"Kel, Your Highness," the young soldier replied. "It is Kel."

"Who did this to you, Kel?" Alexis asked. "Someone stabbed you which caused you to cry out and drop your pike. I would like to know who did this and why."

"I...I...I cannot say," Kel replied. "Please, Your Highness, I need to remove myself and report to my new post."

"Oh, this bores me," the High Guardian said and snapped his fingers three times. Three of the Burdened stepped from the wall and marched over to Kel. "Take him to a cell to await my judgment. This is not how the Burdened behave. He will need to be reeducated, and if that does not hold then eliminated from his position."

"Do not move," Alexis snarled at the three Burdened soldiers. "One more step towards this young man and all three of you will be eliminated from your positions." She turned her attention briefly towards the High Guardian. "And I mean that, Your Holiness, in the same manner you mean it towards this young man."

"Alexis, you will stop this at once," Beumont cried. "This has gone too far!"

"Not far enough, in my opinion," Alexis said.

"Yes, the opinion of a teenage girl," the High Guardian said. "That could never go too far, now could it?"

Many of the Gatekeepers that had stayed to the shadows and out of notice tittered at the High Guardian's words. Alexis visibly stiffened at the insult and response from the members of The Way.

"Move," Alexis said to the three Burdened soldiers. They did not. "Move or I move you."

They still did not move.

"You were warned," Alexis said as she took the pike from Kel's hands and whipped it over her head then settled it under her arm and firmly against her side. "Last chance."

"Oh, Dear Parent, what are you doing!" Bella nearly screamed as she got to her feet and rushed to her daughter. "Alexis! Stop this madness!"

"Alexis! No!" Beumont yelled as he reached for his step-daughter, but was too late as the monarch moved quickly towards the three Burdened that stood and gaped at her like she was a giant grendt that had lost its wings and decided to start telling jokes at Last Meal.

Alexis brought the end of the pike about and slammed it into the side of one soldier's head, then knelt and swept the legs out from under a second. The third soldier regained his composure and thrust forward with his pike, but Alexis expertly parried the attack and whipped her pike about, pinning the soldier's own to the ground.

The mistress raised her foot and stomped on the end of the pinned pike, snapping the blade off easily. She kicked the blade away and returned her attention to the first soldier as that man came at her. Alexis jammed the dull end of her pike into a seam in the man's armor then twisted until she warped the armor and was able to get the weapon against soft flesh.

The man cried out from the force of the blow, but did not drop his weapon. He brought his own pike down and Alexis was barely able to sidestep the attack and avoid the sharp end from ripping into her shoulder. The pike's blade tore half of the right side of Alexis's gown to shreds, which made the young monarch smirk as she spun out and away from the soldier.

"Thanks," Alexis said. "It was getting in my way."

She took several steps back, grabbed the bottom of her gown, and tore it from her body. It ripped easily and revealed a pair of plain, grey breen trousers underneath that had been rolled up and hidden. Alexis looked down at the trousers and grinned wider.

"Now I can really move," Alexis said as she threw the pike at the three soldiers then sprinted to the dining table and retrieved her blades.

Her eyes blazed with fire and violence and she kicked out her legs until the trousers unrolled themselves. The entire banquet hall watched in shocked silence as she casually spun her blades over and over in her hands as she walked back towards the men.

"Shall we continue?" she asked.

"Please stop, Your Highness," Kel said. "I do not need to be defended or—"

"What? Oh, this stopped being about you a while ago, Kel," Alexis laughed. "Trust me, I've been needing this."

"Well," the High Guardian said. "I will have the pleasure of witnessing the Teirmont temper in person."

Beumont and Bella just stood there in the middle of the banquet hall and stared. They did not speak, they did not protest, they did not try to control the obviously out of control young monarch. They simply stared. Both had witnessed the Teirmont temper, and neither wished to come between it and its target.

Alexis nodded to the three soldiers then to the entire contingent of Burdened that lined the walls.

"Ready when you are, boys," Alexis announced. "Let's see how you fare against a mistress."

"Oh, my. . . ." a worried voice said from the entrance to the banquet hall. "What's all of this?"

"Ah, Master Karl, how lovely to see you this evening," the High Guardian said as he stood up from his seat. "You are just in time for the entertainment. It appears that Mistress Alexis here was about to take on my Burdened single handedly. While I fear she has bitten off more than she can chew, I would be a fool to say that she will not succeed. If tonight has taught me anything, it is that when it comes to our young mistress here, assumptions are a silly thing."

"Are we not to dine with you then?" Master Karl asked. A short man with a ruddy complexion and balding head of red hair, the master looked as if entertainment was not something he enjoyed on a regular basis. He turned his attention to Beumont. "Regent Beumont? This is the young woman you want my son to meet? I think not after what I have witnessed so far."

Beumont cleared his throat. "Yes, well, things have gotten out of hand, Master Karl," Beumont said as he found his voice and bowed low. "My step-daughter has been under a lot of strain lately and her nerves may have been pushed past their limits."

"Our apologies, master," Bella said as she walked over to the upset monarch and extended her hand as she curtsied. "You know how some get their blood up on the Planet."

"I do not know such a thing," Master Karl replied as he took and kissed Bella's hand then moved out of the way to reveal a young man that was almost an exact copy of himself, just younger and with dark blonde hair instead of red. "This is not how I wanted my son to be introduced to his possible bride."

"Possible bride?" Alexis asked, still frozen in a battle pose, her body twitching with violence. "That pug?" She looked at her mother then at her step-father. "Is this whole dinner about trying to marry me off?"

"That was the goal, yes," the High Guardian answered from his seat as he lifted a glass of gelberry wine to his lips. He drank the glass dry then slammed it onto the table. "Your parents had expressed concerns about your emotional state and felt that matrimony and the life of a wife and mother may be best suited for you. I was in agreement, since let us face reality and admit that a woman has no place with a crown on her head, but after your show tonight, I am almost of the opinion you should be allowed to rule as you see fit. Helios knows any man that dares to cross and defy you would certainly regret it. You appear to be as fiery an adversary as your grandfather was. I just pray to the Dear Parent you have more reason in your head than your father did or that Teirmont fire could burn out of control."

"I am confused now," Master Karl said. "Should I leave and take my son with me?"

"Helios, no," the High Guardian replied. "Sit, sit, and enjoy dinner with us. Let the two young royals meet and talk. Who knows what the night might bring."

No one moved. The High Guardian sighed.

"Oh, for fuck's sake, sit down, all of you," the High Guardian snapped. "You too, Alexis. Put those blasted shaow stickers down and show some decorum for five seconds. You may wear trousers like a man, but you still have half a gown covering you. I appeal to the feminine half and ask that you join me for dinner without killing any of my Burdened."

"And Kel?" Alexis asked. "He will not be harmed?"

"Harmed? Far from it," the High Guardian said. "He is released from the Burdened and his vows of fealty to The Way are null and void. He is now yours to deal with, Your Highness. I want nothing more to do with the young man."

"Mine?" Alexis gasped. "But, I didn't...I don't...."

"Neither do I," the High Guardian chuckled. "Whatever your babbling may mean. He can no longer be part of the Burdened, Mistress. You have taken that option from him since he will not be trusted by his fellow soldiers. He goes to Station Aelon with you, where you can put him to work as you see fit, or he stays here and is kicked off The Way Prime to make his own life out on the planet. He could be a miner or breen field worker, but his blessed days as Burdened are over."

The High Guardian waited for his glass to be refilled with wine then raised it.

"Welcome to the world of adults, my young girl," he said. "Where actions have consequences and not everyone cares that you are a misunderstood monarch that has been under the thumb of your step-father and conniving mother. Cheers!"

*

Alexis sat in the dark atrium, her butt half asleep as she sat on a stone bench and looked up at the one clear area in all of Helios's sky. The stars shown beautifully through the portal in the Vape clouds that hovered directly over The Way Prime. An entire planet shrouded in combustible clouds except for a single patch; a single patch that was controlled by The Way and its High Guardian and gatekeepers; protected to the death by the Burdened.

Alexis had never felt so small in her life.

"Mistress Alexis?" a voice asked from the shadows at the side of the atrium as a door opened and sliver of light was let into the dark sanctuary. "There is a young man here. He says he doesn't want to bother you, but I knew you'd want to speak to him."

"Thank you, Jex," Alexis said as she stood up from the bench and stretched. She wore a simple tunic over her breen trousers, having been done with the fine trappings of her position hours ago. "Show him in."

"Yes, mistress," Jex said.

The door was opened all the way and Kel walked into the atrium dressed in almost the same outfit as Alexis. He had a small bag in hand and set it down before he took a knee and lowered his head.

"Your Highness," he said. "I have come to ask that you release me from your bond and set me out into the planet so I can make my way in shame as I deserve."

"Seriously?" Alexis laughed then looked at the semi-illuminated face of Jex. "Is he kidding?"

"I do not know, mistress," Jex replied. "He seems fairly serious."

"Maddeningly so," Alexis said as she walked over and smacked Kel on the shoulder. "Stand up, idiot. I fought for you in front of the High Guardian. You're not going anywhere."

"Would you like some privacy, mistress?" Jex asked.

"Please," Alexis said.

Kel looked up in alarm. He whipped his head around and glared at Jex. "You would leave your mistress in the company of a stranger? A man trained in the deadly arts of combat and who has been formally discharged from his duty in disgrace?"

"How old are you?" Jex asked Kel.

"Sixteen," Kel replied.

"Yeah, a man," Jex chuckled. "I should be more worried about your safety than my mistress's." He turned his attention back to Alexis. "I'll be right outside the door if you need me to help remove the body."

"Thank you, Jex," Alexis giggled. "I'll call you if I need you."

"Mistress," Jex nodded then left and closed the door, plunging the atrium back into darkness except for the glow coming from the Vape clouds above in the night sky.

Alexis walked back to the bench and sat down.

"I just made Jex my personal guard," Alexis said. "I think I made the right choice. He takes to it naturally. It is fate."

She turned and was surprised to see Kel still on one knee in his original position.

"Oh, Helios, get up and come sit with me," Alexis said. "Jex was kidding about the body thing." She held her arms up and looked down at her waist. "See? I don't even have my blades on me."

Kel stood up, hesitated, then walked to her and sat down, making sure he was as far to the end of the bench as he could be. Alexis sighed and scooted over until her hip was touching his.

"Listen, Kel, I am not like other girls and do not live in the world of commoners and passengers," Alexis said as she took Kel's hand in hers. "I have all the power of a mistress of station, yet have almost no control over my own life. I am bound by traditions that do not fit me since I am a woman in a man's crown. I am also under the rule of a regent that believes he will stay in power indefinitely. I don't have the time or luxury of waiting for my life to happen. Understand?"

"Yes. . .yes, Your Highness," Kel replied.

"You do?" Alexis asked.

Kel hesitated. "No. I am sorry. I honestly don't."

"Neither do I," Alexis said as she raised her head and looked up at the sky again. "I'd be surprised if you did."

Kel frowned at the strange monarch then looked down at their hands. "Will you let me leave here then, Your Highness?"

"Helios, no," Alexis laughed as she squeezed his hand. "You're coming back to Station Aelon with me where you will train with my Royal Guard. You will be part of my bodyguard contingent and will be in my presence day and night. Except when you need to pee. You can do that on your own."

Kel sputtered and tried to speak, but no words came out.

"Are you alright, Kel?" Alexis asked.

"I don't know," Kel responded after he found his words.

"Well, you better find out soon because my shuttle back to the station leaves in three day," Alexis said. "You are sixteen, Kel?"

"Yes, Your Highness," Kel nodded.

"I'm fourteen, but will be fifteen very soon," Alexis said. "When I am sixteen I can legally be crowned as Mistress of Station Aelon, but I have been told that won't happen until I am eighteen. So instead, I have decided I will marry at sixteen."

"You will?" Kel asked. "Who are you marrying? Not that minor from earlier?" He gasped and shook his head. "I am sorry. I should not have asked that. That was too personal. Forgive me."

"Too personal?" Alexis laughed. "You are sitting with your hip against mine and my hand gripping yours. I think we have passed personal. Plus, you know who I will marry, so don't be silly."

"I do?" Kel asked. "Oh, so it is the Minor of Station Flaen that was in attendance this evening."

"That siggy worm? Hardly!" Alexis guffawed.

It was a loud, raucous laugh that filled the entire atrium. Kel's face lit up at the sound and he unconsciously leaned in against Alexis's shoulder. She leaned back and continued laughing until tears streamed down her cheeks.

"Sorry, sorry," she gasped. "I shouldn't laugh like that. He seemed like a nice young man. Just not my type."

"Who is your type, Your Highness?" Kel asked.

"First, stop calling me Your Highness when my name is Alexis," Alexis said. "Second, haven't you guessed who my type is yet? It's pretty obvious."

"No, I'm sorry, Your—Alexis," Kel replied.

"You are, silly boy," Alexis laughed again. "You are my type and when I turn sixteen you and I will be married. That is what I decided tonight when I was fighting those idiots. That very second I knew you and I would be together forever. It's fate."

Kel sat there, his mouth wide open.

"Trying to catch honey wasps?" Alexis smiled as she reached over and gently pushed up on his chin. Her fingers lingered then moved up and touched his lips lightly. "I don't see why you're so shocked. Have you never read the tales of masters fighting for a maiden's honor and how they fall in love and live happily ever after?"

"Well, I...I mean, uh...Yes, I have read those stories," Kel stuttered. "But, I am not a maiden and those are just stories. No one believes that those come true and people fall in love and get married after one chance meeting."

"I do," Alexis said and she leaned up and kissed him.

There was an instant heat between them that made Alexis grin around the kiss. She reached up and put her hands through his short brown hair and their lips parted and tongues met. They stayed that way for several minutes, just holding each other and kissing passionately then gently then passionately then gently until they finally parted.

"Did that just happen?" Kel asked as his fingers traced her cheeks, down her chin and then outlined her long and graceful neck.

"It happened," Alexis said then abruptly stood up. "That was my first kiss with a boy and I loved it. How did you like it?"

"It was great," Kel replied. "But I have to admit—"

"Not your first kiss with a girl?" Alexis smiled. "I would think not. Despite it being said that the Burdened are as celibate as the gatekeepers, no one actually believes that. You can't have warrior blood in you without it running hot."

She held out her hands and he took them and stood up. Alexis pressed her body close to his and smiled. They almost looked each other in the eye since she was a Teirmont through and through and had inherited the family's legendary height.

"We aren't going to have sex until we're married, alright? I can't risk getting pregnant out of wedlock and, really, I don't want kids until I have my crown secured for me only," Alexis said. "We can fool around, though. It'll be tricky to find privacy and time when we get to the station, but that'll be part of thrill."

She kissed him again then reached around and gripped his ass hard. Kel jumped, making Alexis guffaw once again.

"Relax, Kel," Alexis said. "This is going to be fun. You have to trust fate, alright? Fate is everything to me. Everything."

She slapped his ass then pushed him away.

"Now go find Jex and tell him you are part of my Royal Guard," Alexis said as she once more looked back up at the night sky. "He'll get you settled with the other guards. But don't tell anyone we're getting married, okay? That's our secret. Well, except for Jex. You can talk to Jex. I trust him to keep the secret and I know you'll need someone to confide in or you'll go mad. Now hurry off, my love. You have work to do before we leave the Planet."

Kel stood there for a second then bowed, turned and left quickly. Alexis waited until he was gone then sat right down on the ground and took a deep breath. She didn't know whether she wanted to laugh or cry, shout or be silent. All she knew was she was happy, or at least not angry, and that it all felt right for a change.

She trusted in fate.

*

Jex could hardly contain his smirk as he led Kel towards the barracks where the Aelish Royal Guard was boarded.

"Something you want to ask, Kel?" Jex asked. "Be honest. It's the only way you'll survive around her."

"Is she mad?" Kel asked. "Is she touched in the head a little?"

"A little?" Jex laughed. "A lot is more like it. Why do you ask?"

Kel stopped and Jex stopped with him.

"She says we are going to be married," Kel admitted. "I had never laid eyes on her until this evening and now I am in a secret betrothal with the Mistress of Station Aelon. That's not sane."

"No, it isn't," Jex said. "Married? She said that?"

"She did," Kel nodded. "She said it's fate and I shouldn't fight it and that I need to relax because it's all going to be fun."

"Well, she's the mistress," Jex shrugged.

"That's your answer? She's the mistress?" Kel exclaimed.

"She isn't the same as others," Jex said. "If you are going to make it on Station Aelon then you have to realize that. Most of all you have to admit that you already know that. Go on, be honest. Tell me what you felt when you first saw her enter that banquet hall."

"The Burdened feel nothing except loyalty to The Way and the High Guardian," Kel replied.

"Shaowshit," Jex laughed. "I told you to be honest. What did you feel?"

Kel started to speak then shook his head and looked down at his feet.

"How about I tell you how I felt the first time I saw her as mistress?" Jex said. "It was powerful. There is something about that young woman that just grabs your heart and makes you want to impress her and serve her and lay down your life for her."

"You've known her a long time?" Kel asked.

"I've barely spoken to her until today, man," Jex replied.

"You have to be kidding," Kel exclaimed. "She speaks as if you are her most trusted guard. I'd have guessed you had known each other since you were small children."

"No," Jex said. "But today she connected with me and I connected with her, just as you have. Did she mention fate?"

"Yes, several times," Kel nodded.

"She talked about nothing but fate on the cutter ride from Aelon Prime back to here," Jex said. "Nonstop. She told me she trusted me and that I would be her right hand from now on. And that fate would show her more guards she could trust and that she had plans for us. The girl has no fear and, whether bad or good, no filter."

"She must drive everyone on the station mad," Kel said then held up his hands. "Not that she drives me mad; I just mean the stuffy stewards and other nobility."

"Now, this is where it gets strange, Kel," Jex said and leaned in close. "She has always been brooding and quiet for as long as I have known her and from what everyone on the station has said. But, something happened to her on the prime. She changed. It was like a light being switched on."

"She is illuminating," Kel said then frowned. "But this is all easy for you to say. You're her guard, not her future husband."

"Do you want to marry her?" Jex asked. "If you don't then you better speak up."

"I don't know her," Kel replied. "And until this evening I never even thought of marriage. I was Burdened. The Burdened don't marry."

"But do you want to?" Jex asked.

Kel smiled slyly. "Yes. But I don't know why. I'm not sure I love her."

"You do," Jex grinned.

"Yeah. . .I do," Kel said. "How is that?"

"Fuck if I know," Jex said. "Just like I don't know why I feel like I have been her confidante since I was born. It's as if there is no barrier between us and only trust exists. I would have died for that woman before today, but now? Now I will not only die for her, but I will beg Helios to resurrect me so I could die for her again and again. She may have been born almost fifteen years ago, but I think today was the first day she felt alive which in turn has brought us all alive. Does that make sense?"

"Not at all," Kel said. "But fate rarely does."

"That's the spirit," Jex said as he grabbed Kel by the arm and started walking again. "Because it was fate that made all of this happen." They walked to the end of the passageway and Jex stopped. "By the way, how is your side?"

"My side? Oh, where Ned stabbed me?" Kel said.

"Yes. What was that about?" Jex asked. "Did you owe him credits or something?"

"No, no, it is what the veteran Burdened do to those on their first detail," Kel said. "If you are new to duty then the others will try to bleed you as much as possible to see if you'll break. It's not sanctioned by the Gatekeepers, but it's a tradition."

"Looks like you broke," Jex smiled.

"Yes," Kel frowned. "I did."

"Well, the mistress likes broken things around her," Jex said. "She's not exactly whole herself. It is a good thing you are broken."

"A good thing?" Kel asked.

"Yes, a good thing," Jex said. "Otherwise you wouldn't be marrying a mistress, now would you?"

"Helios. . . ." Kel gasped. "I can't make any sense of this."

"Welcome to being Aelish," Jex laughed. "It never makes sense. Now come on, kid. Let's introduce you to the others. If you thought the hazing with the Burdened was bad, wait until the rest of the Royal Guard get to you. You may be cursing fate before the month is out."

*

"What are you smiling about?" Bella asked, supervising the servants as they packed and prepared the royal trunks for departure back up to Station Aelon. She looked over at her daughter as Alexis sat on the bed and just grinned. "That is a smile, right? It's hard to tell since I rarely see one on your face."

"It is a smile, Mother," Alexis replied.

"So, answer my question," Bella insisted. "What are you up to?"

"One day I'll tell you," Alexis said and glanced at the servants. "Not right now."

"Alexis, what have you done?" Bella asked, narrowing her eyes. "Not that you haven't done enough already. Once word of your little act at dinner the other night gets out to the other stations, which it will, you'll be all but impossible to marry."

"Why do I have to marry, Mother?" Alexis asked.

"Because the crown needs heirs," Bella stated. "You can't have heirs unless you are married."

"So, I can marry anyone then," Alexis stated. "All I need is a man to impregnate me and then I'll have heirs."

Some of the servants looked up quickly from their duties, but the glare they received from Bella got them back to work immediately.

"Alexis, do not say such things," Bella said in a hushed, harsh whisper as she stalked over to her daughter. "You are mistress. You do not simply get impregnated. First, we must find a suitable husband for you from royal stock. No one will take your heirs' claims of legitimacy seriously if the father is not of royal blood as well. It is hard enough for the meeting of stewards to accept a woman with the crown. They'll never accept an heir that doesn't bring titles and holdings from his father's side."

"Or her father's side," Alexis corrected. "Precedent, mother. You are looking at it."

"His or her, makes no difference," Bella said. "The meeting of stewards are not a body to be trifled with. Even with your step-father's arrogance, even he does not underestimate the power of the meeting. He knows firsthand that the power the crown wields is only as strong as what the meeting allows. That was something your true father could never understand."

The smile on Alexis's face left quickly. "I know. He told me."

"He did? When?" Bella asked. "Before he died? Or did he leave a letter? If he left you a letter then you must show it to me right away."

"No, no letter," Alexis said. "His ghost told me on the prime when we visited the house. We had a long talk about the crown and the meeting and fate."

All of the servants stopped working, but Bella did not glare that time. She stared at her daughter and struggled with a response.

"A ghost?" Bella finally asked. "Alexis, do not joke of such things. It's cruel and disrespectful to the dead."

Alexi stood up and shrugged. "He said you'd say that."

Then she turned and left the guest quarters assigned to the royals from Station Aelon. Bella watched her go then sat down heavily on the bed and waved her hands at the servants.

"Get back to work," she said. "And if I hear of any of you speaking about what my daughter just said then I'll have you and all of your relatives jettisoned out an airlock. Are we understood?"

They all nodded and doubled their efforts to pack up the room.

CHAPTER TWO

The council glared at Beumont as he sat at the head of the table in the great hall, the reminders of reigns past depicted in worn tapestries that hung along the walls behind him. Beumont met the hard gazes of the stewards of the council with a hard gaze of his own, more than willing to fight the issues out, if need be. Unfortunately, due to his step-daughter's behavior of late, "need be" had become commonplace.

"She wants a tournament instead of a coronation ceremony," Beumont stated again, since his first try had only been met with the aforementioned glares. "At the end of the tournament she will be crowned as Mistress of Station Aelon pending her true ascension to the rule in two years when I step down as regent."

"This is a farce, Beumont," Steward Corwin Harper of Sector Nenne said. "Have you heard that she intends to compete?"

A slight man with deep brown skin, Steward Harper was known throughout Station Aelon for his ruthlessness in business and deep distaste of the idea of being ruled by a woman. He looked to the others seated and they all nodded that they were privy to the news as well.

The royal council of stewards, an offshoot of the larger meeting of stewards, was made up of Steward Blanton Wulberry of Sector Gwalter, a shy man that usually went with the majority; Steward Emeric Hume III of Sector Twaern, a cocksure young man used to being treated like he was worth more than the other stewards since his grandfather had served on the council under Alexis the First; and Steward Hal Magnaird of Sector Dulby, a man so twitchy that servants knew not to set any plates, cups, or silverware within reach for fear he'd knock them off the table, or worse, knock them towards one of the other stewards.

It was those men that Beumont looked to as he struggled with his dual role of being regent to his step-daughter and being a steward and member of the meeting. The former meant loyalty to the crown, the latter meant loyalty to the nobility and their strength and standing on the station.

"Yes, I have heard she intends to compete," Beumont sighed. "My wife is currently trying to dissuade her of such a foolish notion."

"A woman competing in a tournament?" Harper laughed. "What next? A woman as ruler of a station? Oh, wait. . . ."

"Yes, yes, I have heard it from you before, Corwin," Beumont grumbled. "Yet there isn't a thing that can be done about it. She has turned sixteen and the crown is hers. If she declares she wants a tournament instead of a coronation ceremony then that is within her rights. It has been done before many times with many other masters."

"Masters, yes," Harper sneered. "But she is not a master, is she? She's a bloody woman who wears trousers and walks about with a group of royal guards who nearly worship her! Dear Helios, man!"

"And she talks to herself," Steward Hume huffed. "Everyone knows it. She has been caught more than once having conversations in rooms where she is the only person in attendance. That is madness, Beumont, and grounds for her to lose her right to her title."

"Have you ever witnessed her talking to herself?" Beumont asked.

"Well. . .no," Hume admitted.

"Have any of you witnessed it?" Beumont asked the council. None answered. "Exactly. As far as I know, it is the hearsay of servants and passengers."

"It doesn't make it less true," Harper responded. "All we need is a credible witness, Beumont, and she can be taken down."

"Taken down?" Beumont asked. "Are you crazy? There has never been a ruler of Station Aelon more loved than Alexis. Not in the history of this station has any master, or mistress, had the complete adulation of their subjects like she does. Do you think that news that she talks to her dead father would sway public opinion? I do not, and it is not a risk I am willing to take."

"Her dead father?" Harper asked as he leaned forward and narrowed his eyes at Beumont. "You've witnessed her madness."

Beumont sighed and rolled his eyes. "I live with the girl in the royal quarters, Corwin. I have witnessed most of her day-to-day life."

"Then you can testify against her!" Harper snapped. "You can prove she is not well in her mind!"

"People talk to themselves all the time," Steward Magnaird said. "I agree with Beumont on this. This will open a door to something we do not want. If we accuse her of doing what most passengers do themselves, then we risk turning the whole station against the meeting. It wouldn't take much for the voices she hears to start talking of getting rid of the meeting." All eyes turned on Magnaird and he began to noticeably twitch under the scrutiny. "I'm just saying."

"Then how do we get rid of her?" Harper asked. "Because I will not live under that crazy girl's rule."

"Let me think on it," Beumont replied.

"Perhaps she has an accident during the tournament," Steward Wulberry muttered.

"What was that, Wulberry?" Hume barked. "Speak up, man!"

"I said," Wulberry replied as he cleared his throat. "I said that perhaps she could have an accident during the tournament."

All eyebrows raised at the suggestion, not because it was out of the question, but because it came from a man that hadn't contributed much since being appointed to the council.

"That's good thinking," Harper said. "If maybe her armor was tampered with and she was up against one of the other stations' stronger champions, then things would surely turn for the worse for the girl."

"But if it doesn't work and it is discovered there was foul play, then eyes will be on us," Hume said. "We stand the most to gain from her being removed. Having her taken down because of suspected madness makes us look like we are only doing our duty, but purposefully sabotaging her during tournament combat makes us look like murderers."

"Hume is right," Harper said. "We'll need a scapegoat."

"But who would gain the most from her death other than us?" Magnaird asked.

They were silent for a while then Beumont smiled.

"What?" Harper asked. "Do you know of someone?"

"I do, indeed," Beumont said. "Not only does he have the most to gain, but he also has no supporters that would come to his aide. I'll make the arrangements at once. The tournament goes forward and when it is all done we will have a station to divide."

*

"Uncle Thomas!" Alexis screamed as she ran down the passageway to the shuttle dock airlock. "Uncle Thomas!"

"Alexis!" Kel yelled after her as the royal guards struggled to keep up with the Mistress's long legs. "Dammit, Alexis! Hold on!"

The dignitaries from the other stations that had just arrived all gasped and looked shocked at the informal way Kel called after the mistress. But those from Station Aelon didn't give it a second thought as they were quite used to the way Alexis's closest guards interacted with her.

"Calm down, Kel," Jex said from the man's side. "She hasn't seen her uncle in close to a decade. She is going to be excited and there's nothing we can do about that."

"I don't like all these foreigners around her," Kel said as the bodyguards shoved through the crowd of shuttle passengers to get to their mistress. "All it takes is one hidden blade and she's dead."

"I am well aware of that," Jex said. "Which is why we won't let down our guard, ever. It is our job to protect her, not her job to be protected. I'm getting sick of having this conversation, Kel. We've been at her side for over a year now; it's time you relaxed."

Kel leaned in and put his mouth close to Jex's ear so only the head guard could hear him. "Easy for you to say. You don't love her like I do."

"Don't I?" Jex replied as he raised an eyebrow. "I think the truth is she doesn't love any of us like she loves you. Yet we all will die for her in a heartbeat. Enjoy your position, my friend, because we have your back as much as we have hers. Do you hear me?"

Kel looked at his fellow guard and then nodded. "Yeah, I hear you. Sorry."

Jex clapped Kel on the shoulder and smiled broadly. "Not to worry. We envy you, Kel. I don't think there is a man amongst us that wouldn't trade places with you even it was for only a minute."

The mistress screamed and the conversation was dropped as the bodyguards shoved people out of the way without regard for their well being or safety. They plowed through the crowd until they reached Alexis, who was still screaming, yet not in fright or terror, but in joy as she held a long blade in her hands.

"Kel! Look!" she beamed as she whirled about and showed the blade to the guards. "My uncle got me a hand-forged long blade of Klaervian steel! Oh my Helios! Isn't it beautiful? Don't answer! No need! I know it is! Thank you, Uncle Thomas!"

She tossed the blade in the air and Jex reached out and caught it as Alexis wrapped her arms around the man that stood in front of her, a bemused smile on his face.

"You are more than welcome, Alexis," Minor Thomas Teirmont said as he was nearly bowled over by his niece. "I knew you'd like it, but not this much."

"I can use it during the tournament," Alexis said as she pushed back and took her uncle's arm. "It'll be the perfect symbol from one generation to the next. I'll have my weapon smith check it over, but I know he won't find a flaw. I could see the edge on it. It's amazing!"

"My lord," Jex said as he bowed before the minor. "I am Jex Lemnt, head of the mistress's personal guard. I have been instructed by my lady to assign men to you if you need them." Jex looked past Thomas and towards the airlock. "Which it appears you do. Are you traveling alone?"

"Unfortunately, yes," Thomas nodded. "My position does not come with the income needed to travel with guards and servants. I must rely on the charity of others when I go off station."

"There is never any charity here, Uncle," Alexis smiled. "Just love and affection. What is mine is yours."

"That is kind, Alexis," Thomas replied. "Yet we both know it is more complicated than that."

"I will assign two men to you, my lord," Jex said. "They will be by your side day and night for your protection."

"That is kind, Jex, but not necessary," Thomas said. "My days of court intrigue are done. I live a simple life on Station Thraen." He looked about and frowned. "Did my cousin not care to come see me?"

"Cousin? Oh, yes, Mother," Alexis frowned as well. "She says she prefers to stay away from the airlocks. She doesn't like the crush of people during times like this. She'll meet us in the royal quarters for tea."

"Yes, very well," Thomas said. "I'd like to get to my quarters and change before then if there is time."

"There is all the time in the world, Uncle," Alexis stated then stopped and the crush of people around them was forced to stop also as Jex, Kel and the mistress's guards formed a tight circle of protection. "Uncle? Is that...? Is that the bracelet I gave you all those years ago?"

Alexis pushed up the sleeve of Thomas's cloak and stared in wonder at the worn breen bracelet he wore. She finally tore her eyes away and looked up at her Uncle, tears in her eyes.

"I have never taken it off," Thomas said. "It has come close to wearing thin, but I had my tailor apply some siggy worm silk to the weak areas. It looks worse than it is."

"It looks lovely," Alexis said, tears streaming freely down her face as she smiled so wide that her cheeks looked to bust. "It's the loveliest thing I have ever seen."

"Well, the credit is all yours since you did make it," Thomas said.

"Here, I have another gift," Alexis said as she took Kel by the arm. "This is Kel. He will be one of the guards assigned to you, if Jex does not mind."

"I do not," Jex nodded. "Kel?"

"Whatever Alexis wants," Kel smiled.

"Alexis?" Thomas asked. "That's a little informal for a guard."

"What is formality amongst family?" Alexis asked. "And let me assure you that my guards are my family, Uncle. They say they would roast alive in the fires of Helios for me, but I say it is my duty to roast alive for them. There is no separation between us. We are all warriors that serve Station Aelon, after all."

"That's quite a statement," Thomas said then looked to Jex. "Does she talk like this all the time?"

"She does," Jex replied. "And she has never shown us that she means otherwise."

"Very well," Thomas said. "Kel, is it?"

"It is, my lord," Kel said and bowed. "At your service."

"Show me to my quarters, Kel," Thomas said. "It is going to be a grand few days and I'd like to get settled and ready."

"This way, my lord," Kel responded.

Alexis leaned her head on Thomas's shoulder even though she was equally as tall as he was. "Wait until you see me compete. I have been practicing."

The guards all laughed heartily and Thomas looked about.

"Am I missing something?" he asked.

"Only if you blink," Jex replied.

*

The weapon smith stared at the bag of jewels set before him. He nervously worked at his lip with his teeth as he watched each gem removed one by one and set on his workbench.

"This is half," Beumont said. "A second bag will be delivered once the tournament is over. You will be required to attest that you were ordered by Thomas Teirmont, on pain of death, to leave the long blade be and not examine it as is your duty. No harm will come to you if you do as I say. Once the business is done, then you can take your jewels and go where you want. Stay on the station, emigrate to the Planet, live on a different station—the System is wide open to a man with your riches."

"Yes, sire," the weapon smith replied. "And all I have to do is say I didn't ever examine the blade?"

"That is all," Beumont said. "While also keeping this talk a secret. As well as the fact I must take the blade with me for today. It will be on your workbench first thing in the morning. Can you do all of that?"

The weapon smith continued to chew on his lip, his eyes darting from jewel to jewel.

"Yes, my lord, I can do all of that," the weapon smith said. "But I need to know that the Mistress will not come to harm because of this."

"Come to harm? No, never," Beumont exclaimed. "She'll be using a different blade during combat. This is purely ceremonial. That is why there is no danger in you not examining it."

"Yes, of course," the weapon smith nodded. "You have my word."

"Good man," Beumont smiled as he picked up the long blade. "Like I said, this will be returned in the morning as if it was never gone. Good day to you, sir."

The weapon smith took his eyes off the jewels long enough to watch the regent leave then returned his attention to the riches on his workbench. Just the first half of the payment was more wealth than his entire family had seen in ten generations.

*

"You strike it here," Beumont said as he held the long blade in front of Steward Francis Montgeire's face. "This is the weak point. Make sure that when you do strike, it is while you are in a position to take full advantage of the weakness and end the fight swiftly."

"You want me to make it look like an accident?" Montgeire asked. A tall, broad shouldered man, Steward Montgeire was Station Thraen's strongest bladesman and champion of more tournaments than any other noble in the System. "Even if I do so, I will still be executed. Killing a mistress is a capital offense, accident or no."

"Not with this tournament," Beumont said. "Mistress Alexis has decreed that any deaths arising from the tournament will be considered accidents. She wants all competitors to fight as hard as they can, so she can prove she's one of the boys, as she likes to say."

"She is hardly one of the boys," Montgeire laughed. "Some say she isn't even one of the girls."

"She is a force of nature unto herself, that is for sure," Beumont said as he clasped Montgeire on the shoulder. "You are first cousin to my wife, Francis. It is not only I that asks this, but she as well. Station Aelon will not survive the rule of a woman and neither will Station Thraen."

"Station Thraen?" Montgeire frowned. "Station Thraen will never be ruled by a bleeder."

"That depends," Beumont responded. "Alexis has spoken of making a claim for the crown since she is the granddaughter of Paul the Fourth. Now that his sons have died, and left no heirs, the succession can be contested by her."

"We have a master!" Montgeire snapped. "And that is my brother! She has no claim to the Thraenish crown!"

"No, of course not," Beumont replied. "Any man could see that, but she is blinded by her female emotions and cannot be controlled. Helios knows I have tried over the years. The girl is mad with power and once she takes full control of this station she will set her eyes on Station Thraen and its Prime. And to do that she will have to kill your brother and any other Thraenish nobles that could even be considered a threat. The girl is a Teirmont and you know the violence that dwells within that bloodline. Not to mention the madness."

Beumont leaned in close even though they were the only two men in the room.

"She talks to her dead father," Beumont whispered. "In the open, for all to see. We allow it, the people allow it, only because she is young. Some say she will grow out of it, but I say she will not. She is touched in the head just as her flip father was."

"Abomination," Montgeire spat.

"Too true," Beumont replied. "Too true, indeed."

Montgeire walked a few paces away then spun on his heel and held out his hand. "Let me see the blade once more. I will memorize the flaw and do as you ask. But you will do something for me, Beumont."

"What is that?" Beumont asked. "What more than the safety of your station could you possibly want?"

"You appeal to my patriotism, which you are correct in doing, but neither of us are naïve enough to think this System runs on ideal alone."

"Fine. Name your price," Beumont huffed. "And know that if I pay it, it will buy your silence not just in this life, but in the afterlife as well."

"I want a piece of the lease holdings on Thraen Prime," Montgeire said. "I hold no Vape mining rights and I would like to add some to my portfolio."

"You ask a lot, Francis," Beumont growled. "That is not an easy task. The paperwork alone to make that happen would raise so many red flags that I don't know if it would be safe for either of us to allow."

"That is your problem, Beumont, not mine," Montgeire smirked. "Just make it happen."

Beumont sighed and shook his head. "If it has to be done then it has to be done. What's a little paperwork to keep two stations safe, yes?"

Montgeire didn't respond, just examined the long blade and its undetectable flaw.

"I'll get you your Vape mine," Beumont said. "You get me the corpse of my step-daughter without anyone suspecting foul play."

Montgeire handed the blade back and nodded. "That will not be a problem. She can fight for a long time with this blade despite its weakness. This flaw is masterful, Beumont. I'll only be able to exploit it because I know of it."

"Thank you, Francis," Beumont nodded. "I like to be thorough. I have learned the hard way in life that being anything less means death."

"A lesson too many fail to ever learn," Montgeire nodded. "Now, if you will excuse me, I must prepare myself for tomorrow's tournament. It is not just about physical skill, you know. There is mental and spiritual preparation that must be attended to."

"You are the champion," Beumont bowed. "I leave you to your process. May it serve you well."

*

"Are you ready to explain yourself, Beumont?" Harper asked as he took a seat next to the regent in the royal box overlooking the tournament field that had been set up on the Surface of Station Aelon just outside the walls of the royal Castle Quent. "We have been waiting for days for the tragic accident to occur, yet the girl keeps winning and advancing. If you allow her to go any further then she will have to fight Steward Montgeire."

"Will she?" Beumont grinned. "Is that a bad thing? The man is the best in the System. If anyone can defeat her, he will."

"He is skilled enough that he will not only beat her, but make sure she is not harmed," Harper said. "That defeats our purpose."

"I have it all well in hand, Corwin," Beumont said as he patted the man's arm. "Now, make way, please. My wife is about to join me and you are in her seat."

"Do not botch this, Beumont," Harper said. "She dies today or you do."

"Careful, Corwin," Beumont replied as he stood, forcing Harper to stand as well due to ceremony. "I am no slouch with a blade myself. Keep talking like that and you and I may have our own private tournament."

"Corwin!" Bella cried as she came up to the two men. "I didn't know you were joining us in the box today. What a pleasant surprise. I'll have a servant fetch another chair for you."

"No need, my lady," Harper said as he bowed. "I have other matters to attend to before I take my own seat. I am sorry I cannot join you since your view of what is to come will be superb. Isn't that right, Beumont?"

"We do have the best view of all," Beumont said. "There hasn't been a moment's disappointment yet, I doubt there will be during the next fights."

"I trust that to be true, Beumont," Harper said then smiled at Bella. "My lady, until we meet again."

"Goodbye, Corwin," Bella replied. "Give my love to your family."

Harper smiled, turned and left quickly. Bella waited until he was gone then looked her husband in the eyes.

"What was that all about, love?" Bella asked. "Hard not to miss the double meanings you two were trying to hide."

"No double meanings, my dear," Beumont said as he took Bella's hand and sat down. "Just two politicians sparring with words, is all."

"As long as it stays just words," Bella replied. "We do not need any more trouble. Not on the eve of our daughter's taking the crown."

"Yes," Beumont smirked. "Our daughter."

*

"You have been more than impressive," Montgeire said as he stood in the middle of the tournament field, his polybreen armor shining in the light of the midday sun that shown down through the environmental shield that kept the Surface from being exposed to open space. "That last fight was a work of art, Your Highness."

"I did do fairly well, didn't I?" Alexis smiled, her own armor shining just as brightly as Montgeire's. "But it wasn't too hard. That steward relied too much on his size and not enough on his footwork. He was as easy to dance around as a drunk servant boy during Last Meal."

"Excellent observation," Montgeire said as he looked Alexis up and down. "He believed his armor would save him from your attacks, but it did not. You were able to draw first blood in record time. I fear our duel may last considerably longer, considering our matched skills."

"It makes for good entertainment," Alexis grinned as she turned from her opponent and waved to the crowds that sat in the boxes and bleachers that encircled the field. Everyone stood immediately and cheered with open enthusiasm and joy. "We shall give them their credits' worth today."

"If you had thought to charge for attendance," Montgeire said. "But this is free, which means they do not have anything invested. A long, drawn out fight will bore them eventually. That would be a shameful way to end such a glorious tournament."

Alexis's smile left her face and she turned slowly towards the champion. At six foot two inches, he would have towered over any other woman, but

Alexis was a Teirmont and her height was not only in her legs, but in her genes. She was not any other woman. She stepped closer to the Thraenish steward and cocked her head as she studied his face.

"What do you have in mind, sir?" Alexis asked. "Some type of side-wager we announce to the crowd? Would that make it more interesting?"

"The crowd cares not for side-wagers and the nobility betting sums that they cannot even imagine to ever possess," Montgeire replied. "I propose we alter the rules a bit. We fight not to first blood, but to the surrender. We go as long as we can until one of us quits, no matter how much blood."

"That would take even longer," Alexis said. "Your armor is as strong as mine. We could be here for twelve full revolutions before either of us is weakened enough to give up."

"Then we remove our armor," Montgeire suggested. "That would truly be a show for your people, would it not?"

Alexis took a single step back then stopped and corrected her action by stepping forward and getting even closer to the Thraen.

"If we weren't standing in front of a thousand people, not to mention nobles and royals from all the stations, I'd say you have intentions of killing me, Steward Montgeire," Alexis glared. "But there would be no way you could possibly get away with it. My guards would execute you on the spot for such an action. You do understand that, right, Montgeire?"

"I have zero intention of killing you, Your Highness," Montgeire replied. "I am skilled enough at this game to know the difference between a disarming blow and a killing blow. I am not saying you will not be hurt, for that is the game we play, I am just saying that every witness here will see me fight according to the rules and spirit of the tournament. That will never be questioned."

Alexis studied the man's face for a full minute, all while the crowd cheered and shouted around them, until she finally nodded.

"Very well, Montgeire," Alexis said. "Sans armor it is. Let my people have no doubt that I am the best warrior Station Aelon has ever had."

"That is a bold claim, my lady," Montgeire grinned. "I met your grandfather when I was young once. Longshanks was the perfect specimen of a warrior master."

"Yet even he felt the cut of the blade more than once," Alexis said as she held out her arms. "Whereas I have never been cut, only done the cutting."

With her arms still outstretched, she snapped her fingers and two confused attendants hurried out to her.

"My lady?" one asked.

"We have decided to fight without armor," Alexis said. "Please remove it from me at once."

"Your Highness, no!" the second attendant cried. "You will be exposed!"

"I can handle myself," Alexis said.

"No, my lady," the first attendant said. "You will be exposed to the crowd. All you wear underneath is your upper shift and thin trousers."

"You are correct," Alexis nodded. "I will need to tie up the shift so it does not slow me down by getting tangled. Help me do so, man."

"Your Highness," the first attendant said. "It is not my place to do such a thing. You need a female attendant to help with that. I can help you don and doff your armor, not make adjustments to your under shift."

"Just get the fucking armor off me," Alexis snapped. She watched as Montgeire skillfully removed his own armor without assistance. "And fucking hurry."

The cheering crowd began to murmur and talk amongst themselves as they saw what was going on. Montgeire stepped away from his armor and then removed his tunic, showing everyone his hairy chest and all the scars of previous fights that crisscrossed his skin. Once his attendants had removed his armor from the field he took a knee and watched Alexis closely.

The mistress waited impatiently as the armor was removed from her arms, her legs, and finally unclasped from around her torso. She wasted no time in adjusting the long breen shift that covered her chest and belly and hung down to her mid thigh. As her attendants hurried off the field with her armor she grasped the hem of the shift and sliced several inches off then tied what was left into a knot behind her, pulling the shift tight against her torso. She then cut off the sleeves and flexed her arms, making sure she had the range of movement she wanted.

"Is your attire to your satisfaction, my lady?" Montgeire asked. "I wouldn't want you to be hampered by a simple shift."

"I killed four men in a nightgown once, Montgeire," Alexis grinned. "I do this so as not to embarrass you. How would it look if the System's greatest champion was defeated by a girl in a loose shift?"

"Your confidence is amusing and dangerous, Your Highness," Montgeire said as he stood. "You should be careful. You are all alone out in this field. You cannot call your cult to help you."

"My cult?" Alexis frowned. "I do not get your meaning."

"Here comes a member now," Montgeire sighed. He turned and nodded as a visibly upset Jex stomped onto the field.

"What in Helios's name are you doing, Alexis?" Jex snarled. "I allow you a lot of leeway when it comes to your security, but this I will not stand for. Call your attendants back and don your armor at once!"

"Uh oh, someone's in trouble," Montgeire snickered.

Jex went for his blade and the crowd gasped loudly as Alexis grabbed his hand.

"Jex! Do not move another muscle!" Alexis ordered. "We are fighting until surrender. You will not interfere, you will not allow any of the other guards to interfere, and you will not allow any of the nobles to interfere. Do you understand me?"

"No," Jex said. "I do not understand you. This is reckless and dangerous. He could kill you."

Alexis smiled and leaned in close to the guard. "Do you really believe fate would allow that, Jex? After everything we have been through? Fate has a plan for me and it is not to die on this field." Her eyes were drawn past Jex's shoulder and she growled. "Great. Just great. Here comes my mother. Go and tell her what is happening and get her off the field. This is so embarrassing!"

Jex looked over his shoulder then back to Alexis. He started to speak then stopped and turned his attention to Montgeire. "You will fight like a gentleman and you will fight fair. If I even suspect you are going for a killing blow then I will have a longslinger put a barb right between your eyes. Are we understood?"

"Longslinger?" Montgeire frowned as he looked about the stands. "I was not told any would be in attendance."

"Nor was I," Alexis snapped.

"Good," Jex smiled. "Then that means my men can keep their mouths shut."

"Alexis!" Bella cried as she ran towards her daughter.

"Jex, get her off the field," Alexis ordered.

Jex nodded and turned from the two fighters to intercept the visibly upset Mistress who ran towards them.

"Ready, Your Highness?" Montgeire said as he took six steps back and presented his blade.

"I am, steward," Alexis said, also taking six steps back and presenting her own blade.

They waited for the horn to be blown.

*

The blood poured from the wound so freely that Alexis could hardly believe her eyes. It was as if a faucet had been placed in the steward's body and turned on to full. She stumbled back, letting go of the hilt of the broken blade that stuck from the man's neck, then turned to look at the other part of her blade that lay in the dirt and grass of the tournament field.

The cheers of the crowd had turned to silence then screams as Alexis fell to her knees next to the broken blade. She barely noticed the cries of alarm that came from the stands and edge of the field, all she could focus on was the neatly snapped end of the metal before her.

"Get up, my sweetest girl," a voice said from her side.

Alexis turned her head, but saw no one there.

"Get up, my girl," the voice said again. "Don't let them see you weak. Don't follow in my footsteps."

"Papa?" she whispered. "What have I done, Papa?"

"You did what you were trained to do," the voice replied. "Your blade broke and Montgeire was coming in for the killing blow. Your instincts took over and you moved without thought, struck without hesitation. That is what a warrior mistress does. That is who you are. There is no shame in that."

"But I killed him, Papa," Alexis said as she continued to stare at the long shard of metal. "This was a tournament, not a duel to the death. I was to win with honor, not murder."

"He came at you even after the blade broke," the voice responded. "You saw him, you know he wasn't going to stop. Listen to your instincts, Alexis. Listen to the truth of what happened. This was not a tournament fight;

this was a setup. This was not a simple duel amongst nobles; this was an assassination attempt."

"No, Papa, no," Alexis said as she shook her head.

"Oh, stop it!" the voice shouted, making Alexis jump. "You are not some servant girl! You are Alexis Teirmont the Third of Station Aelon and its Prime! You know what an assassination looks like! And you know that this man did not act alone!"

Alexis shook her head over and over until it felt as if her neck would turn to putty and dissolve from exhaustion. Hands gripped her and yanked her to her feet; she let them. Voices shouted all around her and asked if she was alright, if she was safe; she nodded. Bodies surrounded her and there were calls to arms; she did not argue against.

It took eternity and was over in seconds.

Alexis allowed herself to be taken from the surface and into the safety of Castle Quent. She allowed herself to be cleaned and then dressed in a nightgown. She allowed herself to be led and placed into her soft bed.

"There, there, child, hush now," her mother cooed in her ear as she lay next to the overwhelmed mistress. "Stop with your jabber. Just stop it now."

Alexis hadn't realized she was jabbering, but as her mother kissed her on the cheek she forced herself into conscious realization and stopped saying the words, "Fate is cruel, Papa. Fate is cruel."

She then removed the nightgown and fell into a deep sleep.

*

"Alexis? Are you awake?" Kel asked as he pushed open the door and quickly entered the mistress's bedchamber. "Alexis?"

"I'm awake," Alexis said quietly from the bed.

"It's so dark in here," Kel said.

"Leave it that way," Alexis said. "If you turn on the light then you'll be forced to see a murderer."

"You are not a murderer," Kel said as she shut the door and slowly felt his way over to the bed. He stood there for a second then sat down.

"Crawl up and comfort me, Kel," Alexis said.

"I cannot, Alexis," Kel responded. "I'm afraid I'm not here to comfort you. I have news; news you will not like."

Alexis sighed. "What? Has the meeting decided to strip me of my title? Have they finally found the balls to remove me from my birthright?"

"They have not decided that," Kel said as he reached out in the darkness and found her hand. "But they have decided to hold a trial. Evidence has been discovered and they know who orchestrated the plot to kill you."

"They do?" Alexis asked as she tried to pull Kel to her. "Stop resisting, dammit."

"I resist because I know you will be on your feet shortly," Kel said. "Like I said, you will not like the news."

"Why wouldn't I like to know who ordered Montgeire to sabotage my blade and try to assassinate me?"

Kel was silent.

"Kel? My love? Out with it. Who is the person behind it all?"

"Your uncle," Kel said. "Thomas Teirmont of Station Thraen. He's standing before the meeting right now. They won't give him a full trial and plan on sentencing him within the hour."

"They what?" Alexis shouted as she bolted from her bed. "My uncle? Never. Never!"

She turned on a lamp on a side table and stomped over to her closet.

"Helios, Alexis," Kel hissed as he averted his eyes from the mistress's naked body. "Don't you wear nightgowns?"

"No," Alexis said. "Not since one was nearly used against me on the prime when assassins were sent to kill me."

Alexis pulled an undershirt and tunic from the closet and threw them on then stood there, bare assed and started yanking trousers from the racks. "Dammit! Where are my purple breens? If I'm going to march in there and put a stop to this then I want my purple breens!"

"They're on the chair," Kel said as he pointed across the room. "But you'll want some underpants on first."

"Fuck that," Alexis said as she rushed over to the chair and snatched up her purple breen trousers. "I don't have time for underpants! I only put the undershirt on so the old pervs wouldn't stare at my nips! Now come on, Kel! We have to save my uncle!"

Kel was more than stunned as the mistress stormed from her bedchamber and into the main area of the royal quarters. He watched as startled servants dashed this way and that, desperate to get out of the way of the enraged monarch.

"*Kel!*" Alexis roared.

"Coming!" Kel yelled as he jumped and hurried after the woman he loved.

*

"The evidence is overwhelming," Beumont said as he sat at the end of the long table in the great hall, his eyes locked onto the shackled Thomas Teirmont who was forced to stand at the opposite end of the table. "We have the signed confession of the weapon smith, the evidence in the tampered blade, letters of correspondence between you and Steward Montgeire where you promise him part of Aelon's lease holdings on Thraen Prime, and the fact that you would have the next claim on the crown of Station Aelon should anything happen to your niece."

"All circumstantial," Thomas said. "The weapon smith committed suicide, so you do not have it first hand from him. Montgeire is dead, so you do not have it first hand from him. And I have never once mentioned wanting the crown in all the years I have lived in exile on Station Thraen."

"What the fuck is this?" Alexis roared as she threw open the doors to the great hall and marched over to her uncle's side. "Release him right now! My uncle would never hurt me! He has been set up and you know it, Beumont!"

"I know no such thing," Beumont responded as he stood up and held out his hand. An attendant hurried over and placed an envelope in his open palm. "What I do know is that he just lied to this august body of nobles. He states that he has never in his life mentioned wanting the crown, yet I have evidence to refute that right here."

Beumont opened the envelope and pulled out a letter. He cleared his throat, looked over the paper at Thomas, then at Alexis, cleared his throat again, then looked back at the letter and proceeded to read.

"*Steward Spiggot, I thank you for the loan and for the offer of support. While I had never thought of making a claim before, I believe your case, and my circumstances warrant we both look at the possibility further. As you know from my previous letters, my finances are ruined and I do not know how much longer I can rely on the grace of others. With mother dying, and her fortune tied to the crown of Station Thraen, I am left in a royal limbo.*

- 41 -

REIGN OF FOUR: BOOK III

Perhaps we could meet in a neutral location to discuss what would need to be done to remove my brother from his position and install me as Master of Station Aelon as is my birthright? I look forward to hearing back from you. Your New Friend, Thomas Teirmont."

"Where did you get that?" Thomas gasped.

"The Spiggots' belongings were confiscated by the crown as soon as they were killed," Beumont said. "Do you deny you wrote this?"

"No, I do not deny it, but I do have an explanation," Thomas replied.

"No explanation is needed," Beumont smiled. "You just told this meeting that you have never once mentioned wanting the crown yet here we have direct proof against that statement. How can we believe anything you say when you have already lied?"

"Uncle?" Alexis asked. "Did you want my father's crown?"

"No, Alexis, I did not," Thomas stated firmly. "That was a dark time for me and I was in deep debt. Herlen Spiggot contacted me and offered to finance my return. But I swear I never took him up on it." Thomas looked at Beumont and smirked. "Read the next letter I sent where I refuse Spigott's offer, Beumont."

"Next letter? We did not find a next letter," Beumont said. "I'm not saying you did not write one, just that I have no evidence of it."

"Convenient," Thomas said and looked at his niece. "You see what they're doing, don't you?"

"I don't know," Alexis said. "You lied about that letter. . . ."

"I forgot about the letter," Thomas snapped. "I would never have plotted against my own brother! And, as Helios as my witness, I would never plot against you!"

"If that is so, then please tell me where you were the last days of Alexis the Second's life, Thomas?" Beumont asked. "Because you certainly were not on Station Thraen."

"Don't," Thomas said quietly. "What you are about to say means nothing. It is not related to my brother's death."

"Is that so?" Beumont asked as he picked up a piece of paper from the table. "Then what an amazing coincidence that you happened to be on Planet Helios during the same time when Master Alexis died in such a horrible tragedy."

"Many people were on that planet then, you fool!" Thomas shouted. "That proves nothing!"

"Fine then tell us all what you were doing there," Beumont grinned. "Please. We would love to hear your explanation."

Thomas opened his mouth then closed it.

"Uncle? Tell them," Alexis said. "Just tell them who you were with on the planet."

"What I was doing on Helios, and who I was with, has nothing to do with the plot against you, Alexis," Thomas said. "Don't you get it? They are trying to blame me for one murder in order to prove I plotted another. Don't let them trap you in their thinking."

"But you can tell us who you were with, can't you?" Alexis asked. "Just so I know you had nothing to do with my father's death."

"A death that was ruled an accident by Aelon's very own regent," Thomas said. "But now he says it was deliberate and accuses me of having something to do with it."

"I accuse you of nothing, Thomas," Beumont said. "I am only allowing you to clear your name and prove to us that your word is worth listening to. Who were you with?"

"A woman," Thomas sighed. "A noble woman who I will not name for fear that her husband would retaliate and kill her."

"Oh, how chivalrous of you," Beumont said. "You choose to protect a woman's honor by sacrificing your own. Perhaps you could write her name down and the meeting could contact her privately to get her statement corroborating your alibi?"

"I cannot give you her name," Thomas said.

"Because her husband is a noble of Station Thraen and will harm her if he finds out she was unfaithful?" Beumont asked.

"No," Thomas said, swallowing hard. "Because her husband is a steward here on Aelon and is sitting at this table."

Many stewards shoved their chairs back and stood yelling at Thomas, their fingers pointing and mouths frothing with rage.

"Oh, dear," Beumont laughed. "I believe we touched a nerve here. Gentlemen? Gentlemen! Sit down!"

It took a few moments, but the enraged stewards calmed themselves enough to retake their seats.

"You certainly do not have any allies at this table, Thomas," Beumont said. "Oh, I believe your only hope is for a royal pardon from your niece. The very niece you plotted to have killed by a Thraen nobleman."

"Alexis, you have to believe me," Thomas said as he turned to the mistress. "I would never want a single hair on your head harmed. Not ever."

"Alexis," Kel whispered from her side. "We must talk before you say anything."

"Hush," Alexis snapped at him as she wiped tears from her cheeks. "Go stand against the wall with the others."

"Alexis?" he asked, shocked by the order.

"Just do it, Kel," Alexis said. "This is a matter for the crown, not for the Royal Guard."

"But, Alexis, you have to listen—"

"Go! *Now!*" Alexis roared, making the man take a step back as half the table jumped in their seats. She took a couple of deep breaths and calmed herself. "Please go stand over there, Kel. Please."

Kel started to speak then closed his mouth and bowed. He turned and walked away, taking his position by the doors to the great hall.

"Alexis. . .please," Thomas pleaded.

"Did you write that letter?" Alexis asked her uncle.

"Yes, but—"

"Were you on Helios when my father died?" she asked.

"Yes, but like I said, I was there—"

"Then I cannot help you," Alexis said. "I'm sorry, Uncle, but I cannot be objective in this. I must leave it up to the meeting to decide the evidence against you. If I overrule them, then I will look like a woman that lets her emotions rule her. I cannot be that mistress. The meeting is here for a reason, and matters such as this are part of that reason."

"Alexis. . .you'd just abandon me?" Thomas asked. He grabbed her by the shoulders. "Please!"

She pulled away from him and held out her hands as guards rushed forward. "I'm fine." Then she looked at his wrists and frowned. "Where is my bracelet?"

"What?" Thomas asked as he looked down at his wrists. He pushed up his sleeves then frowned and shook his head. "I. . .I don't know. I've never taken it off. Not ever. You know that."

"You mean this?" Beumont asked as he reached into his pocket and pulled out the worn and old breen bracelet. "The bracelet a servant girl found in the refuse bin in your chambers, Thomas? Why, after all these years, would you cut it off? Perhaps because you knew that your niece did not have long to live? Or perhaps due to your overwhelming guilt for what you conspired to have done to her?"

"I didn't take it off," Thomas said as he turned a pitiful and pleading look to his niece. "Alexis, I swear to Helios I am being framed."

"You gave me the blade," Alexis whispered. "You wrote that letter, then lied. You took off your bracelet."

"I didn't!"

"No, Uncle, no," Alexis said as she shook her head. "I cannot defend you. I am sorry."

She turned and hurried from the great hall. Kel paused briefly, his eyes locking on Beumont's before he followed her out.

"Well, gentlemen, I believe we have a verdict to deliver," Beumont said to the stunned meeting of stewards. "Thomas? Any last words?"

"May I sit while you read the verdict?" Thomas asked.

"No, you may not," Beumont smiled. "Your days of comfort are over, Thomas Teirmont."

*

Alexis sat on her bed, her legs crossed as she wrung her hands over and over. There was a light knock at the door, but she didn't answer, just kept twisting her fingers in between themselves.

"Alexis? Sweetheart?" Bella asked quietly as she opened the door. "Alexis? Can I come in?"

"No," Alexis said. "Go away, Mother."

"I will not," Bella said as she walked inside and closed the door behind her. "My Helios, look at this bedchamber. I am going to fire your attendants immediately."

"I told them to go away and not come back or I'd slice off their tits and feed them to each other," Alexis said. "They haven't come back."

Bella sighed as she walked over to her daughter. "You can't hide in here forever, Alexis. You are Mistress of Station Aelon. You have duties to perform and a job to do. The people need to see that you are strong and capable of handling your crown. Hiding like a broken hearted teenager does not help your cause."

"My cause, Mother? What cause is that?" Alexis snapped. "The cause of trying to navigate this den of scrim vipers I live in? The cause that even if I have the most loyal guards in the history of Station Aelon, someone, somewhere can hatch a plot to get to me? The cause that no matter how much I trust someone that trust can be shattered just like a long blade? Please, Mother, tell me what cause you mean."

"The cause of the crown, Alexis," Bella snapped. "The cause that every single master before you has had to deal with. The cause of keeping the passengers happy while keeping the meeting of stewards satisfied. The cause of running a station that holds more power than half the other stations combined. The cause of proving that a woman is not just a brood shaow and is as capable as any man to lead her people to greatness. How about those causes? Do any of those sound worth your time and energy?"

"No," Alexis said.

She never saw the slap coming.

Alexis's head rocked back and she was on her feet and towering over her mother in an instant, her fist pressed against the older woman's belly. Bella looked down and smiled.

"There she is," Bella said as she took her daughter's fist in her hands. "There is the girl that was raised to rule. Good thing I had Jex remove your blades from the room the last time he checked on you. I had asked Kel first, but apparently you are not talking to him. Why is that, Alexis?"

"I don't know," Alexis replied as she relaxed. "I may have yelled at him in front of the meeting."

"I know," Bella said. "I just wanted to hear you say it. Don't you think you owe him an apology?"

Alexis looked up at her mother and frowned. "Really? You have never approved of my feelings for Kel. Nor have you approved of my closeness with my guards. What are you up to?"

"Nothing," Bella said and sat down next to her daughter. "I've just realized that I have made a huge mistake with you. I have built walls between us by trying to force you into a space that doesn't fit you. No matter how much the reality that you are a ruling mistress slaps me in the face, my upbringing and life try to insist that you are like me, just a woman who must sit back and listen to the men around her. But that is not you, Alexis. You have power and opportunities that I never had. I should never have tried to lessen that power or those opportunities."

"So, if I were to marry Kel, then you wouldn't object?" Alexis asked.

"Marry him? Right now you won't talk to him, so I don't think marriage is in the picture," Bella laughed. "I can understand a teenage crush, Alexis. Trust me, I can. But when it comes time to marry, I believe you have better choices out there than one of your guards."

"I don't," Alexis said. "Fate decided that I would marry him and I listen to fate. Plus, well, I love him more than I love anyone else in the System. I love him more than I loved Papa."

Bella leaned back and studied her daughter for a few seconds.

"You're serious," Bella said. "You actually mean to marry him, don't you?"

"Yes," Alexis said. "I always have. Since the night I met him I knew he was the one."

"Because of fate?" Bella asked.

"Yes, because of fate and because of Papa," Alexis replied.

"What do you mean? What does your father have to do with you marrying a guard?" Bella asked.

"He told me that Kel was the right one," Alexis said. "When he speaks to me in his voice, he tells me things. They always come true. He told me Kel was the man that I would love forever and that we had to get married for the sake of Station Aelon."

"Alexis? You don't really believe you hear your father, do you?" Bella asked. "You understand that it's just your own mind you are hearing, right?"

Alexis stood up and turned to her mother, her brow furrowed.

"It is Papa," Alexis stated. "I know the difference between my own voice and Papa's voice. I'm not crazy."

"I wasn't saying you were," Bella replied. "I'm just worried that maybe the stress of being mistress is taking its toll and you—"

"Don't," Alexis sighed as she walked over to her closet and rummaged around until she found a cloak and a short blade. "I knew he didn't find all of them."

"Wait, Alexis, what are you doing? Where are you going?" Bella asked as she stood and hurried over to her daughter. "We're not done talking yet, young lady."

"Yes, Mother, we are," Alexis said. "Thank you for trying to comfort me, but we have to face the fact that you can never understand me and that I never want to understand you. I love you, but we live in different worlds. I'm going for a walk." She looked about her bedchamber. "Please have the servants come back and clean up. I'm ready to face the station and the meeting again. Don't bother waiting up for me; I may be late."

Alexis strode to the door and left the bedchamber quickly before her mother could utter another objection.

*

The environmental shield shimmered in the night as Alexis lay on her back, nestled in a soft patch of grass in one of the many courtyards of Castle Quent. She pulled her cloak tight around her as the night chill tried to get to her. Even with the feint shimmer of the shield, Alexis could see star after star twinkling in the sky, teasing of other systems far, far away from hers.

"Alexis?" Kel whispered from the dark. "Are you out here?"

"Yes," Alexis said. "Sorry."

"For what?" Kel asked as he crossed the courtyard and sat down next to her, unsheathing his sword so he didn't jam it into the dirt. "What are you sorry for?"

"For yelling at you," Alexis said.

"You shouldn't be sorry," Kel said. "I'm the sorry one. Sorry for not telling you what I know sooner."

Alexis turned and propped herself on her elbow. "So tell me. What's the big secret that you felt compelled to interrupt my Uncle's trial to tell me?"

"You're not going to like it," Kel said. "And you aren't going to like me for keeping it from you. But, in my defense, it is only a rumor I heard from some of the veteran Burdened. And since Burdened are never supposed to spread rumors, I just figured that they were messing with me."

"And...?" Alexis prodded. "Out with it, my love."

"You called me your love again," Kel grinned. "You have no idea what a relief that is."

"I have a short blade with me, Kel," Alexis growled. "I'll use it if I have to, so start talking."

"Fine, calm down," Kel laughed.

"Mistress!" Jex shouted as he burst into the courtyard and hurried over to them. "Alexis! You're being summoned to the meeting!"

"The meeting? At this hour?" Alexis asked. "What's happening?"

"The lowdeckers," Jex said. "They are revolting and have started moving up the decks. Klipoline is saying that he should be the Master of Station Aelon since no woman should ever hold the crown."

"Son of a grendt," Alexis snarled. "Damn lowdeckers. They picked the wrong time to come after me." Kel stood up and Alexis leaned in and kissed him quickly. "We'll talk later, alright? You can tell me your secret then."

"Yeah, sure, go," Kel said. "I'll get the rest of the guard together and meet you two at the great hall."

"Sounds good," Alexis said as she took off running with Jex. "Love you!"

"Love you too," Kel called back.

CHAPTER THREE

The great hall was packed with nobility. Instead of the usual simple majority, the meeting held almost every single steward from every single sector on Station Aelon. The massive space was filled with the excited voices of men preparing for war.

"Please! Everyone quiet down!" Beumont shouted as he rapped his knuckles on the table six times and sat down. Soon the refrain was taken up and the nobles began to take their seats and rap their knuckles as well until no voices were heard, only bone on wood. "Thank you."

Instead of sitting at the head of the table, as was his usual custom as regent, Beumont sat just to the right so that the main chair could be occupied by Mistress Alexis. All eyes fell on Beumont, then Alexis; back and forth until Beumont cleared his throat and stood back up.

"I thank all of you for coming to court on such short notice," Beumont said.

"We had notice, Beumont," Steward Hume said. "The disgusting lowdeckers rampaging through the bottom levels of our Middle Decks was all the notice we needed."

"What is the crown going to do about this?" asked Steward Nitting, an older, heavyset steward from Sector Fennlane. "These lowdeckers have been a thorn in our buttocks for generations now, Beumont. Part of the agreement—"

"Yes, Chaz, I know," Beumont interrupted. "We all know the history of the lowdeckers and their constant troubles. And, for the most part, Master Klipoline has kept things under control. But, again as we all know, lowdeckers are fickle, untrustworthy people and never content with the graciousness we have shown them."

"Middle Decks Seventy-Five through Sixty-Eight have been overrun!" Steward Claxton yelled. He was an average man, of average height and average age, that rarely spoke out in the meeting. Many of the stewards had to search their memories for his name since he was so easy to forget and overlook. "I lost three factories and an entire year's worth of breen blankets ready for shipment to Ploerv! Do you know the penalty I will have to pay for not fulfilling that shipment? I expect the crown to reimburse me for every credit lost!"

Many stewards stood and began demanding the same from Beumont as the besieged regent rubbed his face and looked on. Instead of interrupting them he just let the men shout their grievances and demands until they realized he was not going to respond and reluctantly took their seats with grumbling voices and half-concealed insults.

"There, are you finished, gentlemen?" Beumont asked. "Or do you need to whine some more like little children that dropped their dollies in a puddle?"

"Puddles," Alexis said.

"I beg your pardon?" Beumont asked.

"Puddles," Alexis said. "If there are children and there are dollies then there are puddles. Plural."

"I don't think that matters much," Beumont said.

"Sure it does," Alexis grinned. "If you are going to talk about dollies then at least get it right. I would know since I'm a girl. That's a subject I can speak on. Dollies in puddles. Dollies in beds. Dollies in dresses. That's why none of you have looked to me for an answer, right Step-Daddy? Because you have been busy talking man talk and don't want to involve the girl sitting at the head of the table. You know, the one that is mistress of this station? Don't bother her. No, no, no."

Beumont stared at her for a few seconds then frowned and turned back to the meeting.

"Don't look away from me, Beumont," Alexis said.

Her tone of voice made Beumont pause just as he was about to speak. He closed his mouth and looked back at the mistress then bowed his head.

"My apologies, Your Highness," Beumont said. "Is there something you'd like to say that is not doll related? Would you care to address the meeting and offer your words of wisdom?"

"I thought you'd never ask," Alexis smiled as she stood up.

Many of the men seated at the long table rolled their eyes and let out long, exaggerated breaths of contempt while others just leaned back in their chairs and stared up at the ceiling high above. Alexis smirked at the lack of respect she was shown and made a point of standing there silent until one by one the men were forced to look at and acknowledge her.

"Hello," she said and waved. "I'm Alexis Teirmont the Third, Mistress of Station Aelon and its Prime. I just want to make sure you all are acutely aware of that. I'd hate for there to be a misunderstanding when I make my declaration."

"Declaration?" Beumont asked, looking worried. "Alexis, we haven't discussed any—"

"Mistress," Alexis said. "It is customary to address me formally when the meeting is in session. You may call me Alexis when we are in the royal quarters, but here I would prefer to be addressed as mistress or Your Highness. Is that too much to ask, Steward Beumont?"

Beumont looked more than confused, a look that was equally matched by the majority of men at the long table.

"My apologies?" Beumont replied, completely off balance. "No disrespect meant."

"Good," Alexis said. "May I share what I have in mind now?"

"Yes, of course," Beumont nodded and waved a hand at the assembled nobles. "By all means."

"Gentlemen," Alexis said. "As you may or may not know, care or care not, I have been making changes to the Royal Guard over the past year. Many of the men have become more than just security for the crown and are my most trusted allies and protectors."

There was a snort from far down the table and Alexis leaned forward, placing both hands on the wood and cocked her head. "Does someone have something to say?"

All eyes turned to Steward Harper.

"No offense, Your Highness," Harper said. "But shouldn't your allies be the meeting of stewards and not a group of uncouth, uncultured guards?"

"Yes, you would think that to be true, wouldn't you?" Alexis smiled. "Yet, for me, I prefer that my allies actually be willing to die for me instead of hoping I die on a tournament field."

There were several gasps and cries of shock.

"Mistress," Beumont cautioned through gritted teeth. "None of these men had anything to do with that unfortunate incident. The perpetrator of the crime was found, convicted, and executed. You know that."

"Of course I know that, Beumont," Alexis replied. "I will always know that. What I meant was that I highly doubt any of the men sitting here today would have been saddened by my death on that field. I can see many advantages it would have had for half of the stewards present. Not to mention the advantage you'd gain, Step-Daddy. Think of all that power."

"Mistress," Beumont growled. "I would be heartbroken if anything happened to you. I have known you for many years and like to think of myself as more than just regent, but as a father figure. Especially since you never truly had a positive role model in that respect."

"Positive? No, I suppose I never did," Alexis admitted. "Loving? More than you can comprehend, sir. Never presume to put yourself in a place where you have no business and may not be welcome. My heart is not open to all."

"Your highness, this is not a conversation for the meeting," Beumont said. "I believe you have gotten off track."

"Have I?" Alexis smirked. "I don't think I have. I am more on track than I have ever been."

Beumont sighed and rubbed at a spot between his eyes. "Then please, tell us all what it is you are thinking."

"The mistake you men are making is that you think the crown is here to serve you, to make your lives and existence better," Alexis said. "Whereas I say it is you that is here to serve the crown and lay down your lives to make the station's existence better. That is why I am asking that each of you volunteer twenty of your best men from your militias. Between all sectors, that will give us more than enough soldiers to descend on the lowdeckers and clip Klipoline's wings once and for all."

Silence.

Not a sound could be heard in the great hall.

"And, so none of you question my commitment, and the commitment of the crown, to this cause, I will be leading this fighting force myself," Alexis announced. "I think I have proven on more than one occasion that I am capable of handling myself in combat. Now I will prove it to the lowdeckers and the usurper Klipoline."

Silence. Then slowly, as a small bubbling at first, the laughter began. Soon the entire table was chaos as men guffawed at the idea Alexis presented. They slapped backs and wiped at eyes, none taking the teenager seriously at all.

None except Beumont. He ignored the cacophony and leaned in close to his step-daughter.

"Do you have any idea what you just proposed?" Beumont asked. "You are saying you will lead the assault against Klipoline yourself and that you expect the stewards' men to follow you into battle. If you were ten years older and a man that would be quite the task. But, you are neither of those. You are a sixteen-year-old girl that has been trained to duel and fight in a controlled setting. War is not controlled, Your Highness. It is chaos and blood and never what you expect."

"So is life, Beumont," Alexis replied. "Or have you forgotten how I saved our lives on Helios that night? I understand danger, I understand killing, now I want to understand victory."

"There is no victory in war, Alexis," Beumont said and held up a hand before she could object to the use of the familiar. "You may win and send the lowdeckers back down to their holes in the station, but you will not be victorious. They are your people, too. Fighting them will win you no new allies and will more than likely make enemies for life. I advise you rescind your plan and we look at a diplomatic solution. Namely, we bribe the Helios out of Klipoline until he quits and goes away. That's what he wants anyway. The man could care less about his people. He has always wanted title and riches."

"He has been given a title," Alexis said. "He is Master of the Lower Decks. I no longer believe he deserves that. As for riches? Not the crown's problem."

"Everything is the crown's problem," Beumont replied.

"Not for long," Alexis said then slammed her hands down on the table. The great hall quieted down and many mocking, bleary eyes turned her way. "I would like to put this to a vote, as a courtesy to the meeting."

"A courtesy?" Harper asked. "I believe you to have that backwards, Your Highness."

"No, I do not," Alexis said. "According to the charter of this station, the master, or mistress, has all authority in matters of war and station defense.

I ask that you vote, so that I may see who stands with me and who stands against me."

"Voting *nay* does not mean we would stand against you, mistress," Steward Hume said. "It just means we are not willing to sacrifice our men on a fool's fight. It will be less bloody, and less costly, if we just pay the idiot man off and be done with it."

"But you look for the crown to pay, is that not correct?" Alexis asked.

"Naturally," Hume said. "Klipoline only has power because of the title he was granted by your father. The meeting of stewards did not approve of that course of action and you can now see why."

"But what is to stop the man from rising up again as soon as his pockets are empty? What will stop him from extorting the crown at every opportunity he gets?" Alexis asked the meeting. "Nothing will stop him. It is no different than rewarding a toddler with candy for throwing a tantrum. No, gentlemen, Klipoline needs strict discipline, not another lolly."

As one, the meeting looked to Beumont.

"We put it to a vote," Beumont shrugged. "All in favor?"

More silence then slowly hands were raised and "Ayes" were called out. In seconds a surprising majority was revealed.

"Well," Alexis grinned. "That was unexpected."

"At the end of the day, Your Highness, you are the Mistress of the Station," Beumont said. "We are bound by duty to follow you." He looked at the meeting. "Let us adjourn immediately so that preparations can be made. Twenty of your best men will need to be ready for deployment by the end of the week. Do not dally, gentlemen. If the mistress is to have our support then she deserves to have it in a timely manner."

"Thank you, gentlemen," Alexis said. "You will not regret this. I will prove to you all that I am a Teirmont through and through. If you'll excuse me, I must speak with my guards. I expect them to take leadership roles within each regiment and I must prepare them for that. May the Dear Parent bless you all."

The meeting watched as she turned and hurried from the great hall. Once she was gone, Stewards Hume, Harper, Magnaird, Gwalter and Wulberry caught Beumont's eye. He nodded his head towards a small door between the tapestries on the far wall. They nodded back, excused themselves from the men around them, and each made their way to the door.

*

"How in Helios's name did you get her to agree to that?" Hume asked. "This couldn't be more perfect."

"She truly believes she can lead men into battle," Harper laughed.

"She believes she not only can lead them, but that she can win," Wulberry added.

"I must say, Beumont, the failure at the tournament had me worried," Gwalter said. "We put our faith in you and you let us down."

"But this?" Magnaird said. "This is brilliant."

Beumont looked at the men as they stood in the cramped antechamber just off the great hall. He almost was willing to take credit for it all, but he calculated the risks of deceiving the council and decided that honesty, in that occasion, was the best course.

"I did nothing," Beumont said. "I never spoke to her about going to battle. My plan was to have the meeting pay Klipoline off, just as I said. He would have come back for more and more and soon the treasury would have been bankrupt and the businessmen of the Middle Decks would have called for her head when the crown was forced to raise taxes to make up for the deficits. I had abandoned the direct route and was looking at a more long term solution to our mistress problem."

"Wait, Beumont, are you saying the girl came up with the idea on her own?" Harper asked. "That she got it into her head that she could lead a fighting force into battle against the lowdeckers down in their own turf where no other master has ever truly succeeded before?"

"Yes," Beumont grinned. "The girl is mad like her father."

"And rash like her grandfather," Hume added.

"And a useless ruler like her great-grandfather," Magnaird said.

"It seems her only qualities are her legs," Hume chuckled. "Which she may lose quite soon."

"To be serious, Beumont," Harper said. "If she is to fall, then are we still in agreement that the crown remains empty and the meeting takes full control of the station? Even with a loss, this battle will stir up patriotism amongst many of the passengers. It will be hard to dissolve the monarchy if that happens."

"We dissolve nothing," Beumont replied. "The monarchy will remain, but we will have full control over the person that takes Alexis's place."

"How can you be sure of that, Beumont?" Hume asked.

"Because the person that the meeting will put in my step-daughter's place will be none other than her grieving mother," Beumont grinned. "My wife."

"Brilliant," Hume laughed. "She is a royal and the passengers will have nothing but sympathy for her during her grief for her late daughter."

"And since she is a woman, the meeting will not look like it is going backwards," Harper said. "Another move that will shore up passenger support. I could almost thank Klipoline for his treachery."

"But what if she escapes death again?" Gwalter asked.

"I think some carefully chosen words to your men will assure that that does not happen," Beumont suggested. "I'm not saying they should revolt, but perhaps not give their all at crucial moments in the battle."

The men all smiled at the idea.

*

"Alexis!" Bella shouted as she marched into the Royal Guard barracks. "Alexis Tiermont!"

"Uh oh," Kel frowned as he stepped aside so Alexis, encircled by her most trusted guards, could see her mother come at her. "Should we leave?"

"No, stay," Alexis said as she left the circle and hurried up to her mother. "Mother. What are you doing here? This is a strategy meeting with my men. I need to focus right now."

"Did you actually think I would allow you to go into battle against Klipoline and his lowdeckers? Have you lost your teenage mind, girl?" Bella shouted.

"Hardly, Mother," Alexis smiled. "I am Mistress of the Station, so it is my duty to lead the charge against the insurgents."

"Alexis, you are talking nonsense," Bella snapped. "Your father never tried to take on the lowdeckers, and there was a reason for that. Do you know what the reason was?"

"Yes," Alexis nodded. "The reason was even his father couldn't fully defeat the Lower Decks. He reached an accord with them, but it just barely kept them in line. My father gave them everything that has led to this mess.

Now I will finish what my grandfather started and clean up what my own father never could."

"You will die, is what you will do," Bella exclaimed. "The men down there will have your head before you get past the first passageway. They do not fight with long blades, but with heavy blades that even you cannot wield with two hands. One swipe will cut a man in half. You are not a man, Alexis, so it will take even less force to sever your legs from the rest of you."

"They can try," Alexis beamed. "I welcome the challenge."

Bella grabbed her daughter by the upper arm and pulled her close. With her other hand she touched Alexis's forehead.

"You aren't feverish, so this is not a physical ailment," Bella said. "So it can only mean an affliction of the mind. I forbid you to go through with this until I have had the physicians look you over."

"You don't forbid anything, Mother," Alexis said as she pulled free. Her eyes narrowed and her voice grew cold. "You have no power over me on this station. And don't even think of protesting to your husband. I have the full support of the regent and the meeting of stewards. It has been decided and there is no turning back from this."

"No, it has—"

"Yes, it has!" Alexis roared. "I am mistress and you are not! I rule Aelon and you do not! Now, leave me so I can prepare with my men!"

"Alexis, you are not thinking straight," Bella said.

"Yes, Mother, I am," Alexis replied. "I am thinking straight enough to consider throwing you in the Third Spire if you do not leave my sight in ten seconds."

"Alexis!" Bella cried.

"Ten."

"You wouldn't dare."

"Nine."

"Do not test me, child."

"Eight."

"Alexis, stop that at once!"

"Seven."

"You are serious."

"Six."

"Oh, for Helios's sake, knock off that childish counting," Bella snapped. "I'll leave. But do one thing for me before I go."

"And what is that?" Alexis frowned.

"Hug your mother," Bella said as she held out her arms. "This could be the last time I see you."

Alexis's entire demeanor changed. Her aggressive posture, defiant attitude, and willingness to imprison her own mother flew out the door as she gladly embraced Bella, almost lifting the older woman off her feet.

"I love you, Mother," Alexis said. "Don't you worry. I'll be safe. I have some of the strongest men in the System fighting for me. Not to mention the full backing of the meeting and the men the stewards will provide."

Bella just squeezed her eyes closed and hung onto her daughter for as long as she could.

*

"Where are they?" Alexis screamed as she retreated down the passageway towards the lift. "Harper's men and Hume's men were supposed to flank Klipoline while we drove him back! We aren't supposed to be the ones being driven!"

"Alexis!" Kel shouted. "Behind you!"

Alexis dropped to a knee and spun about, her long blades slicing into the thighs of the lowdecker that had just swung his heavy blade where her head had been only a second before. The man screeched and fell forward, but Alexis rolled out of the way before he could crush her. She slashed out with a blade and the man's head tumbled from his neck.

It rolled down the passageway and Alexis watched its progress in horror. Not because of the decapitation and trail of blood the severed head left in its wake, but because she saw just how badly outnumbered her men were. All were excellent fighters and would have stood against any soldier from any station in the System, but the number of lowdeckers that came at them was too much.

Just too much.

"Where is Jex?" Alexis yelled as she jumped to her feet and sprinted down the passageway with Kel. "He should be here by now!"

"We'll meet him at the next junction," Kel said, pushing Alexis to the side as a hatchet flew through the air between them.

Kel drew a short blade from his belt and threw it at the man that had stepped from the alcove in front of them. There was a brief shriek then a strangled choke as the man fell to his knees, his hands trying to pry the blade from his throat. Kel kicked him square in the face as they ran past.

"Rally on me!" Alexis yelled over her shoulder, hoping some of her squad still had life enough to hear her. "To me!"

She risked a quick glance, and wished she hadn't as she saw not a single allied soul standing, let alone rushing to join her. All she saw were angry lowdeckers, smeared with her comrades' blood and guts. Even the most hardened of soldiers would have been close to breaking at that sight, but Alexis turned back around and shoved it from her mind, knowing she'd have to revisit the images later.

If she had a later.

She and Kel skidded to a stop when they reached the junction of the last two passageways before the lift that would take them back up to safety. Both of them were stunned at the sight of pure ferocity they witnessed. Man after man from the royal guard was cut down as they desperately tried to retreat. Heads rolled, arms fell, legs collapsed as heavy blade after heavy blade met their marks.

"Helios," Kel whispered, his voice lost amongst the screams and pleas for mercy.

But there was no mercy. Lowdeckers chopped Alexis's men to pieces then stomped on the dead mens' heads, laughing as the brains exploded onto the floor and against the walls. They used the massive pommels of their heavy blades to break bones and crack open skulls. They gouged out eyes and ripped lips off faces. Throats were torn open with bare hands.

Blood coated every square inch of the passageway including the one man still left fighting.

"Jex!" Alexis screamed as she rushed into the fray. "Jex!"

"Dammit, Alexis!" Kel called after her as he dodged one sword swipe and then another, burying his long blade up to the hilt in the ribs of a huge lowdecker who stood almost a foot taller than him. The man coughed blood all over Kel's face and he barely wiped his eyes clear in time to duck and roll from the double attack that came at him from two more lowdeckers.

"Alexis!" Kel yelled as he kicked out and snapped one man's knee, then used the man's falling bulk to shield him from the heavy blade that came at his head. "Alexis!"

The Mistress ignored her love's calls and dodged between the berserker lowdeckers to get to the head of her Royal Guard. She jammed a blade into the soft flesh under one man's chin then twisted, pulled down, spun about and gutted a second man who rushed her from behind. She grabbed onto the man's freed entrails and threw them into another man's face just as she thrust her blade into his groin and tore down, sending his manhood, and half his blood supply, falling to the floor.

"Jex!" Alexis yelled. "Jex! Duck!"

Without thinking, Jex dropped his head and let the heavy blade fly over before he thrust his own blade into the man's belly. He tried to pull it free, but it was lodged in the man's spine, so Jex let it go and reached down for a small blade he had tucked into his boot. He ducked to the side and slashed out with the blade, cutting a man's forearm open from wrist to elbow. Blood sprayed in a high arc and coated the ceiling.

"Here!" Alexis yelled as she shoved one of her blades into Jex's hand. "Come on! We have to get back to the lift!"

"You go!" Jex shouted. "I will keep them from following!"

Alexis pressed herself against the man and shouted right into his ear. "Fuck that! Come with me now, asshole! That's a fucking order!"

Jex couldn't help but smile as every fiber in his body obeyed, unable to refuse the woman that had captivated him since she first spoke to him down on Aelon Prime. He nodded once, raised his blade to block a killing blow, parried the attack and then let his blade continue its momentum until it came back around in a full circle and severed the hands of the attacker.

Alexis pulled at his polybreen armor and they made their way back to Kel, fighting for every inch. The three warriors closed ranks and dodged, slashed, thrust, parried, ducked as one unit, each anticipating theirs and their opponents' movements as if they somehow could see them before they happened.

Fifty bloody feet, thirty bloody feet, ten, five, and they were at the lift.

"It won't open!" Kel shouted as he slammed his fist against the lift controls. Then he cried out as he fell to the floor, a blade protruding from his back. "Fuck!"

"No!" Alexis yelled. "Kel!"

"Protect him and I'll get the lift open!" Jex shouted.

Alexis went to pull the blade from Kel's armor, but Jex kicked her hand away.

"He'll bleed out! Leave it!" Jex yelled. He used his blade to pry open the lift controls and then went to work.

"Fuck off!" Alexis screamed as she hooked a blade with the toe of her boot and kicked it at two men coming for her. The blade sliced off half of one man's face, causing him to fall and trip up the second man.

Alexis found more stray blades and started tossing them as hard and fast as she could. Men threw themselves against the walls of the passageway to get clear of the flying metal. Some slipped on the offal and blood that coated every inch of the floor while others tripped on the body parts that were scattered everywhere. It gave Alexis just enough time to get her hands up under Kel's arms as the lift doors finally opened.

"Get his legs!" she shouted at Jex.

"Got them!" Jex yelled as he grabbed Kel's legs and the two of them lifted the wounded man and carried him into the lift. "The controls had an override in place, Alexis!"

"They what?" she cried as she set Kel down.

"There was an override!" Jex said, turning around so he could hit the inside controls and close the doors. "Someone above must have—"

His voice cut off and Alexis screamed as a heavy blade burst out his back. A lowdecker sneered in at them just before the lift doors closed. Alexis immediately saw what was going to happen and she tried to get to the lift controls to stop, but she was too late. The lift started to ascend and the blade that was caught in the doors, and in Jex, was pulled down quickly, splitting the man down the middle from chest to groin.

"*Jex!*" Alexis screamed as she dove for her protector and friend. "*No!*"

She hit the floor of the lift and yanked Jex into her lap, but the man was already dead. His organs spilled out of him and all over Alexis as she cradled his corpse in her arms. She didn't care as she rocked the man back and forth, her lips kissing his cheeks, his forehead, his eyes.

"Nonononono," she whimpered. "Nonononono."

"Alexis?" Kel whispered. "Alexis? Are you there?"

"Kel?" she gasped, reluctantly letting Jex's body slump from her so she could crawl over to the man she loved. "Kel? Don't move, baby. Don't move or the blade could do more damage."

Kel lay on his belly, the blade sticking straight up from between his fourth and fifth rib. Alexis lay down with him, her face pressed to his, her breath hot and strong against his lips, his breath barely a puff of weak air.

"Alexis, listen," Kel said.

"No, no, be quiet," Alexis said. "Save your strength."

"No, I have to tell you this," Kel insisted. "You have to know the truth."

"What truth, my love?" Alexis asked. "That you are the world to me and that you won't die? That Helios has written it in the stars that we are fated to marry and have many beautiful children? You don't have to tell me that. I know it all."

"Beumont killed your father," Kel said. "The Burdened, on the High Guardian's orders, helped him make it look like a fire. They killed all witnesses."

Alexis's breath stopped. Her eyes studied Kel's, looking for the lie, looking for the delusion. But she saw none. Only sincerity stared back at her.

"I heard about it from the others," Kel said. "I didn't think it was true, but as time went on, and I learned more about Beumont, I knew it was. He killed your father. I'm sorry, Alexis."

"How?" was all she could say.

"You don't want to—"

"*How?*" she screamed.

The rage that came off Alexis in waves made Kel draw back and he cried out in pain.

"Oh, no, no, I'm sorry," Alexis said immediately and started kissing his lips over and over. "I'm sorry, I'm sorry. I love you. It's not your fault. Thank you for telling me. Please don't let my anger be the last thing you remember."

Kel smiled weakly. "Your anger would never be the last thing I remember. It would be those damn legs and that dimple on your chin."

Alexis laughed and cried at the same time. Her body shook with sobs as she reached out and stroked Kel's face over and over.

"Hang on, love, hang on," she cooed. "We'll be up top soon."

"I won't make it to the top," Kel whispered. "I can tell, Alexis. We have to say goodbye."

"I will not say goodbye," Alexis snapped as she pushed herself to her feet and went to the lift controls. "I will find help."

"Alexis, no," Kel said. "We don't know who to trust below the surface. Some of the Middle Decks may be helping the lowdeckers."

"Not this Middle Deck," she said as she pressed a button and waited.

It was a long, painful hour until the lift began to slow. Alexis checked Kel constantly, waiting for him to take his last breath, but the man hung on, if just barely.

When the lift stopped, Alexis held her blades in front of her and waited for the doors to open. As soon as they did, she was greeted by the black holes of a dozen longsling barrels.

"Mistress Alexis?" one of the men asked. "Is that you?"

"Yes," Alexis said as she looked out at the men of Middle Deck Twenty. "My man is wounded and I need your help. I know you are not lovers of the crown after the way my father and the Spiggots disrespected you, but I come as a woman in need who only wants help saving the man she loves. Forget I am mistress, forget about the crown, and please, please just help me."

The longslings wavered, wavered, then lowered.

"Get him to the physicians," a man ordered. "Be careful with him."

Several men pushed past Alexis and gently lifted Kel up, carrying him out of the lift and down a passageway towards the main atrium of Middle Deck Twenty.

"I'm Claevan Twyerrn," the man said as he held out his hand. "It is an honor, Your Highness."

"The honor is mine," Alexis said as she curtsied in her blood coated polybreen armor. "I will be forever grateful."

"Do not shame yourself, mistress," Claevan said. "We are your loyal subjects and would do anything for you."

"I do not believe your deck boss would say the same," Alexis said. "My father was not a favorite of his." She paused and looked at the man. "Wait...Twyerrn?"

"Yes, Your Highness," Claevan smiled. "My father was the one that refused to help your father. He was deck boss at that time."

"Was?" Alexis asked.

"He passed six months ago, leaving the job to me since Steward Beumont has been too busy as regent to appoint another," Claevan nodded. "I am the youngest deck boss in the history of Middle Deck Twenty." He looked past

Alexis at Jex's corpse and frowned. "Would you like me to have his body secured down here while you return to the Surface?"

"Return," Alexis said, more to herself than to Claevan. "Yes, I would appreciate that. Thank you."

"You need not thank me," Claevan said. "Your willingness to fight for the station and for your crown is all the thanks I need. I have two infant daughters, twins just born, and you will be the example that they can do anything on this station, even if they are female."

Alexis tried to smile then frown then grimace then cry, but her emotions wouldn't settle, so she just patted Claevan on the arm and turned to look into the lift.

"Help me get him out," she said. "I believe the time to return is now."

*

When the lift doors opened, the soldiers that had been stationed by them to ensure no lowdeckers made it up to the Surface all gasped at the sight of the mistress that was painted in blood from head to toe. She held long blades, one in each hand, and just nodded to the men as she casually walked past them.

"Mistress?" one finally was able to muster the strength to say. "Are you injured?"

"No," Alexis said as she kept walking from the lift and down the passageway in the direction of the great hall.

"Should we call Regent Beumont for you?" the soldier asked.

"No," Alexis said. "I'm going to find him right now."

*

The great hall doors burst open and the council seemed to be caught in mid toast as the horror that was Alexis the Third stalked towards the long table where they were seated.

"Alexis?" Beumont asked, barely recognizing the girl. "Is that you? My Helios, child, you are injured!"

"It's not my blood," Alexi said as she walked over to a side table and poured herself a large glass of gelberry wine. She drained it and poured another then walked to the long table and sat down next to Steward Hume, tossing her blades up onto the surface in front of her. "It's my men's blood. And the blood of quite a few lowdeckers. But mostly it is Jex's and Kel's."

"Are they with you?" Beumont asked as he looked about the great hall and realized there were no guards present as he had sent them away so he and the council could speak freely in private. "I hope they are as unhurt as you."

"I never said I wasn't hurt," Alexis said, sipping from her glass. "Believe me, Step-Daddy, I am deeply, deeply hurt."

She set her glass down and picked up a blade. Steward Hume's head was off and rolling across the great hall before the other men knew anything had happened. His decapitated corpse spewed blood like a geyser up into the air. It gushed then spurted, spurted, and stopped.

"Helios!" Beumont cried.

The others leapt to their feet. Harper and Wulberry reached for blades on their belts, but both stopped short of pulling them.

"Please," Alexis said as she continued to stay seated. "Draw your weapons, gentlemen. I am upset, exhausted, and traumatized from having to fight my way through the Lower Decks because none of your soldiers showed up when they were supposed to. I am also emotionally defeated since my dearest friend, Jex, was split in two by a heavy blade. Actually, he was impaled by the blade; I believe the lift did the actual splitting."

She sipped some more wine, her eyes moving slowly back and forth from one man to the other.

"What? No one is going to apologize for leaving me to die?" Alexis asked. "I'm not my father or my grandfather. You'd be surprised how far an apology goes with me."

"I'm sorry," Gwalter said. "I never wanted to be a part of the betrayal."

"You lying fuck," Harper hissed.

The blade flew from the table and landing square in Gwalter's chest. He coughed blood across the table then collapsed to the floor.

"Apparently my blade goes further than an apology," Alexis grinned. "Who's next?"

The men watched her for a second then turned as one and bolted for the doors.

Alexis was up and chasing them down with her long stride before they even got a quarter of the way. She tackled Harper around the legs and had his blade out of its sheath and imbedded in his skull just as his face slammed into the floor from the fall. She rolled off Harper and jumped at Magnaird, sweeping the man's legs out from under him then she sprang into the air and collided with Wulberry, taking his blade and slitting his throat wide open in almost one motion.

Alexis got to her feet and flicked the blood from the blade.

"Step-Daddy," she called after Beumont as the regent was almost to the doors. "You'll never be able to hide from me."

Beumont reached the doors and threw them open. "Guards! Help!"

"I know you killed my father," Alexis said as she walked towards the man. "But I don't know how. I'd dearly appreciate it if you would tell me the method in which you murdered my Papa. Do you think you could do that for your beloved step-daughter?"

Beumont was out into the hall and ready to sprint away when Alexis's words sunk in.

"Alexis, mistress, sweetheart," Beumont said. "I don't know who you heard that from, but I can assure you it is not true. I would never do anything to cause you harm."

Alexis looked down at her armor then looked back at the regent and raised an eyebrow. "Really? That's what you're going with? You'd never do anything to cause me harm?"

She followed Beumont out into the passageway, making sure to take slow, even steps so she didn't spook him. The sound of boots on the station's hammered metal floor echoed from the far end of the passageway and Beumont turned his attention to the sound.

"It's not too late to fix this, Alexis," Beumont said. "Just let me explain everything and you'll see that I had no choice but to go along with the council. It has been their decisions I have been following."

"You lying sack of shaowshit," a stunned Magnaird said from the great hall's entrance. "You orchestrated all of this! From day one it was your plan to murder the master and then take the crown from the mistress! Don't you dare say different, Beumont, you slimy bog toad!"

"That's why I didn't kill the whole council," Alexis said as she grinned at her step-father. "I needed one steward left alive to tell everyone that you are a traitor and a murderer." She looked over at Magnaird. "Are you willing to testify in front of the entire meeting, steward?"

"I am," Magnaird said. "For immunity."

"Immunity from what?" Alexis asked.

"Conspiring to withdraw our soldiers from the Lower Decks," Magnaird replied. "And for plotting your death during the tournament."

"Idiot!" Beumont yelled. "She knew nothing about that!"

"She does now!" Magnaird shouted.

"Oh, I had a feeling," Alexis said. "But it is good to know my feeling was right." She nodded her head at Magnaird. "Immunity granted." She turned and looked past Beumont at the squad of guards that ran towards them. "Go deal with them, steward. I don't want to be disturbed for this next part."

Magnaird looked briefly from Alexis to Beumont and then at the guards. He took off running and waved his arms over his head as he shouted for the guards to stop.

"Alexis, please," Beumont pleaded. "What are you planning on doing?"

"Hurting you, Step-Daddy," Alexis said as she pointed the blade at Beumont. "Tell me how you killed my father and I'll make the hurting short."

"You aren't going to kill me, Alexis," Beumont said. "You already revealed that when you said you needed Magnaird to testify. Kill me and there's no reason for his testimony."

"Sure there is," Alexis said as she took a step towards Beumont. "Someone has to say why I was justified in executing the entire council. I mean, they aren't going to let me stay mistress if I'm killing stewards for no reason. They may forgive a master for homicidal rage, but no one will forgive a mistress. They just aren't that enlightened." She grinned from ear to ear. "Yet."

"I'll tell you how your father died," Beumont said. "But you can't kill me. Lock me up in the Third Spire forever, but don't kill me."

Alexis lowered her blade and cocked her head. "The Third Spire? That's a thought."

"It is, it is!" Beumont cried. "It is a horrible place! I've been imprisoned there before! It is a fate worse than death!"

"Oh, you've been there before?" Alexis asked. "That's right. I forgot."

She rushed him and jammed her blade in his gut, tilted it and continued pushing so that the tip came up out just below his throat. Beumont coughed blood all over her face, but she didn't care. It was just more to add to the already thick layers that painted her features.

Guards yelled from down the passageway as Alexis leaned in and gave her step-father a quick peck on the cheek then shoved him away, opening his belly wide as she withdrew her blade.

She ignored the shouts and calls, and turned around to go find the communications room. She couldn't remember if she'd ever been there before and she hoped she could find it since she wanted to get the business of the day finished and go shower so she could get back down to Middle Deck Twenty and check on Kel.

*

"Your Holiness?" a gatekeeper said from the bedchamber door. "Your Holiness?"

"What?" High Guardian Diel the First mumbled. "What is the matter?"

"You have an urgent call on the communications system," the gatekeeper stated. "It is Mistress Alexis of Station Aelon."

"I know where Mistress Alexis is from, fool," the High Guardian snapped. "What does she want? Did she tell you?"

"Yes, Holiness."

"Then what does she want?"

The man swallowed hard, but didn't answer.

"Out with it, idiot!" the High Guardian barked. "What does the stupid woman want?"

"She said she wants either a formal apology for your collusion in her father's death or your head," the gatekeeper whispered. "She said it could be your choice."

The High Guardian bolted from his bed, threw on his robes, and rushed from the room, leaving the gatekeeper standing there, shaking with fear and confusion.

ACT II

FATE CHOOSES A CHAMPION

"The astounding feat that Alexis the Third accomplished was that, not only did she become one of the most powerful monarchs of her day, but she never wavered in being who she was: a woman. Some dismissed her ability to balance the crown with motherhood and marriage as a product of living an elite lifestyle, but I must differ, since most male monarchs were horrible fathers and husbands. Alexis the Third had it all, almost until the very end."
    —Dr. D. Reven, Eighty-Third Archivist of The Way

"When the Righteous Anger fills you, it is one's duty to listen to that call and respond with Fire and Wrath."
    —Conflicts 2:9, The Ledger

"I, nor my brothers or sisters, ever wanted for affection from Mother. We just wanted more time with her. The same with Father. It was one reason I became the fighter I am known as, so I could spend my time with my parents on the battlefield as we waged war for Mother's birthright."
    —Journals of Alexis the Fourth, Master of Station Aelon and its Primes

CHAPTER FOUR

"Put the globe down, Alexis," Kel snapped as he chased after his four-year-old son. "That is an antique and belonged to your grandmother!"

"My great-aunt," Alexis said as she watched her husband run about the royal quarters after their son. "My father's Aunt Melinda had left it in one of the libraries in the royal estate on Aelon Prime. I found it in the crates of furniture and books that were moved before Beumont killed my father and torched the estate house."

Kel looked over at his wife and frowned. "That's a bit morbid, Lexi."

"Most of my family history is," Alexis said a she reached out and snatched the globe from the Minor Alexis as he rushed by just a little too close. She tossed it in the air and caught it easily as she relaxed back into her chair. "Do you know what this is, Alexis?"

"It's a ball, Mommy!" Alexis yelled.

"No, it's a globe of Planet Helios," Alexis responded. "It shows all of the primes of all the stations—Flaen, Ploerv, Klaerv, Haelm, Thraen, and ours, Aelon. Although, one could argue that Thraen Prime is ours as well since I do have a claim to the crown of that station."

"Not while your cousin is still alive," Kel said. "He has vowed to fight with all of Thraen's resources if you even hint at coming at him."

"He's barely a cousin," Alexis replied. "He's more like a fifth cousin, once removed. I'm the granddaughter of Paul IV. As soon as my uncles died without heirs, that crown should have gone to me. But instead it went to what's his name."

"Lionel," Kel said.

"Lionel? Who follows a master named Lionel?" Alexis laughed.

"He's actually the third one in Thraen history," Kel stated. "Lionel the Third."

Minor Alexis jumped onto his mother's lap and grabbed for the globe, but she kept it out of his reach easily.

"You little bugger," Alexis giggled. "You think you can take this from me? I'm Mistress of Station Aelon. No one takes what is mine."

Minor Alexis leaned in and kissed his mother on the cheek then nuzzled his nose against hers.

"Oh, that's no fair," Alexis smirked as she handed the globe to her son. "No fair at all, you little cutie."

The boy took the globe and hopped down quickly, rushing from the room as fast as his legs would carry him. Just like his mother, the boy had blonde hair and bright blue eyes. He was tall for his age, nearly seeing eye to eye with kids several years older than him.

But, unlike his mother, and more like his father, he did not have that Teirmont fire burning inside of him. Instead of a determined drive, Minor Alexis was easy going and always watching out for others' feelings. He could tell a person's mood within seconds of being around them and catered his behavior to suit. If an adult was angry then he'd be angry with them, if a child was upset then he'd be upset with them, but never in a mocking way, always sincerely and supportively.

"There goes my little empath," Alexis said, shaking her head as she stared at the doorway her son had just bolted through. "He's going to break so many hearts."

"Mostly his own," Kel said, finally taking a seat since he no longer had to chase his son. "One day that deep well of feeling in him will be his undoing."

"It didn't undo you, my love," Alexis sighed. "It made you who you are."

"I was lucky, Lexi," Kel replied. "I had you. If I hadn't then I would have been lost in the Burdened's ranks."

"And Alexis has us and the whole of Station Aelon," Alexis said. "They will watch out for him just as he will watch out for them."

"Mistress?" an attendant asked from the doorway. "You have a message."

"Well, bring it here, Lara," Alexis said to the young woman. "You don't have to announce that you have a message for me. You can walk in and set it down."

"Yes, well...." Lara said as she stepped to the side to reveal Claevan Twyerrn standing behind her. "The message has been delivered in person."

"You cheeky snot," Alexis grinned at her attendant. "You and your flair for the dramatic."

Lara gave the mistress a small grin then hurried off as Claevan stepped into the room.

"Your Highness," he said as he took a knee and lowered his head. "It has been too long since I last saw you and I apologize for not having come to the Surface sooner."

"It is I that should apologize," Alexis said as she stood and walked to the man. She took him by the shoulders and pulled him to his feet. "I owe you and your people everything good in my life. I have failed you by not addressing you all in person."

"You have been busy, Your Highness," Claevan said. "Busy sealing the Lower Decks from the rest of the station. That is not an easy task."

"It was the least I could do," Alexis replied. "Literally the least I could do since I do not have the support of the meeting to wage another campaign against Klipoline and the lowdeckers."

"Yes, well, that is why I am here, Your Highness," Claevan said.

"Call her Alexis," Kel said as he crossed and offered the man his hand. "And call me Kel. You are almost family, considering the life debt I owe you."

"I could not do such a thing," Claevan replied, shaking his head. "I would be dishonoring your titles by—"

"Shut up, Claevan," Alexis smiled. "Do as my husband says. He is the Master of Station Aelon, you know."

"I thought I could only be a minor since I'm a commoner," Kel said.

"No, that only applies to passengers," Alexis grinned. "I looked it up. Since you are a commoner from the planet, the rules don't apply. It's a pretty stupid loophole, if you ask me, but one we can take full advantage of."

"The High Guardian is good with this?" Kel asked.

"The High Guardian is good with whatever I tell him to be good with," Alexis replied. "Diel has wisely stayed quiet on all matters of station when it comes to Aelon's crown. I have a holy blank check in that department."

"Interesting," Kel nodded. "I'll have to flex my new royal muscles."

"You'll flex them for me later, love," Alexis said as she leaned in and gave her husband a kiss. "Oh, yeah, that's happening."

Claevan gave a small squeak of embarrassment and looked away.

"Sorry, for that," Kel said as he pointed to chair by a small table. "Have a seat, Claevan, and tell us what has brought you here."

"Are you thirsty? Hungry?" Alexis asked as she patted her belly. "Because I could eat something. I'm starving. Lara!"

"No, Your Highness," Claevan said. "I ate lunch in the lift on my way up here. My wife packed it for me."

"Yes, Your Highness?" Lara asked as she came to the door.

"Cakes," Alexis said. "And tea. But, mostly cakes."

"Any specific flavor?" Lara asked.

"Something with heavy shaow cream on it," Alexis replied. "And salt. Sweet, creamy and salty."

Lara glanced at Kel quickly and saw his eyes go wide.

"Heavy shaow cream and salt?" Kel asked.

"Yes," Alexis frowned. "That's what I said."

Kel looked back at Lara and the attendant nodded then left.

"What was that about?" Alexis asked. "What are you two up to?"

"You really don't know?" Kel asked.

"No and you are being rude to our guest by not explaining," Alexis snapped.

"I'll explain later," Kel said, then turned to Claevan. "I hope you don't mind. It's a private matter."

"I could leave," Claevan said and started to stand up.

"No, sit," Alexis said as she sat down across from the man and gave her husband a sharp look. "You came here for a reason and our mysterious family issue is not it. Please, Claevan, tell me what is on your mind."

"It is Klipoline, Your Highness," Claevan stated.

"Alexis," Alexis corrected.

"I cannot," Claevan said, wincing. "I hope I do not offend you."

"Not at all," Alexis sighed. "But now it is a goal of mine to get you to call me by my first name. You should be warned that I take my goals seriously."

"Yes, that is why I am here," Claevan said. "It is one of your goals that needs addressing. The goal of stopping the lowdecker rebellion once and for all."

"Have they breached the seals?" Kel asked, alarmed. "If they have, then we should have been alerted at once."

"No, they have not breached the seals," Claevan replied. "Nor do I believe they will. It's that Klipoline has died and one of his bastard sons has taken his place."

"Klipoline is dead?" Alexis gasped. "When? How?"

"This morning," Claevan replied. "It is said he died of a heart attack, which everyone believes since he was very obese and never stopped eating, really."

"It is said?" Kel asked. "But you don't believe that?"

"I do not," Claevan responded. "Mainly due to the fact that the bastard son that has taken his position is Noomis Jaeg."

"Jaeg. . .Jaeg," Alexis mused. "That name sounds familiar. Why?"

"He is head of the Drive Mechanics Union," Claevan said, nearly spitting out the name. "A bunch of thugs that have threatened to shut down the rotational drive several times the past couple of years. Klipoline always kept them in line, but now I fear that with his passing, the threats may become reality."

"If he shuts down the rotational drive then the station will be nearly torn apart," Kel said. "The Lower Decks would be affected just as much as the other decks."

"But not as much as the Surface," Claevan said. "Which is what he is betting on."

"What could he possibly want that warrants such a threat?" Alexis asked. "Credits? The treasury is nearly empty. The tariffs the other stations have placed on the importation of our breen has almost bankrupted us. Why? Because it is the only way they can strike out at a woman running a station. Bunch of grendt hole bullies."

"It's not credits, Your Highness," Claevan said.

"What does he want if it isn't credits, Claevan?" Kel asked.

"His father's title," Claevan replied. "He wants to officially be recognized as Master of the Lower Decks. He knows that the charter signed by the late Alexis the Second only applied to Kliopline and any heirs that bore his name. He wants that changed or he shuts down the drive."

"Then this is something I must bring before the meeting," Alexis grinned. "It looks like I have the perfect excuse to justify forcing the lowdeckers in line with the crown."

"Don't get ahead of yourself, Lexi," Kel said. "Signing a new charter is cheaper than waging war against the lowdeckers. We both know the meeting will do whatever is cheapest."

"Fine," Alexis said. "Then let them think that is what they are approving." She looked at Calevan. "How did you come by this information? Why are you the intermediary coming to speak to me of this?"

"My youngest brother's wife is Jaeg's niece," Claevan said. "Once Jaeg learned of that he sent word to me knowing I might be granted a special audience with you."

"So no one else knows about this?" Alexis asked, leaning forward so her elbows rested on her knees, her eyes filled with fire. "This is all through back channels?"

"So far, yes," Claevan said.

"And Jaeg had you tell me in hopes I would immediately see a chance to go to war and bypass the meeting," Alexis said. "Then he can whip up the fervor of his people and convince them that stopping the drive is the only way to stop Surface aggression. It's a smart move."

"If that's his move," Kel said.

"Oh, I think it is," Alexis responded. "He doesn't even need me to come down there, just act like I am. Then not only does he have the support of the lowdeckers, but he can play victim in the eyes of the other stations and throw more shame onto the rule of the woman holding Aelon's crown. The man is good."

"That is a lot of assumptions," Kel said.

"Then we should meet the man and find out if my assumptions are correct," Alexis said. "Claevan? Could you arrange a private meeting on your deck?"

"A private meeting?" Claevan asked. "In secret? Without the meeting of stewards' knowledge?"

"That would be ideal," Alexis replied.

"I believe so," Claevan nodded. "But if anything were to go wrong, then Middle Deck Twenty's reputation would be damaged in the eyes of the entire station. We are not a rich people, Your Highness. Anything that could damage trade with other Decks or with other stations would crush us in weeks."

"No harm will come to your Deck, Claevan," Alexis assured him. "You have my royal word on that. Just set it up so I can meet with Jaeg face to face, please."

"Yes, Your Highness," Claevan nodded.

"Ah! Cakes!" Alexis cried as Lara came into the room with a cart of many different cakes and several pots of tea. "But why all the tea?"

"You have a hard time deciding when you're pregnant," Lara said.

"When I'm what?" Alexis laughed. "What the Helios are you talking about?"

"Lara? Really?" Kel sighed. "You can't help yourself, can you?"

"I, uh, should take my leave, Your Highness," Claevan said as he got to his feet quickly then almost fell over as he bowed low. "I'll send word with the time and day that I can arrange."

"You won't stay for cakes?' Alexis asked.

"No, Your Highness, my apologies," Claevan said, then nodded at Kel. "Master. You will hear from me soon."

The man took his leave as fast as possible, leaving Alexis to look back and forth between Lara and Kel with frustrated amusement.

"That was a horrible joke to play on the man," Alexis said. "Telling him I'm pregnant. Did he offend you in some way, Lara?"

"My lord?" Lara asked, looking to Kel for help. "Can you explain to your wife what she obviously doesn't know yet?"

"Who the Helios are you to tell me what to tell my wife?" Kel asked.

"Just the woman that helped wipe your private area when you were recovering from your wounds five years ago," Lara said. "Then the woman that put a damp cloth on your head when you fainted during your own son's birth. Oh, and that time you got that rash on your—"

"Shut up," Kel grimaced. "You made your point."

"She's made her point that she owns your ass," Alexis laughed. "But not the point that I'm pregnant. I haven't missed my period, Lara, so I'm afraid you're wrong."

"You haven't missed your period yet," Lara said as she poured a cup of tea and handed it to the mistress. "But you will miss the next one, I can assure you. Have a sip."

"I love you like a sister, Lara," Alexis said. "Only because you are shaowshit crazy like a sister of mine would be if I had one." Alexis took the tea and was about to sip from the cup when she turned up her nose and handed it back. "Ugh! What is that crap? Is there a new cook in the kitchen?"

"It's mallow berry, Your Highness," Lara grinned. "Your favorite."

"That is not mallow berry," Alexis said. "It smells like Vape gas."

"That's what you said last time," Kel sighed. "When you were pregnant with Alexis."

Alexis started to argue then stopped and her eyes went wide. Her hands instantly went to her belly. "Shit, you're right. I'm pregnant. Lara, call the midwife so we can confirm this."

"I already have," Lara said as she stepped away from the cart and gave a slight curtsey. "Congratulations, Your Highnesses. It will be a great joy to have another little minor or minoress running around Castle Quent. I'll leave you two to your discussion."

Lara left quickly and Kel and Alexis locked eyes.

"Pregnant," Kel said.

"Maybe," Alexis cautioned. "We won't know until we have the official test."

"It's been four years," Kel said. "I was starting to think Alexis would be an only child."

"As was I," Alexis nodded.

"Rotten timing," Kel said. "Especially if we can't work things out with Jaeg diplomatically."

"Oh, I'll still go to war with the man," Alexis said.

"Leaving me to lead the force down there," Kel said.

"Hardly," Alexis laughed as she rubbed her belly. "This little one will get to go to war with Mommy."

"Are you insane?" Kel snapped as he jumped to his feet, his finger pointed at Alexis. "There is no way in Helios I will let you fight while pregnant!"

"You don't have a choice in this," Alexis stated. "I'm the ruler of Station Aelon, so I lead the troops into battle. That's how it's worked for millennia and that's how it will work now."

"Alexis! I will not stand by—"

"Yes, you will," Alexis said as she stood up and faced her husband. "You will stand by my side while we fight the lowdeckers. I can trust no one else to watch my back, love. Too bad Alexis isn't old enough yet or we could have the whole family down there."

"Insane," Kel whispered. "Fucking Teirmonts are all insane."

"Kel, that's not like you to say such a thing," Alexis frowned and wrapped her arms around her husband. "Come on, let's go to our bedchamber. All this talk of pregnancy has me thinking of how I got pregnant in the first place. I say we get sweaty and work our worries out with some good, hard, pounding sex. How's that sound?"

"Insane," Kel said, but there was a smile on his lips. Lips that Alexis quickly kissed before she took her husband by the hand and led him to their bedchamber.

*

Fit, athletic, with sharp features and an eye that strayed to every female servant that walked past the meeting table that had been set up in a side hall off the Middle Deck Twenty main atrium, Noomis Jaeg sat with his back straight and feet firmly planted on the metal floor as he waited for Mistress Alexis to respond to his demands.

But, instead of responding, Alexis only watched the man, her eyes studying every detail of the self-proclaimed leader of the lowdeckers. It was several excruciatingly long minutes before she finally answered him.

"No," Alexis said.

Jaeg, able to play the game as well as Alexis, waited a full minute before he responded.

"No? Well, that is unfortunate," he said as she stood up and nodded to the mistress. "It is a shame our time was wasted."

"Sit down, Jaeg," Alexis said. "I may have said no, but that does not mean your request to be Master of the Lower Decks in perpetuity will not happen. It just means I am not ready to grant you the title at this time."

"Yet my request is for the title *at this time*," Jaeg said, still standing. "As you know, I am not a legitimized heir of my father's, just a bastard from one of the many servant girls the fat fuck enjoyed raping on a nightly basis."

"Such a sad story," Alexis said. "But I believe you have the Alexises mixed up. It's my four year old son that has the bleeding heart. The boy cries when a siggy worm gets stepped on. I, on the other hand, am a cruel bitch. Or so I have heard it rumored."

"I have heard no such thing, Your Highness," Jaeg said. "Compared to the cruelties of masters past, the fact you have left the Lower Decks alone for five years has said much to your lack of cruelty."

"Oh, that was not by choice, Jaeg, I can assure you," Alexis stated. "The meeting has been more than reluctant to grant me the men and funds needed to come down and obliterate you. That is the simple truth. Without the stewards' men I cannot fight you and your heavy blade wielding rebels. I could buy the men needed, but the meeting has frozen the treasury and the exchequer is no longer under the control of the crown thanks to the mistakes my father made."

"And thanks to Regent Beumont's usurping of royal powers," Jaeg said. "You'd think that disemboweling the man would have granted you certain privileges that are yours by birth. You'd also think that, being mistress, you'd take those privileges just as masters have in the past."

"You seem to enjoy bringing up masters of the past," Alexis said. "Are you a student of station history, Jaeg?"

"I am a student of all that is relevant to my needs," Jaeg said. "I learn what I need to in order to keep one step ahead of those that oppose me."

"You were certainly one step ahead of your father," Alexis said. "I have no idea what physician you bribed, and I am sure later killed, to procure the potion needed to stop your father's heart, but I applaud you. No, let me step back for a moment, if I may. I applaud you for applying such potion without getting caught. Procurement is easy, but application takes patience and careful planning. I'd consider you a worthy opponent if it wasn't for your one flaw."

Jaeg stood for a second then took his seat again, propped his feet up on the table, and smiled at the mistress.

"Let's dance," Jaeg said.

"I beg your pardon?" Alexis asked.

"I said let's dance," Jaeg repeated. "It means that you and I—"

"I know what it means," Alexis said. "I'm just wondering why you said it since we've been dancing for a long while now. Would you care to know what your flaw is?"

"I would," Jaeg nodded.

"It's that you see yourself already in a position of power," Alexis said. "You believe that the threat of shutting down the rotational drive is leverage when it is the opposite."

"How so?" Jaeg asked. "And I'm being sincere in asking that. I think Station Aelon being without power and gravity is quite a bit of leverage. Decks would tear themselves apart in hours. There would be nothing left of the station in days."

"Exactly," Alexis said. "Which is why it's no leverage at all. It's a cataclysmic solution, when a more subtle one is called for."

"I am sure you can tell me what that subtle solution is," Jaeg smirked.

"Yes, I can," Alexis said. "But, it will mean you leaving the station and going down to Helios and The Way Prime."

Jaeg watched the mistress for a moment then burst out laughing. "That's what you have to say? After all this time where I have heard of your diplomatic skills in dealing with the meeting as well as other stations and even the High Guardian, your solution is to get me to leave the station so you can have me killed down on the Planet while you waltz into the Lower Decks and take it all back? I honestly don't know how to respond."

"Oh, I am so sorry, Jaeg," Alexis laughed. "I'd be accompanying you, of course. The High Guardian would never grant a passenger an audience without the sponsorship of nobility. And being a lowdecker, it will take the presence of a royal to get the High Guardian to even consider listening to your plea."

"My plea?" Jaeg asked, looking about the room at the men and women from both sides that stood there in silence. "Did I step into some other meeting? You are speaking in riddles and circles and mysteries, woman! I have no plea to give the High Guardian. I only have a demand of the crown and that is to give me the title I deserve!"

"There you go," Alexis said and then clapped. "The title you deserve! You are the son of Master Klipoline and should be recognized as such. What I propose is that I accompany you down to Helios so you can petition the High Guardian for full recognition of your heredity and legitimacy."

"You what?" Jaeg asked, befuddled. "You want to help me become master, not by the meeting's decree, nor by your signing of a new charter, but by a holy proclamation directly from the High Guardian himself? While I am pleased with the idea, I do not see how it benefits you in any way."

"You don't have to see that, Jaeg," Alexis said. "You just have to be open to it." She leaned forward and patted Jaeg's hand as if he was her four year old son. "Listen Jaeg, I'm going to let you in on a secret, alright?"

"If you must," Jaeg said as he pulled his hand away.

"Oh, I must," Alexis smiled. "You see, your true leverage is that once mastership was granted to the Lower Decks, there was no going back. It was the grand mistake my father made. The lowdeckers have a taste for the noble now and they always will. I could fight you, and probably win, but it would make no difference. Someone else would step up and make his claim. I'd kill him and another would step up then another and another."

"You are assuming quite a few victories for yourself considering you have yet to manage one," Jaeg sneered. "Which is where I think my real strength lies."

"Oh? What strength is that?" Alexis asked.

"That you have never been victorious in battle," Jaeg said. "Whereas I have."

"Have you?" Alexis asked. "When?"

"I was part of the fight those five years ago," Jaeg said. "I remember with crystal clarity the moment you escaped into the lift and the Lower Decks were no longer beholden to the Surface and the crown. I know what winning tastes like. You only know what defeat stinks of."

"Watch your tongue," Kel said from his seat by the wall, his anger getting the better of him. "One of the best men to grace the System with his presence died that day."

"Oh, yes, Jex Lemnt," Jaeg smiled as he kept his attention on Alexis. "Maybe you can petition the High Guardian to officially make Jex a martyr while you accompany me to the planet."

"My husband can be emotional," Alexis said. "It's one of the many traits I love about him."

She turned and looked over her shoulder, making sure to catch Kel's eye. They held each other's gaze for a long while then Kel turned his eyes down to the floor and Alexis returned her attention to Jaeg.

"Alright, I'm exhausted and tired of dancing," Alexis said. "In order for me to deal with the meeting effectively, I need the whole business with the Lower Decks to be over. I help you gain your legitimacy and you end your campaign against the Surface. You get to be master down there, I get to be mistress everywhere else, and we go about our lives. It makes the station stronger and I can put my energy into keeping the meeting in check. Don't forget that my step-father had many more conspirators than just the few I executed. It's a den of scrim vipers above. Believe me, you are better off down in your Lower Decks."

"Ah, there it is," Jaeg said. "By helping me you show the meeting, and the entire station, that you can deal with a threat without plunging Aelon into violent chaos like your father and grandfather."

"Exactly."

"Makes me almost want to say no, just to mess up your plans," Jaeg laughed. "But I'd be an idiot to pass this up, wouldn't I?"

"Oh, you most certainly would be," Alexis smiled. "But after it is all said and done, the majority of passengers will think I'm the idiot for letting it happen."

"Now, that will make it all worth it," Jaeg laughed again and extended his hand. "I believe the dance is over and we can wish each other a goodnight."

"I believe so," Alexis said as she took Jaeg's hand and gave it six hard shakes. "Master Jaeg."

*

"You ever going to let me in on what you are really thinking?" Kel asked as the lift made its way back to the Surface.

"In here? With all the guards?" Alexis asked.

"Their loyalty cannot be questioned," Kel said. "They'd never repeat what you say."

"Which is not something I can fully rely on," Alexis said then turned to the men around her. "No offense, gentlemen. Your honor is above reproach; I just have trust issues."

The guards all nodded and gave her reassuring smiles as she turned back to her husband.

"I am going to keep this one to myself, love," Alexis said as she leaned in and kissed Kel's cheek. "Mainly because I want to see the look on your face when it all happens."

Kel shook his head, but didn't push the matter. He knew better. They all did.

*

"How are you feeling?" Kel asked as the royal cutter sliced through the large waves of Helios's poisonous sea. "Do you need a bucket?"

Alexis shook her head, but didn't open her mouth to respond for fear of throwing up all over the deck of the ship.

"Mommy!" Minor Alexis cried out as he pressed his face against the shield dome that covered the top deck of the cutter, protecting all inside from the deadly atmosphere of Helios. "I see land! Is that home, Mommy?"

"It was for me, once," Alexis sighed as she willed herself to her feet and walked slowly to her son. A hand gripped hers and she looked over through bleary eyes to see Lara at her side. "Thank you."

"Of course, Your Highness," Lara said. "It wouldn't do for the mistress to take a fall and force a miscarriage of another Aelish heir."

"Aelish heir! Aelish heir! Aelish heir!" Minor Alexis singsonged as he tapped his fingers against the shield dome surface. "I'm an Aelish heir too!"

"Yes, you are," Alexis said as she stopped at the dome and placed her free hand on her son's head. "The heir to a crown that will one day be unquestionably the most powerful in the history of Helios, whether System or Planet or even God."

"Lexi," Kel hissed as he joined her. "Don't blaspheme." His hand went to her belly. "We do not need bad luck right now."

"I know, I know," Alexis said, her eyes locked onto the approaching coastline of Aelon Prime, a place she lived for several years "for her safety." A place where her mother desecrated the holy vows of her marriage and started the affair with Steward Beumont. A place where Alexis first learned that killing was not as hard as everyone had made it out to be, whether physically, psychologically, or spiritually. "It's just hard coming back here after all these years."

"Then why come back if it's so hard?" Kel asked. "Why torture yourself?"

"Because I must," Alexis stated. "As deadly as the prime can be, it is still the land that our ancestors left during the Cataclysm. They fled here, not by choice, but because they were forced to. This land is in our blood."

"Like family," Minor Alexis said.

"Yes, sweet boy, like family," Alexis smiled.

*

The environmental suit felt tighter than she remembered and Alexis continually tugged at the seams about her armpits and crotch.

"I think I picked the wrong size," Alexis said as she carefully made her way through the burnt out ruins of the old Aelish estate house. "I don't remember these things being so stuffy and clingy."

"It's your condition, Your Highness," Lara said. "You get claustrophobic when you're with child. You hate lifts, you hate small rooms, you even hate Castle Quent. Do you not remember riding skids on the station's Surface for most of your pregnancy last time?"

"Apparently, I don't remember much of anything from my last pregnancy," Alexis replied. "Good thing I have you and Kel to remember for me. I probably don't have to think at all over the next nine months with the two of you around. Let me know when you get the lowdeckers' situation figured out, will you?"

Lara looked at her mistress through the foggy visor of her environmental suit's helmet and pursed her lips. "I'll let you wander on your own."

"Lara, I'm sorry," Alexis said as the attendant walked off after Minor Alexis as the boy jumped from one scorched strut to another. "Lara! Oh, blast it all to Helios!"

"Making friends?" Kel laughed as he wrapped his suited arms around his wife. "I can see this place truly brings out the best in you."

"It has in the past," Alexis replied. "It's just that my best isn't exactly my nicest."

"We can't stay long, you know," Kel said. "We have maybe a half an hour before we'll need to be on the cutter back to The Way Prime. A dinner audience with the High Guardian is a rare privilege, especially since he's also allowing Jaeg to dine with us and present his case."

"You have never believed in my sway over the High Guardian, have you?" Alexis asked as she turned around and faced her husband, pressing her helmet's visor against his. "You think this is all just part of my Teirmont ego."

"The Teirmont ego is a better explanation than you blackmailing the holiest man in The Way," Kel said. "Don't forget, my love, that I was once of the Burdened. This planet is my birthplace and The Way was once my family. I have never known of any High Guardian to ever willingly submit to a master's, or mistress's, orders."

"But, he isn't doing it willingly, now is he?" Alexis smiled. Then she burped and looked back through the ruins to the far off dock and the cutter. "I think the tour of my childhood past is coming to a sudden end."

"Don't puke in your suit, Lexi," Kel warned.

"I'll try not to," Alexis said as she pushed away from her husband and took off running towards the dock. "Don't hurry Alexis. Let him play for as long as possible. I want him to have good memories of this place for when we return and rebuild."

"Wait...rebuild? Lexi! The meeting will never allow the funds to rebuild the estate house!" Kel called.

"Sure they will," Alexis said. "I just have to win a war first and then they'll give me everything I want."

"Dammit, Lexi!" Kel yelled. "No wars! Not while you're pregnant!"

*

"Congratulations," High Guardian Diel the First said from his seat at the head of the intricately ornate dining table set in the middle of one of The Way's smaller banquet rooms. He raised a glass of gelberry wine. "Another heir is always good to have on hand. You never know what might happen to the first one. Helios knows I've said more than my fair share of words at royal funerals where the singular dreams of a station lay dead in a casket before me."

"Are you trying to anger me, High Guardian?" Alexis asked as she lifted her own glass of gelberry wine in acknowledgment of the initial congratulations. "Are we to spar all evening? If so then please allow me to have my attendant fetch my blades. Or is this just your version of gentle ribbing?"

"You get offended too easily," the High Guardian sighed as he set his glass down. "Although, not as easily as your grandfather, from what I have heard."

"We Teirmonts are a touchy bunch," Alexis said. She took a long drink from her glass then set it down as well. "Ahhhh, that's the first thing I've had today that didn't taste like Vape gas. I may have to be careful; this heir could come out with a bottle of gelberry wine in hand and a penchant for drink."

"Wouldn't be the first," Jaeg said from his seat far down the table.

The High Guardian reluctantly turned his attention to the lowdecker.

"Something about only speaking when spoken to comes to mind," the High Guardian smirked as he eyed the rebel master.

"That is a phrase for children," Jaeg replied. "Not for men."

"Then I used it correctly," the High Guardian responded. "Because you are nothing but a child trying to play at an adult's game, Noomis Jaeg."

The lowdecker started to stand in protest, but Alexis waved her hand at him and frowned.

"Calm down, Jaeg," she said. "The High Guardian likes to have his fun with his guests. I can attest to that."

"How about we all cool down and talk about the issue at hand?" Kel asked from his wife's side. "It has been a long day and I'd like to return to our quarters in time to read to my son."

"How is the heir that has already been born?" the High Guardian asked Kel. "In good health? Showing signs of greatness already?"

"He is on both counts," Kel smiled. "He is also the kindest soul I have ever met."

"Kindest soul?" the High Guardian grimaced. "That's not always a good trait in a master."

"Then you will not have to worry about legitimizing my claim," Jaeg interrupted. "I've been told I don't have a kind bone in my body."

"I didn't say a damned thing about kind bones, fool," the High Guardian spat. "I was talking about souls. Bones can be broken and mended, souls not so much."

"Alright, alright, you don't like him," Alexis sighed. "We get it, Diel. Now, can we stop with the time wasting barbs and get down to business? I'm in agreement with my husband and would like to get back to our quarters as soon as possible." She shoved the plate of barely touched food away. "My energy isn't what it should be and I'd like to lie down."

"You test our relationship, Mistress Alexis," the High Guardian said. He glanced at the row of Burdened that stood silently along the wall. "It is not always a good idea to test me."

"Empty threats," Alexis said as she nodded to the Burdened. "As you well know."

"Address me properly," the High Guardian said. "And there will be no need for threats, empty or full."

"To business?" Kel interrupted.

"That would be wonderful," Jaeg said as he held up his empty glass and waited for a servant to fill it. And waited. And waited.

The High Guardian finally nodded ascent to the closest servant and the man hurried over and filled Jaeg's glass.

"Thank you," Jaeg said. "Now, where do I stand in The Way's eyes as to my claim of legitimacy as an heir to my father's title?"

"The Way's eyes are my eyes, Jaeg," the High Guardian said. "And from where I sit, I see no reason to grant your request. To open the door to bastards staking claim on titles would be a slippery slope indeed."

"You do not have to open the door wide," Alexis said. "Just enough that it pertains to the Lower Decks of Station Aelon. Our station is an anomaly amongst the stations of System Helios, so I do not believe that any of the multitude of royal bastards on the other stations, and perhaps even down here on the primes, would see it is their chance to grasp at crowns. In fact, you could say it in such specific terms as to only apply when a legitimate heir, one born of matrimony and sanctioned by The Way, is not available. This lessens the chance of fratricidal conflicts amongst siblings."

"I doubt anything can lessen those tendencies," the High Guardian said, snorting a little in his glass after taking a long drink of wine. "No other people are more murderous than royalty."

"Except, perhaps the clergy," Alexis smiled.

"So am I a legitimate heir or not?" Jaeg snapped.

"Helios, you are making this hard," Alexis said. "I should have left you on the station, but I wanted you to see that I hid nothing during the negotiations." She drained her glass. "Not that we are doing any negotiating. More like wasteful banter and measuring of cocks. You both win. Your cocks are longer than mine. Yippee."

"Vulgar, but accurate," the High Guardian said. "Very well. If it means I never have to deal with your kind again, Jaeg, then I grant you your legitimacy. I'll make an announcement tomorrow as to The Way's new view of bastards. It will, unfortunately, have to apply to all titles in all stations, not just the masterships. I am sure you understand that if I am too specific it will show favoritism towards Aelon, which would undermine my authority as the unbiased word of Helios, our Dear Parent."

"Understood," Alexis nodded. "Jaeg?"

"Understood," Jaeg said.

"Good," Alexis smiled and stood up. She patted her husband on his shoulder and curtsied to the High Guardian. "With that finally done, my love and I will retire and put our son to bed."

"Before you go, mistress, I believe we should conclude our own business," the High Guardian said. "I consider granting this meeting and making this change to be the end of our relationship. From this night forward, you are only a mistress, equal to the masters of all stations, and no longer hold anything over my head. Do you agree?"

"Of course," Alexis said, curtseying again. "I know that the only thing over the High Guardian's head is Helios. Neither mistress nor master can ever come between your relationship with the Dear Parent. From this night forward we are even. I thank you for granting us this audience and wish you a long and holy life, High Guardian."

"Good," the High Guardian smiled. "I feel much better about this then. Goodnight, mistress and master."

Alexis and Kel slowly made their way from the banquet room, leaving the High Guardian with Jaeg.

"What's for dessert?" Jaeg asked.

"Guards? Show this man to his quarters and make sure he is on the next shuttle to Aelon as soon as the planet's rotational window allows," the High Guardian said, snapping his fingers at the Burdened.

*

"When will you tell me what you are up to, Lexi?" Kel whispered in the dark as the two royals lay together, their bodies entwined and sweaty. "My stomach is in knots with worry."

"Well, after that hard fucking, my stomach is finally not in knots," Alexis said as she twirled her fingers in her husband's chest hair. "So don't ruin this for me, Kel. Let a woman enjoy a healthy orgasm."

"I still don't think we should make love so forcefully while you are with child," Kel stated. "The physicians warned us against you doing anything strenuous. The shuttle ride down to the Planet was testing fate enough."

"We do not test fate," Alexis said. "We only serve fate. You know that, my love. Fate has been our friend and protector since we met. I have all of my faith in fate's capable hands."

"So, you'll tell me your grand plan then?" Kel pushed.

"Not yet," Alexis said. "But I will tell you that part of my plan involves rebuilding the royal estate house and compound, on Aelon Prime to a level that has never been seen before. It will be a place of wonder and awe for all that visit."

"Which brings me back to the point that the meeting will never give you the funds to do it," Kel said. "Unless you expect some windfall in revenues to come in."

"There will certainly be an increase in revenue," Alexis admitted. "But not enough for what I have in mind. I'll need to petition certain stewards for added funds. But only the ones I can trust with my life and the true honor of Station Aelon."

"Why in Helios would stewards contribute from their personal credits to rebuild the royal estate?" Kel asked. "What possible motivation could you give them to agree with that?"

"Eternal glory and the loyalty of the crown," Alexis said. "Isn't that what motivates all nobles?"

Kel shook his head and laughed then leaned in and kissed his wife. He was about to progress to more passionate activities, despite his previous worry, when there was a knock at the bedchamber door.

"What?" Alexis barked in frustration as her hand hovered just above her husband's crotch.

The door opened and Lara peeked her head in. "There is a certain heir to the crown that refuses to go to sleep and insists on seeing his mommy and daddy."

"Hand us our robes, Lara," Alexis said as she sat up, disregarding all modesty. "Then send in the little gully fish."

Lara kept her eyes averted as she handed the royals their robes then stepped out of the bedchamber and returned with Minor Alexis.

"This place stinks," Minor Alexis said as he climbed up into bed with his parents. "It smells like pretty farts."

"That's because of all the incense," Kel said as Minor Alexis snuggled down in bed between his parents. "And all the Vape. You get used to it."

"I don't want to get used to it," Minor Alexis said, waving his hand in front of his face. "I like the way the station smells."

"You'll learn to appreciate the smells of the planet," Alexis said, stroking her son's hair.

"No, I won't," Minor Alexis replied petulantly. "I'm never coming back here."

"Oh, I believe you will be," Alexis said as she snuggled up to her son and draped her arm across him so she could grasp her husband's arm. "We all will be, Son, and when that happens the entire System will know it."

"Great," Kel sighed. "More to worry about."

CHAPTER FIVE

The levels of anger directed at Alexis ranged from pure, unadulterated rage to simple fury, as she walked into the great hall and took her seat at the head of the long table. Only a couple of faces seemed to keep their composure as the meeting of stewards erupted into shouts and calls for the deposition of the mistress. Alexis waited calmly until the last of her detractors were silent and she could address the meeting without competing against venomous vitriol.

"Is that all out of your systems?" Alexis asked. "Because I expect your full attention while I speak to you today and do not want to revisit the idiotic notion that I should be deposed. Let me make it perfectly clear that no monarch of Station Aelon will ever be deposed again. That is a tool for traitors and conspirators, not men of noble breeding such as you gentlemen. Am I clear on that?"

There were quite a few grumbles and low protests, but no one raised their voice in true opposition.

"Good," Alexis said. "And to show I hold no ill will, I promise that not a single member of the meeting will be tried for sedition for their heated words spoken today. I want this meeting to be free of intrigue and backstabbing. Let us work together to build Station Aelon to its former glory, as well as push it to new heights."

"It will be hard to accomplish that, Your Highness," a short steward of middle age said as he stood and bowed his head towards the mistress. "You were willingly complicit in the legitimization of Noomis Jaeg's claim to a crown that should never have existed in the first place. You must see how this august body views that as a betrayal of all that Station Aelon stands for."

"Steward Mournlang is correct in his account of my complicity," Alexis conceded, resulting in more than a few gasps. "But, he is wrong in the motivation and intent of the action. If you gentlemen would care to hear my side of the plan, then perhaps we can come to an understanding of how we proceed and handle the situation that is about to erupt below us."

"Situation that is about to erupt?" Steward Blairdton asked. He was a young man about Alexis's age and dark in all ways, from his physical appearance to his temperament. He sat with his back ramrod straight in his chair, his hands folded neatly before him on the long table. "So, you admit you have increased an atmosphere of conflict and aggression amongst the lowdeckers towards us."

"I admit no such thing, Blairdton," Alexis replied. "At least, I admit no such thing when it comes to the conflict and aggression being directed towards us. Yes, it is true, since you have all heard or read the reports coming up from the Lower Decks, that the people below have been agitated to a state we have not seen since my grandfather's rule. But what those reports forget to mention is that the agitation is directed amongst the lowdeckers, not up here at the Surface."

"That is not the impression I got when I read the reports this morning, Your Highness," Steward Lunting stated. An older steward, the man was wracked with arthritis and kept himself wrapped in a heavy breen blanket for warmth. One of the wealthiest and stingiest of the stewards, he was mocked by many and called "the Cocoon" behind his pained back. He pretended not to know about the slight since he really did not care what he was called. "The reports were very clear that calls to arms have been raised in every single sector of the Lower Decks. It is only a matter of time before the lowdeckers try for an all out assault once more. There has been a tenuous truce these last five years and now your willful ignorance has destroyed even that thin margin of hope."

Alexis smiled then clapped her hands slowly. "Bravo, Lunting, bravo. Willful ignorance? Did you come up with that or was it one of your more talented advisors that coined the term? I love it and reserve the right to steal it from you and use it at a later date. A date where it actually applies, not at a time like this, where in seconds it will make you appear to be the ignorant one."

The great hall doors opened and Kel hurried inside and over to Alexis. He leaned down and whispered in her ear for a few seconds then stood back and fixed his gaze on the meeting.

"Well, gentlemen, it sounds like lowdeckers may be on the eve of their own destruction," Alexis announced. "I have urgent matters to attend to, so let me make this brief."

"Urgent matters?" Blairdton asked. "What is more urgent than addressing the meeting and explaining yourself so that we do not call for your removal?"

"Perhaps a Lower Decks civil war?" Alexis replied as she stood up and placed both hands on the table.

She wore her customary comfortable tunic and trousers and it was apparent to all in attendance that she was beginning to show her condition as an expectant mother. Many of the stewards averted their eyes from the belly that pressed against the breen material of Alexis's tunic. She did not let the aversion go unnoticed.

"Eyes up here, gentlemen," Alexis said as she nodded her head. "Pay attention to the words coming from my lips, not the fetus that grows and will one day come from between my legs."

Kel sighed and shook his head, but kept his mouth closed.

"I petitioned the High Guardian to grant legitimacy to all bastards of Master Klipoline," Alexis continued. "This also has far reaching implications to all nobles when it comes to their lineage, but I could care less about that. If you don't want to deal with bastards laying claim to your lands and title then stop fucking whores and servant girls. It's pretty simple, gentlemen."

"Alexis," Kel warned. "We are on the clock."

"Right, sorry, love," Alexis said. "The reason I petitioned the High Guardian is not so Jaeg had a claim, but so that all of his half-brothers, and even half-sisters, had a claim as well. There must be a dozen bastards down below rallying their men to arms, all wanting nothing more than to be Master of the Lower Decks, even though that title holds almost no power."

"It holds enough power to control the rotational drive," Lunting said.

"I would hardly call that power," Alexis nodded. "It would be like saying my chef holds power over me because he controls my food. Or that my maids hold power over me because they control my clean sheets and dry towels. At the end of the day, I can cook my own fucking food and make my own fucking bed. Their power means nothing unless I grant it to them."

"The rotational drive is not clean sheets or a honey wasp liqueur tart," Blairdton stated. "But, I assume it is your gender's nature to not see the difference."

Kel's hand instantly went to his wife's arm and held her in place. She looked down at it with fury in her eyes then followed the path up his arm to his shoulder and finally to the tranquil features of his face. He took a deep, calming breath and she followed suit.

"It is my gender's nature to cut through the shaowshit and get to the heart of the matter," Alexis finally replied to the smug steward. "You see things as vastly more complicated than they are. Because at the end of the day this does come down to food being cooked and clean sheets and dry towels, none of which the lowdeckers will have, once the bastards begin their war."

"But how does a war help us?" a thin steward asked. His voice was raspy and his throat had a long, jagged scar across it; a sad result from the crueler days under Alexis the Second's reign. "When the dust settles there will still be a Master of the Lower Decks, and one stronger than before because of the legitimacy granted to him by The Way."

"Steward Grommet," Alexis smiled. "That is a very good point. But all of you seem to be ignoring what war does to a people. Before a victor is even close to showing himself, the lowdeckers will want an end to the death and fighting. They will want hot food and clean sheets, dry towels and the ability to step outside their quarters without risking a blade in their empty bellies or across their parched throats. Will the Master of the Lower Decks control the rotational drive? Yes. But we control everything else, including their oxygen supplies."

"You'd threaten to kill an entire people?" Steward Grommet asked.

"I only threaten to kill those that stand against the crown," Alexis said. "Which is exactly how I will present it once I take my forces down there in support of the bastard I see as the most worthy of my attention and compassion."

"You're going to let them kill and weaken themselves, then swoop in as the hero, mistress," Steward Mournlang said. "But you forget that you cannot offer them anything without the meeting's permission. Castle Quent is well-stocked, but not enough to feed the entire Lower Decks."

"Which is the only reason I stand before you, gentlemen," Alexis said. "I expect each of you to provide your fair share of supplies to the lowdeckers when I call upon you. When this is all over there will still be a Master of the Lower Decks, but only because I—nay, we—allow it to happen. As I said, I have urgent business to attend to. I'll leave you to cast your votes. I am sure you will all do the right thing and support my plan. To not do so would be to oppose fate, and we all know how that turns out for stewards on this station."

Alexis stepped away from the table, turned and left without so much as a bow or curtsey to the meeting. All of them noticed the slight, but they were so stunned by her news that none took it to heart. They had bigger plans.

"Good day, gentlemen," Kel said as he did bow and followed his wife from the great hall.

*

"Should I check your feet, love?" Kel asked as he closed the door to the communications room, having just ordered the techs to leave.

"Check my feet?" Alexis asked as she turned on the video screen that one of the techs had indicated would be receiving the signal. "What in Helios are you talking about?"

"You're walking the razor's edge with this, Lexi," Kel said. "There is no way you'll get away unscathed."

"Cute," Alexis said as the video screen warmed up from a single bright dot in the middle to a grainy picture of an obviously furious Jaeg. "Noomis, my good friend! Sorry it took me so long to return your communication. Pressing meeting business. But here I am now. What can I do for you?"

"You fucking whore bitch!" Jaeg snarled. "You set me up!"

"What? I did no such thing," Alexis said as she leaned back in her chair. "I did as you asked and had your bastard status legitimized."

"As well as every fucking other bastard down here!" Jaeg shouted. "Do you have any idea how many that is? My father's cock was in anything that would hold still for thirty seconds! At last count there are fifteen claimants to the title of Master of the Lower Decks!"

"Fifteen? Yikes," Alexis replied. "That'll be a lot of Last Meal cards to add to my annual list. I'll make sure Lara gets a full count from you so I don't leave anyone out."

"You cunt. You stupid, shaow bitch," Jaeg growled. "If I manage to get through this in one piece then I swear I will come hunting for your head."

"Helios," Alexis grinned. "Those are quite the scary words, Noomis. Especially since they hold zero weight. If you make it through this in one piece you'll be lucky to have the strength to wipe your own ass, let alone come up here and kick mine. But, hey, my lowdecker friend, I applaud your enthusiasm and passion for what you feel is right."

"Do you think this is a joke, Alexis?" Jaeg asked, his face turning a dark grey with rage, not red, since the video monitor was in black and white only. "Have you forgotten my original threat that started all of this?"

"No, Noomis, I haven't forgotten at all," Alexis replied. "As you said, it is what started all of this. Um, I'm assuming you mean your threat to shut down the rotational drive, right?"

"Yes, I fucking mean my threat to shut down the rotational drive, you fucking bitch!" Jaeg screeched, his voice nearly cracking with rage.

"Listen here, Jaeg—" Kel started.

"I've got this, love," Alexis said and winked at her husband. "Trust me."

"You've got nothing but a death wish!" Jaeg shouted as the image began to crackle and break apart then steadied itself. "As of this moment I am ordering the drive be halted! If I'm going down then this entire station is going down with me!"

"First, you are not going down," Alexis said calmly. "I have the utmost faith in your tenacity and abilities as a leader. You'll rally your men to fight off those that are staking claim on what is rightfully yours. You are the oldest heir after all."

"I actually am not the oldest heir," Jaeg admitted. "Just the one with the most men and the first to try to make a claim."

"Oh, I see," Alexis frowned as she turned to Kel. "Did you know that?"

"I did not," Kel grinned. "But then it is not my job to keep track of lowdeckers and their hierarchy in the bastard line of succession."

"I love you," Alexis said as she leaned in for a quick kiss. "Now, back to your threat, Noomis. I have had many consultations with engineers and it has come to my attention that it is impossible for one man to shut down the rotational drive. It takes an orchestrated effort by a minimum of three sectors. While I know you have an iron grip on your sector of the Lower Decks, I am less than certain you have two other sectors willing to go along with you now that your claim is being challenged. You had leverage before, but now, ironically, that leverage has evaporated due to your legitimacy. Who'd have ever guessed that would happen?"

"I love you," Kel said as it was his turn to lean in and get a quick kiss.

"You. . .you. . .you. . . ." Jaeg stuttered and spat as he struggled for words.

"Yes, *me*," Alexis replied, all joking gone from her face. "*Me*, Jaeg. I am the mistress of this station and the only true heir to any crown on Aelon. When this is all over, I will allow a lowdecker the illusion of being master, but I will also yank every single tooth out of that person's mouth so they have zero bite whatsoever."

"Metaphorically speaking," Kel said.

"No promises," Alexis responded as she tapped the video screen. "With this asshole, I might literally yank his teeth out."

"You will regret this, Alexis," Jaeg said. "Hatred for the Surface goes so much deeper than you can comprehend."

"That may be true, Noomis, but I'll deal with that issue down the line," Alexis replied. "For now, I'm going to sit back and watch the fun happen. Then I'm going to march down there and take my station back. Now, if you'll excuse me, I have several more calls to make." She turned to Kel. "How many are on the callback list?"

"Eighteen," Kel said.

"Eighteen?" she asked then returned her attention to Jaeg. "Uh-oh, sounds like your list of fifteen is already outdated. You'll want to rip your advisors new ones for that oversight."

"I'll fucking kill you for this, Alexis!" Jaeg shouted. "You are a dead—"

Alexis reached out and switched off the connection. "Well, that was the most fun I've had in a long time."

"More fun than last night?" Kel asked.

"No, not more fun than that," Alexis smiled. "But don't distract me with sexy thoughts, my love. Help me figure out how to dial up the first lowdecker on that list."

"Should I fetch a tech?" Kel asked as he stared at the buttons and knobs on the communications console. "I'd hate to break this equipment."

"No, we can figure it out," Alexis said. "We're the Mistress and Master of Station Aelon. We should be able to work our own communications equipment."

"Yeah, we should. . . ." Kel said, then stood up. "I'm getting a tech."

"Quitter!" Alexis laughed as she put her hands on her belly and rubbed softly. "You better not give up as easily as your daddy."

"Hey!" Kel said. "No influencing the fetus!"

"Love, I'm mistress," Alexis smiled broadly. "It's my right to influence everyone. Get used to it."

"Oh, I am," Kel said as he opened the door. "Trust me, I am."

*

Claevan Twyerrn looked about the great hall with wonder and awe. His eyes were drawn to a particularly bloody tapestry that hung on the wall and he shivered slightly.

"Yeah, that's usually the reaction to that one," Alexis smiled as she walked into the hall with Kel by her side. "It's good to see you again, Claevan."

"You as well, Your Highness," Claevan said as he jumped to his feet and bowed low.

"Stop that," Alexis said as she hurried over to him and gave him a big hug. "You are to call me Alexis. No arguing."

"But—"

"No arguing," Alexis insisted. "A mistress isn't supposed to have favorites amongst the decks, but I am happy to admit that I do. Care to guess which deck?"

"You flatter me, Your—Alexis," Claevan said.

"What? Oh, I was talking about Middle Deck Fifteen," Alexis said, taking her seat at the head of the table. "Did you think I meant your deck?"

"She's kidding," Kel said as he moved to a cart and poured three glasses of gelberry wine. "Ignore her."

"I could never ignore her," Claevan said. "She is Mistress of Station Aelon."

"This is true," Alexis smiled. "Being mistress means my duty is not only to rule this station and its prime, but also to lead the military forces of this station in battle."

"We'll see," Kel said as he set the glasses down and took his seat next to Alexis. "Sit, Claevan, and drink your wine. You should get comfortable as this could take a while."

Claevan hesitated then sat down, his eyes going from the wine to the mistress and back.

"It's all I can stomach, except for cakes," Alexis frowned then sipped her wine. "The physicians don't like it, but the midwives say as long as I don't drink to drunkenness I won't harm the baby. Plus, my nausea has lessened considerably since the battles began down in the Lower Decks."

"It has been weeks now," Claevan stated. "My sources say there is still no clear winner. However, the field has been thinned considerably."

"Yes, that is what we hear as well," Kel said. "It is down to just four factions—Jaeg, of course, a man called Listrom, another known as Halburt, and the final one is...is...." He snapped his fingers as he tried to recall the name, his eyes on Claevan.

"Diggory. Bostman Diggory," Claevan said. "He is the grandson of Moses Diggory. That name still holds power in the Lower Decks. If he can keep enough men on his side then he could end up taking the crown."

"Yes, Diggory," Alexis nodded. "What else do you know about him?"

"To be honest, Your—ugh, *Alexis*," Claevan laughed. "I am surprised he is in the running at all. The man is not known for bravery or ambition. I believe his wife and her family are behind his push for the title. Once the Klipoline line took the mastership, the Diggorys fell from grace and turned to, well, more illicit activities."

"They run the black market in the Lower Decks," Alexis stated.

"Yes, that they do," Claevan said, surprised.

"Which is why Diggory's mother seduced Klipoline and got herself pregnant," Kel said. "In order to curry favor with a master and keep the Diggory family close to the crown."

Claevan frowned and looked from the mistress to the master then leaned back in his chair.

"You already know Diggory's story, I can see," he stated. "I just confirmed what you knew."

"Sorry," Alexis said. "We just needed information that wasn't biased or influenced by what someone may have thought we wanted to hear. We didn't mean to deceive you."

"No deception," Claevan shrugged. "Don't forget that I am a deck boss. I know my way around political intrigue."

"More importantly, you know your way around longslings," Kel said.

"Which is really why you are here," Alexis said. "That and to catch up with a friend of the crown."

"Thank you," Claevan nodded. "How can I be of service? Or, more precisely, how can my longslingers be of service?"

"I was hoping you'd ask that question," Alexis said. "Because I learned a few things from my first foray into the Lower Decks. One thing was that I can get my ass handed to me."

"It's a fine ass, if I do say so," Kel smiled.

"Thank you, love," Alexis said. "But as fine as it may be, it's not an ass that deserves to be stared at as it retreats into a lift for its very life. It's an ass that should be standing triumphant as it supports my spine in victory."

Claevan chuckled then stopped and his face went white. He pushed his glass of wine out of his way and leaned onto the table, his eyes boring into the mistress's. "You aren't thinking of leading an assault on the Lower Decks yourself, are you?"

"I am," Alexis replied. "It's always been the plan."

"But you are nearing your second term of pregnancy!" Claevan exclaimed. He looked to Kel. "How is this being allowed?"

Kel held up his hands in surrender. "Trust me, Claevan, you are not the first person to voice this objection. There has been a long line before you, with me at the head of that line."

"If it means you leading an assault yourself, then I withdraw my support, Alexis," Claevan frowned and crossed his arms. "I will not contribute to the possibility of yours or your unborn child's death."

"Yeah, I've heard that one," Alexis said. "But guess what? In the end I get my way, whether people like it or not. My way involves the longslingers, Claevan. So, take a minute to get your thoughts and emotions under control and then I'll lay out my plan and reasoning."

"I do not need a minute," Claevan said. "I would not be considered a man if I allowed you to come to harm. My entire deck would shun me if they find out I am even considering this."

"Your entire deck will hail you as the greatest deck boss to ever serve your sector," Alexis said. "Once I show the lowdeckers that they can fight all they want, but it is my crown that reigns supreme on this station."

"No," Claevan said.

"Will you at least listen to what I have to say?" Alexis asked.

"You should listen, Claevan," Kel said. "It may not make you feel better, but it does make sense."

Claevan grumbled for a couple of seconds then shrugged. "Fine. I'll listen, but I won't promise I'll change my mind."

"Which is completely fair," Alexis said. "So, imagine what it would be like for the lowdeckers if I went down there, trounced all sides of their conflict then made the declaration of who I wanted as their Master. Just think about it. Be sure to picture me in my armor, tailored to my new physique, standing in one of their atriums while surrounded by my Royal Guards and your longslingers. Quite a picture, don't you think? It would dispel any notion that I cannot lead a force into battle and win."

"But if you've already won then why would you need that notion dispelled?" Claevan asked.

"No spoilers," Alexis replied. "That is for a different discussion. But, just imagine the scene I've set. Striking, yes?"

"Well. . .yes," Claevan admitted. "It would be a thing of legend."

"Exactly!" Alexis cried. "But I prefer to call it a thing of fate, manifested for all to see."

"Legend is shorter and rolls off the tongue better," Claevan grinned. "But you are the mistress and call it whatever you want. The only problem I have, is you getting to that point. The lowdeckers are savages when it comes to battle. Those heavy blades, as you know, can tear a man in half with one swipe. I shudder at what one would do to you, my lady."

"True, but what are the heavy blades' fatal flaw?" Alexis smiled.

"They are heavy," Claevan replied.

"And they are slow," Kel added. "Even in capable hands you cannot swing one with the speed of, say, a particle barb."

"They also need to be in close to be effective," Alexis said. "Another advantage particle barbs have over heavy blades. Do you see where I am going?"

"I believe so," Claevan said. "But I'd prefer to hear it straight from your mouth."

"Very well," Alexis said. "I intend to have your best longslingers train my best men in the art of shooting. Many know how to use the small slings, but those have limited range and do not do the damage that longslings, with their particle barbs, do."

"We take four regiments down to the Lower Decks," Kel stated. "Each regiment will be comprised of your men and ours. The regiments attack one of the four factions still left simultaneously. We push them back until they surrender or are defeated. Then Alexis gets her striking moment of glory."

"You see, Claevan," Alexis said. "I learned the hard way, and many great men paid with their lives, that if you engage a lowdecker directly, you are not likely to survive. I don't intend on engaging them. I intend on killing them before they can even raise their lousy heavy blades."

Claevan shook his head. "You are talking about fighting a battle entirely with longslingers, aren't you?"

"We are," Kel nodded.

"But wouldn't that go against the code of honor for combat?" Claevan asked. "Longslingers have always been there for support, but never as the main, and only, offense. You're changing the rules of battle, even if the battlefield is the Lower Decks."

"Claevan," Alexis chuckled as she patted her belly. "My whole existence has been one long rule change. Everyone really does need to get used to it."

*

"You'll have my backing, Bostman," Alexis said as she looked at the grainy image of a demur man on the video screen. "All you need to do is make sure that the men you trust the least are in front."

"But they will die," Bostman Diggory said, his voice somewhere between a whine and a cough, as if he had a complaint permanently lodged in his throat. "I'll be sending good men to their deaths."

"Not good men, Bostman," Alexis sighed. "Untrustworthy men. Those that your gut tells you may not have your best interests at heart."

"My gut?" Bostman asked, making Alexis sigh.

"Yes, your gut," Alexis replied, her voice changing from her mistress tone to her mother tone. "Your instincts, that little voice that tells you what to do, that feeling you get just before you make the right choice."

"I'm sorry, mistress, but I do not hear voices and only get feelings in my gut when I need to use the privy," Bostman responded.

Kel snickered as he stood out of view by the communications room door. Alexis snapped her fingers and he went quiet. Well, almost quiet, since he had to cover his mouth and bite his lip after the next thing Bostman said.

"I'll check with my wife," he announced. "She may hear voices that I do not."

"No, Bostman, you can't check with your wife," Alexis said. "If you do that, or check with anyone else, then the deal is off. And the deal I am offering is all that stands between you and defeat. Jaeg is going to win, Bostman. All of my sources say that lowdecker opinion is blowing in his direction. He has the resources and the ability to take the Lower Decks. Maybe not now, maybe not next year, but eventually he will win. I'm your only chance here, Bostman. Most people are pleased when the crown comes to their aid, yet you're looking at me like I just bludgeoned your pet to death."

"Oh, I don't have pets," Bostman replied quickly. "Allergies."

"I have to leave," Kel snorted as he turned and bolted from the room. Alexis could hear him burst into laughter as soon as the door was almost closed.

"What was that?" Bostman asked.

"Just some kids out in the passageway," Alexis replied. "I'll deal with them as soon as I am done speaking with you." Alexis took a deep breath and slowly let it out.

"My wife does that," Bostman said.

"Most women do," Alexis smiled. "So, Bostman Diggory, what will it be? Certain defeat at the hands of Jaeg?"

"I hate him," Bostman stated.

"Me too," Alexis agreed. "Or, will it be victory with my assistance? My covert assistance, of course. No one will know we have spoken, no one will know that I supported you, it'll just happen to be that your men, not all of them, will be the ones left standing at the end. I reward that by giving you the position of Master of the Lower Decks and you in turn reward my kindness by pledging fealty to me and the Aelish crown from now until eternity."

"Eternity is a long time," Bostman said.

"It is, but it goes by so fast when you are being carried along by fate."

"I won't be harmed and my family will not be harmed?" Bostman asked. "You promise?"

"I promise," Alexis nodded. "The only ones that will be harmed are those you choose to put on the front line when those lift doors open. They will die, Bostman, I'm not going to lie to you. But it is the only way that our *alliance* will not be found out."

"I think I know of some men," Bostman nodded. "They are always whispering as I walk by. I'll choose them and their friends."

"Excellent!" Alexis exclaimed and clapped. "You're making a wise choice, not just for yourself, but also for your people!"

"You think so?" Bostman asked.

"I know so," Alexis replied. "Trust me, I'm a mistress; I know all about this kind of stuff."

"So, I can ask you questions when I become master?" Bostman asked, his eyes wide with hope. "Get your opinions and advice on the best way to be an effective leader?"

"Oh, Bostman, I am counting on it," Alexis grinned.

*

Lara stood in front of the door, her arms crossed and legs braced against the frame.

"Five months," she snapped as she watched the ever changing custom armor be placed onto her mistress. "You are five months along and you think I am going to let you out of this room to go fight some stupid battle? That is not happening, Your Highness. You'll have to cut me down before I move."

"Stop being melodramatic," Alexis frowned as her breastplate was snapped in place. "I know this all took a lot longer than I thought it would—"

"A lot longer?" Lara snorted. "It took two months longer than you thought. Two months is a long time when you are pregnant! That child in your womb isn't as protected by fluid as it was eight weeks ago. Now all it will take is a hard blow to your abdomen and it could be harmed or worse."

"I know that, Lara," Alexis said. "But I can assure you I will be fine."

The attendants finished with the armor and all stood back, waiting for Alexis's approval. She moved to the mirror and grimaced.

"My Helios, I look like a shaow in this," she said. "All the extra padding and plating makes me look huge!"

"Your pregnant belly is what makes you look huge!" Lara shouted, causing the other attendants to cringe at her impertinence. "And that ass of yours isn't helping, either! If you're wondering where all those cakes go, I can point it out pretty fast."

"You're a cruel bitch," Alexis growled then looked at the attendants. "The armor fits fine. Thank you. You may leave and go to your families. You'll be called when I return to the castle."

The attendants bowed and hurried from the room, forcing Lara to break her word and step aside.

"I'm not going anywhere," Lara said.

"You've already stated that," Alexis replied. "But we both know that's not true. You'll be with Alexis the whole time."

"He has nurses and nannies to keep him safe and occupied," Lara countered. "He'll be fine without me."

"Except that he is going to Castle Helble to be with my mother," Alexis said.

"You don't trust your own mother to keep her grandson safe?" Lara asked.

"Oh, I trust her to keep his body safe, but it's his mind and soul I worry about," Alexis replied. "I love my mother and we have come to an understanding over the years. Enough of an understanding that I freed her from the Third Spire and gave her her own estate. She is not a bad person, but she does blame me for quite a lot of her own troubles. I don't want that blame worming its way into my son's ear."

"And you think I can stop her from doing that?" Lara asked. "She may no longer be Mistress of Station Aelon, but the woman is a Minoress of Station Thraen. I'm a royal attendant and apparent sucker. I won't stand a chance."

"You are one of the very few people I can trust, Lara," Alexis said as she walked over to the woman. "You know me, you know my family, you know this station. When I speak of trust it means so much more than when your average passenger speaks of trust."

"What about when nobles speak of it?" Lara smirked.

"The nobles don't know how to spell trust let alone speak it without irony," Alexis replied. "And there will be nobles sniffing around Castle Helble. My mother is not without her own callers and own confidantes."

Lara growled then let her shoulders slump. "Fine. I'll let you leave, but you have to promise me you'll change your will so that if anything happens to you and Kel, Alexis is left in my care."

"That's quite a lot to ask. Especially hours before I descend into battle. I don't think I can have the papers drawn up in time," Alexis replied.

Lara's eyes went wide and she took a step back. "I was joking, Your Highness. I would never be serious about such a thing."

"Yet I am serious," Alexis said. "That should tell you how confident I am that I'll return since there's no way I'd risk my son actually being left to be raised by you."

"You snotty twat," Lara glared. "You so set me up on that one."

"You walked right into it," Alexis laughed. Then she grabbed her crotch and frowned.

"Alexis? What's wrong?" Lara asked, alarmed. "Is it the baby?"

"No, well, sort off," Alexis said. "It's pushing on my bladder and now I have to pee."

"Guess you should have thought of that before you got all dressed up for war," Lara smirked as she turned and left the room.

"Hey!" Alexis shouted. "Get your ass back here and help me out of this shit! Lara! Lara come back! If I piss my armor I'm going to lock you up in the Third Spire, but without the chance of us ever coming to any kind of understanding! Lara? *Lara!*"

*

"There you are," Kel said as he stood in the passageway outside the main lift. The longslinger-trained guards stood behind him and all took a knee at the sight of the mistress, their polybreen armor clunking and clinking. "What took so long? Is the baby alright?"

"I wish people would shut the fuck up about the damned baby," Alexis snapped. "The baby is just fine. It's a fucking Teirmont and about to go into its first battle! The damn thing is doing somersaults!"

"We could postpone this, my lady," a guard said as they all stood up. "It can still be done."

"He's right," Kel said. "Or you could just not go with us. I'm more than capable of leading this campaign."

"The only way it will work is if I am there and seen participating," Alexis replied. "The fighting is only one step in the plan, Kel. I have to see it all through or there is no point."

"Mommy!" Minor Alexis cried from the end of the passageway.

"Alexis! Come back!" Lara shouted as she chased after the boy.

"Hey, sweet boy," Alexis grinned as she crouched and took the boy in her arms, lifting him easily up. "You know you're supposed to be on a skid heading to your grandmother's estate, right?"

"I want to come with you," Minor Alexis whined. "I want to go down and fight the lowdeckers with you and Daddy."

"I don't think so," Kel laughed as he walked over and tousled the boy's blonde hair. "It's way too dangerous down there."

"But Lara says that lowdeckers are just shaows that walk on two feet," Minor Alexis replied. "That they don't think further than what to eat next."

"She said that, did she?" Alexis asked, looking at Lara. "Well, don't believe everything that Lara says. Lowdeckers are people just like us and they are subjects of the crown, so Mommy has to go down there and talk with them and remind them of that fact."

Minor Alexis looked at the polybreen clad guards. His eyes fixated on the longslings that each of the men held.

"If they are people like us then why are you going to kill them?" Minor Alexis asked.

"I said I was going to talk with them," Alexis responded. "I won't kill them unless I have to."

"I don't believe you," Minor Alexis replied as he shook his head back and forth. "I can see it in your eyes, Mommy. You have killing eyes."

"Do I?" Alexis asked. "I think those are just called Teirmont eyes, silly boy. You have them too."

"No, Mommy," was all Minor Alexis said.

Alexis tried to smile, but it came out a weak grimace. She then set the boy down and took a couple of steps back. Kel picked him up immediately as Alexis put a hand to the wall.

"Lexi?" Kel asked.

"Just gas," she smiled, her eyes on her son. "I'm good to go."

"Are you sure?" Kel asked, handing Minor Alexis to Lara. "I can call a midwife or physician. We can wait an hour or so before we go down."

"No, it's all coordinated," Alexis said. "We need to be in place so we strike as one."

"We can use the com to contact the other regiments," a guard suggested. "They can wait until we give the order."

"No com," Alexis said. "Too risky on the station. The lowdeckers could easily tap into the channel and overhear us. Com silence is mandatory, that's a royal order."

"Yes, Your Highness," the guard agreed.

"I'm, fine," Alexis said as she stood tall and smacked her fist on her armored chest. "Fit and ready to fight." She pressed the button to the lift and the doors opened wide. "In we go, gentlemen. Time to go to war."

"War means killing," Minor Alexis whispered and Lara put his head to her shoulder.

"He'll be fine," Lara said. "We leave for your mother's the second you get on that lift."

"Then leave now, Lara," Alexis said as she walked into the lift and turned around. "May Helios be with you."

"And you," Lara said as she backed away from the lift.

Kel entered and stood next to Alexis while the guards filed in and shielded both of them from the doors. Lara and Minor Alexis watched as the doors slowly slid closed and a quiet chime indicated the lift was descending.

"Come on, you little bugger," Lara said. "Let's go see your grandmother. I'm sure we'll have just as much of an adventure with her as your mommy and daddy are going to have down in the Lower Decks. So don't you worry, alright?"

"They'll be fine," Minor Alexis said then yawned. "Grandpa told me so."

Lara hesitated as she started to walk away from the lift. She opened her mouth to ask what the boy meant, but thought better of it and let the subject drop. There was already too much drama to the day, she didn't need a specter of Masters past added to it.

*

"He'll be fine," Kel said, taking Alexis's hand in his. "The Surface will be safe from what we are about to start. As far as the lowdeckers know, they are still only dealing with each other. Our attack will be a complete surprise."

"It better be," Alexis said. "If anyone has talked then we could all be lowering down into an ambush."

"No one would dare talk," Kel replied. "Our guards are loyal, I trust Claevan to keep his people quiet, and Bostman Diggory is too much of a fool to open his mouth and spoil everything. The man is a quaking, little grendt. He's more likely to lay an egg than to reveal our plans."

"Never underestimate stupidity," Alexis warned.

The guards chuckled which brought Alexis out of her head and worries and into the present moment.

"Everyone knows their jobs?" Alexis asked.

"Yes, Your Highness!" the guards replied as one.

"You fire the second the doors open then you press forward, firing at anyone you find," Kel stated. "You do not stop firing until you are ordered to, or your run out of particle barbs."

"The lifts will be locked down once we hit the Lower Decks," Alexis said. "No one can escape to the Surface until I have called the engineers and given the code. That also means we cannot retreat unless I give the code. Understood?"

"Understood, Your Highness!"

"Good," Alexis said. "Then prepare yourselves. Clear your minds of chatter and focus on your duties. You are no longer men, but extensions of the longslings you hold; you are no longer my royal guards, but soldiers in a fight that will decide the fate of this station. The station is the priority, not my safety. If I fall, you keep fighting. That is your sworn duty to me."

"Yes, Your Highness!"

"I may not be able to keep that promise," Kel said. "If you fall, I will be forced to stay by your side."

"Disobeying your mistress during a time of war is an executable offense," Alexis said as she leaned in and kissed him lightly.

"Oh, is it?" Kel smiled. "And how am I to be executed?"

"With long, slow passion," Alexis said and bit his lip softly. "It's an extremely pleasurable way to go."

"Well, the punishment must fit the crime," Kel replied, his hand going to Alexis's belly.

There were more than a couple of throats cleared in embarrassment in the lift.

CHAPTER SIX

Flesh was torn.

Blood was spilled, sprayed, expelled.

Bones were broken, fractured, shattered into fragments that pierced the flesh, that spilled the blood.

Men screamed.

They called for their god, Helios, to save them, to show mercy. They pleaded for the Dear Parent to tell them why they were dying, why they were doomed to a shortened life. They looked up at the sky, the grey, grey sky, and begged to be spared.

But Helios did not listen; the Dear Parent had closed the door and the men were left to fall to the ground as their environmental suits filled with Vape gas and their bodies began to combust and burn, their insides started to liquify and leak from their orifices.

And Alexis smiled at it all, smiled like the mistress she was—the bringer of death and destruction.

She looked to her papa and he smiled at her as he stood next to her, his body engulfed in flame.

"Your fate," he said. "It is the fate of all. Do not waste it."

"No, Papa," she said. "I will not."

"Do you know who you are?" he asked.

"Yes, Papa," she smiled as she realized she was naked and did not wear an environmental suit, yet her skin did not burn, her insides did not leak from her. At her feet were her children, naked with her, unharmed just as she was.

Alexis knew in that moment who she truly was.

She was Helios. She was the Dear Parent.
And she was to show no mercy.

*

Alexis's eyes opened wide and she saw Kel staring at her, his head cocked, his features questioning.

"Dream," she sighed as she looked about the lift. "I must have dozed off."

"You were mumbling," Kel said and nodded to the guards that were busy trying to pretend they noticed nothing.

"What was I saying?" Alexis asked as she took a deep breath then slowly let it out.

"No mercy, Papa," Kel replied. "Over and over until you woke up."

"And you didn't think to give me a nudge so I'd stop?" Alexis frowned.

"Not when you're whispering 'no mercy' over and over," Kel said. "I figured it would be safer to let your mind work itself out."

He glanced down at Alexis's hands as they gripped the hilts of her blades. Her knuckles were white with tension. Alexis followed his gaze and relaxed.

"Yeah," she smiled. "Probably a good call."

"I thought so," Kel said then kissed her cheek. "So, what are your waking thoughts? Shall we truly show no mercy?"

"Do we have a choice?" Alexis asked. "We don't know friend from foe. Once these doors open it will be us versus them. If we hesitate and try to discern motivations and intent then we will be cut down by heavy blades as we always have been. I do not intend for today to be the same as it always has been. That is no longer the fate of my rule. This day will show them that Alexis the Third is the strongest of the Teirmonts and those that have ever questioned that will be sorry."

Slowly, despite their training, the guards turned and looked over their shoulders at their mistress. She caught their eyes and nodded.

"Today, you will be a part of history," she said. "You will accomplish something that not even my grandfather could accomplish. Today we retake the lowerdecks and unite this station once again. Your actions, guided by fate, will become the stuff of legends. You will be honored, whether you stand or fall, at the end of the day. Today is about immortality. Today is about victory."

"Today is about Aelon," a guard said, then looked shocked that he'd spoken.

Alexis moved forward and gripped the man's polybreen armor, spun him about, and pulled his face close to hers.

"Yes," she hissed. "Today is about Aelon."

"Today is about Aelon," another guard said as he turned and pushed in close to the guard and Alexis.

"Today is about Aelon," a third guard said, moving in close as well.

"Today is about Aelon."

"Today is about Aelon."

"Today is about Aelon!"

"Today is about Aelon!" they all shouted, their arms draped across shoulders, their heads bowed and touching. *"Today is about Aelon!"*

"Today is about Aelon," Alexis said to them and stepped back.

"Today is about Alexis," Kel said in the following silence and all eyes focused on the mistress.

She was about to object, to scold her husband for ruining the moment, for making it about her, but the words never left her lips as the guards all fell to their knees and lay their longslings at her feet. The image of her dream children, naked and expectant, rushed through her mind and she gasped.

"Alexis," the men said, then retrieved their longslings, stood and turned back to the lift doors.

Kel leaned in and kissed her ear just before whispering, "Alexis, our mistress, our mother, our wife, our fate."

Then the lift stopped, longslings were raised, and the doors opened unto the future.

*

Flesh was vaporized.

Alexis was amazed at the destructive power of the particle barbs when shot from longslings that were wielded by capable hands.

The second the lift doors opened, the war cries of the lowdeckers filled her ears and she had to force herself not to think of the last time she'd heard their calls of violence. Instead, she focused on the guards that stood between her and dozens of enraged men rushing at them with heavy blades lifted, already in mid-swing.

The first row of guards dropped to their knees and fired as the second row of guards stayed standing and fired over their heads. The particle barbs flew from the lift and out into the passageway, projectiles of certain death that found their marks, did their jobs, and ripped through the simple breen armor the lowdeckers wore and tore through flesh, bone, blood as the barbs split into a million particles until they destroyed the men on an almost molecular level.

The passageway was soon filled with a blood mist that coated polybreen armor and coated throats that were open as the royal guards issued their own war cries and left the lift to push the attack. Due to the very nature of the particle barbs, there was not much left of the first wave of lowdeckers except for scraps of breen cloth, random chunks of flesh and shards of bone, and the fallen, forgotten heavy blades that lay as gravestones on the metal floor of the passageway. It was this detritus that the guards stepped over and around as they sprinted into place a few yards into the passageway.

"Steady!" Kel shouted from behind them all, a blade in one hand and his other raised in anticipation. "Fire!"

Alexis, both of her long blades drawn and still shining bright and clean despite the blood mist that wafted this way and that, watched as a second wave of lowdeckers charged her men. She watched as her guards pulled triggers and sent more particle barbs towards their targets. She watched as the large men of the Lower Decks, with their impossible blades held high, were stopped in mid stride, parts of them disappearing, adding to the blood mist that seemed to be as ever present as the Vape clouds on Planet Helios.

"Forward!" Kel yelled as the second wave of lowdeckers were reduced to nothing. "Press on!"

The guards stood and marched down the length of the passageway, their eyes watching as the junction to the next passageway was filled with more and more lowdeckers. Those lowdeckers met the gaze of the longsling wielding guards then looked past at the destruction that coated every inch of every surface. There was no wavering, no fear, no turning back for either the guards or the lowdeckers.

Fate had come to the Lower Decks and fate would have its way.

"Drop and fire!" Kel ordered and the first row of guards did just that then they were replaced by the second row.

Over and over the rows of guards fired and moved, fired and moved, forcing the lowdeckers to run or die in the face of their onslaught. Stray particle barbs hit the surface of the walls and ripped into metal, shredding the passageway as the guards systematically moved forward. The shards of metal that randomly exploded from the walls nicked and sliced the bare cheeks of the guards, drawing the only blood from the Aelish patriots.

The lowdeckers could never get close enough for their mighty heavy blades to even send a breeze at the men.

"Halt!" Kel yelled as the last lowdecker fell into a pool of his own blood and vaporized organs. "Reload!"

The men immediately began to reload in shifts so that the regiment was never without protection. All the while, Alexis watched from behind them, her eyes clear and bright, her heart full of pride and soul full of fire. Kel looked over his shoulder at her and his own heart swelled with pride as he saw true beauty. The two royals' eyes met and the connection was so strong that even some of the guards paused in their reloading and looked up to see what was happening.

"For Aelon," Alexis whispered.

"For Alexis," Kel whispered back.

*

Claevan Twyerrn slammed the butt of his longsling into the lowdecker's midsection then shoved the man away and spun the weapon up to his shoulder and fired. Without hesitation he turned about and fired at the two men that rushed him, heavy blades coming down at him in deadly arcs of bloody metal. Their chests blossomed and bloomed with their lifeblood before they collapsed onto the floor, joining the dozens of their brethren that had met the same fate.

More skilled with the longslings, but less disciplined in combat than the royal guards, the longslingers of Middle Deck Twenty had made a brilliant first attack, but then found themselves boxed in and surrounded. The advantage of surprise was soon lost to the lowdeckers' advantage of position and numbers, not to mention brute strength.

The middledeckers cried out as they were cleaved in half. Men screamed as they were forced to watch their own limbs fall from their bodies just before their eyes were torn from their heads. Heavy blades thrust into chests, hacked against necks, sliced open bellies. The lowdeckers roared with triumph as they literally cut down those that dwelled above them.

Claevan saw the way the battle turned against his men and did not hesitate as he called to them to fight as if their women, their children, their legacies were standing right there in the passageway, blades to their throats. It was those thoughts that pushed Claevan on as he dodged the swipe of a heavy blade and jammed the barrel of his longsling up under the attacker's chin. Claevan pulled the trigger and the top of the man's head splattered the ceiling of the passageway, painting it with abstract clumps of grey matter and bone.

But the particle barb didn't stop its destruction with just the contents of the lowdecker's head, it kept going as it decimated the ceiling, tearing a massive hole in the illuminated metal. Bits of the station rained down on Claevan and he realized that the reverse would be true.

"The floor!" he yelled to his men. "Take out the floor beneath their feet! Follow me!"

He backed his way towards the passageway that led to the lift and provided cover for the dozen or so middledeckers that still stood. Lowdeckers fell under his expert marksmanship and he almost thought that his traditional training could save the day, but as he watched in horror as one of his men was pierced through the spine by a thrown heavy blade, he knew that his new discovery would have to be what saved him and his men from certain defeat.

"Get behind me!" Claevan yelled as he took a knee and fired into the floor directly in front of the approaching lowdeckers.

The large men laughed, thinking Claevan had missed, then they began to holler and try to retreat as the metal in front of them was nearly dissolved, revealing the substructure below. A couple of lowdeckers lost their balance and tumbled into the substructure, their cries for help cut off as they collided with beams and posts, their necks and backs snapping from the impacts.

Claevan's men turned and joined him on their knees as they steadied their weapons and fired not just in front of the lowdeckers, but directly at their feet and behind them. The more accurate of the longslingers were able to place particle barbs in strategic spots so that the lowdeckers were forced to group together in an ever tightening clump.

In minutes the battle went from being in the lowdeckers' favor to an almost certain win for the men of Middle Deck Twenty.

"Drop your blades and surrender and you will be allowed to live!" Claevan called across the micro-chasm that lay between him and the lowdeckers. "Declare your loyalty to Station Aelon and Mistress Alexis and I will spare you!"

"We are to show no mercy," a man said from Claevan's shoulder. "They do not deserve second chances."

"Nor will they take them," Claevan said. "Look at their eyes, look at how they hold themselves. There is not a man there that will surrender. But, being a man of honor, I must give them the option, whether they take it or not."

The lowdeckers lifted their blades as one, ready to send them flying with all their might at Claevan's men, but none got the chance to complete their throws as longsling after longsling barked death at them. The particle barbs raced to meet their targets and in less than a second all that stood on what solid portions were left of the passageway floor were empty boots surrounded by the drippings of dead men.

The middledeckers lowered their longslings and stared at what they had done. Blood spilled over off the edges of the floor and down into the depths of the substructure below. The few shapes that were identifiable as body parts just lay there, attached to nothing anymore, reminders of how the face of combat had just changed in a matter of minutes.

*

"You will not prevail!" Jaeg yelled as he dove and rolled across the floor, letting the particle barbs fly over him harmlessly, then came up swinging, his heavy blade taking men out at the legs, their bodies tumbling over him as he leapt and dove again. "This day is not for the Surface!"

The rebel lowdecker, bastard heir to the Lower Deck crown, impaled two longslingers at once and yanked their weapons from their hands. He left his heavy blade in the guts and put one of the longslings to his shoulder, turned and fired. He marveled at the particle barb's destructive ability, having never witnessed it before.

"Take this," he snapped as he picked up the fallen longsling and shoved it into the hands of one of his men. "Tell the others to gather them as they fall. If Mistress Alexis wants this to be a war of fancy gadgets and new toys then we will join her in that. Kill and retrieve, that is your new order. Spread the word."

The man looked at the longsling for a second until Jaeg had to slap him across the face to get his attention.

"Sorry, my liege," the man said. "I've never fired one."

"Neither had I until just now," Jaeg said. "It's easy. You point and shoot. Do you need to know more?"

"No, sire," the man said as he nodded and then ran off to inform the others.

Particle barbs whizzed past Jaeg's head and he glared at the longslingers that knelt far down the passageway. He returned fire, but knew his aim wasn't true as he saw no blood splatter and heard no cries of pain. Instead of risking being caught out in the open, Jaeg retrieved his heavy blade from the corpses before him, sheathed it quickly, and fled the passageway, not in cowardice, but so he too could spread the word that the rules of the battle had just changed.

*

"Where are we?" Alexis asked as her regiment stopped by the junction of two passageways. "Is this where we meet Bostman? Or is it the next junction?"

A guard stood next to Kel and they both looked up from a schematic of the Lower Decks, neither appeared happy at what they had discovered.

"We should have rendezvoused with the man two passageways back, if this is correct," Kel said. "Perhaps the coward decided not to risk his skin today and believes hiding in his bedchamber is the best strategy for winning his crown."

"He was never to win anything," Alexis said. "We were to win it for him, which it appears we still must do, just without the reinforcements of his men."

"Do we press forward or go back to the junction?" Kel asked.

Alexis looked back and forth from one end of the passageway to the other. Her inclination was to push on and take the fight to the next sector, knowing that Bostman Diggory was not a real threat. But her instincts gnawed at her, making her wonder if Bostman's failure to appear as planned was more than just a coward saving his own skin.

"We go back," she said. "I don't like the idea of a surprise rear attack that could box us in."

"Neither do I," Kel said as he handed the guard the schematics and put his longsling to his shoulder. "We find Bostman and see what the little twerp is thinking by not meeting us as he was supposed to." He started to move then stopped as he caught Alexis looking at him. "What?"

"That," she said as she waved a hand towards him. "It's a good look."

"Covered in blood and gore?" Kel asked.

"No, the longsling," Alexis said. "It's kinda sexy."

"Really? That's what you're thinking about right now?" Kel laughed.

Alexis frowned. "Shut up. I can't help it if you look good."

"Well, thank you, my love," Kel smiled. "You're not so bad yourself."

"Not so bad?" Alexis huffed. "That's your return compliment?"

She turned and walked past the guards, taking lead down the passageway that was littered with the remains of lowdeckers.

"I believe you have the hardest job on the station," a guard said quietly from Kel's side.

"I heard that!" Alexis yelled over her shoulder. "Whoever said that better hope I'm in a good mood when this day is done!"

Everyone took a deep breath, lifted their longslings, and followed after their striking, yet somewhat erratic, mistress.

*

Jaeg and his men moved from passageway to passageway, taking longslingers by surprise, attacking not with heavy blades, but with the very weapons the invading forces had thought would win them the day.

Men gathered in Jaeg's wake, picking up longslings and adding to the lowdeckers' arsenal.

From one sector to the next, Jaeg began to dominate the war. He knew the layout better than the forces from above and he knew that he had surprise on his side in those brief few seconds before the middledeckers and Surface guards realized they weren't going up against just heavy blades.

"These would have ended it all months ago," Jaeg said as he turned a corner and put two particle barbs in a startled middledecker's belly.

The man turned to mist and jelly before Jaeg's eyes and he smiled at the work as his men swarmed past him and opened fire on the unsuspecting longslingers who were waiting for howling madmen, not calculating, albeit amateur, marksmen.

"With these I will not only drive Alexis back to the Surface, but I will follow her and take it as my own," Jaeg laughed. "She is right; there should only be one Master of Station Aelon. And that master shall be me."

The screams of dying men spurred him on and he joined in the attack on the middledeckers that tried to regroup and change their tactics.

"Drive them back!" Jaeg yelled. "Drive them back to the heights they came from! Let them see the view from up there before I push them to their fall!"

*

Having sent the first wave of his men up in the lift, Claevan waited with the last of his men for its return so they could join them several decks above. He did not consider what he was doing a retreat, so much as a rethinking of his entire battle strategy. If what he had learned was to be put into use for the mistress's benefit then he needed to get the information to the mistress or join her himself.

But the order of com silence made it impossible for him to relay his new found use of the longslings without actually being in her presence. So his hasty backtracking was nothing more than necessity, not a lack of resolve or will to take the fight to the lowdeckers.

He hoped the mistress saw it the same way when he finally reached her.

*

"Bostman!" Alexis shouted, despite Kel's insistence that she stop. "Bostman! Show your cowardly face, you piece of shaowshit!"

Several men rushed from a doorway to her side and she spun towards them, blades out, ducking under one blade swing then dodging to the right as another came down at her. She was only able to disembowel one man before her guards opened fire and obliterated the lowdeckers.

"Bostman!" Alexis roared. *"I will hunt you for eternity!"*

"My husband is a Diggory as well as a bastard of Klipoline's!" a woman screeched as she stepped out from a doorway several yards down the passageway. "He will be addressed as such!"

Alexis shook her head in surprise, not only because the woman was brash enough to declare such an absurdity, but also because she wielded a heavy blade in both her hands and stood there ready to fight.

"Are you serious?" Alexis asked once the shock wore off. She looked over her shoulder at her husband. "Kel? Is this woman serious?"

"I believe she is," Kel said. "Ma'am? You'll want to put down the blade."

"I will do no such thing!" the woman yelled. "I will fight for my husband's honor and spill my blood and life to show him my devotion!"

The royal guards started to move forward, their longslings at the ready, but Alexis held out her hand and stopped them.

"What's your name, woman?" Alexis asked.

"Chevan," the woman replied. "Chevan Diggory."

"Well, Chevan Diggory, your husband made an agreement with me that he has not lived up to," Alexis said as she sheathed her blades and slowly walked towards the agitated lowdecker. "He was supposed to meet me several junctions back with his men and we were to make our way to Jaeg's sector and end that man's campaign for the Lower Decks crown."

"You were going to make my husband a puppet!" Chevan shouted. "You were going to parade him around like your toy, telling him what to do and what to say, while you get all the glory and power and privilege!"

"Well, yes," Alexis nodded. "That was the plan. But, look at it this way, Chevan: your husband would have been a puppet with a crown. He would have been a master and you would have been a mistress, just like me."

"I would never want to be like you!" Chevan spat. "Real women know their place and that is by their men's sides, not ruling over them like some cocksure strumpet!"

"Says the woman holding a heavy blade," Kel whispered.

"Quiet," Alexis sighed. "I think I know what this woman wants. It sickens me that I do know, but we don't have much choice. Without Bostman, we will not be able to get the lowdeckers to fall in line once this day is done."

"Do whatever you need to, my love," Kel said. "I'll just stand here and be ruled over."

"You are not funny right now," Alexis said as she cleared her throat. "Chevan? I think you are reacting to a misconception. The previous Master, Kliopline, was never allowed to have the true power that his title suggested. His greed may have gained him a crown, but it lost him a voice. Now, as you say, your husband is a Diggory. Well, Moses Diggory was a steward, with all the rights and privileges, including a seat in the meeting of stewards. I intend to extend that honor to your husband as well. Not only will he be Master of the Lower Decks, but he will be Steward Diggory and be allowed a voice in the meeting that is equal to all the other stewards."

"That's your plan?" Kel asked.

"Hush, you," Alexis snapped. "What do you say, Chevan?"

"I say that the stewards are nothing but a nest of honey wasps, is what I say!" Chevan shouted, oblivious to her repetition. "You can take that stewardship and shove it up your pregnant twat!"

"And that's my cue," Kel said as his finger moved to squeeze his longsling's trigger.

"Stop," Alexis said. "Chevan? Is that your final response?"

"It is!"

"I am sorry to hear that," Alexis said. "Because I like your spirit and your loyalty to your husband. I think we would have had great conversations when I visited you in your estate house on the Surface."

The heavy blade faltered as Chevan's arms started to relax.

"My estate house?" she asked.

"Your estate house," Alexis nodded. "All stewards have estate houses on the Surface, not to mention quarters within Castle Quent for when they stay at court. But I understand you are a woman of principle and wouldn't dare let things such as that sway your opinion of this pregnant twat. I am sorry we could not see eye to eye, Chevan. Guards?"

"Now hold on!" Chevan protested as she quickly let the blade fall from her hands and clatter to the floor. "I didn't exactly mean all of what I just said. You people have me flustered and confused. Completely understandable since you never bothered to speak to me directly. If you'd communicated your intentions before, then there wouldn't be this misunderstanding, now would there be?"

"Your are completely right, Chevan," Alexis said as she held out her arms and walked towards the woman. "My apologies for not having you be part of the discussion I've had with your husband. I, of all people, should know that a woman's opinion is as valuable as her husband's. If not more so, am I right, Chevan?"

"Well, yes, yes, I think so," Chevan said as she was taken into the mistress's arms and hugged tightly.

"Now, Chevan, where is your husband?" Alexis asked.

"He's hiding under our bed," Chevan admitted freely.

"Excellent," Alexis smiled as she pushed away from the woman and took her by the shoulders. "You have done him a great service today and I promise your loyalty to your husband, as well as to me, will be rewarded." Then Alexis slammed her fist into the woman's face, crushing her nose into a bloody pulp. "But if you ever call me a twat again, I'll slice your tits off and feed them to you. Are we understood, Chevan?"

"And she's back," Kel said as he pushed past the woman and through the door into the Diggory quarters. "Men? Seize her."

"No need," Alexis said as she grabbed Chevan by the collar and pulled her in close. "You aren't going to ever be a problem again, now are you Chevan?"

"No, mistress," Chevan said, her voice choked with blood. "Do I still get the estate house?"

"Oh, Chevan, you still get the estate house and all the headaches that come with it," Alexis sighed. "Trust me, being royalty is no picnic." She looked around at the passageway. "You'll miss your old life faster than you think."

Kel came out of the quarters quickly with Bostman in his grip. The lowdecker cringed at the sight of his wife's bloody face, but made no move to go to her assistance.

"Hello, Bostman," Alexis said. "Your wife and I were just talking about your future as a royal of Station Aelon. As you can see we had a disagreement, but we worked it out. Do you believe you and I will have a disagreement? Or is everything already worked out?"

"It is worked out," Bostman said. "It's all worked out. We can proceed to the main atrium where most everyone is waiting. I have heard from my sources that Jaeg is close to defeat already. That's good, right? You probably won't have to lift another finger today."

Alexis looked past Bostman at the shadowed figure of her father that stood against the passageway's wall. The apparition shook his head back and forth and Alexis nodded in response.

"Lexi?" Kel asked. "Are you alright?"

"Fine, love," Alexis said. "Just mulling over what Bostman just said. While I'd love to believe him, my gut is telling me that it won't be such a simple victory today."

"General reason could tell you that," Kel said. He looked from Bostman to Chevan. "Do we bring them with?"

"We have to," Alexis said. "If we march into that atrium without him then we are invaders. With him we are liberators. Fine line, I know, but a line we are forced to walk."

Kel shoved Bostman away and then gave him a hard kick in the ass. "Lead the way, worm," Kel snapped. "And be sure you aren't leading us into a trap."

"I'm not, I'm not," Bostman said as he scuttled down the passageway. "I can assure you that the day is yours. Long live the mistress!"

Alexis rolled her eyes and walked alongside her husband as they followed the toady to the main atrium.

*

Men hurried to and fro as they worked at fortifying the main atrium, setting up barricades and barriers, hides and cover. The general population of the Lower Decks had long since retreated to their quarters and hovels. None wanted to be present when the lowdecker forces met the Surface forces in one final clash.

"Set up on that level!" Jaeg shouted as he directed men with longslings towards a balcony that overlooked the main entrance to the atrium. "You keep those things trained on that entrance! The second you see Alexis's men, you fire until you are empty!"

Several men shouted back their understanding, but most just hurried into position, not wanting to upset their leader more than he already was. Jaeg watched them go then turned his attention to the large group of men that stood off to the side, heavy blades held firmly in blood encrusted hands.

"Once the bitch shows her face, the men above will start firing," Jaeg stated. "Alexis and her guards won't know what is happening since they will not expect longslings to be used against them. They'll scatter and break ranks in their confusion. That is when you men descend on them and cut them down. Separate and destroy. That is how we will win."

"You're sure she is coming this way?" a man asked.

"I am," Jaeg said. "Diggory has assured me he will lead her here. It was the only way I would agree to let him live."

"You're going to kill him as soon as we kill the mistress, right?" the man asked.

"Oh, I'll kill him as soon as I see him," Jaeg smiled. "No need to wait until the royal cunt has stopped breathing. In fact, I'd love for her to see me take the slimy bastard's head off just before I tell her that she was set up. Then she'll know all of her careful planning was pointless and no Surface whore can beat the true heir to the Lower Deck crown."

*

Alexis held up her hand and her regiment halted at the junction of passageways just before the entrance to the Lower Decks' main atrium.

"This is where the lowdecker masses await me?" Alexis asked the man that cowered by her shoulder. "Can I ask you a question, Bostman?"

"Yes, of course, Your Highness," Bostman nodded.

"Have you ever been around a mass of people?"

"I'm sorry, mistress?" Bostman asked. "Did you just ask if I had ever been around people?"

"Around a *mass* of people, Bostman," Alexis said. "You know, a large group of passengers, or in your case, lowdeckers, all gathered together in a space such as an atrium."

"I-I-I don't quite understand," Bostman said.

"She wants to know why we aren't hearing the sounds that a large crowd makes when it is tense and waiting," Kel explained. "We may be a passageway off from the atrium, but we should be able to hear voices and chatter. We don't. It's silent."

"Oh. Well...." Bostman replied then broke down into tears. His wife went to him, placed her arm across his shoulder, and gave Kel and Alexis a scornful look.

"Is this how you treat your allies?" she asked. "By punching them and interrogating them until they break? I pity those that you call friends."

"So do I," Alexis said. "Being around royalty is never easy." She turned to her men and frowned. "Our brave guide is obviously setting us up. The atrium is an ambush, but unfortunately, it's an ambush we have to face head on, since the side entrances are no doubt barricaded."

"We rush in fast and hard and unload everything we have on them," Kel added. "If it turns to blade to blade and hand to hand then so be it. Our longslings have served us well, but once we get out in the open we run the risk of shooting each other as much as we shoot the enemy."

"Fire at anything and everything just like we have been all day," Alexis said. "Then cut down anything and everything. Do not worry about killing innocents. If they are in that atrium then they are no longer innocent."

"And if any lowdecker doesn't know to hide and take cover by now then we are doing the gene pool a favor by removing them from the mix." Kel smiled and the men laughed at his joke as they checked and double checked their weapons. He leaned in to his wife and whispered in her ear. "Speaking of gene pool, how is our little one doing?"

"She's been asleep for most of it," Alexis said, sounding disappointed. "I'd have thought that all my adrenaline would have kept her wide awake."

Kel leaned back and studied his wife. "She?"

"What?" Alexis asked.

"You're referring to the baby as she, Lexi," Kel smiled. "You haven't done so until just now."

"Huh," Alexis smiled back. "Interesting."

"Very," Kel said then kissed her and looked at the regiment. "Ready, men?"

"Ready!" they shouted.

"Are we to go with you?" Bostman asked.

"Not with the ambush waiting for us," Alexis said and pointed at two men. "Hang back and secure them then hurry on and join us."

"Yes, mistress," they said in unison as they came forward, took the Diggorys by the arms, and led them over to a set of large pipes in the corner by the wall.

"Are you ready, my love?" Alexis asked Kel.

"I've been ready since the moment I saw you," Kel replied.

"Good answer," Alexis grinned as she pulled both long blades from their sheaths and pointed towards the atrium entrance. *"Now!"*

*

The noise of compressed Vape gas combusted within the chambers of the longslings was overwhelming. Never before in the history of Station Aelon, nor in the history of the System, had so many longslings been fired at the same time. The lowdecker atrium echoed with the release of the deadly particle barbs from both sides.

Royal guards screamed as they were ripped apart. Many fell to the floor in agony as the wild shots from the untrained lowdeckers tore into arms and legs instead of torsos or heads, lucky to have hit a target at all. The clatter of falling weapons was almost as loud as the concussions of the particle barbs being fired.

"To the sides!" Kel shouted as he aimed at one of the weaker barricades where several lowdeckers hid, obviously only armed with heavy blades and not longslings. "Take them out and take their cover!"

The royal regiment split and dashed for various points of cover, some abandoning their longslings for the more familiar feel of the blades that hung at their hips. They slashed and hacked their way over and behind barricades, dispatching the lowdeckers quickly so they could hunker down from the continual onslaught of particle barbs that showered down from the levels above.

"Lexi!" Kel shouted as he cracked open a lowdecker's skull with the butt of his longsling then whipped it about and fired point blank into the groin of another. "Lexi!"

Alexis Teirmont, Mistress of Station Aelon and its Prime, was not amongst those that ran and hid behind the hastily built barriers and barricades. She did not fight and scramble for a place of safety. She did not try to dodge the particle barbs that exploded next to her feet, shredding the metal instantly. Alexis simply walked down the middle of the atrium, her long blades held out, ready to get to work.

As lowdeckers saw that she was not going to flee their ambush, the braver of them stepped out to confront the monarch that many saw as only a mere woman. She may have been tall for her gender, but she was female and not worthy of any respect when it came to fighting, despite her reputation. A half dozen lowdeckers, heavy blades held high, came at her in an arrogant rush of testosterone and foolishness.

Two heads had hit the floor, their former necks spewing blood high into the air, before the other men realized they may have underestimated the young mistress. Already committed to the fight, the remaining lowdeckers changed their tactics and tried to circle and trap Alexis, instead of taking her head on. But, unlike the men, Alexis was not a muscle-bound behemoth who relied on brute strength. No, she was agile and lithe, the picture of style and grace, as she spun about from foot to foot, then down onto knee to knee, her blades whirling, striking, slashing, killing.

Up and around, in and then out, the woman could not be contained, her power could not be trapped, her skills could not be matched, even by the warriors that outweighed her by a hundred pounds.

Alexis Teirmont butchered every person in her path and she did it with a sly smile and a happy twinkle in her eye. Her grandfather was a man quick to rage who fought battles again and again his entire life. Her father was a man that preferred the finer things, a simpler, easier way of living, and that was how he died. But, for Alexis, life did not exist unless death was right at hand.

She craved the heat of battle and that craving pushed her on as she decimated the lowdecker forces almost single handedly while her royal guards, with Kel, provided what cover they could with their longslings from the sides.

"Jaeg!" she roared as she skipped over a pile of stray intestines that blocked her path. *"Jaeg! Show yourself!"*

A particle barb nearly clipped her leg, but her instincts turned her body just at the right time. She followed the trajectory of the barb back to its origin and found herself staring eye to eye with Noomis Jaeg as he lowered his longsling and stepped from behind a barricade. He looked shaken, but he tried to maintain an air of confidence despite the fact that a woman just marched down the middle of the atrium he held, killing his men casually as if she was simply picking flowers in a Surface field.

"Hello, Jaeg," Alexis said, her blades hanging from her hands, blood dripping steadily from their tips. She looked around at the battle that raged and smiled. "Good day to die, don't you think?"

Jaeg started to raise his longsling then thought better of it and tossed it aside as he held out his hand. One of his men handed him his heavy blade and he slowly gripped it and raised it to his shoulder.

"You are impressive," Jaeg said. "But impressive doesn't win wars, Alexis. Impressive gets songs sung and tales told, but it also digs graves and writes epitaphs. I am sorry that a woman of your skill must meet her end by my hand. I would have preferred to kill a master; there's no honor in killing a woman, but at least I will have the favor of slaying the monarch of Station Aelon."

"Possibly," Alexis shrugged. "But I don't think you have it in you, Jaeg. I think there is a weakness to your soul that won't let you truly give me your all when you charge with that blade."

"Is that what you think?" Jaeg sneered, his face red with furious indignation. "You think I am afraid to kill a bitch cunt like you?"

"No, I think you're afraid this bitch cunt will kill you," Alexis laughed. "I mean, come on, Jaeg, that's way scarier than just killing me. I'd be afraid of me if I weren't me."

"You won't be you for long, whore!" Jaeg shouted as he rushed towards Alexis.

"No, I won't," Alexis said calmly as she dropped to the floor just as a volley of particle barbs flew past her and ripped into Jaeg's head, chest, belly, and legs.

The lowdecker was obliterated in less than a second, leaving only a heavy blade to fall to the floor and splat in his remains.

Alexis smiled as she pushed up on her hands and looked over her shoulder at her husband and men as they still held their longslings to their shoulders, all trained in her direction. She got to her feet and walked the couple of feet to the bloody pile of clothes and miscellaneous body parts that didn't get molecularly destroyed. Alexis nudged the remains with her toe and sighed.

"None of us are the same person for long, Jaeg," she said. "Change is part of life. The difference is I get to live mine and you don't."

The sounds of battle intensified as Jaeg's men realized that their only chance at survival was to kill the royal guards and make sure the mistress and her master did not leave the Lower Decks alive. They were all well past the point of surrender and any chance of being granted mercy.

Alexis looked up at the levels above her and calculated how many lowdeckers remained. Her heart skipped a little as she realized that even with her confidence, and Jaeg dead, her men were so vastly outnumbered that it was only a matter of time before they were overwhelmed and beaten. For the first time that day, Alexis felt fear and worry that she would not prevail.

She immediately thought about ordering her men to fall back and head to the lift. They could regroup above and then plot a new course of action. But as she turned to look at the main entrance to the atrium she saw lowdecker reinforcements pour into the space, heavy blades gleaming in the artificial light.

"Lexi!" Kel shouted.

"I know!" Alexis shouted back. "Everyone on me!"

Kel and her men rushed to her, creating a protective circle as the lowdeckers charged. Several of the guards' longslings clicked empty and were tossed aside for long blades. The weapons looked small and weak compared to the heavy blades that were being wielded by the screaming, enraged, bloodthirsty lowdeckers.

"I love you!" Kel yelled over his shoulder as he braced himself.

"I love you too!" Alexis replied, her blades gripped so tightly that every knuckle on her hand cracked louder than the few longslings still firing. "We die together, my love! We *all* die together!"

"Together!" the guards roared. *"For Aelon! For Alexis!"*

But, just as the two factions were about to collide, the sound of a world being ripped apart nearly forced everyone to their knees. Many of the men, royal guards as well as lowdeckers, dropped their weapons to clamp their hands over their ears. The aural assault was so great that in seconds half the atrium fell unconscious as their heads were overwhelmed.

Alexis, down on one knee, looked up at the ceiling of the atrium and gasped. Where there should have been hammered metal and massive struts, there was only open space revealing the internal structure of the station. And out of that open space dropped Claevan Twyerrn and his men, all clipped to thick cables, their longslings firing at every lowdecker they could see.

It was all over before Claevan's men landed boots on the floor. Only a few lowdeckers remained awake and able to fight, but they were dispatched quickly by the middledeckers that swarmed over them. Claevan unclipped himself from the cable he had slid down and hurried over to Alexis.

"Mistress? Mistress, are you alright?" he asked. "I am sorry for the noise. We had no idea that would happen."

"It is alright," Alexis smiled as she was helped to her feet. She shook her head slowly and winced at the massive headache that quickly grew. Then she stared up at where there should have been a ceiling. "I believe, even though it was excruciating, I would still endure that discomfort just to watch you do that again. Amazing, Claevan. Simply amazing."

"Lexi?" Kel asked as he stumbled over to her and took her in his arms. "Are you harmed?"

"Nothing a healthy dose of honey wasp liquor won't cure," Alexis sighed as she pressed her face into her husband's shoulder. "And a long sleep in my own bed."

"I'll be right by your side for both," Kel said as he held her tight.

"Is it safe to come out?" Bostman asked from the atrium entrance. "Did we win?"

"Why must there always be someone to ruin the moment?" Alexis asked as she pushed back from Kel and looked over at the weak man she intended to give the Lower Decks crown to. "Yes, Bostman, it is safe to come out. Why don't you have a seat over there and I'll be with you shortly, alright?"

"Where?" Bostman asked. "Everything is covered in blood."

"Helios, kill me," Alexis mumbled.

"I'll handle him, Your Highness," Claevan nodded. "You tend to your men and regroup." He looked about at the wounded and unconscious lowdeckers. "What would you like my men to do with this filth?"

"Kill them," Alexis said. "I don't want a single witness left who can talk about what you did, Claevan. Do you understand what I'm saying? Your men I trust. The lowdeckers? Never. The way you used those particle barbs will change this System more than the longslings ever could. I want that tactic to be held in the strictest confidence."

"Understood, Your Highness," Claevan bowed.

"And Claevan?" Alexis asked.

"Yes, Your Highness?"

"It's Alexis, remember?" the mistress grinned. "Don't make me tell you again."

Claevan started to respond then just nodded and bowed again.

"When do we parade Bostman about?" Kel asked.

"Now," Alexis replied. "We find the communications room on the deck and make a station wide announcement. As of this moment, Bostman Diggory is the new Master of the Lower Decks. And his ass is mine forever."

Kel smiled and kissed her, wiping a glob of gore from her cheek, then got down on one knee and raised his blade.

"For Alexis!" he called out.

Everyone present, including Claevan's men, all followed suit and soon the atrium was filled with men, blades raised, swearing their ever dying fealty and loyalty to Alexis the Third, Mistress of Station Aelon and its Prime.

*

Servants and attendants stepped to the side and lowered their heads as the mistress marched down the grand hallway of Castle Helble, her armor still coated with blood. She quickly reached the double doors of the castle's library, but hesitated, pulling her hand back from the handle.

"Once you go in there, you will not be able to go back," the apparition of Alexis the Second said from Alexis's side. "She is not to be trusted. Fate does not smile on that witch."

"She is my mother," Alexis replied quietly. "And I need her."

"She will betray you," her father said. "She will let you down. You know that. Bella looks out for Bella, that is her way."

"That is the way of all royals," Alexis responded, her hand hovering over the library door's handle. "Until now. It is time it changed."

"You may not be the one to change it," her father sighed. "It may not even be possible to change."

Alexis rubbed her belly and shook her head.

"No, I do not believe that," she said. "All things change."

"Your Highness?" an attendant asked as he stepped out of a doorway a few feet from the library. "Were you addressing me? I apologize that I did not catch what you said."

"Tea," Alexis said, turning and fixing her gaze on the young man. "Lots of it. And some towels and a basin of water. I'd like to wipe myself clean while I speak with my mother."

The attendant's face blanched as he took in her full state.

"Yes, of course, Your Highness," the attendant bowed. "Shall I have a bath prepared as well? Are you remaining at the castle for the night?"

"No," Alexis said. "I'll be leaving soon. Just the tea and towels, if you please."

The attendant bowed again and hurried back through the door he'd just come through.

Alexis looked about, but the ghost of her father was gone. She took a deep breath and turned the door's handle then shoved it open and stepped into the library.

"Mommy!" Minor Alexis cried as he jumped down from his grandmother's lap and rushed to Alexis. "Mommy, you're alive!"

Alexis was overjoyed to see her son, but his words stopped her short and she fell to her knees as great sobs ripped up from her soul and took her over.

"My lady!" Lara cried out as she hurried to the mistress. "Are you wounded?"

"Only in spirit," Bella Herlect Terimont Beumont said as she got to her feet and made her way to her daughter. "Lara, please take the minor to his quarters, will you? I believe my daughter is here to see me."

Lara scooped up Minor Alexis before he could get to the mistress, and her blood coated armor, and quickly left the library, despite the boy's protestations.

"Get up, Alexis," Bella said as she placed a hand on her daughter's shoulder. "This is not how a mistress celebrates a victory such as yours."

Alexis struggled to get herself under control, but it took another minute before she could find the strength to stand and walk over to one of the chairs by the wide windows that looked out onto the Surface of Station Aelon.

"We'll have to burn that once you're gone," Bella said. "There's no getting that blood out of the upholstery."

"I'm not here to talk about how I have ruined furniture you do not own, Mother," Alexis said, her voice still shaky with emotion. "I am here to talk about the next step in my rule."

Bella nodded to a large, and dusty, video monitor on a table in the corner of the library. "Yes, I saw your announcement of the end of the Lower Decks conflict and your installment of Bostman Diggory as the new master down there. It was a fine speech and very impressive, even if your choice of men is questionable. That Diggory is weaker than a siggy worm and has even fewer brains."

"Which is why he is perfect for my needs," Alexis replied. "He is a place holder, Mother, and I make no allusions otherwise."

"Good for you," Bella said. "So, my dearest daughter, tell me what your next move is. What does the Mistress of Station Aelon have in mind?"

"My birthright," Alexis said. "That is all I want. To secure my birthright, and the birthrights of my children, so that Station Aelon reigns supreme in System Helios."

"Your birthright?" Bella frowned. "You already have the crown and have just defeated the usurpers below; what more could you possibly want, Alexis?"

"Everything," Alexis said. "All of it. What should be mine, but has been taken by some pretender that wouldn't know true royal blood if it was pumped into his veins by physicians."

"Everything? All of it?" Bella asked. "Sweetheart, you can't mean what I think you mean. I do not think you are ready. I do not think Aelon is ready."

"I do not think that either, Mother," Alexis said. "But Aelon will be ready, as will I. It may take years, possibly a decade, but the time will come when I make my move and those that have laughed at a mistress as monarch will be forced to see the error of their opinions."

"And you want my help to achieve this why?" Bella asked. "Look about, my dearest, I am in exile. What use could I be?"

"You are a Thraen, Mother," Alexis said as she leaned forward and fixed her Teirmont fire fully on the woman that had birthed her more than twenty years before. "And I will need the advice of a Thraen if I am to become the Mistress of Station Tharen and its Prime."

"Oh dear, Alexis," Bella said, shaking her head. "I fear you are mad like your father."

"I may be mad," Alexis laughed. "But I am not wrong. I am the daughter of a minoress of Thraen and that crown is my birthright. I will have it, no matter the cost."

"Be careful Alexis," Bella said, her eyes going to her daughter's pregnant, and armored, belly. "The costs may be greater than you are prepared to pay."

"No, Mother, they are not," Alexis said as she stood and rubbed at her belly. "I intend to make sure that my son, and my daughter, and all of my future children understand the costs. I intend for them to be the most powerful royals this system has ever seen. When the time comes for me to strike, I will have all the Teirmonts by my side. This family will be legend for all of time as we take what is ours and show the System that Station Aelon cannot be held back."

The attendant rolled in a large cart with the tea service, towels, and a basin of steaming hot water.

"Out," Bella snapped.

"No, stay," Alexis said, her eyes on her mother. "I plan on having a cup of tea and wiping this grime from me while we discuss the parameters of your role in the fate of this station, Mother. Unless you are outright refusing my request for assistance?"

The attendant looked from Alexis to Bella, frozen in place as he waited for the battle of royal wills to come to a conclusion.

"Tea will be fine," Bella said finally and stood up. "Leave us, Villene. I'll pour the tea myself.

"Yes, my lady," the attendant bowed as he turned and hurried from the library, closing the doors behind him as he left.

The two women stood there, eyes locked, neither moving towards the cart or towards each other, as the fate of Station Aelon hung between them.

ACT III

THE CENTURY WAR BEGINS

"With the distinct boundaries of sovereignty we adhere to today, it is always astounding to look back on a time when all it took was superior resources, and an immense amount of luck, to overtake one's neighbor. It would be unheard of today to march onto a prime and declare it as one's own and only have to fight, and win, to make the statement the truth."
   —Dr. D. Reven, Eighty-Third Archivist of The Way

"Then Helios looked down upon the Planet and declared the Cataclysm as Holy. The Dear Parent cleansed the land of the Evil and the Unjust, leaving it clean once again for those with Faith."
   —Book of Remembrance 8:11, The Ledger

"Love could be considered its own prison. It binds and constricts and controls. One is never free when one is in love. But, then, who cares? You have love."
   —Journals of Alexis the Third, Mistress of Station Aelon and its Primes

CHAPTER SEVEN

The two single hover skids raced through the breen fields at speeds that no one would have considered safe, except for the fact the fields had just been harvested and all that stood in the dirt were the occasional broken stalk or two. They zipped in and out of each others' paths, turning just in time, always so close to disaster. The machines, their riders laughing and taunting each other, were pushed to the limits of their technology.

"You almost didn't cut that turn, A," Alexis chuckled over the com. "Maybe we should head back to the compound for your nap."

"I'm fourteen, Mother," Minor Alexis replied. "I do not take naps."

"Perhaps you should start," Alexis snickered. "Then you'd have the energy to keep up with your mother."

"No one has that kind of energy, love," Kel said as he sat on a large hover skid at the edge of the field, his legs dangling above the dirt and wisps of Vape gas that floated across the landscape. He watched the gas twist and turn around itself, not missing the obvious parallel between it and how his wife and son drove their skids. "Except perhaps Natalie, but then she is the freak of the family."

"Daddy!" the ten year old minoress yelled over the com as she walked up to the hover skid. "That was a mean thing to say!"

"Oh, hey there, baby girl," Kel laughed. "I didn't know you were in range otherwise I wouldn't have said perhaps. Everyone *knows* you're the freak of the family."

"You think you're being cute, don't you?" Natalie sighed as she climbed up next to her father. "Mother, Daddy is being cute again. Tell him to stop. He's no good at it."

"Oh, I don't know, Nats," Alexis replied. "I think he's extremely cute. If I didn't then none of you little buggers would be here."

"Gross," Natalie replied as she watched her mother and brother cut their skids at the same time and almost collide. "Ooh, an inch closer and I would have just become the mistress of the station. Go faster, you two; getting the crown would be the perfect Decade present."

"Don't be morbid," Kel scolded. "Helios knows this family has enough of that without your jokes, Nats." He looked about then frowned. "Where's your skid?"

"I walked," Natalie replied. "It's a nice enough day for it."

Kel looked up at the never ending grey sky and shook his head. "You're a true girl of the prime, if there ever was one. I can't imagine considering this dreary world nice enough for anything."

"Yet this is your birthplace and home," Natalie said. "I doubt The Way could imagine a Burdened saying anything of the sort. Aren't you people bred to love the clouds and tumultuous seas?"

"How old are you?" Kel laughed. "Tumultuous? What ten year old uses the word tumultuous?"

"The same ten year old that crushes you at chess and can disarm her brother with the flick of a wrist," Natalie grinned behind her environmental suit's visor.

"I slipped!" Minor Alexis protested as he braked his skid hard and let his Mother shoot past just before they were going to collide. Again. "I told you that the servants had just mopped the workout room, yet you insisted we spar."

"Yet *I* didn't slip, did I?" Natalie replied. "I stayed on both feet and sent your blade flying against the wall. Clatter, clatter, clang, clang. That's your new fanfare, A. Every time you enter a room at court they'll play those sounds. Clatter, clatter, clang, clang. It's catchy. Could be a top hit with the disc traders."

"Shut up, you shaow," Minor Alexis snapped.

"Hey, be nice, you two," Alexis warned over the com. "We are all down here for a family vacation, not so you two can bicker like you do on the station."

"Why we thought it'd be different, I don't know," Kel said. "They never stop bickering up there so I doubt they'll stop down here."

"They will if they want to sleep in the castle tonight," Alexis responded. "Otherwise they can stay in their environmental suits all night and bunk with the harvesting equipment."

"You wouldn't dare, Mother," Natalie said. "Grandmother would throw a fit and toss you out the airlock. She loves me more than you. I'm like the daughter she never had."

"Oh, for Helios's sake," Kel sighed. "You had to go and say that, didn't you?"

Alexis whipped her skid around and sped over to her daughter and husband. She stopped just an inch short of running into Natalie's legs as they dangled from the large hover skid, yet the minoress didn't even flinch. "You better watch yourself, little girl, or I'll cancel your Decade celebration."

"Please, Mother," Natalie smiled. "We all know you wouldn't even think of doing that. My Decade celebration is just your excuse for inviting half the System's nobility to see our new prime estate. You are way too proud of your castle to cancel now and make everyone go home."

"Sometimes I wonder who is the mother and who is the daughter in this relationship," Alexis smiled back at Natalie. "Oh, wait, the mother is the one that can tell you to scrub the suits when we get back to the castle. Have fun with that."

"No way!" Natalie yelled. "It's my birthday! You wouldn't dare make me clean the suits on my birthday!"

"Oh, I think I would dare," Alexis said as she gunned her skid's drive and sped off. "And be sure to do a good job, Nats, or I'll make you do it again."

"Mother!" Natalie shouted. "Mother! Come back here right now!"

Alexis kept going, her body hunched over her skid's handlebars as she raced across the land and back towards the Aelon Prime estate and castle.

"Daddy! You aren't going to let her do that to me, are you?" Natalie whined. "Tell me you'll talk to her."

"I can tell you I'm going to talk to her," Kel shrugged. "But you know as well as I that talking to your mother when she has made a declaration is like talking to the clouds above. Nothing will make them change except Helios the Dear Parent."

"This is so unfair!" Natalie shouted and jumped down from the large skid. "It's my birthday!"

"And you'll have an amazing Decade celebration starting tomorrow morning," Kel said as he got up and went to the skid's controls. "Now get up here so I can give you a ride back. You have some suits to clean."

"I am not riding with you unless you promise to make Mother change her mind," Natalie insisted. "Fathers protect their daughters; they don't let them get thrown to the Vape gasses."

"You know I can still hear both of you, right?" Alexis said over the com. "You should remember to change channels if you're going to bad mouth me. Maybe the cooks need some help scrubbing out the ovens, as well. I'll ask them when I get to the castle. Isn't that great, Nats? Now you'll have that to look forward too!"

"Argh!" Natalie shouted. She stomped away through the cut and broken stalks of the breen field, headed not back towards the Aelon castle, but out into the open expanse of the Aelon Prime continent.

"Nats! Knock it off and get back here!" Kel yelled, but the beeping in his ear told him she had switched off her com. "Dammit!"

"I'll get her, Father," Minor Alexis said. "Go on back with Mother. We won't be long."

"Try to calm her down, will you? We don't need her coming into the castle all rage pissed. It'll ruin the spirit of the surprise."

"I know, I know," Minor Alexis replied. "I got it handled."

"*Have* it handled," Kel corrected. "I may be low born, but you are not. Speak properly or others will think less of you. You cannot afford that when you are next in line for the Aelish crown."

"With how much Mother spent on the prime castle and estate fortifications, I doubt I'll be able to afford anything once I get that crown," Minor Alexis replied. "And how much is she spending on Nats's Decade anyway? Where do we get the credits from?"

"Not your concern," Kel said. "You just worry about your training."

"And my sister," Minor Alexis said. "And the rest of my siblings. And the future of the station and its prime. And—"

"Stop," Kel ordered. "You'll have many, many years before the crown is yours and you need to worry about any of that stuff."

"That's not what Mother says," Minor Alexis responded as he turned his skid and started off slowly in the direction his sister was hiking. "She says now is when I should begin paying attention since she wasn't too much older than me when she took the crown."

"Your mother's situation and your situation cannot be compared," Kel laughed. "Trust me, you spoiled little royal." He started the large skid's drive and aimed the vehicle back towards the castle. "But I will talk to her about filling your head with worries. You don't need that. Leave the serious stuff to us, A. You just be a kid."

"I'm fourteen," Minor Alexis said. "I'll be legally able to take the crown in two years. Not much time left to be a kid."

"Which is why you should stop worrying," Kel countered. "Now go get your sister so she can get back to the castle and her surprise."

"Fine," Minor Alexis said as he gunned his skid and shot across the landscape. "See you in a little while."

"Be safe," Kel said.

"I always am," Minor Alexis replied.

Kel laughed at the ironic interchange. No Teirmont was ever safe. It was a lesson he had learned the hard way over and over.

He pushed the large skid's propulsion drive as hard as it would go, eager to catch up to his wife. It took him a couple of minutes, but he came up behind the mistress on her single skid and started scanning the com channels until he found hers.

"Your daughter just turned hers off," Kel said. "Instead of setting it to a private channel that no one would think to look for."

"Well, our daughter isn't mistress, is she?" Alexis replied. "I don't have the luxury of turning mine off, do I?"

"Wait, are you actually mad?" Kel asked. Alexis didn't reply. "You are! Oh, you have got to be kidding me."

"I am not mad," Alexis replied. "I'm just disappointed that you didn't defend me harder."

"Defend you? Against what? Our daughter?" Kel laughed. "She's ten, Lexi. You don't need defending against a ten year old. And it wouldn't matter what I say, anyway. That girl gets her mind made up before anyone even opens their mouths. I could have promised her the glory of Helios in a box and she would have still been ready to argue against it. Let it go, Lexi. There are other battles to fight."

"Yes, I know," Alexis sighed. "It's just so hard sometimes. I see so much of myself in her and so much of my mother in me. Those are not fun visions to have, love. Believe me, I do not want to ever turn out like my mother and I surely do not want Nats to ever turn out like me."

"What's wrong with turning out like you?" Kel asked. "I love the way you turned out."

"That is because fate interceded on our behalf," Alexis said. "Without fate you would have seen me for the mess that I was and run screaming."

"I doubt that," Kel said. "Not with the way your ass looks in armor."

"Used to look," Alexis laughed. "Five kids later and I'm lucky my ass even fits in my armor."

"Ha!" Kel laughed. "Half the women in the System would give their firstborns to have your body. Five kids and you can still outfight most of the men of the Order."

"Oh, Helios!" Alexis exclaimed. "The Order! We are supposed to meet tonight!"

"No, no, I postponed that until after the Decade celebration tomorrow," Kel said. "I saw what a mistake that would have been. We have too much on our plates, as it is. No need to pile the Order of Jex business on top of it all."

"Well, I guess they have to be here for the celebration anyway," Alexis said. "And the shuttle window back to Station Aelon isn't until the end of the week. Good thinking, my love."

"I've been doing this for a while, Lexi," Kel said. "I know how to handle our schedule in order to keep us from going mad."

"You mean you know how to handle me," Alexis smirked.

"I didn't say that," Kel laughed. "You can't prove a thing."

"I'll get you to confess later, my love," Alexis said. "I have my ways."

"Yes, you do," Kel replied. "And do I love those ways."

They drove their skids in silence from there, each lost in their heads as they worked out the minutiae of arrangements for the next few days.

*

"Nats!" Minor Alexis yelled as he aimed his skid at his sister. "Nats! Hold up!"

Having turned her com off, Natalie didn't acknowledge her brother until he got up next to her, and even then she only gave him a glance and just kept hiking across the damp, post-harvest breen field.

"Dammit, Nats," Minor Alexis swore as he tried to cut her off with his skid. "Stop!"

His sister just kept moving, dodging his attempts to block her path, turning as he turned, stopping quickly so he'd overshoot and rush past her.

"Nats!" Minor Alexis roared, ditching his skid so he could jump down in front of her and grab her by the shoulders. "Knock it off!"

She only stared blankly at him.

"Turn your com on!" he shouted, pantomiming for her to hit the button on her wrist so he could talk to her, voice to voice. "Turn it on, or I'll turn it on for you!"

Having grown up going from the station down to the prime for most of their lives, the siblings both knew how to read lips through their environmental suits' visors. Minor Alexis was confident that his sister knew exactly what he was saying and his legendary calm and patience quickly ran thin as Natalie insisted on ignoring his orders.

"Fine! I warned you!" Minor Alexis said as he grabbed his sister's wrist and flipped open the control band. "Better hope you have the volume turned down or this is gonna hurt!"

Natalie struggled against her older brother, but he outweighed her by close to a hundred pounds, having grown tall and broad early. Not that Natalie was spared the growth of the Teirmonts. Just like her mother, she was mostly legs with a powerful stance and a solid frame. Coupled with a belligerent attitude, Minor Alexis had his work cut out for him.

"Ow!" Natalie yelled as her brother finally got her com turned on and she was greeted by an ear piercing squeal of feedback. "Jerk!"

"Hey, you're the jerk," Minor Alexis replied. "You're the one acting like a snot and marching halfway across the prime. Where are you headed? Are you planning on swimming across the sea to the Thraen Prime lease holdings?"

"Maybe," Natalie growled. "I could do it."

"Hardly," Minor Alexis said. "That suit is so outdated, you wouldn't even make it to the coast before the Vape starts breaking down the seams."

"It's not that bad," Natalie said. She tried to step around her brother, but he just moved to block her with each try. "Stop that."

"Come on," Minor Alexis said as he took her by the elbow. "I promised Father I'd get you back to the castle for your surprise."

"For my what?" Natalie asked, yanking her arm free of his grasp. "What surprise?"

"Uh...huh? I didn't say surprise," Minor Alexis frowned. "I said I'd get you back in time for your chores. You know, scrubbing the suits and all that."

"No, you said, surprise," Natalie said, her eyes narrowed and suspicious. "What's the surprise, A?"

"There isn't one," Minor Alexis said quickly. "I misspoke."

Natalie crossed her arms and planted her feet firmly in the soft earth of the breen field. Minor Alexis knew his day was lost the second she started to wiggle her boots deeper and deeper into the mud. He'd never get her free, or if he did, it would only be after an hour of wrestling which would put them both at risk in the poisonous air. All it would take was one sharp rock to rip open one of their suits and expose them to almost instant death.

"Fine!" Minor Alexis shouted. "You don't have to scrub out the suits! You're getting one of the first of the new type of environmental suits Mother had made. Plus, and I'm not happy about this, you're getting the latest model of hover skid. Father helped design it so it would run faster and maneuver better down here on the prime. It is specifically calibrated for the planet's atmosphere. Not that it wouldn't work on the Surface of Station Aelon, just that down here on Helios it will work better."

"A new suit and new skid?" Natalie gasped, her eyes twinkling with anticipation. "What are you waiting for, jerk? Get me back to the castle!"

"Alright, but do not tell Mother or Father that I ruined the surprise," Minor Alexis pleaded.

"Oh, please, A," Natalie laughed. "One look at your face and they'll know. You are a shit liar."

"We'll see," Minor Alexis replied as he helped his sister up onto his skid. "I've been working on my lying. Grandmother says all royals need to be proficient liars if they want to live to their thirtieth year."

"Then I should be able to live forever," Natalie joked as she waited for her brother to hop onto the skid so she could wrap her arms around his waist and steady herself for the skid ride back to the castle. "I'm the best liar in the family. Or will be, once Grandmother dies"

"Nats!" Minor Alexis exclaimed. "Take that back! I'd make you spit six times against the bad luck, but you're in your suit. You be sure and say a prayer of forgiveness tonight before bed."

"I always do, A," Natalie laughed. "It's why Helios hasn't smitten me yet."

"If we didn't look so much alike, I'd wonder if we were even related," Minor Alexis said.

"Oh, quit being so soft and move this skid," Natalie ordered. "I want to see my surprise!"

*

"What do you mean, they are impervious?" Bella asked as she eyed the new environmental suit her granddaughter was busy shimmying into. "Impervious to what?"

"Almost everything," Alexis grinned. "They can withstand fire, acid, the concussive force of a Vape explosion; they even self-repair if torn. The best part is sling barbs can't damage them; they just roll off the surface. Their only weakness is a blade. A direct stab would go right through, but at least the hole would seal around the blade."

"But there'd still be a blade sticking in you," Bella said. "Hardly impervious."

"What about particle barbs?" Kel smirked.

"We are still working on that, Kel," Alexis frowned. "As you know."

"Why would a suit need to stop sling barbs?" Minor Alexis asked. "I know Nats acts like she's always going to war, but I don't think she's going to come across any longslingers down here on the prime."

"You never know when an assassination attempt might occur," Bella stated. "I applaud your mother's preparedness. It appears she has thought of everything on the eve of such an important occasion."

"*Mother*," Alexis growled. "Not here."

"What, sweetheart?" Bella asked, obviously feigning innocence. "I was talking about our dear Natalie's Decade celebration tomorrow. I'm sure she'd like to show her new suit off to the other royal children in attendance."

"I'm sure she would," Kel said as he grabbed one of the larger suits and began to put it on. "How about you two go have a final talk over the last minute details, alright? I'll take Nats and A outside to try out the suits."

"Don't be long," Alexis said. "Lara has her hands full with the twins and Richard."

"Lara has three attendants of her own now," Kel replied. "She's the only attendant in the System with attendants. I think she'll be fine."

"Not to mention that lovely nurse that was just hired," Bella said. "What is she? Ploervian? Haelmish?"

"She's actually a middledecker from Aelon," Alexis said. "Middle Deck Twenty and a second cousin or niece or something of Claevan's."

"Oh, right, Middle Deck Twenty," Bella nodded. "That explains the accent. Beautiful girl, if not a little thick in the head, as well as the rest of her body."

"Go," Kel said, shooing his wife and mother-in-law out of the airlock area and into the castle. "I've got this."

"Thanks, love," Alexis said as she gave him a quick kiss then took her mother's elbow and pulled into the rear entry hall of Castle Aelon Prime. She waited until the light above the airlock door behind her turned green and the audible hiss of air told her that the door was sealed until she spoke again. "Out with it."

"What?" Bella asked. "I have no 'it' to be out with."

"Mother, you obviously want to tell me something," Alexis said. "So just tell me and then we can move on to the details of the Decade celebration."

"Well, that's just it, Alexis, my dear," Bella said. "The details of the Decade celebration are what I want to talk to you about. I have heard through back channels that there might be an attempt on your life, or possibly the minor's, tomorrow."

Alexis stared at her mother as if the woman had suddenly started to produce Vape from every orifice.

"Oh my, have I broken you?" Bella smiled. "Or is it the shock that your precious Order of Jex didn't hear about this first that is troubling you?"

"What back channels?" Alexis asked. "Tell me now, Mother."

"Dearest, you are an amazing diplomat and quite possibly the greatest warrior Station Aelon has ever seen," Bella said. "So, you above all, should know that protection of one's sources is key to surviving as a royal in this System. I will not divulge a single detail of who has been speaking to me. Otherwise that person will be of no use later when we may need him or her the most."

"Just a single person?" Alexis asked. "Hardly reliable. You know you need at least two, if not three, sources to corroborate rumors. As an *amazing diplomat*, I would be a fool to listen to just one voice."

"It depends on the voice," Bella stated. Her entire demeanor changed and she grew pensive, wary. "Alexis, please listen. I know we have our personal issues, which is why you have decided I shall be exiled down here on the Planet once again, but—"

"You are not exiled, Mother," Alexis snapped. "I need you here, watching the completion of the fortifications, so when the time comes I can make my move without worry of our home position. This isn't exile; this is management."

"I'm a royal, a minoress, and former Mistress, Alexis," Bella frowned. "Not some sector warden or deck boss. Management, no matter how important, is beneath me, even considering how far I have fallen."

"I'm not going through this with you again," Alexis said as she threw up her hands and began to walk away. "I'll be in my quarters with my other children when you decide to tell me your source."

"Alexis Teirmont!" Bella shouted. "Don't you walk away from me when lives are on the line! I will not be treated like a crazy woman! My source is beyond reproach and the second your Order arrives this evening, you will want to gather them so I can give them the facts! Do with those facts what you will, but do not ignore me!"

Alexis turned and looked back at her mother. The woman was visibly shaking with emotion and Alexis had to wonder just what was really going on. Threats on her life, and on her family's lives, were commonplace, but always ended up to be empty and false. So the fact that Bella was so upset meant something at least.

"Alright, Mother, who has ordered the attempt?" Alexis asked.

"I cannot say, right now," Bella replied, holding up her hands. "But I will say that I do not doubt that this person would make such an attempt. To say more would put Aelon at risk, you must believe that, Alexis. If I thought you knowing more than that would make any difference then I would tell you."

Alexis studied her mother for several long seconds before replying. "I'll call for the Order to meet tonight. We will make sure that the Decade celebration is as secure as it possibly can be. Which, if I may say so, it was going to be anyway. I am a Mistress of Station, Mother. I know the dangers my position brings on myself and on my family."

"I know you do, sweetheart," Bella said. "But knowing and experiencing are two different things."

Alexis walked up close to her mother, not in a menacing or aggressive way, but so her mother would be forced to pay full attention to what she said. "You seem to forget my days down on this planet during your true exile, Mother. I have experienced it all."

"Yes, of course," Bella said then curtsied low. "You were baptized in blood before you ever took the crown. How can I forget."

Alexis bopped her mother on the top of the head. "Oh, knock of the fake formal crap. You said your piece and I listened. The Order will keep us all safe tomorrow, I guarantee it."

*

Close to twenty men sat around the large oval table in a side dining hall off the main banquet hall of Castle Aelon. Many were young, only in their mid-twenties or early thirties, but there were a couple of exceptions, one of which stood and called for the meeting of the Order of Jex to begin.

"We are here because we have shown perfect loyalty to the crown and to our Mistress, Alexis Teirmont," Claevan said as he stood to the right of the head of the table where Alexis was seated. "We are not just chosen, but tested by combat and by commitment. Where we go, the crown is protected. We are the Order of Jex and nothing in this System, not even Helios the Dear Parent, can break our vows of obedience and devotion. Long live the crown, long live Alexis, long live the Order!"

"Long live them all!" those around the table cried.

"Our lives and our loyalty!" Claevan shouted.

"Our lives and our loyalty!" the men repeated.

"Thank you," Alexis nodded as she stood and bowed. "Your lives and loyalty are under my protection and shall be until the day I die. Now, let us get on with the business at hand."

Claevan nodded and sat down, letting Alexis take over from there.

"You are all here for my daughter's Decade celebration, and I thank you for that," Alexis smiled.

"We're here to see our investment," a man a few seats down laughed. "I didn't pledge half my newborn son's inheritance to the building of Castle Aelon just for a few shiny pictures and a hearty promise."

"Understood, Steward Maglion," Alexis grinned as she looked about the dining hall. "And what do you think so far? I believe the architects have outdone themselves and delivered on their promises. Not only is Castle

Aelon an example of royal luxury, besting all other castles on Planet Helios, but it is nearly impregnable."

"Nearly?" Steward Maglion smiled. "The brochure said it would be completely impregnable."

"Well, you know brochures," Alexis replied and the table of men chuckled. "But, seriously, yes, you are here to see what your money has purchased, and why being a part of the Order of Jex is not just a title on paper, but a physical duty that we all know will become reality within the year. You, gentlemen, have been tested by combat in my many tournaments and have shown your commitment with your generous donations to the crown. Yet soon your loyalty will be tested with blood, not just credits and competitive glory. The war will start, and possibly sooner than we think."

"Why is that?" asked Steward Vast, a man in his mid-thirties with long, brown hair and a jagged scar running from his left eye, across his cheek, and to his left ear. "Is there a new development we are not aware of?"

"Possibly," Alexis said. "A trustworthy source has informed me that there may be an assassination attempt on either myself or Minor Alexis. I know we have all heard these rumors before, but considering the amount of people from the other stations and primes that will be attending my daughter's Decade celebration, this rumor could hold weight. The sheer numbers that security will need to deal with could easily lead to the assassin slipping through. I call on all of you, and your men, to be vigilant through the entire day tomorrow. We do not have the luxury of getting lost in drink and revelry if there is even the chance that my son can be hurt."

"Or that you could be hurt," Kel said as he walked into the dining hall. "I apologize for being late, but the twins just would not go to sleep."

"Hello, love," Alexis smiled as she kissed her husband and gestured for him to take his seat to her left. "Are they fine?"

"Just high-strung, like all six year olds the night before a big event," Kel said and the fathers at the table chuckled. "It took three bedtime stories and a promise that Steward Kinsmon would do his High Guardian impression tomorrow to finally keep them under the covers."

"I'll do it, but only once the actual High Guardian has left the celebration," Steward Kinsmon, a young man in his early twenties with wild, curly red hair, said. "Helios knows I don't need His Holiness mad at me or my family. Not with the tariff negotiations coming next month."

"None of us need that," Kel smiled.

"No, we do not," Alexis agreed. "Now, gentlemen, my husband has been informed of the details, of course, and if you open the folders in front of you, you'll find all information I have been given. If there is an attempt, it will happen just after the banquet during the chaos of the guests beginning to leave. This presents a different type of problem for us, since it is easy to screen guests as they come into the castle, but not so easy to detain them as they try to leave."

"Detain?" Steward Neggle asked. A short, but muscular man, Neggle always had a suspicious squint to his eye, making him look like he disapproved of everyone he met. Which, on general principle, he did. "Are you saying that nobles and royals from the other stations will be prisoners by default? That is going a bit far, mistress, even for you."

"No, none will be prisoners nor will they actually be detained," Alexis said. "We will just need to take care to monitor the comings, and especially the goings, of the guests."

"I highly doubt the assassin will be a noble," Neggle stated. "Too conspicuous."

"No, not a noble or royal, but perhaps one of their attendants or guards," Alexis said. "Although not even nobles or royals are above suspicion. Helios knows that there's enough bloodlust running cold in royal veins. Present company included."

The table laughed, but only briefly as each of the men mulled over the myriad of opportunities a killer could have during the Decade celebration.

"We will have extra guards posted everywhere, but they are not as trained as any of you or your men," Kel said. "While I would never say to not enjoy yourselves tomorrow, please do so with caution since you may be called upon at a moment's notice."

"So much for finishing that bottle of Klaervian whiskey I'd been saving," Neggle groaned. "It'll have to wait until I retire to my quarters, then."

"I am sure you would have more than a few volunteers to help share that burden with," Alexis said. "That way you can enjoy the libation yet not compromise your clarity."

"Where's the damn fun in that?" Neggle growled as he held up a finger. "And no one is touching my whiskey. I want that to be known now."

"Not even your mistress?" Alexis asked as she put her hands on her hips.

"Oh, how you try my loyalty, Your Highness," Neggle replied, but with a sly grin. "I may be convinced to part with a snifter, but that all depends on my mood at the end of the day."

"Then I hope that mood is jolly," Alexis smiled. "Because I haven't had decent Klaervian whiskey in ages. Those bottles the Master of Station Klaerv sent for mine and Kel's anniversary were subpar, to say the least. He is obviously hoarding the good stuff."

"So, are we all in agreement about our duties tomorrow?" Claevan asked. Everyone at the table rapped their knuckles on the surface six times in acknowledgement. "Good. Let's move on to other matters, specifically the movement of supplies from station to prime. Has anyone had troubles getting their shipments past The Way? My last inventory of the armory showed we are about fifteen percent shy of our goal."

"I have had to sacrifice some goods in order to make sure the proper crates made it from The Way Prime to here," Steward Fleurtine said. "Their inspections have increased considerably over the past few months. It's as if they are looking for hidden weapons. I know the gatekeepers are always on the prowl for new ways to extort extra tithes, but this is out of the ordinary, even for them."

Quite a few voices were raised in agreement.

"Too coincidental," Claevan said to Alexis. "No issues for years, but now that we are only a few months from the possibility of going to war over your birthright, the gatekeepers decide to tighten up their inspections? And a valid threat to your life, and possibly Minor Alexis's as well, is revealed? I do not buy it, Alexis."

"Nor do I," Kel said. "Pieces are moving, my love, and not just by our hands. While we will all be busy making sure you are safe tomorrow, it would be wise that you use your powers of persuasion and see if perhaps Master Lionel has been alerted to our intentions."

"Oh, I certainly intend on doing just that, my love," Alexis said as she looked down the table at the worried and determined faces of the Order. She shook her head and sighed. "But let us not forget that it is also Minoress Natalie's Decade tomorrow. We cannot lose sight of the fact that we'll have a highly excited ten year old on our hands. Life does not stop for royal intrigue and station maneuvering."

"Nor should it," Kel said. "Do not worry, love, I will make sure our daughter has the greatest day of her life."

*

The grand banquet hall was filled to capacity, and possibly over capacity, as nobles and royals from all stations and primes mingled amongst themselves. Having relaxed enough from drink and food to mix outside their delegations, many nobles were drawn into raucous, and usually good natured, conversations and debates with members of their class from the other stations. Belts and sashes were gradually loosened to make room for the free flowing barrels of gelberry wine and happy voices filled the hall to its rafters.

"Quite the success, Alexis," Master Lionel the Third of Station Thraen said as he took a seat next to the mistress at the table at the head of the grand hall. "I haven't seen this congenial an atmosphere in quite some time. Certainly not at one of my children's celebrations. How did you manage to pull it off?"

"Pull it off?" Alexis asked, her eyes watching as Minoress Natalie danced with her father across the hall. "How do you mean, Lionel?"

"Well, so many differing viewpoints and cultures," Lionel said as he casually swept a hand towards the revelers. "Usually there would have been at least one call for a duel over some insult or other by now. Yet, look: not an aggressor in the bunch."

"I spike the wine," Alexis said as she leaned in conspiratorially to the master. "My court apothecary is well versed in concoctions that cannot be detected by taste or smell."

Master Lionel drew back in shock at her words then caught himself and laughed. "Alexis, Alexis! Your sense of humor is certainly morbid."

"I try," Alexis grinned then nodded at the celebration before them. "The truth is, Cousin, that I honestly want my guests to be happy. I let all petty slights and disagreements fall away and encourage others to do the same. As monarchs, we set the tone and mood in all aspects of our duties, not just the administration of our stations, Lionel. I happen to believe revelry is as important to royal life as business and political negotiations. We have to live a little, Lionel, not just rule."

"A very interesting philosophy, Alexis," Lionel nodded. "It is not one I personally subscribe to, but if it serves you well then who am I to argue?"

"It does serve me well," Alexis said. She glanced at the line of attendants that stood against the wall behind them. "Speaking of serving, it appears you brought your entire staff with you."

"I do hope that isn't an inconvenience," Lionel replied. "As you know, we came straight from The Way Prime to here and didn't have a chance to go to Thraen Prime. Normally, I would have left half of my attendants in my own castle, but it just seemed pointless to have my cutter make the journey twice. If they are a burden then I will gladly loan them to you for the night to assist with celebration duties."

"No need," Alexis smiled and patted the master's arm. "I was just curious. Mainly because I was hoping the additions to your retinue were not some new trend amongst the royals. I already have the smallest staff amongst the monarchs, due to my stubborn nature of self-sufficiency, so to have that staff look even smaller would be a bit embarrassing, even for me."

"I assure you it is nothing of the sort," Lionel chuckled. "Just a product of circumstance for the evening only."

"Good," Alexis said. "I probably wouldn't have noticed except that my guards alerted me to the addition of names to your guest roster. Those men work so diligently to keep me and my family safe that I always feel guilty when their jobs are made any harder than they already are."

"Guards' lives are meant to be hard," Lionel replied, a frown playing at his lips. "It keeps them vigilant. You should see this as a test of their readiness, not a weight on their shoulders."

"Yes, of course, you are right," Alexis said. "But we all run our courts slightly differently, do we not? I consider my guards almost family, and you know my reputation when it comes to my family."

"Fierce and protective are the more diplomatic words used," Lionel replied. "Deadly and dangerous are probably more accurate."

"Too true," Alexis agreed. "If anyone were to hurt my family I would think it would take an act of Helios for me not to declare war immediately."

"War? Well, that certainly takes one outside of the protective descriptor and firmly into the dangerous," Lionel said. "Any level headed monarch knows that revenge is never a reason to declare war."

"Oh? Then what would be a reason to declare war?" Alexis asked.

"Personally, I could not think of one," Lionel responded. "Wars are so bloody expensive. Why bother with all of that nonsense when you can be so much more effective in other ways?"

"Spoken like a true Thraen," Alexis said. "Always looking for an alternative to fighting. You people certainly prefer your back channel intrigue, don't you?"

"I'm sorry, mistress," Lionel said. "But is there a point I am missing? It almost feels as if you are dancing around a specific issue." Lionel nodded towards Kel and Natalie out on the dance floor. "Although, you are not quite as graceful as other members of your family."

"My apologies, Your Highness," Alexis nodded. "I'm just a bit tipsy and rambling on. It's so rare, and refreshing, to be in the company of one's equal that I sort of forgot myself for a second there. I hope you will forgive me."

"Of course," Lionel said as he stood up. "And I hope you will forgive me, as well. I believe I need to find the facilities. All that wine will have its way in some form or another."

"That it will," Alexis nodded. "We'll talk again later."

"I look forward to it," Lionel nodded then bowed quickly and hurried off past his row of servants.

Alexis followed his progress with her eyes as he made his way through the crowd and out of the grand banquet hall. Her instincts told her nothing of the Master's intentions, which frustrated her considerably, and she was about to let her suspicions go when she caught sight of familiar skirts hurry past the doorway just as the master exited the hall.

The mistress stood, making sure to look as casual as possible, and gestured for the closest guard to come over.

"Have my children left the nursery?" Alexis asked. "I could have sworn I saw their nurse go by out in the hall just now."

"I do not believe so, Your Highness," the guard replied. "But I will be more than happy to check for you."

"No, that is alright," Alexis said. "I'll check on them myself. I could use the walk as it has become a bit warm in this gown. I can't wait to get this off and back into trousers the second this celebration is over."

"I am sure you can't, Your Highness," the guard smiled, well used to the mistress's candor. "Are you sure you would not like me to look in on the minors and minoress?"

"No, thank you," Alexis said as she walked away from the table. "I'm on my way now."

It took Alexis much longer than she would have liked to get from the head of the hall to the entranceway since she was forced to acknowledge every single person that came up to her. The only reason she was able to hurry as fast as she did was because of a growing unease that slowly crept into her belly. It took all of her willpower not to panic as that unease turned into true fear when she looked about and realized she didn't see the Minor Alexis.

"If you'll excuse me," Alexis said, as she removed herself from the presence of a Flaenish steward who insisted that moment was the time to nail her down on her intentions towards trade agreements over the next year's breen crops. "I have an urgent matter to attend to. I'm sure you understand."

She did not wait for an answer as she began to push through the crowd, her eye catching the attention of members of the Order that she could see. Alexis did not wait to see if the members of the Order were following her or not as she burst from the grand hall and into the wide hallway, her head turning this way and that for signs of the nurse.

"She may have just needed something from the pantry," Alexis mumbled to herself as she turned, hiked up her gown, and moved quickly down the hall. "I'm sure she left one of the other attendants with the children."

Her foot slipped and she steadied herself, ready to keep moving, at least until she glanced down and saw the red smear on the ornately decorated tile. Her heart leapt into her throat as she knelt slowly and wiped at the smear with her fingers. A quick sniff told her exactly what the red substance was and she was off and running before she consciously knew it.

Her eyes caught the many drops of blood that grew in size and frequency until she was following an obvious trail. Alexis was in an all out sprint when she came around the corner of a passageway that led to one of the service entrances of the castle. There, just ahead of her and slumped on the floor, was the body of her children's nurse, a pool of blood haloed about her.

"No!" Alexis yelled as she whirled about and almost ran into Stewards Neggle and Vast. "The children! Not me, but the children!"

The men's eyes went wide and they began to shout orders and call for their men as they followed the mistress as she ran as fast as her legs, and attire, would allow her. Reflexes kicked in and Alexis barely thought of the route to the nursery, just let her feet carry her where she was supposed to go. There were yells and finally a raising of the alarm by the time she reached the partially open doors of her children's quarters.

Alexis burst through the doors, a scream ready in her throat. That scream let loose as soon as she saw her eldest son standing in the nursery, cradling two small bodies in his arms. Alexis rushed to the minor and wrapped herself about him, hoping in some way that her presence would fight back the truth that her mind struggled to believe.

"Tell me they live," Alexis cried. As she pulled back and locked eyes with her son, intentionally keeping her gaze from the two still forms wedged between them. "Alexis, please tell me my babies live."

The minor, his eyes empty and lost, shook his head. "I cannot tell you that, Mother. I cannot."

"No...no, no, no, no!" Alexis screamed as she reached down and took the lifeless corpses into her own arms, forcing Minor Alexis to fall back to the blood-soaked rug beneath them. *"No! No no no no nooooooooooooo!"*

Half of the Order of Jex stood at the edge of the doorway, their eyes cast down in grief and sorrow as their mistress wailed in soulful agony. None dared to move until Kel forced them aside and rushed into the nursery.

"Oh, Helios! Oh, Dear Parent! What has happened here? What has happened?" Kel screamed. "Oh, why? *Why?*"

The Master fell to his knees and nearly dove at his wife and dead children, but stopped himself just short of collapsing upon them. His hands shook violently as he reached out to stroke their deathly white cheeks, his wife's tears dripping down onto them like a heavy rain.

Minor Alexis scooted himself away until his back hit the far wall. He looked from his wailing parents and then down at his clothes that were drenched in the blood of his siblings. He had never seen so much blood before in his life, not even when he had visited a shaow slaughterhouse down in one of the Middle Decks on Station Aelon. The color of the blood was so much darker than he had expected it to be.

There was shouting from the nursery doorway that pulled Minor Alexis from his shock and forced him to his feet.

"What is happening?" Minoress Natalie shouted as her way was blocked into the room. "You will stand aside this instant! I am a Minoress of Station Aelon and I order you to stand aside!"

"Nats, no," Minor Alexis said as he pushed through the wall of stewards and out into the hall. "No. You don't want to see what is in there."

"The Helios I don't!" she yelled. "Today is my Decade celebration! People are supposed to do what I say!"

"No," was all Minor Alexis said in reply.

"Stop saying that!" Natalie yelled. "Get out of my way, A! Is that Mother? Do I hear Mother crying? Why is she crying, A? Tell me why she is crying!"

"The twins," Minor Alexis replied as he shook his head.

"The twins? What about the twins?" Natalie asked.

"They are hurt," Minor Alexis sighed. "Hurt so bad, Nats...."

"How hurt?" Natalie asked, but Minor Alexis couldn't answer her. "What about Richard? Is he hurt as well?"

It was like a slap to the face for many in the hall, not just Minor Alexis, as the realization that one royal child was still unaccounted for hit them all.

"Richard," Minor Alexis gasped. "We have to find Richard! He's with Grandmother! And she's...."

"Stay here, my lord," a steward said. "We will find him. I promise."

The minor had no idea which steward made the promise, but soon almost every man in the hall was rushing away, the name Richard exploding from their throats.

*

"There, there," Bella said as she cradled the small boy to her breast. "You're safe. We're safe. That nasty woman will not find us in here."

Bella could hear the boy's name being called and she smiled with relief, knowing that help was so close. She tried to get her feet under her and stand up in the small closet she'd hidden in with her grandson, but for some reason her legs would not obey. She hadn't moved in quite some time, so she assumed she just needed to get the circulation going again to stand, but when she reached down to smack at her legs and get the blood moving, she realized that there was quite a bit of blood on the outside of her legs, not inside where it was supposed to be.

"Richard? Richard, are you hurt?" Bella exclaimed as she quickly checked the boy over in the dim light of the closet. The minor whimpered at the hurried and rough treatment and Bella pulled back, satisfied that he was not the source of the blood.

Which led her to the conclusion that the blood must have been hers.

"You hear that, Richard?" Bella asked as the sound of boots clomping down the hall echoed through the door. "I believe we are safe now."

The boots hurried past the closet and Bella cleared her throat. She felt exhausted, more exhausted than she'd ever felt in her life, which was saying a lot. But she summoned the strength to call out at the top of her lungs.

"In here!" she shouted. *"We're in here!"*

She tried one last time to move and stand just as the closet door was yanked open and almost ripped from its hinges. Stewards and guards stood at the doorway and many stepped back at the sight.

"Dear Helios. . . ." one guard muttered, before turning and throwing up on the boots of those behind him.

"My lady?" Steward Neggle asked as he stepped forward and crouched before Bella. "My lady, can you hear me?"

"Of course I can hear you, Neggle," Bella snapped. "It's my legs that won't work, not my ears."

"Your legs?" Neggle asked as he gratefully tore his eyes away from the woman's face. "What is wrong with your legs?"

"They have fallen asleep," Bella said. "I just need some assistance to stand and everything will be fine."

"Yes. . .of course," Neggle said. "But let me take the minor from you, if I may. We'll hand him to the physicians then see about getting you up."

"I'll keep ahold of my grandson, thank you very much," Bella snapped. "I did not escape that demon woman just to hand this child over to anyone. Help me up, man, and I'll give Richard to the physicians myself."

"Minoress, you need to give me the boy," Neggle insisted. "It will be better if I take him from you so you are not burdened with his weight while you try to stand."

"Are you even hearing me?" Bella growled. "This child does not leave my grasp!"

Neggle sighed then looked over his shoulder. "Fetch me a mirror." No one moved. "Fetch me a mirror, now!"

Two guards hurried off and were back in seconds, having yanked one of the ornate mirrors directly from the wall.

"Thank you," Neggle said as he took the mirror, but kept the reflective surface to his chest. "Minoress? I am going to show you why I need you to give me the boy. He appears to be unharmed, but you, well. . . ."

"Oh, just show me," Bella said.

"As you wish," Neggle nodded then spun the mirror around.

Bella stared at the stranger in the reflection, if a stranger it could be called. More like a monster. A monster that was missing most of its face. Bella reached up and the monster reached up as well, both hands feeling at the strips of skin that flopped loosely at her jaw.

"She came at me so fast," Bella whispered as she realized there was no stranger to see, just her own hideous reflection. "But I came at her just as fast, even with that blade in her hand. I didn't feel anything. Not a thing. I don't now, either."

"You're in shock, my lady," Neggle said. "Your body has shut down. That is why you cannot stand."

"Oh," Bella said. "I thought for a moment that I had been stabbed and that was where the blood came from. But I hadn't been stabbed, had I? I had been slashed and sliced. Like a fine cut of shaow, carved into nothingness for the Last Meal feast."

Neggle gently pried Bella's hands away from her grandson. When he had the boy out of her lap he spun about and handed off the child to the guards directly behind him. Then he turned his attention back to the minoress that was still talking about fine cuts and hunks of meat.

"My lady?" Neggle asked, taking Bella's hand in his. "I am going to sit with you until the physicians get here. I don't think you should move right now."

"No, I suppose not," Bella agreed. "We'll wait together for the physicians. That is the best course of action." She leaned her head back against closet wall and was about to close her eyes when a hard reality slammed into her mind. "The twins! Alexis! Natalie!"

"Minor Alexis and Minoress Natalie are well," Neggle stated.

What he didn't state hung there between them like a Vape cloud, combustible and poisonous.

"Oh...." Bella whispered. "I understand."

"Do you, my lady?" Neggle asked as he too leaned against the closet wall. "Because I do not. I do not understand any of it."

*

The door to the royal chamber opened slowly as Alexis made her way into the darkened room.

"Did he speak with you?" Kel asked from a chair in the shadows. "Did the bastard grant you an audience?"

"He would have been a fool not to," Alexis said as she began to strip the mourning gown from her body until she stood only in a pair of pantaloons and a chemise. "Even that greedy grendt wouldn't refuse a grieving mother on the day of her children's funeral."

"And?"

"And he says he has no knowledge of which station hired the nurse," Alexis replied. She walked over to her husband and crawled right into his lap. "In fact, the asshole even suggested that we should look at Claevan Twyerrn as the suspect since the woman came from his deck."

"It has crossed my mind," Kel admitted.

"Mine as well," Alexis said. "It crossed my mind and kept going. There is no way that Claevan would harm us. It serves him not and the man is one of the very few I trust completely."

"As do I," Kel said. "So where does that leave us?"

"It leaves us with my instincts and fate," Alexis said. "Both tell me Station Thraen was behind this."

"Why?" Kel asked. "What benefit does Lionel get from attacking us?"

"I don't know," Alexis said. "Maybe he thought to strike first. Maybe he knows we are planning to take Thraen Prime from him."

"But killing our children?" Kel choked. "That gives us more reason to fight!"

"I know," Alexis replied. "None of it makes any sense."

They sat there, wrapped in each others' embrace for several minutes.

"Now what?" Kel asked finally.

"Now we do what we have been planning for," Alexis said. "I have already sent word to the Order to make preparations. I will announce my intentions of claiming my birthright as the true heir to the crown of Thraen. Lionel will be given one chance to abdicate and give me what is mine."

"And if he doesn't?" Kel asked, sounding so exhausted that his voice was nothing but a lonesome whisper. "Do we take the prime?"

"We take the prime," Alexis nodded. "And then we take the station. We will be at war by the end of the month and I will have the Thraen crown by the end of the year. So says fate."

A small laugh from the opposite side of the room caught Alexis's attention, but she could tell by the lack of response from her husband that the sound was only meant for her.

"Be careful," her father said. "That may not be fate you hear, sweet girl. That may be folly and pride."

"How do I tell the difference?" Alexis asked.

Kel frowned at her and was about to respond, but quieted when Alexis shook her head at him.

"Tell the difference?" Alexis's father asked. "How should I know? There's a reason I met such a grisly end, child."

Alexis nodded and then lowered her head to her husband and nuzzled his neck. She may not have known the difference between folly and pride over fate at that moment, but she did know the difference between comfort and safety. Comfort was what she felt as Kel held her and safety was something she never expected to feel again.

Never again.

CHAPTER EIGHT

High Guardian Victor the Eighth sat there, his hands folded across his lap, his wrinkled brow furrowed, making his already aged features even more craggy, more stern.

"It's been well over a decade since you've granted an audience to a High Guardian," he stated. "Why now, Mistress? Why change your mind?"

"You know why," Alexis replied as she set the cups of tea down on the small table that split the distance between two couches, while also splitting the difference between two of the most powerful people in the System of Helios. "I refuse to be the one to say it."

"Yet, as I made perfectly clear in my correspondence, The Way will never admit to any wrongdoing in regards to your children's deaths," the High Guardian said as he picked up his cup and took a sip of the bitter brew. "Oh, not a fan of sweetener?"

"I lost my taste for sweetness a long time ago, Victor," Alexis responded as she took her seat and eyed the holy man. "But maybe, just maybe, I will find it again once our chat is done."

"You are too familiar with me, mistress," the High Guardian frowned. "I may be the eighth Victor to hold the seat of High Guardian, but that doesn't mean I am not due the full respect of my office."

"Is that what it is?" Alexis laughed. "An office? And here I thought service to The Way was a calling."

"It is a calling, a duty, and a job, mistress," the High Guardian replied. "It is the job aspect that brings me to Castle Aelon. This war of yours must stop. It put my predecessor in an early grave despite his being twenty years younger than me. Do you know how Diel the First died?"

"He bled out his anus," Alexis said and sipped her tea slowly, slurping until the High Guardian winced and looked away. "It was a strain of the wasting sickness. Some new bug that crawled up his asshole and found a nice, happy home there. Too bad it decided to rearrange his intestines without permission."

"Your mockery of that man's suffering will not be forgotten by Helios," the High Guardian snapped. "You will burn in the fires of the star for your blasphemy."

"I am sure I will burn," Alexis nodded. "But not for my words against Diel. The man worked against me at every turn despite my warnings to him. He conspired with Lionel the Third of Station Thraen to have my children murdered. He refused to allow my troops to descend on the planet so I could claim my birthright. Unfortunately, he had no idea that I'd been bringing down weapons and men for years as I built this castle. Did you know that a crate of longslings weighs as much as a crate of nails? No? Well, neither did Diel. By the time I struck Thraen Prime, it was too late for him to back down from his decree. His fate was his own, and not of my making."

"Yes, his decree," the High Guardian said as he cleared his throat. "That is what I am here for today. Aelon has been at war with Thraen for a decade now. You have nearly conquered their entire prime and only need to complete your siege of their castle to finish what you started. I would like to hasten that goal."

"Would you?" Alexis asked, amused. "Why? What does The Way stand to gain by supporting me?"

"No, you have misunderstood, mistress," the High Guardian replied. "The Way could never formally support Station Aelon; that would be a step towards legitimizing your claim to the Thraenish crown. It is The Way's, and my, fervent opinion that no monarch can stake claim on another monarch's holdings or title. Helios allowed us to escape the Cataclysm to the Six Stations for a reason, the consolidation of power is not that reason."

"You talk to me of consolidation of power?" Alexis chuckled. "The Way is the epitome of the consolidation of power. Do not kid yourself that your ambition and greed are any different than mine. We are cut from the same cloth, Victor, it's just that your cloth was tithed to you, while my cloth was grown, harvested, and woven on this very prime. Take my cloth away and there is plenty more. Take your cloth away and you are naked until someone else hands you the rags you need to cover your pitiful junk."

The High Guardian coughed on his sip of tea and nearly dropped his cup. It took all of his self-control to set the cup down without spilling the remainder of the contents.

"You cannot speak to me that way!" he snapped once he found his voice. "I am the High Guardian! I am one step from Helios, the Dear Parent! You would do well to—"

"Blah, blah, blah!" Alexis yelled as she set her cup down as well. *"Blah!"*

There was knock at the door and Lara peeked her head in.

"Everything good, Your Highness?" Lara asked as her eyes settled on the High Guardian.

"It is not polite to stare, miss," the High Guardian stated. "Please avert your eyes unless you are addressed."

"Yes, of course," Lara said and bowed her head, turning her attention back to Alexis. "Shall I have him shot and his body tossed out the airlock?"

"Lara, what a horrible thing to say," Alexis smirked. "We wouldn't waste a particle barb on this siggy worm; we'd use a blade so he suffers and dies slowly."

"My Burdened are just on the other side of that door!" the High Guardian shouted as he jumped to his feet. "You will threaten me no longer! Men!"

The High Guardian waited, but there was no response.

"Men! To me!" he yelled once more.

Still no response.

"Yes, about your precious Burdened," Lara grinned as she pushed the double doors of the study wide. "They are occupied at the moment."

The High Guardian stared into the hallway at the scene. His privileged mind could barely comprehend what he saw. The dozen Burdened he brought with him were unmoving as they stared into the barrels of two dozen longslings. All eyes, except for the longslingers', turned to look at the High Guardian as the old man struggled for words.

"I believe he gets the picture, Lara," Alexis said. "You may close the doors again. Have the Burdened removed to the barracks. They may rest there and wait for their boss. If they are hungry or thirsty then fetch them refreshments, after disarming them, of course."

"Of course, Alexis." Lara smiled, her eyes locking onto the High Guardian's. "A pleasure, Your Holiness. Next time don't bother bringing men. It just makes my job harder."

The doors closed and Alexis poured more tea.

"I can fetch sweetener, if you'd like, Victor," Alexis said. "If that will make your visit more pleasant."

"You can't do this," the High Guardian sputtered. "Taking the High Guardian hostage will be seen as an act of war against *all* the stations! I will open the portal to any and all that wish to attack you!"

"Alright, I have a few issues with those words," Alexis said. "First, you are not my hostage. Feel free to leave at anytime. Second, if you think that any of the other stations will want to try their might against my longslingers then you have not been paying attention. And third, but possibly not last, how can you give the order to open the portal if you've been taken hostage? That just doesn't make sense. Not that you are a hostage, Victor. I refer to my first point on that one."

The High Guardian could only stare at the forty-two year old monarch. His mouth was so dry that even if he'd wanted to speak, it would have only come out as a weak croak. After several minutes of complete indecision, while Alexis just sat patiently and waited, the High Guardian finally took his seat once more.

"Now, are we ready to get down to it? Are we finally at that place where you stop acting like you hold all the power and I stop acting like I don't know why you're here? I do have a war to run, you know, and I'd like to get back to that."

"Yes, well, I don't have much choice, do I?" the High Guardian asked.

"We all have a choice, Victor," Alexis replied. "It's just that sometimes those choices get taken from us. Yet, fate is always there to fill the void of choice. Or that's how I see it."

"Your belief in fate over Helios's will is troubling," the High Guardian admitted.

"I don't see the difference between the two," Alexis replied. "I call it fate, you call it Helios's will. Same thing. But, you aren't here to debate the verbiage of my devotion to the Dear Parent. Tell me why you are here, Victor, so we can get on with it and then part ways. I do have a war to run."

"Yes, as to that war," the High Guardian said. "I am here to offer a deal between Aelon and Thraen. The Way will once again allow direct shuttling of supplies from Station Aelon to the planet if you withdraw your troops from around Thraen Prime's castle. You may hold all the lands you have captured, with all Vape rights intact, but the castle is to be left alone and all inside guaranteed safe passage if they desire to leave."

"He's lying," Alexis's father said as he stood in the corner of the study, hidden from the High Guardian's sight by shadows and reality. "Once you withdraw your troops, the Thraens will gather their forces and launch a counterattack. That is why they want your forces gone, nothing else."

"I know," Alexis replied, causing the High Guardian to give her a quizzical look.

"I'm sorry?" the High Guardian asked. "How could you know what I was to offer? I only finished discussions with Station Thraen this morning."

"Oh, my apologies, Your Holiness," Alexis smiled. "I was responding to my father. Surely you've heard how the Mistress of Station Aelon is mad and speaks to the ghost of her murdered father. I've never kept it a secret. We all have our ways of coping with times of stress."

"Is your speaking to me stressful, mistress?" the High Guardian asked. "Perhaps that is your soul struggling against your reluctance to embrace The Way as the one true ordained power on this planet."

"Yeah, I doubt that's it," Alexis chuckled. "More like the fact I am waiting to hear from my son about the results of his attack. He should have launched it an hour ago. I'm terribly worried that it has taken so long for him to contact me. He's never late for a call to his mother. Not that boy."

"The Dark Minor is a pillar of honor and integrity," the High Guardian nodded. "No one in the System would argue otherwise."

"Too bad his mother is a raving bitch, though," Alexis laughed. "That's the second part of what everyone says in the System, is it not?"

"Too be honest, I have not heard that," the High Guardian reluctantly admitted. "Quite the opposite, I'm afraid."

"Exactly," Alexis said. "That is why your offer to end the embargo against Aelish shuttles bringing supplies directly from my station is not much of an offer at all. I have trade treaties in place with all the other stations, excluding Thraen and Ploerv, of course. I don't know why those Ploervians hate me so much, but they do. Bastards won't so much as trade a fart for a pallet of finished breen cloth."

"Yet they are one of the top markets for breen cloth," the High Guardian said. "If you were to listen to reason and pull back your troops then perhaps the Ploervians would be open to—"

"They'll be open to my boot inserted up their asses," Alexis laughed. She leaned forward, her elbows resting on her knees, and fixed the man with her cold, blue gaze. "I don't want to waste any more of your time,

Victor, but you will not get a deal from me today. Maybe in a month or two the tides will change and we can talk again, but for now, I am on top. And when I'm on top I do not get down until I finish. It's a rule of mine. Ask my husband."

"I could stop the proxy shipments from the other stations," the High Guardian threatened. "While your self-sufficiency is admirable on your prime, there are items you need that you cannot manufacture yourself."

"That's your move? To stop the proxy shipments?" Alexis laughed. "I would end diplomatic travel before ending my supply shipments from the other stations, if I were you. It's much easier to stop my men from boarding a shuttle than it is to inspect every single box, crate, and container that is unloaded from the shuttles."

The High Guardian did not respond.

"Right, because once you stop the movement of people then you'll have all the stations worried that you'll use that against them next," Alexis continued. "Taxing, I mean *tithing*, shipments is one thing; it's expected since that is how The Way is able to finance all its charitable endeavors, but to stop diplomats, nobles, and royals from freedom of movement would isolate The Way instantly. Everyone would be shuttling to and fro from station to station and no one would come down to the planet anymore. How lonely for you that would be."

"Your idea of how things work is warped, mistress," the High Guardian said. "You run on misconceptions and suppositions."

"Blah!" Alexis yelled, making the man jump. "Now you sound more like a lawyer than a holy man. Are we done? My answer to any of your proposals, unless it's The Way's recognition of my birthright to the crown of Station Thraen, will always be no. Just no."

The High Guardian started to speak, but stopped and stood. He looked at the closed doors with trepidation.

"I'll call the barracks and have your men released," Alexis said. "They'll meet you at the main airlock. No need to look so frightened, Victor. We may not be friends, but I am always respectful of my guests. Be well, Your Holiness."

"Be well," the High Guardian nodded as he opened the double doors and quickly left the study, his long robes trailing behind him as he hurried down the hall.

"That was uneventful," Alexis's father said. "A High Guardian finally agrees to speak with you and it results in nothing."

"You see, Papa, that is why you were never a good ruler," Alexis said as she sipped at her tea some more. "I thought that was far from nothing. If the High Guardian is willing to come all this way to Aelon Prime, instead of waiting for me to obey one of his summons, then there is some pressing matter that affects The Way as well as Station Thraen."

"Oh, clever you," Alexis's father nodded. "You do have a way of getting to the heart of the matter, don't you? I wonder what the old man really wants."

"It'll be fun finding out," Alexis said as she drained her tea cup, stood and left the study, the ghost of her father fading out as soon as she crossed the threshold.

* * *

Alexis Teirmont, the Dark Minor, stood with his back to the platoon of longslingers under his command. There were close to five hundred men, armed and ready for his orders to attack. They had been waiting all day, long past the scheduled time they were supposed to unload their particle barbs on the castle that loomed before them in the Vape mist that covered Thraen Prime.

"My liege?" Steward Fleurtine asked from Minor Alexis's shoulder. "Why do we wait? We're about to lose the light, sire. Your mother is waiting anxiously for your report."

"My mother can keep waiting," Minor Alexis replied. "This is my campaign and I will give the order to attack when I feel the time is right."

The young man, twenty-five and decked out in almost pitch black polybreen armor that was hidden under an environmental suit that was equally as black, kept his eyes on the castle. There was something about the place that worried him immensely. He couldn't put his finger on it, but the second the battle skids had stopped and unloaded his longslingers, he knew that the day was not the day for an attack.

"Who do we have for reconnaissance?" Minor Alexis asked. "I want the castle inspected thoroughly before a single barb is fired."

"That would have been an order to give hours ago when the light was better," Fleurtine said. "Perhaps we should have the men return to camp and approach tomorrow instead?"

"No," Minor Alexis replied. "We will attack, just not until I know for sure that it is worth it." He placed a hand to the side of his helmet. "Do you hear that?"

"No, sire," Fleurtine responded. "I can only hear what is coming over the com."

"Turn on your ambient," Minor Alexis ordered. "Listen hard, Fleurtine. Listen very hard. Tell me when you hear it."

The steward adjusted his com's settings so he could hear outside his suit and waited. After several minutes he shook his head in defeat.

"I am sorry, sire, but I hear nothing except for the restless shuffling of our men behind us," Fleurtine said. "I hope I have not let you down."

"No, you have not," Minor Alexis smiled. "Because there is nothing to hear. No sound of any movement within the walls of that castle. No sound of soldiers preparing for a siege or machinery or weapons being moved into place. The castle is silent, Fleurtine. Castles that are about to be attacked are never silent, even with protective shields muting the noise."

The steward studied Minor Alexis for a second then turned his attention back to the castle. The lack of any sound did trouble him, once alerted to it, and he tapped at the com controls on his wrist until two soldiers ran up to him.

"Send a small squad to reconnoiter the castle walls," Fleurtine ordered. "Watch for traps and listen carefully for any signs of life. I want you to report what you don't find as much as what you do. You have thirty minutes; use them wisely."

The soldiers nodded and hurried back to the main platoon.

"Thank you, Fleurtine," Minor Alexis said. "I know everyone worries I'll be talking to ghosts like my mother, but I can assure you that my instincts are more mundane than supernatural."

"No one thinks you touched, my liege," Fleurtine stated. "Not that anyone thinks the mistress is touched, either. We all know she has her ways of coping with life, just as we all do. Personally, I cannot go to sleep at night without making sure all of my boots are in a straight line in their closet. I don't know why, but I've been like that since I was a child."

"Ha!" Minor Alexis laughed.

It was a genuine laugh, full of shared camaraderie and honest happiness. Despite his name as the Dark Minor, Minor Alexis was known for his compassion, openness, and quick, infectious laughter. He was much loved amongst the Aelish, both on the station and the prime, and his presence was always a welcome sight.

"I'm afraid my middle daughter has picked up my habit," Fleurtine smiled. "Except it's her hair bows she must line up each evening once she's out of her bath. Drives her mother to fits."

"I'd think a mother would want her daughter to be neat and tidy," Minor Alexis said.

"Not my Viola," Fleurtine admitted. "She works her fingers to the bone to keep a great estate, which is why she has no patience for work or nonsense that is not productive. I'm afraid that mine and my daughter's habits are not seen as productive."

"Unproductive nonsense is the best nonsense," Minor Alexis chuckled. "Tell her that I said that. Maybe some royal influence will change her mind."

"That could well be," Fleurtine said as he kicked his right boot against a clump of scrim grass at his feet. "Although she would be considerably more responsive if you told her in person. When do you plan on returning to the station, sire? I would be more than happy to host a party for you."

"It all depends on what happens here this evening, I suppose," Minor Alexis replied. "If I'm gutted and left to die in the Vape mist, then I don't think I'll be returning to Station Aelon anytime soon."

"That is not funny, my liege," Fleurtine frowned. "Here we were having a nice chat and you have to get all morbid."

"Oh, I'm just playing, Fleurtine," Minor Alexis grinned. "Everyone knows my sister is the morbid one, not me." Minor Alexis finally looked over his shoulder at the rows of longslingers that waited in their environmental suits. He scanned the men and the grin evaporated. "Where is Natalie anyway? Shouldn't she be up with her men?"

"Yes, well. . . ." Fleurtine trailed off.

"Out with it," Minor Alexis sighed. "What has she done now?"

"Your sister has taken her team and gone scouting on her own," Fleurtine replied.

"Of course she has," Minor Alexis nodded. "How long ago?"

"About the time you began staring at the castle instead of attacking it," Fleurtine said. "The minoress is not known for her patience, sire."

"You don't need to tell me," Minor Alexis chuckled. "I've known the woman her whole life. I'm fairly certain she came two weeks early, she was so eager to leave the womb."

"Shall I contact her over the com and call her back, sire?" Fleurtine asked.

"No, let her have her fun," Minor Alexis said. "Hopefully, she'll discover the source of my unease."

*

"Lang, on the left. Buck, on the right. Baise and Jay, watch our asses," Minoress Natalie whispered as she stood up from the airlock controls. The outer door slid open and Natalie had her longsling up to her shoulder and sweeping back and forth as she stepped inside. "Let's see who's home."

"Your brother is not going to be happy we are breaking into the castle," Lang said. "He was quite explicit about his desire for a frontal assault."

"I don't think anyone is even here to assault," Natalie said as she started to work on the controls to the internal airlock door. "We would have been discovered by now. He can knock on the front door all he wants, but no one is going to answer."

She motioned for Baise and Jay to join them in the airlock and once the outer door was sealed she hit the controls for the inner door. It slid open as klaxons blared and red lights spun.

"We're about to find out who's here," Blaise said, his longsling at the ready.

The five Aelish warriors hurried into the castle, each taking a position just inside the passageway, their eyes and ears scanning for signs of an attack. After several minutes, and no signs, Natalie disabled the klaxons and lights, plunging them into a dark silence.

"That should have brought them running," Natalie said. "Let's move out and cover as much ground as we can. We'll make our way to the docking bay and see what ships are still here. I'll lay credits the bay is empty and everyone retreated before we got here."

"Then why not just blow it up?" Lang asked as the team moved out. "They could have opened the airlocks and let the Vape hit the oxygen. This place would have been flaming rubble by the time we got here."

"Because they intend to come back," Buck said. "They ran; they didn't surrender."

"So they want us to occupy the castle?" Natalie asked.

"Or they want us inside the castle then they plan on blowing it up," Baise said.

"Shit," Jay grumbled. "I really don't want to be blown up."

"We get to the docking bay," Natalie said. "That decides what we do next."

*

"Have you reached him?" Alexis asked as she stepped into Castle Aelon's communications room. "Kel? Have you reached A?"

"Not yet, love," Kel said as he leaned back in a chair while several com techs worked the various control consoles that lined one wall. "We've got a Vape storm approaching and it's causing havoc with the signal."

"A Vape storm?" Alexis asked. "No one once mentioned a Vape storm was coming."

"It just appeared, Your Highness," Steward Maglion said from another chair. "You know how the planet can be. It is as unpredictable as a teen girl's affections."

"Yeah, I'll forget you said that," Alexis grinned. "I was a teen girl once and my affections were very predictable. Weren't they, my love?"

"I wouldn't say predictable, sweetheart, but certainly persistent," Kel grinned back. "There is nothing predictable about you, Lexi."

"Mother?" Minor Richard asked from the hall. "Is there any word?"

"No, son, there is not," Alexis said. "And it's about to drive your mother insane."

"Too late," Richard smirked then dodged a swipe from Alexis. "Hey! No nails!"

"Lucky you were fast enough to get out of my reach," Alexis laughed and then spread her arms wide. "Come give your mother a hug."

"You're gonna smack me, I know it," Richard giggled.

Unlike his brother and sister, Richard was not tall for his age. In fact, he was considered on the shorter. But, just like his siblings and mother, he was agile and quick on his feet. It was that agility he relied on as he went in to hug his mother, knowing full well it was a trap.

Alexis started to swing and Richard tackled her about the waist, knocking her to the floor and into Kel's chair.

"Not in the com room!" Kel barked. "How many times have I had to say that?"

"Too many for my taste," Maglion said as he rolled his eyes. Then he sat bolt upright and grabbed one of the techs by the shoulder. "Stop! What was that? Did you hear that?"

The tech adjusted his earphones and started backtracking through the frequencies.

"There!" Maglion exclaimed. "Tell me you hear that!"

Everyone froze as the tech turned up the volume and the sound of voices over static filled the room.

"What is that?" Alexis asked as she untangled herself from her son and stood up. "Is that our people?"

"No," Kel said as he too stood. "Those are Thraen codes!" He cocked his head and tried to decipher the meaning of the coded orders being barked. He shook his head in frustration. "I don't know what they are saying. They must have changed codes recently."

"Why are they running along the coastline?" Richard asked. "There isn't much coast by their castle, is there?"

"You understand it?" Alexis asked as she whirled on her son. "How much can you make out?"

"Only a little," Richard said. "It's not code, it's a dialect from one of the Thraenish Middle Decks. Grandmother taught it to me after, well. . . ."

"Dammit," Alexis snapped. "Of course, when I need my mother the most, she's up on Station Aelon as regent in my absence."

"I told you that would backfire," Kel said and easily dodged the smack aimed for his head. "Sorry. It was just too easy."

"Why are they running on the coastline?" Richard asked again. "If we haven't attacked yet then why run at all?"

"Show me a map," Alexis ordered and one of the techs brought up a map of Thraen Prime. "Thank you. Alright, so the castle is there and our forces are here. We have them completely cut off and their only chance of retreat is to take their cutters across the sea to Haelm Prime. But, if they are actually on the coastline, like Richard has said. . . ."

Her finger traced out from the castle and then over to the coast. She followed it and quickly saw what was going to happen.

"Helios! They are flanking us! The Thraenish bastards are actually mounting a counter attack!" Alexis shouted. "Those gutsy fuckers!"

"Mother, language," Richard frowned.

"Fuck off, kid," Alexis replied.

"You get that information to our people now!" Kel ordered the techs. "Broadcast it on every single channel! I don't care if the Thraens know we've found them out, got it? I want my son to know what's about to bite him in the butt!"

"Yes, sire," a tech said and started barking his own orders at the other techs.

Kel and Alexis looked at each other then looked at Maglion.

"How many more troops do we have ready on Thraen Prime?" Alexis asked. "Can we get them across the continent in time to help?"

"Minor Alexis took a platoon of longslingers with him, leaving three platoons of longslingers and six of ground troops at the ready," Maglion replied. "But only one platoon of ground troops are close enough to him to make a difference. We can order the others to head his way, but they won't reach him until morning at least."

"Do it," Alexis said. "Order them to move. He may need the reinforcements. We just don't know."

"Your Highness?" a tech asked. "We are broadcasting on all channels, but there is no way to know what is getting through and what isn't. That Vape storm has settled between the primes and the static is increasing by the minute."

"Just keep trying," Alexis said as she hurried from the com room.

"Lexi! Where are you going?" Kel asked as he chased after her.

"I'm going to take a cutter over to Thraen Prime," Alexis stated. "Then I'm going to go help my son!"

"Like Helios you are," Kel snapped, grabbing her arm and yanking her to a stop in the middle of the hallway. "Did you miss the part about the Vape storm? Right now that thing is out on the open water, but if it turns this way we will be in for a really bad night."

"And if it heads A's way then he could end up dead!" Alexis yelled as she tried to free her arm from her husband's grip. "Kel, let go of me."

"No," Kel said. "You are staying here in the castle. Your battle days are over. Your son runs the campaign now and you have to get used to that."

"He won't be running anything if he's caught in the open with a Vape storm bearing down on him!" Alexis shouted. "And Nats! She's with her brother right now!"

"He'll find a way," Richard said as she walked up to his parents. "Or Nats will. They know what they're doing. You taught them both well."

"We wait to see what the storm is doing," Alexis said. "Once we know then we take a cutter to Thraen Prime and I go find my son and my daughter."

"Now you are thinking clearly," Kel said. "Let's go to our quarters and have a rest. Maglion will send someone as soon as there is word."

Alexis took a deep breath then nodded and allowed her husband to lead her down the hallway and towards the royal quarters. Richard hesitated then decided to go back into the com room, just in case he could make out more of what the Thraens were saying.

*

"Gone," Natalie said. "All of their cutters are gone."

"Except one," Buck added as the team stood staring out through the airlock porthole that looked out onto the Thraenish castle's docking bay. "And that's military."

"So there are still soldiers left inside?" Lang asked, watching everyone's backs with Baise. "If there are then they're the quietest soldiers out there."

"Maybe they aren't in the castle," Jay said. "It wouldn't make sense for them to guard someplace that's empty."

"Then where are they?" Baise asked.

Natalie stood and studied the cutter, her mind working a mile a minute to figure out what they stepped in.

"We head back," Natalie said. "We head back to the platoon and let my brother know what we found."

"We didn't find anything," Lang said.

"Exactly," Natalie agreed. "He needs to know that."

*

"The troops are reporting back," Fleurtine said to Minor Alexis. "No sign of a single Thraen. No sign they left on foot."

"So they all just piled into their cutters and took to the open sea?" Minor Alexis asked. "Why abandon their castle now? Why make it so easy for us?"

"I don't know," Fleurtine replied. "It's not a trap, as far as the men can tell. They swept for explosives and didn't find a trace. If the castle is booby-trapped then it must be deep inside."

"That's not hard to do," Minor Alexis said then turned his attention from the castle and back to his men. "We move in. Get them all ready. We take the castle and go from there."

"I don't like it," Fleurtine said.

"Neither do I," Minor Alexis replied. "But our mission was to claim this castle for Aelon and that's what we're going to do even if there's no fight in doing it."

Fleurtine nodded and went to convey the marching orders to the platoon.

*

Natalie and her team passed the castle's communications room and she paused.

"Now, why the holy Helios would they do that to their own gear?" Natalie asked as she looked in the room to see the control consoles smashed to pieces. "What's the point of that?"

"So we can't use it," Lang said.

"Right, I get that, but why would we want to use it?" Natalie asked. "We have our own communications gear."

"It's short range, though," Baise said. "It requires a boosted signal from the base of operations to get across the sea to Aelon Prime."

"Right," Natalie nodded. "Which is easy enough. Unless there's a storm. A Vape storm would mess with all signals even the ones from us to BOP. If that happens then this room would have been nice to use."

"Has anyone checked the weather?" Buck asked as he stepped into the com room and knelt down by a torn piece of paper.

"Yeah, it's cloudy and grey," Lang laughed. "Just like yesterday and just like tomorrow."

"No, out over the sea," Buck said. "Where we wouldn't notice unless we were looking for it." He picked up the piece of paper and shook it in the air. "Weather print out. A huge storm is massing over the sea off the coast, just a few miles from BOP."

The men all looked at each other then back at Natalie as realization hit them.

"We won't be able to call for reinforcements," Natalie said as she started to run down the passageway towards the main airlock. She switched on her com and discovered her brother's voice trying to hail her. "Sorry! Sorry!"

"Nats? Finally!" Minor Alexis said over the com. "Where the Helios are you?"

"Inside the castle," Natalie replied. "But we're coming to you. I think the castle was abandoned for a reason. Have you heard from BOP? Is there a Vape storm on the coast behind them?"

"We tried getting through, but we couldn't," Minor Alexis said. "How'd you know there was a Vape storm? What did you find in there?"

"It doesn't matter," Natalie replied. "Just get the men ready. We're coming out now."

"Don't worry," Minor Alexis said. "We're coming in to you. We'll sweep the castle properly then use it to bunk down in overnight. We'll reassess—"

His words were cut off by loud shouting over the general com channel. Men were calling for help and crying out in pain.

"Shit!" Natalie yelled. "It's started! Come on, we have to get everyone inside! We have no idea what force we're up against!"

*

Minor Alexis spun about, his longsling firing again and again at the barely perceptible shadows that rushed at the platoon.

"What the Helios are they?" Minor Alexis yelled. "I can hardly see them!"

"They have disguised their suits!" Fleurtine shouted. "They've been waiting right here for us all along!"

"Disguised their suits? Why would they do that?" Minor Alexis asked. "What cowards hide to fight?"

"Smart ones!" Fleurtine yelled as he watched three men get cut down by Thraenish long blades, their attackers dashing in then back out into the gloom of the approaching night. "They're using the twilight to confuse us!"

"We retreat into the castle!" Minor Alexis yelled. "We regroup in there and fight again in the bright, morning light!"

"Sire, once we get inside those walls we could be trapped! We are supposed to be laying siege to the castle, not the ones under siege!"

"We don't have much choice, Fleurtine!" Minor Alexis shouted. "We have no idea the numbers we are up against or even where the fuck those numbers are coming from! They're like ghosts, rising out of the scrim grass to strike!"

"Fine," Fleurtine yelled, putting two particle barbs in the chest of a Thraen that hadn't been in front of him a second before. He was lucky he was facing that direction or he would have been impaled on a Thraenish blade. "I'll sound the call to retreat!"

He tapped at his wrist and a general alarm rang through every Aelish helmet in the platoon.

"This way!" Fleurtine yelled over the com. "Into the castle!"

"We better be able to get inside," Minor Alexis said.

"Not a problem, brother," Natalie's voice replied. "I have the main airlock open and secured. Just get your asses in here. Now!"

"You heard the lady," Minor Alexis said. "Let's get our asses in there now!"

*

The two siblings stood on the ramparts of the castle, their eyes studying the landscape as the Thraen troops massed below them.

"Any word from Castle Aelon?" Natalie asked as Fleurtine came up behind the royals. "Has the storm slackened at all?"

"No on both," Fleurtine said. "But our scouts tell us there are close to ten thousand Thraenish troops down there. They must have moved around us as we approached the castle. That's why all the cutters were gone."

"All except one," the Natalie said. "Why would they leave just one cutter?"

"For us," Minor Alexis replied. "For me and you, Nats. I'm sure Thraenish ships have the sea behind us cordoned off. They'll use us as bargaining chips. If Mother agrees to withdraw from Thraen Prime then you and I get to go free."

"The storm isn't expected to pass for days," Fleurtine said. "There's no way to get a message to us, if that is the plan."

"They want the delay," Natalie said as she looked at her brother. "They want us under siege, desperate and hungry, so when the time to discuss terms arrives, we'll be weak and in no position to fight."

"Then we don't wait," Minor Alexis said. "We fight now."

"Ten thousand troops, sire," Fleurtine said. "We have five percent of their numbers."

"Yes, but we have position," Minor Alexis replied. "In five days we won't, but right now we do."

"What are you thinking?" Natalie asked. "We take them head on? If we leave this castle we'll be ripped to shreds. Our longslingers are good, but not against ten thousand troops."

"We don't need to take them head on," Minor Alexis smiled. "Not when we're already over their heads. Gather everyone, and I mean everyone. I have an idea that could work."

Natalie and Fleurtine shared a look of worry, but neither voiced it.

*

The longslingers stood shoulder to shoulder, several rows deep, filling the ramparts and walkways of Castle Thraen. The night sky was an oppressive black, darker than even the Dark Minor's armor and environmental suit. The Vape clouds above swirled unseen as the sounds of the Thraenish army on the field below echoed everywhere.

"It is dark, I know," Minor Alexis said as he addressed the men before him. "But that is to our advantage. You have all been battle tested and I know that, even with both eyes closed, not a single one of you can miss. Tonight we prove that. Under the cover of darkness we will rain death down upon the Thraens. We will not let up until they cry for mercy. And even after that, we will not stop. To live, they must leave. Stay, and they die. That is a promise I make tonight to each and every one of you."

The longslingers watched Minor Alexis with reverence and awe. What they were going to try had never been done in modern military history. No one had ever thought to try.

"The first row fires down on the field," Minor Alexis continued. "The next four rows fire up. You send those particle barbs arching through the air and deep into the Thraenish ranks. Split them, send them running in panic, and destroy them all."

"Destroy them all!" the longslingers cheered.

"Nats?" Minor Alexis asked, turning to Natalie. "Would you like the privilege of giving the order?"

"No, A, it is all yours," Natalie grinned. "This was your thinking, so you deserve the glory."

"Very well then," Minor Alexis nodded. "Longslingers? *Fire!*"

*

Alexis jumped from the couch she had fallen asleep on the instant she heard the door open.

"Alexis? Natalie?" Alexis asked as Kel walked into the royal quarters. "Please, love, give me good news."

"I cannot," Kel replied. "Because I only have great news."

"They escaped? Oh, Helios! I knew my children would not die today!" Alexis cried as she lunged at her husband and wrapped herself in his arms. "They are Teirmonts and Teirmonts always find a way."

"They did not escape, Lexi," Kel said, gently pushing his wife away. "You need to sit down."

"Oh, no," Alexis said as Kel led her back to the couch. She took a seat and grabbed Kel's hands, squeezing them with a mother's worry. "You said you have great news. If they did not escape then what great news could you possibly have? The last report was there were ten thousand Thraenish troops besieging them. They couldn't have won, that's not possible. Did they surrender? But that wouldn't be great news. Kel, you must—"

"Hush, Lexi," Kel laughed. "You are worked up over nothing."

"You are the one that told me to sit down!" Alexis snapped, her nails digging into her husband's hands. "Stop fucking with me, Kel! Tell me what has happened!"

"We won," Kel said. "Our children won."

"The main force came and rescued them?" Alexis asked. "They got there in time?"

"No, my love," Kel grinned. "By the time reinforcements arrived, it was all over. Our son led five hundred longslingers against ten thousand Thraenish troops. And he beat them all. Not a single Thraen lived through the night. Five hours of constant firing and it was all over."

"Kel, I do not understand," Alexis responded. "How can five hundred longslingers take on ten thousand troops? Even if what you say is true, we must have suffered massive casualties."

"We didn't lose a man," Kel said. "Every longslinger that entered that castle alive also left it alive. Our son used the higher position to defeat the Thraens. Five hours of longslings sending particle barbs into the Thraenish troops. From the reports, it sounds as if the landscape is nothing but craters and blood. Alexis has done something no one else has ever done. He has changed the System as we know it."

"They were on top of the castle," Alexis stated as realization hit her. She quickly pictured the positions of the longslingers and smiled. "The Thraens have their own longslings, but their men are not trained like ours. They had no way to defend themselves as the particle barbs came at them."

"Exactly," Kel replied. "Apparently our Alexis figured out how to create waves of barbs. The Thraens couldn't escape. Everywhere they turned they were met with death. There is video in the communications room, if you would like to see it."

"I would," Alexis said. "Very much. But before we watch that we must do one thing."

"I have already given the order," Kel said as he kissed his wife. "Our children are coming home. We'll see them in about three days, just after they secure Castle Thraen and make sure it cannot be retaken."

"Who would dare try?" Alexis laughed. "It is part of Family Teirmont now and shall be forever!"

CHAPTER NINE

The two monarchs faced each other across the table. The threat of violence hung heavy in the air and would have manifested itself if not for the presence of the High Guardian, who sat at the head of the table with Mistress Alexis on his right and Master Lionel on his left. He sighed, his old bones aching as he beheld the two royals.

"We can glare for weeks," Victor said. "But it will do neither of you any good. We are well past the time of glaring and are now in the time of sharing." He sighed and turned to a gatekeeper who sat a few feet away and was busy writing and recording the minutes of the treaty conference. "Strike that last line, please. Horrible prose. Replace it with, let's see. . .Glaring solves nothing; only words and honesty can heal the wounds that the System has suffered over this conflict. Yes, that will do nicely."

"Conflict?" Master Lionel growled. "This *woman* has butchered tens of thousands of my men for nearly two decades!"

"I wouldn't have to butcher them if you didn't keep sending them at me," Alexis smiled. "It's been five years since the Slaughter of the Storm. I'd think you would have learned from that massacre that you cannot take on my longslingers. Do you know how many of my men have died in the last five years?"

"Not enough," Lionel snapped.

"One hundred and six," Alexis said. "Compared to your thirty-seven thousand, give or take a thousand here or there."

"Your disrespect for the dead is disgusting!" Lionel shouted as he shoved away from the table and jumped to his feet. "Those were loyal men that died! They do not deserve your sarcasm!"

"Helios knows that no one deserves the mistress's sarcasm," Victor sighed. "Yet we all suffer under it at some point in our lives."

"I will not sit with this woman unless she shows me, and all Thraens, some respect!" Lionel yelled as he pounded a fist on the table. "This meeting will be over before it begins otherwise!"

"Sit down, master," Victor said. "The mistress will apologize for her unfeeling words and then we will begin. Mistress?"

"You are right, Cousin," Alexis said as she nodded to Lionel. "I let my baser nature get the better of me. It will not happen again. My apologies."

Lionel fumed for a few seconds then retook his seat. He rested his arms on the table and looked to the High Guardian.

"I want this all to end now," Lionel said. "I want no more war with Aelon. It has taken too many good men from my station and nearly emptied my treasury. You must tell her to give back my prime. That is the only way Thraen can save face."

"I will not give back something that you have no right to," Alexis responded. "That prime is more mine by blood than it is yours. The same can be said for your crown."

"We are not here to talk about the crown," Victor interrupted quickly. "This treaty conference is strictly about Thraen Prime. The crown is not an issue I want to tackle anytime soon. Are we understood? No more talk of the Thraenish crown."

"Fine," Alexis said.

"Fine," Lionel agreed. "So, High Guardian, tell us how we resolve the issue of my prime?"

"*My* prime, you mean," Alexis said. "It has been in my possession for five years now."

"Yet you have done nothing with it except squat over it like a grendt over her eggs!" Lionel yelled. "Billions of credits worth of Vape is left to be mined because you are more interested in claim and title than in keeping our stations running!"

"If you would stop sending your troops to die then maybe I would have time to manage the prime instead of defending it," Alexis countered. "If you stop the attacks I may be convinced to sell some of that Vape to you."

"You will sell all of the Vape to Station Thraen," Victor said. "In return for official recognition of your claim to Thraen Prime as a descendant of Paul the Fourth, late Master of Station Thraen and its prime."

"Excuse me?" Lionel almost choked. "I will not have this woman's madness legitimized! I am the only heir to the crown of Thraen!"

"Did you not hear me before?" Victor shouted as he slammed his palms down on the table. "We are not talking about the crown! This is only about the prime! And, if you will let me finish, about the future of the prime for both stations!"

Lionel began to speak again, but Alexis cut him off. "What do you mean I will sell the Thraens all of the Vape?"

"Ah, one of you was paying attention," Victor responded after a couple of deep breaths. "Good. Let's focus on that part first. I propose that Alexis Teirmont is officially declared Mistress of Thraen Prime due to her direct bloodline to Paul the Fourth."

"Thank you, High Guardian," Alexis nodded. "That is certainly a step in the right direction."

"In return for that declaration," the Victor continued. "Station Aelon will manage and operate all Vape mining and production on the prime. They will also sell all of that Vape to Station Thraen at a discounted price below full market value. Station Thraen will then be free to sell the Vape on the open market at a slight profit. This way we can put the issue of lineage to bed as well as any issues of Vape production and profit."

"But what is to keep her from backing out once I withdraw my troops?" Lionel asked. "If I allow her to start Vape mining and production, then she will have all the credits she needs to keep me from my prime forever."

"It will no longer be your prime, Your Highness," the Victor corrected. "It will be Aelon's. But, as part of the deal, none of the Vape mined from Thraen Prime will be allowed off Helios unless it has been sold to Station Thraen. Mistress Alexis can mine and produce it all she likes, but if she wants to make anything close to a profit she will have to sell it to you and only you."

"And if he refuses it?" Alexis asked. "That is a loophole we have not addressed. He could bankrupt my treasury if he does not purchase the Vape. I would have nowhere else to sell it."

"If he refuses the Vape then The Way will purchase it and sell it," Victor stated.

"You must be joking," Lionel laughed.

"I am not," Victor replied. "I want this treaty to be done with, so I am willing to go to extraordinary lengths to make it happen."

"And Aelon keeps Thraen Prime in perpetuity? Is that it?" Lionel huffed. "My people will not stand for it. Thraens are prideful and will always see the loss of Thraen Prime as a reason for war. Once I die, then my heir will declare war on Station Aelon. This treaty will only be a bandage on a wound, not a cure for the ailment."

"That is why we must join Aelon and Thraen together so that blood will heal the wound," Victor said. "The time for bloodshed is past, now we must look to the future and create bloodlines."

Alexis studied the High Guardian for a minute then shook her head. "I will not sell my daughter into slavery. She is a warrior, not a bargaining chip to be married off to some Thraenish heir, and she is committed. Even if she weren't, and I allowed this, she'd chew him up and spit him out before the vows were even finished."

"Again with the insults!" Lionel shouted.

"Be quiet, both of you!" Victor yelled. "I was not speaking of the minoress, Mistress Alexis. At least not the Minoress of Station Aelon. It's the Minoress of Station Thraen that will be married to the Dark Minor of Station Aelon. They are of the same age and I believe of the same temperament. The two royals will be a good match. They will be appointed joint rulers of Thraen Prime and Aelon Prime, to live in the two castles throughout the year. This gives Station Aelon official claim to Thraen Prime while also putting a Thraen's claim on Aelon Prime by marriage, and once children are born, by lineage."

Alexis leaned back in her chair, a look of pure shock on her face. "You've gone mad, Victor."

"That I will agree with," Lionel said.

"I have not gone mad," the High Guardian said. "It is the only way the two stations can move on from this war. This is for the good of the entire System. A perpetual war serves no purpose. The time to end it is now."

"And if I refuse?" Alexis asked. "What happens then, Victor? You cannot possibly think that I will agree to whoring my son out to Station Thraen. He is a grown man and I have refrained from arranging his love life. I do not believe I will begin now."

"While I do not believe you will be whoring anyone, since arranged marriage is how you came to exist in this world, Helios help us all," Victor responded. "I am not without my own teeth and claws, mistress. If you refuse the terms I have put forth—if either of you refuse—then I will be forced to get involved personally."

"How?" Lionel laughed. "Do you intend to stand on the prime and wave your staff about, hoping Helios will make you invulnerable to particle barbs? Trust me, Your Holiness, many of my men have tried just that. It does not end well."

"No, Your Highness," the Victor answered. "I will take the prime myself using all of the Burdened. They will kill every single person on the continent, no matter which station they hail from. If you doubt my commitment to ending this ridiculous war then let those words sink in. My Burdened will show Station Aelon and Station Thraen what true butchery is."

The High Guardian leaned back in his chair and steepled his fingers in front of his chin.

"Do we have an accord?" he asked after letting it all sink in. "Will there be a wedding or won't there?"

Alexis looked across at Lionel and the master met her eyes. They watched each other for several minutes while the High Guardian waited patiently.

"We have an accord," Alexis said finally as she stood and offered her hand to Lionel. "The way I see it is Station Aelon gains a prime while I also gain a daughter. The win is mine."

Lionel stood and took Alexis's hand, a smirk on his face "This is a treaty and a truce. There are no winners here. I am sure your son will say the same thing once you break the news to him. I know love is something you value dearly in your household. Too bad he will not get to experience it."

Alexis tightened her grip and pulled the master to her across the table. "My son has the capacity to love anyone," she growled. "His heart is bigger than Helios. He will be happy, I swear it."

"We shall see," Lionel said, taking his hand back. He resisted the urge to rub it as it throbbed with pain. "We are royals, Alexis; happiness is not always our destiny."

"But it is our fate," Alexis countered then turned and curtsied sarcastically to the High Guardian. "Have the papers drawn up and I will sign them immediately. I must return to Castle Aelon and break the news to my son. He will need time to prepare himself for his new future."

"Of course," Victor said. "May Helios be with you and your family, Mistress Alexis."

Alexis only nodded in response as she hurried away from the table and out of the room before the two men could see the tears well in her eyes.

*

Minor Alexis stared at his image in the mirror, unsure if he was seeing himself or some impostor dressed like him. Not that he would normally wear the formal attire that choked at his neck and restricted his movements.

"You'd think a tailor could create an outfit that not only looked regal enough for a wedding, but could move and breathe for combat as well," Minor Alexis said.

"I do not think combat is in the cards for you tonight," Kel said as she placed his hands on his son's shoulders. "At least, I certainly hope not."

"No, no, that's not what I mean," Minor Alexis sighed. "Minoress Rebecca and I have already discussed our duties and we know what is expected of us."

"You have? How modern of you," Kel laughed. "I was pretty much told what my duties were going to be. Not that I would have argued much otherwise. Your mother is quite persuasive when it comes to the art of love."

"That is not what I needed to hear before my wedding, Father," Minor Alexis replied. "The image of my parents on their wedding night is not what I want to picture on mine."

"Sorry, Son," Kel laughed. "I'm just saying that life gets thrown at us, whether we want it to or not, and it is how we handle that life that defines our future."

"And our fate," Minor Alexis added. "Let us never forget that part. It is what rules us."

"It is what rules your mother, that's for sure," Kel stated. "While I agree with her that fate always has a hand in things, I am not quite as devoted as she. You still have free will, A. If at anytime you want to back out of this, just say the word. I will support you even if that means hijacking a shuttle and fleeing this planet."

"Why couldn't we have the wedding on Station Aelon like all other royal weddings?" Minor Alexis asked.

"Because it needed to be here on The Way Prime so that the vows occur on neutral ground," Kel said. "This is more than two royals getting married. It is the binding of bloodlines over a new way of ruling the primes. You are making history."

"Great," Minor Alexis said. "That should be put on our family crest, since making history seems to be the Teirmonts' true business."

"I don't know," Kel laughed. "Making trouble is right up there with you people."

"Us people?" Minor Alexis asked. "Do you not consider yourself part of the family, Father?"

"I am, of course," Kel said. "But if you haven't noticed, I took your mother's name in marriage, not the other way around. This is the story of the Teirmonts."

"Only because you were never given a surname, having been born into the Burdened," Minor Alexis said. "It wouldn't do for a mistress to be referred to as Her Highness, Alexis Blank."

"There is power and freedom in anonymity," Kel said. "Or so they say."

"So they say," Minor Alexis sighed then turned from the mirror and looked his father in the eye. "Shall we?"

"We shall," Kel said then hugged his son fiercely. "Are you sure you don't want to steal a shuttle? We still have time."

"We wouldn't get far," Minor Alexis laughed as he hugged his father back. "Mother would send Nats after us. Or she'd send Grandmother, which is almost scarier."

*

"I do not understand what the problem is," Bella exclaimed as she sipped at her tea. "If the parts fit then a child should be made."

"Mother, please," Alexis replied, nearly coughing on her own tea. "I do not need to think of my son's and daughter-in-law's parts fitting."

"Well, maybe your Alexis is a flip like his grandfather," Bella said. "Helios knows that is one way to prevent a child from being conceived. Hard to make babies if you don't engage in the activity that makes babies."

"Can we not talk about this?" Alexis sighed. "It is all I hear about from the meeting of stewards, the meeting of passengers, from the High Guardian, from the Order of Jex, and even from my own husband."

"Oh dear, if Kel is worried, then we are in trouble," Bella said. "Have the children seen a physician or midwife?"

"Yes, they have," Alexis replied. "Nothing is wrong, as far as the experts can tell. And stop calling them children, Mother. Alexis is thirty-one and Rebecca is twenty-nine. They left childhood a long time ago."

"They are about to leave child-making, as well," Bella said. "Having children at their age is dangerous. The poor thing could come out with four legs or something grotesque."

"Your understanding of science is frightening," Alexis said. "Many monarchs sired children up into their forties and fifties."

"Shaowshit," Bella said. "Monarchs rarely live that long."

"I'm almost fifty, Mother."

"Yes, but you aren't talking of having more children," Bella countered.

"No, having five was plenty," Alexis said. "At least three still live."

"Oh, darling, I am sorry," Bella said. "How cruel of me to bring up this subject so close to the anniversary of our dear twins' deaths."

"No, it's fine, Mother," Alexis said. "It's not like I don't always have my children on my mind."

"Yes, of course," Bella nodded. "Speaking of, have you heard from Richard lately?"

"They are," Alexis said. "Has he not written to you? After you gave him your right to that estate, which was not yours to give, by the way."

"Details, details, my dear," Bella grinned.

"Well, anyway, he was supposed to write to you regularly," Alexis said. "That was the arrangement we made."

"Oh, he needn't bother," Bella said. "I am sure he is busy learning the estate. Helios knows he is not the most mentally together boy."

"Mother!" Alexis exclaimed. "I do not want you saying that again. If one of the servants heard and it got back to him, he would be devastated. He worships you."

"Does he?" Bella smiled. "Best to worship the living than how you worship the dead."

"Helios, Mother, you have no shame," Alexis sighed. "And I haven't spoken to Father in ages."

"There is no shortage of gratitude for that," Bella said. "You have done well, Alexis, despite your uniqueness. You found great love with Kel. It still breaks my heart that our Alexis could not find that on his own."

"They love each other plenty," Alexis said. "Just in their own way."

"Hardly their own way," Bella snorted. "More like the way of a thousand monarchs before them. You dodged a particle barb, my dearest daughter. You found your love and took it without waiting for anyone to give it away."

"That could be said for most things in my life, Mother," Alexis laughed as she went to pour more tea. "Dammit, the pot is empty. Have we drunk this much already?"

"My bladder says we have," Bella laughed as she slowly pushed herself up out of her chair. "How about you call for another pot while I relieve myself? At the rate I walk, the tea will be done and here before I return."

"Should I get Lara to help you?" Alexis asked.

"That woman is slower than I am with her gout," Bella said. "Don't disturb the poor thing. I am a royal of Station Aelon and Station Thraen, I am quite capable of going pee on my own."

"Very well," Alexis nodded as she rang a small bell. "Don't take too long, I still want to talk about what we are going to do with the new domed gardens down on the Aelon Prime estate."

"I'll hurry, I promise," Bella said as she slowly made her way across the library and to an inconspicuous door against the wall. "I walk slow, but I pee fast."

"Good for you, Mother," Alexis laughed. "Good for you."

Alexis watched her aged mother close the door behind her then turned her attention to the servant that had answered the bell. "More tea, please. And do we have any of those gelberry cakes with the cream frosting? If so then bring me one."

"Would the Minoress Bella like one as well?" the servant asked. "I know she is supposed to watch her blood sugar, but she hasn't eaten much today, so it should be fine."

"She hasn't eaten much today?" Alexis asked. "Have the physicians put my servants on their payroll?"

"Master Kel informed us all about the health needs of Minoress Bella," the servant said. "He has been worried since she received her news."

"News? What news?" Alexis asked, her eyes going to the bathroom door. "I haven't been told anything."

"Oh...my apologies, Your Highness," the servant said and curtsied quickly. "I have spoken out of place."

"Stand up, silly girl," Alexis said. "You aren't in trouble. Go fetch the tea and cakes for both of us. I'll speak with my mother and get to the bottom of all this."

"Yes, Your Highness," the servant said and curtsied again, then hurried from the library.

"News," Alexis mumbled as she watched the bathroom door. "I'm mistress of this station. No one keeps news from me." She looked at the door the servant had left by and frowned. "I should probably have found out what the news was from that girl before she left. Dammit. I'm getting old. Only a few years ago I would have had that girl telling me her deepest, darkest secrets with just an angry look."

"You're losing your touch, sweetheart," her father said from the chair Bella had just occupied. "But, I am afraid you are about to lose more than that."

"Papa? Speak of Helios," Alexis said. "I am only having tea with Mother. No need for you to pop by with your weird words of wisdom."

"I come when you need me the most," her father said then looked at the bathroom door. "Now is one of those times."

"Mother's urinary habits are not cause for you to appear,"Alexis laughed. "I need you when fate speaks to me, not when my mother is—"

There was a loud crash and a thud from the bathroom and Alexis bolted to her feet. She glanced at the chair, but her father's ghost was nowhere to be seen.

"Mother!" Alexis cried as she rushed to the bathroom door. "Mother, are you alright?" She got to the door and could hear a low moaning. "Mother!"

Alexis yanked the door open and screamed. A trail of blood led from the toilet to the collapsed form of Bella. The woman was pale and shivering as she lay there, her eyes looking up at Alexis, filled with pleading and regret.

"Oh, Helios, Mother!" Alexis cried as she fell to the floor and took her mother in her lap. "Help me! *Someone help me, please!*"

*

"There was never a question of your fate, dearest girl," Bella Herlict Teirmont Beumont whispered as her daughter lay in bed with her, both of them covered with several comforters and propped up by a mountain of pillows. "It has always been in your hands since the moment you were born. Helios, since the moment you were conceived. That was a trial, I tell you."

"Shhhh," Alexis whispered back, tears spilling onto her cheeks. "Save your strength. Don't waste your energy talking about me. Tell me about you. Tell me about what your dreams were before you married Father."

"My dreams?" Bella muttered. "Helios knows what those were. That was so long ago, Alexis. So very long."

"We never forget our dreams, Mother," Alexis said. "Tell me yours so that they can live on."

"I don't honestly know, sweetheart," Bella said. "At some point I let them go and never found them again. It's better that way. Not all of us...."

"Not all of us what?" Alexis asked as she nuzzled her face into her mother's soft shoulder. "Don't leave it like that. Not all of us what?"

Bella did not answer, just let out one last breath as the life left her.

"Mother?" Alexis whispered. "Mother...please. Not now. Not yet. I haven't had my grandchildren yet. I need your help, Mother. I need to know how to love them the way you loved yours. I know my children, I know how to show them to fight and be fierce and be rulers. But grandchildren? They want play and hugs and treats, not armor and longslings and blades."

Alexis kissed her mother's slowly cooling cheek over and over.

"Please, Mother," Alexis said. "I'm not ready. I don't understand growing old! Mother? Mother, please! Do not leave me! I'm sorry! I'm so sorry for everything I did to you! I'll take it all back if you just stay a little longer! I'll apologize for banishing you and for killing your husband! Mother! Mother! Mother! *Mother!*"

Hands grabbed at Alexis and helped her from the bed as she cried for her mother again and again. She wanted to fight off the hands that pulled her away from the woman that bore her and raised her and tried to do best by her. But the hands knew how to hold Alexis back, they knew how to handle the aged mistress and keep some, if not all, of her wildness in check.

"Shhhh, love," Kel said as he wrapped himself about his wife. "She knew you were sorry. She never needed you to say it; she just needed you in her life. You did that, Lexi. You made her happy for years and in the end you were there for her. Just like our children will be there for you."

"Too much, Kel," Alexis said as physicians rushed into the room. "There was too much to say for her to know."

"She knew, trust me," Kel said. "You could see it in her eyes and hear it in her voice every time she looked at you. You were her pride. You were her everything, except for her grandchildren, of course."

"The children,"Alexis gasped. "How do we tell them?"

"With love, Lexi," Kel said, kissing her softly. "Just like with everything else in this family. We tell them with love."

*

Minor Alexis could hardly believe the words that had just been spoken. It took all of his strength to keep his knees from buckling.

"But, Mother, that would ruin your honor as a monarch," Minor Alexis said. "Abdication is only for the disgraced."

"You are confusing abdication with deposition. I know the difference between the two, believe you me," Alexis laughed as she motioned for her son to sit. "Take a seat, A, before you fall on your ass."

"That would be the real disgrace," Kel smirked, his hand firmly in his wife's. "Sit down, Son."

Minor Alexis felt behind him for the chair he believed to be there, but wasn't sure until his hand found the breen upholstery. He was barely sure *he* was there, having been whacked upside the head with his mother's shocking news.

"But what about the Treaty of the Primes?" Minor Alexis asked. "If I become master then who will live on Helios? It is required that someone live there, moving between the castles of Aelon Prime and Thraen Prime. Master Lionel will be enraged by this change."

"Master Lionel is enraged when his bowel movements refuse to appear by command," Alexis scoffed. "I could care less about that stupid man and what he wants. The Treaty of the Primes is perfectly clear and you becoming master will not break that treaty."

"Your mother and I will take yours and your wife's places down on the Planet," Kel said. "We will retire to the primes and live out our days on the wild frontier of breen farming and Vape mining."

"It's where your father was born, after all," Alexis added. "And I spent much of my youth down there, not to mention quite a bit of my adulthood during the war. I am my father's child and do feel slightly more comfortable on the prime than up here in the station."

"But no skid riding," Kel scolded. "Not at our age."

"I'm Mistress of Station Aelon and its Primes," Alexis replied. "I'll ride as many skids as I damn well please."

"But you won't be mistress. I will," Minor Alexis said. "I mean, I'll be master. Either way, you won't be mistress."

"I'll still kick anyone's ass that tries to stop me from riding skids," Alexis smirked.

"None of us doubt that, love," Kel laughed. "Just keep the speed down, alright? For me?"

Alexis leaned in and kissed him on the cheek, then on the lips. "Anything for you, my dearest love."

"Have you told Nats?" Minor Alexis asked, hoping to break up his parents' kissfest. "What does she think?"

"She does not know yet. She is off with Petro," Alexis replied. "We wanted to discuss it with you before we mentioned it to anyone else. If you are dead set against it then we'll act as if it was never brought up. You can take the crown when I die, just like every other master before you."

"Is this really so you can retire and enjoy your later years? Or is it because you absolutely refuse to do things they way everyone else has?" Minor Alexis asked. "Because I'd rather not take the crown if it's just so you can stick a middle finger in the air once more and tell the System to go fuck itself."

"Alexis!" Alexis replied, feigned shock on her face. "How could you think of such a thing? I am the picture of tradition, you know that."

"Right," Minor Alexis grinned.

"You have underestimated your mother," Kel said. "She's actually sticking up both middle fingers while dropping her drawers and showing the System her ass."

"That sounds more like it," Minor Alexis nodded. He sat there for some time before he nodded again and then stood up. "Fine. It's settled. I'll be master."

"Well good," Alexis smiled. "As long as it's settled." Then she frowned as she looked about the sitting room. "Although, it would be more settled if your wife had joined us as requested."

"Yes, well, the physicians suggested she not travel right now," Minor Alexis said. "Which means we'll need to postpone the coronation for a few months."

"A few months?" Alexis exclaimed. "I could be dead in a few months. What in Helios's name could she be sick with that takes a few months? Did she grow a third arm?"

"Think it through, love," Kel said, his face aglow with realization. "Let what your son has said sink in."

"Let it sink in? Basically he told me his wife is a weak little...Oh, dear," Alexis said. "Is she pregnant?"

"There we go," Kel said. "You've caught up."

"Don't be an ass," Alexis said as she swatted at her husband. "Is she, A? Is your wife pregnant?"

"She is," Minor Alexis smiled. "Three months along now. Far enough that even the midwives suggested against shuttle travel."

"Three months?" Alexis growled. "You kept this from me for three months?" She whirled on Kel. "Did you know? Have you been keeping this from me as well?"

"Hey, now! I just found out too," Kel said. "Don't get mad at me. Keep that anger for your close-lipped son."

"Thanks, Father," Minor Alexis frowned. "Throw me under the skid, why don't you."

"Oh, how I wish your grandmother had lived to see this," Alexis said. "If she could have hung on for one more year."

"You get to be the grandmother now," Minor Alexis said. "And I think one is plenty around here."

"What does that mean?" Alexis asked. "Kel? What does he mean by that?"

"That you are more than enough for any baby to have," Kel said.

"Whatever," Alexis said as she rolled her eyes. She rang a bell and waited for a servant to arrive. "Wine, please."

"Mistress? It's just after breakfast," the servant girl said.

"Thank you for your marvelous timekeeping skills, but my son just announced he is to be a father and I want to toast the child's good health with wine. Is that too much to ask, young lady?" Alexis snapped.

"Yeah, she is more than enough," Minor Alexis smirked.

"Oh, shut up, you," Alexis replied then smacked herself on the forehead. "I know! We'll have the coronation down on the prime! You can be crowned before your child is born; that way if something happened to you, Helios forbid, the baby would be the undisputed heir. Helios knows that we don't need any more heredity issues with this family."

"Wow, uh, when?" Minor Alexis asked.

"The sooner the better," Alexis said then fixed her eyes on the servant girl. "That goes the same for the wine. Move your ass, girl!"

*

The room swelled with royalty and nobility almost as much as the mistress's belly swelled with child.

"Are you alright, dear?" Master Alexis asked his wife as they sat before the throng of well wishers that lined up to pay them honor on their new titles. "Do you need to go lie down?"

"She is fine, boy," Master Lionel said from Mistress Rebecca's other side. "Thraen royalty do not need to be coddled. We are here to be examples of proper behavior, not examples of weakness."

"Says the man that has never had an eight pound weight pushing at has nether regions," Alexis said from her son's side. She leaned across Master Alexis and placed her hand on Mistress Rebecca's. "If you need to excuse yourself, dear, then feel free to do so. Helios knows it won't be the first time half these people have seen a mistress bolt from the room. I remember one time when I had eaten too many meat pies and I thought my ass was going to—"

"Lexi," Kel scolded from her other side. "Rebecca isn't as fond of poop stories as you are."

"Well, she better get fond of them," Alexis said. "She's about to pop out a poop machine in a week or so, if the baby is anything like its father."

"Thanks, Mother," Master Alexis sighed. "Of course, it wouldn't be a coronation if we didn't talk about my bowel movements as an infant."

"Infant? A, you were in diapers until your—"

"Lexi!" Kel snapped. "Stop it!"

A few of the nobles in the receiving line looked away, trying to pretend they hadn't heard the whole conversation.

"I think I will go lie down," Mistress Rebecca said. "I'm so very tired and my belly is sore all over."

"Is it?" Alexis asked, suddenly serious. "I'll come with you and we'll fetch the midwives."

"No, no, I'm fine," Mistress Rebecca said, giving a quick apologetic glance to her father. "It's probably just my own bowel issues."

"How wonderful," Lionel sneered. "Now she's gone native."

Mistress Rebecca stood up and all stood up with her as she politely excused herself from the room.

"How long has she been in pain?" Alexis asked her son.

"Pretty much the entire pregnancy," Master Alexis replied. "It has not been a fun nine months."

Alexis was about to open her mouth when her husband's hand clamped over it.

"You don't have to tell him that his wife is having less fun than he, Lexi," Kel said. "He was only answering your question, not making a statement on the suffering between the sexes. Ow! You bit me!"

"Damn right I bit you," Alexis said. "That's what you get for covering my mouth."

"You know, I expect the child to be in attendance at court regularly," Lionel said, leaning over the empty chair at Master Alexis. "If our Treaty of the Primes is to hold then that is the least you can do. What say he spend at least four months of the year with me?"

"Are you fucking mad?" Alexis barked.

The whole room went quiet.

"Mother," Master Alexis hissed. "This is between me and my father-in-law. This is not your business."

"If it's his business then it's my business," Alexis snapped. "He may be the grandfather, but I am the grandmother. That child is a Teirmont and Teirmonts spend their time on Station Aelon or its Primes, not on some Thraenish stink hole with Lionel the Numbskull!"

"How dare you!" Lionel shouted and jumped to his feet. "You will apologize this instant!"

"I'll apologize by shoving a blade up your asshole!" Alexis yelled, getting to her feet as well. "Kel! Hand me my blades!"

"Your blades are packed away along with your armor, love," Kel sighed. He looked at Master Alexis and frowned. "Sorry, Son."

"Well, we almost made it through the day," Master Alexis said, his head in his hand. "I'm fairly certain the Order of Jex had a pool going that said we wouldn't make it through the first half of the coronation."

"Is this how you allow family to be treated?" Lionel shouted down at Master Alexis. "If you have any honor you will—"

A blood curdling scream interrupted him and the room turned to look at the main entrance to the grand hall as the distinct sound of several boots could be heard. Several guards burst through the doors, led by Steward Vast, the scar across his face bright white against his blood red skin.

"Your Highness, come quickly," Vast said as he reached the master. "You must hurry."

"Rebecca!" Master Alexis cried and instantly stood and ran from the room.

Kel stood up and grabbed hold of his wife as her legs weakened. They both looked over at Master Lionel and saw a look of terror mirrored back at them.

*

The blood was hot and thick, even if the stillborn infant in Master Alexis's arms was stone cold. But the blood hadn't come from the dead child, but from the barely conscious woman that lay on their bed, surrounded by physicians and midwives.

"Give her here, A," Kel said softly as he approached his shocked son. "I'll take her and they can prepare her properly."

"She has Mother's eyes," Master Alexis said. "She would have been so beautiful."

"She *is* beautiful," Kel said. "Always remember that. When years from now you think of your daughter, think of her as the beautiful child she is, not what she would have been."

"No, Father," Master Alexis said as he handed the corpse over. "We both know that is not how this day will be remembered."

"Your Highness?" a physician asked from the bed. "You are needed. It is time."

Master Alexis looked about the room. "Where's Mother?"

"She wouldn't come in," Kel said. "She's out in the hallway, if you want me to fetch her."

Master Alexis waved his hand at his father and shook his head. "No, she can stay, but tell her not to go anywhere. I will need to speak with her."

"Of course, Son," Kel said. "She isn't going anywhere."

"Thank you," Master Alexis said as he slowly walked over to the bed and took his dying wife's hand.

Kel watched his son for a moment then looked down at his dead granddaughter. Something inside of him tried to break, but he refused to let it. There was too much broken already and his family needed him to be strong and whole.

*

The windows of the East Library looked out at the vast expanse of Aelon Prime and the Teirmonts all stood there, watching the scrim grass blow in the wind of an approaching Vape storm.

"Three days is not enough time, A," Natalie said. "You need to mourn and let your pain lessen before you do anything official like return to the station and call the meeting of stewards together."

"Three days or three years, there is never enough time, Nats," Master Alexis said. "Right, Mother? You've lost your parents, your uncle, two children. Did you have enough time with them?"

"No," Alexis replied. "I did not."

"There you have it," Master Alexis stated. "Three days is long enough."

"What are you planning, Son?" Kel asked. "I can tell by the tone in your voice that you are about to do something very reckless. You sound more like your mother than yourself."

"Well, fuck you too, my love," Alexis responded. "That wasn't a very nice thing to say."

"I know," Kel replied. "That's why I said it. I hoped it would snap him back to reality and pull him out of whatever grief stricken fantasy he has fallen into."

"A, talk to us," Natalie said. "Tell us what you are thinking."

"I am thinking that my legacy just died without a single chance to fight for life or even let out a whimper," Master Alexis said. "She just died. *They* just died. I have no heir and I have no wife to produce more heirs. I am an empty master. I need something to fill my rule, to make me remembered for all of history."

"You were the Dark Minor," Natalie said. "You led one of the greatest battles ever fought. That will always be remembered."

"Yes, well, the Dark Minor died the second I was crowned," Master Alexis said. "Maybe it is time for something darker to appear."

"Darker?" Kel asked. "Alright, Son, I think I'm going to take you back to your quarters. You haven't slept and you haven't eaten a thing. You need to do both before you say anything else."

"No!" Master Alexis shouted as he yanked his arm free from his father's grasp. "I need to do this before anything else! I need to tell you what my plans are for Station Aelon!"

"When you have rested," Kel insisted.

"Love, let him speak," Alexis said. "Whatever it is, it's eating him up inside. Helios knows he doesn't need anything else eating at him."

Kel started to argue then nodded and looked at his son. "Go ahead, A. What plans do you have?"

"Nothing short of all out victory," Master Alexis said, his eyes drawn back out the window to the bleak and nearly empty landscape. "Nothing short of my birthright."

"A? What are you saying?" Natalie asked.

"I'm saying that it's time Family Teirmont took what they are truly owed," Master Alexis said. "Not just Thraen Prime, but the very crown itself." He turned his back on the window and smiled at his family. "I plan on taking Station Thraen. That crown will be mine."

Kel and Natalie both took a step back at the news, but Alexis moved forward and placed her hands on her son's cheeks.

"Yes," she smiled. "Now you are talking, my son. That crown will be yours, I know it. It is your birthright. There may be great grief flowing through you, but there is also something much greater than that. There is fate!"

REIGN OF FOUR

Book IV

Act I

A Dark Minor is Born

"He was known for his compassion in his early years. Even when called the Dark Minor, he was still a man of great caring and understanding. But life changes everyone eventually and, like so many of the Teirmonts, his end was one of confusion and violence."
— Dr. D. Reven, Eighty-Third Archivist of The Way

"When you open your heart to Helios, you open your being to the Dear Parent and allow Him to dwell inside you. There is where you know the meaning of the Planet, the System, The Star, The God."
— Book of Opening 1:3, The Ledger

"At no point did I believe I could ever live outside my mother's shadow. And I was fine with that for a very long while."
— Journals of Alexis the Fourth, Master of Station Aelon and its Primes

CHAPTER ONE

Helios, the star that burns eternal, lit up Station Aelon, its powerful rays penetrating the shield dome that protected the Surface, allowing the natural marvel of life and growth and the technological marvel of a man-made machine to mimic an actual planet.

Station Aelon, one of the Six Stations of the system, orbited above Helios the planet, with hundreds of thousands of Aelish lives in constant motion and industry on its many decks. From the upper sector decks of the nobility, down through the Middle Decks of the working class and gentry, and into the Lower Decks of the laborers and, as many above believed, the lesser of the Aelish passengers, the power of Helios could be felt everywhere.

But it was not Helios the Planet or Helios the Star or even Helios the System that the passengers felt. No, it was Helios the God. The Dear Parent's presence encompassed all and gave them the strength to continue on in the void of space where no human being was meant to live.

It was to that Helios, the God and Dear Parent, that Bella Herlect Teirmont Beumont, Minoress of Station Thraen and former Mistress of Station Aelon, prayed as she watched her four year old grandson whipped about the fields of Castle Helble's estate on a single skid, its hover drive propelling it at speeds which made the older woman gasp repeatedly.

"Mother, calm yourself," Alexis the Third, Mistress of Station Aelon and its Prime, laughed. "He is a Teirmont; he knows how to handle himself on a skid."

Bella turned to her daughter, who was the first female monarch in all the System, and frowned deeply. "You take liberties with his life, Alexis,"

Bella stated. "As of right now he is your only heir to the crown. If he were to crash and be killed, then the station would be thrown into chaos."

"It would not," Mistress Alexis replied without looking at her mother. "My reign is far from over. If anything happened to my Alexis, this station would endure, just as it has for thousands of years. I would endure as well, as difficult as that would be."

"I hear the fear in your voice that you are trying to hide," Bella said. "You know you should not let him be so reckless on that vehicle. Your instincts tell you that you are taunting Helios. And why? To prove to the nobility that a woman, a female monarch, can produce an heir that is strong and masculine?"

Bella looked about at the some of the stewards and stewardesses who sat upon picnic blankets, food and drink being offered and removed by the many servants and attendants afforded to a castle of Helble's standing.

"Or are you trying to make up for your father's inadequacies as a ruler and man?" Bella asked, her stomach doing flip flops as her grandson, the Minor Alexis, nearly lost control of his skid, pulling it out at the last second.

Mistress Alexis ignored her mother's jabs and smiled as she watched her son let out a full throated laugh. She could see the pure joy on the child's features as he faced the danger, and conquered it, all on his own.

"I do not want to talk about Father," Mistress Alexis said. "You should know by now that the subject of my father is off limits to you." She turned and looked her mother full in the face. "Please do not bring him up unless you want to bring up all the memories that go with him."

Bella nodded and took a step back. "My apologies, Your Highness, I have overstepped."

"Oh, knock it the Helios off," Mistress Alexis sighed. "You are not funny."

"What's not funny?" Kel, Mistress Alexis's husband and Master of Station Aelon, asked as he walked up next to the two women. "Did I miss a joke?"

"Of a sorts," Bella grinned. "It is good to see you, Kel. I was not told you would be joining us."

"It was last minute," Kel said. "The meeting of stewards completed their budget conference early, so I decided to grab a royal skid and come see my son play around your estate."

"Yes, my estate," Bella sneered. "It feels so much like home."

"Would you prefer the Third Spire, Mother?" Mistress Alexis asked. "That is always an option if all of this open air and free land is too much for you to handle."

"Stop it, you two," Kel sighed. "You have come so far in your relationship. There is no need to always start bickering when you first see each other. You both know that you'll be thick as thieves in just a couple of days. Neither of you can help it. Despite your history, you two are very much alike."

"Which can present its own problems," Bella said.

"Exactly," Mistress Alexis nodded.

"See? You are agreeing already," Kel laughed.

"The minor's lunch is ready, my lady," Lara, Mistress Alexis's personal attendant, stated as she walked up behind the tense royals. "Shall I have one of the royal guards fetch him?"

"No, no, I will do it myself," Mistress Alexis said as she looked over at a row of parked single skids. "Let's see what the heir to the crown of Station Aelon can do."

"Alexis!" Bella gasped.

"Lexi," Kel warned.

"I'll alert the physicians," Lara smirked.

"Nothing will happen to him," Mistress Alexis sighed. "Trust in fate. Fate will not let me down when it comes to my son. He will live a full, rich life, and will rule this station with strength and compassion."

"If he lives to do so," Bella replied then turned and walked towards a large blanket set out for the royal luncheon.

"Don't push fate, my love," Kel said as he looked at his wife.

She benefitted from the Teirmont stature and was tall, with long legs. Her blonde hair blew across her face and she casually brushed it out from in front of her bright blue eyes as she looked back at him.

"I never push fate, sweet husband," Mistress Alexis grinned. "It is fate that pushes me."

Kel turned from Mistress Alexis and looked over his shoulder at his retreating mother-in-law. "Have you told her yet?"

"Not yet," Mistress Alexis said. "But she knows I am hiding something; it's why she's being short with me."

"She is not going to like the news that you plan on leading our forces into the Lower Decks to put their mastership squabble to rest," Kel said, his hand going to her belly. "Especially when you are with child."

"No, I suppose she is not going to like that news at all," Mistress Alexis agreed. "But she will like the fact that I am going to trust my son's life in her hands. She has never had Alexis to herself before."

"Lara will be with him," Kel said. "So Bella will not truly have Alexis to herself."

"But neither I nor you will be here," Mistress Alexis said. "That is quite the distinction."

"You're sure about all of this?" Kel asked.

"I am," Mistress Alexis replied. "Fate makes me sure."

"I know it does," Kel said then pointed at his son. "Better get him before Lara has to remind you again. You know the attitude that woman gets when you make her job more difficult than it has to be."

"I sometimes wonder who the mistress is on this station," Mistress Alexis laughed. "The way Lara orders me about, you would think it is her."

"You insist on familiarity," Kel shrugged. "It is a bed of your own making."

Mistress Alexis leaned in and kissed her husband. "Perhaps we can enjoy a bed of our making later."

"In your condition?" Kel asked.

"Please," Mistress Alexis laughed again. "If you think pregnancy is going to stop me from mounting you when I feel like it then get ready for disappointment, Husband."

"I think our definitions of disappointment are slightly different," Kel smiled around the kiss.

Mistress Alexis pulled back then smacked Kel on the ass before hurrying over to one of the skids so she could fetch her jubilant son and heir.

*

Alexis watched as his mother and father, along with a flank of royal guards, stepped into the main lift, ready to descend below and put an end to the lowdecker nonsense that had plagued Station Aelon for generations.

Not that the minor understood what was truly happening. He was not yet five and only had a basic understanding of the politics and warfare of Station Aelon; he had zero concept of the politics and warfare of the Six Stations of the System.

Lara, her hand holding Alexis's in her grasp, looked down at the boy as the doors to the main lift slowly slid closed and a quiet chime indicated the lift was descending.

"Come on, you little bugger," Lara said finally, once the chime's echoes had faded. "Let's go see your grandmother. I'm sure we'll have just as much of an adventure with her as your mommy and daddy are going to have down in the Lower Decks. So don't you worry, alright?"

"They'll be fine," Alexis said then yawned. "Grandpa told me so."

Lara hesitated as she led the minor away from the lift. She opened her mouth to ask what the boy meant, but thought better of it and let the subject drop. There was already too much drama to the day, she didn't need a specter of masters past added to it.

Yet the boy was not to let the subject drop.

"You don't believe me," he stated, his voice confident and strangely mature for a child his age. "He said you wouldn't."

"Did he?" Lara asked, trying to sound casual. "The ghost of your dead grandfather specifically said my name?"

"No," Alexis admitted. "He just said that not everyone believes in fate like Mommy does."

Lara stopped, and the few royal guards that did not leave to fight below, stopped as well, keeping their distance so as not to crowd the royal attendant and the minor. Kneeling down, Lara looked Alexis in his blue eyes.

"You know ghosts are not real, right Alexis?" Lara asked. "What you see is just how your mind deals with stress when things get tough."

"Then Mommy has a lot of stress," Alexis replied.

A couple of the guards chuckled, but not in a mocking way. Lara looked to them and rolled her eyes.

"Yes, young lord, your mother has a lot of stress," Lara said as she stood and led the boy down the passageway once again. "I doubt there is a person in this System with more stress than her."

*

The news of the mistress's triumph over the Lower Decks raced through Station Aelon. And no other place was it received with such joy and relief than in the sitting room of Castle Helble.

"Oh, praise Helios," Bella cried. "I knew she could do it, but it is still good to hear this news. Now maybe these old bones will rest again."

"Your bones aren't old, Grandmother," Alexis said, sitting on her knee as the attendant that delivered the news left the royals to themselves. "You have young bones. Strong bones. Teirmont bones."

"Well, no, Alexis, I do not," Bella smiled. "I am a Teirmont by marriage. Or was. But that was a long time ago. A lot has happened to these bones in that time."

"Like what?" the almost five year old asked expectantly. His bright blue eyes locked onto his grandmother's and she couldn't help but smile down at him.

"Well, young minor, I have lived on two different stations, been a minoress on both and a mistress on one," Bella replied.

"This one!" Alexis clapped. "Station Aelon! This one! This one! This one!"

"Yes, this one," Bella chuckled as she gently gripped her grandson's hands. "But I am no longer the mistress of this station. That job belongs to your mother. It is a job she was born for and her father had to fight to get her."

"My grandfather?" Alexis asked. "He died poorly."

Bella frowned down at the precocious child, a child so well spoken considering he was raised around a mother that was almost more soldier than monarch.

"Yes, your grandfather died poorly," Bella said. "That is very true. Some said he had it coming, though."

"Did you say that?" Alexis asked, his eyes wide.

"No, I did not," Bella said. "No matter what your mother may believe, I never once wished that kind of end on Alexis."

"That's my name too," Alexis said, patting his chest. "I'm Alexis the...."
He counted on his fingers quickly. "The Four!"

"Fourth," Bella corrected. "You are Alexis the Fourth and your mother is Alexis the Third."

"And my grandfather was Alexis the Two!" Alexis nearly shouted, proud of his own math.

"Second," Bella corrected again. "I was married to Alexis the Second. He was your mother's father. He wasn't meant to be a master. Or not a master in this time. Maybe one day the stations will be more enlightened."

"You just turn them on," Alexis stated.

"What?" Bella asked, puzzled.

"You turn on lights," Alexis said. "Then turn them off. Then turn them on again. Off and on and off and on and off and—"

"Yes, I know how lights work, Alexis," Bella smiled. "But that is not what enlightened means."

"No?" Alexis frowned and then looked up at the chandelier that hung in the center of the sitting room's ceiling. He squinted his eyes together and pursed his lips.

"What are you doing, child?" Bella asked.

"Changing the lights," Alexis said. "So I can see Grandfather again. He's nice to me."

Bella froze, almost afraid to breathe. She had to force herself to take slow, even breaths before she passed out from lack of oxygen. Her hands shook, so she waited until they were steady before taking Alexis by the chin and turning his face to hers.

"What do you mean see him again?" Bella asked. "Your grandfather passed away before you were born."

"Yep," Alexis nodded and tried to turn his face away. Bella gripped harder. "Ow!"

"Oh, I'm sorry, my little love," Bella said and kissed his chin quickly. "All better?"

"All better," Alexis said.

"Can you tell me what you meant?" Bella prodded.

Alexis sighed in a way only four year olds are able to and his whole body seemed to deflate. "Why does everyone bother me?"

Bella couldn't help but laugh at the serious and dejected way the boy responded to her. She wrapped him in her arms and kissed the top of his head over and over.

"Your mother talks to your grandfather a lot," Bella said. "It is no wonder you want to as well."

"I don't want to," Alexis replied, squirming in Bella's embrace. "He's kind of sad. I don't like to see him sad."

"Your mother never liked to see him sad, either," Bella said, easing up on the hug, but refusing to fully let the boy go. "She loved her father so much. I wish you could have known your mother before he died. It changed her."

"Made her sad too," Alexis nodded. "That makes me sad."

"Don't be, my boy," Bella said. "That is the last thing your mother would want. Let's change the subject, shall we? What would you like to talk about?"

"The new baby!" Alexis shouted. "I'm going to have a brother! A baby brother! We will wrestle and ride skids and fight and shoot longslings and eat and eat and eat!"

"I suspect you will," Bella said. "But what if you have a sister? Will you do all of that with her too?"

"No," Alexis said quietly.

Bella was shocked by Alexis's answer. She held him out slightly at arm's length so she could study him clearly.

"Your mother likes all those things, so why wouldn't your sister?" Bella asked.

"She will," Alexis said and crossed his arms. His lip stuck out and he furrowed his brow. "But I don't want her to."

"Helios! What a thing to say," Bella scolded. "Why do you say that?"

"Because she'll be better at them than me," Alexis answered. "Just like Mommy is better at those things than Daddy."

Bella began to laugh so hard that she was afraid she'd knock Alexis off her lap. She wrapped him up again, but he struggled against her, obviously mad at the source of her mirth.

"I'm sorry, Alexis, I'm not laughing at you," Bella said as she struggled to stop laughing. "I really am not. One day you'll understand just how funny that is."

The doors to the sitting room opened and Lara strolled in, her face bright and happy.

"Have you heard?" she asked.

"Lara, as much as you like to consider yourself an equal amongst us, and Helios knows my daughter encourages it, you do not barge into a room like that and blurt out questions," Bella snapped, her mood changing in an instant. "You present yourself with decorum and you address me properly. You will also address the minor properly."

"My apologies, minoress," Lara said and curtsied. Then she put both hands to her mouth. "Or is it former mistress? The dowager mistress? What is your official title? My poor, tiny attendant's brain can't seem to keep up."

"She's playing with you, Grandmother," Alexis whispered loudly.

"Yes, I am well aware of that," Bella said, fixing her eyes on Lara. "And to what do we owe this pleasure of your so-respectful appearance?"

"It is time for the minor's blade lessons," Lara replied. "The mistress was adamant that he keep up his studies even when here at Castle Helble."

"Does he train so vigorously at Castle Quent?" Bella asked. "I do not understand why he must be pushed so hard. The boy can barely tie his own laces!"

"He has nannies to tie his laces for him," Lara said. "But he will not have nannies to fight his wars for him when he is master." Lara held up a hand and bowed her head before Bella could reply. "Those are your daughter's words, not mine, my lady. Please do not kill the messenger."

Bella glared for a second longer then took a deep breath and let it out quickly. "Fine," she huffed, lifting the young minor off her knee and setting him on the floor. "Take the child to his murder lessons. I guess if his mother hadn't been so well trained then she wouldn't be mistress today."

"Nor would she have bested the lowdeckers while pregnant," Lara smiled. "The woman is hero to us all."

"Mommy is a hero!" Alexis shouted as he sprinted past Lara and out of the sitting room. "Mommy is a hero! Mommy is a hero!"

"It'll be a shame when he discovers she is also only a woman," Bella said sadly.

"A shame for him or a shame for her?" Lara asked.

Bella studied the royal attendant for a second. "Well put, Lara," she said, finally then waved her hand. "You had better chase after him. He could easily be heading for the pantry instead of the training wing."

"Of course, my lady," Lara said and curtsied quickly. "Good day."

"Good day to you as well," Bella said as she watched Lara leave.

She sat there for a few minutes then straightened her back and stood up.

"Well, if my grandson is to train to be a fighter then I should probably watch him," Bella grumbled to herself. "I may not be a warrior like my daughter, but I have watched many a minor and master fight. It would do me well to see how my grandson measures up."

*

The long blade came at him faster than he anticipated, forcing Alexis to stumble backwards and parry wildly. His feet almost went out from under him, but he maintained his footing and shifted his weight, dodging a second thrust and spinning about for a side attack on his opponent.

His blade was knocked aside and his opponent grinned from ear to ear.

"That new polybreen armor makes you slow," Mistress Alexis said. "Perhaps you should take it off until you grow into it a bit more?"

"No," Alexis frowned as he went at his mother again. "I only just got it for my Decade celebration. I'm still getting used to it, Mother."

"Proper-fitting armor can make all the difference between success," Mistress Alexis said as she lunged, feinted left then came in fast on Alexis's right. A loud thunk could be heard in the training room as her long blade met the minor's armor. "...and failure."

"My armor protected me," Alexis stated.

"Only because I let it," Mistress Alexis replied, grinning at her ten-year-old son. "And it won't protect you for long if it's falling off you."

"If it's what?" Alexis asked then cried out as half his armor tumbled from his midsection. "Mother! That's cheating! You broke one of the buckles!"

"Mommy doesn't cheat!" five-year-old Minoress Natalie yelled from the side of the training room while she sat on her father's lap. "Take that back, shaowshithead!"

"Whoa, whoa, whoa," Kel growled as he looked down at his daughter. "Where did you hear that?"

"From the guards," Natalie responded, "and the cooks and Nanny Halpa and Lara and you and Mommy and—"

"Alright, alright, I get it," Kel chuckled. "You live with rough-talking people."

"I live with Aelish people," Natalie stated.

"Yes, my sweet girl, you do," Mistress Alexis said as she walked to her son and tried to help him pick up the pieces of his armor that fell.

"I can do it," Alexis snapped. "I will not have my mother on the battlefield with me, as you have told me many times."

"You are a long way from being ready to fight on the battlefield, Son," Mistress Alexis laughed. "Now, stop being stubborn and let me help get your armor put back together."

"The buckle is broken, Mother," Alexis complained. "We will need an armorer to repair it."

"It is not broken," Mistress Alexis said. "It is merely undone. Do you think your mother would be callous enough to break her own son's armor, armor he received as a present from his grandmother on the day of his Decade celebration, just to prove a point?"

"Yes," Alexis replied without hesitation.

Kel chuckled from the wall and Natalie reached up and tweaked his nose.

"No laughing at Mommy," she scolded.

"Ow," Kel said and gently smacked her hand away. "Careful, little girl, or I'll take you out on that training floor and teach you a lesson just like your mother taught your brother."

"She did not teach me a lesson," Alexis pouted. "She cheated."

"There is no cheating in war, Alexis," Mistress Alexis said, ignoring her son's stubbornness and helping to put his armor back on. "If you get anything from today's lesson, know that there is never any cheating in war. You do everything you can to win, no matter the cost."

"Now, hold on," Kel said. "Don't teach him that. Our son needs to know there is always a cost to war. Always."

"I didn't say there was not a cost, my love," Mistress Alexis replied. "I said to do whatever you have to no matter the cost. If you are going to go to war then you better be ready to go all the way."

"I'm ready!" Natalie shouted as she jumped up and raced onto the training floor. She picked up a long blade before anyone could stop her. The thing was longer than she was tall, but she was able to heft it up and keep it from falling over. "Come at me, shaowshitheads!"

"Little girl," Kel said as he got up and went after his daughter. "That is not a toy for five year olds. You are still learning with short blades."

Natalie swung the long blade at her father and he had to jump back to keep his shins from being sliced.

Everyone in the training room—Mistress Alexis, Alexis, Kel, and the couple of royal guards hanging back by the door—all stared at the over-exuberant, and blade-wielding, minoress.

"Do that again," Mistress Alexis said, watching her daughter very carefully.

"What?" Natalie asked. "This?"

She swung the blade from left to right then moved towards her mother, swinging it back from right to left. The little girl didn't lose her balance at all. In fact, she seemed steadier on her feet with the long blade in her hands.

"Lexi, no," Kel said as he saw the look in his wife's eyes. "Just take it from her before she gets hurt."

"Hush, lover," Mistress Alexis said and she hooked a toe under her long blade and flipped it up into the air. She caught it easily and pointed the tip at her daughter. "Let's see what you got, Minoress Natalie."

The girl was well used to seeing her mother's tricks with blades, so she didn't even give the toe flip a second thought as she rushed forward.

Mistress Alexis sidestepped the attack easily and whacked her daughter's blade. The tip of the blade dug into the thick breen mat covering the floor, stopping Natalie's progress instantly. But instead of running right into the pommel as Mistress Alexis expected, Natalie turned her body and used her momentum to yank the blade free. Unfortunately, due to the weight of the blade, she couldn't slow herself enough to stop from twisting and falling on her butt.

"Ha!" Alexis laughed. "Good thing your trousers are padded."

"Shut up!" Natalie yelled, tears welling in her eyes. "That was mean!"

Natalie started to cry hard from the embarrassment of the fall. Before his mother could say anything, Alexis was already hurrying to his sister's side. He plopped down next to her and hugged her around the shoulders.

"I'm sorry, Nats," Alexis said. "Don't cry. I didn't mean it."

"Yes, you did," Natalie sniffed.

"No, no, I didn't," Alexis said, hugging his sister tighter and tighter until the girl started to giggle.

"Stop it," Natalie laughed. "Stop it, you shaowshit—"

"Yeah, that's enough of that," Kel said and lifted his daughter up into his arms. "Let's go have a talk about that potty-mouth of yours while your brother and mother finish training."

"Finish?" Alexis asked. "Aren't we done?"

"Nice try," Kel said as he walked towards the exit. "You still have an hour on the mat."

"Great," Alexis said.

"I think it is," Mistress Alexis said as she handed him his long blade. "It gives us time to be together."

"You should spend that time with Nats instead," Alexis said. "She's better than me already."

"Oh, knock it off," Mistress Alexis said as she sent a thrust at Alexis's midsection. "Don't be a baby."

Alexis parried the thrust. "You saw her," he said, moving his feet to the side, looking for an opening. "I wasn't that good at her age."

"No, you weren't," Mistress Alexis said. "But Natalie is wild, Son. She doesn't have the self-control that you do. It was impressive, what she just did, but that was only strength and instinct. Skill and training can beat that any day. That's why you are still in here and she's going down for her midday nap."

The two royals trained for the rest of the hour, their blades meeting each other over and over, with Mistress Alexis's blade meeting her son's armor more than a few times. By the end of the session they were both sweating heavily and huffing and puffing.

"You're getting old, Mother," Alexis grinned.

"You cheeky shit," Mistress Alexis smiled. "I'm not old, I'm just a woman who has the burden of a station on her shoulders and has given birth to four children." She glanced at a clock on the wall. "Speaking of, I'm betting the twins are waking from their naps right now. They'll be hungry for their afternoon feeding. I better shower fast so they don't taste sweaty boobs."

"Helios, Mother!" Alexis cried out. "I do not need to hear that!"

"Oh, get over it," Mistress Alexis said as she put her long blade away and grabbed a towel from a table by the wall. "You used to latch onto these sweaty boobs when you were their age. Don't act like you are something special."

Mistress Alexis let her armor fall to the ground and an attendant hurried over to retrieve it. She looked at her son as he stood alone in the middle of the mat.

"Aren't you going to go shower?" Mistress Alexis asked. "You have studies with your tutor in twenty minutes."

"I'm going to skip my shower and keep practicing," Alexis said. "There is no way I'm letting my little sister get better at the long blade than me."

"Well, even if she does get better, don't let it worry you," Mistress Alexis said. "There are a lot more weapons than just long blades. Always remember that."

*

The target disintegrated instantly as the particle barb ripped it apart on a molecular level.

Alexis let the longsling ease away from his shoulder and surveyed the far end of Castle Aelon's shooting gallery.

"Twelve for twelve," Natalie smiled, sipping from a bottle of gelberry soda. "And you beat your time too. Way to go, A."

"Thanks," Alexis said as he set the longsling on the table and started to reload it. He got halfway done then turned to look at his sister. "Hey, aren't you supposed to be getting ready? Today's your Decade celebration. I'm surprised Mother let you come watch me shoot."

"She didn't," Natalie shrugged. "I'm hiding."

"She's going to be mad," Alexis said. "This Decade celebration is a big deal. Not just for you, but for all of Aelon. Half the royals from the stations have come down to Helios for it so they can see our new castle on Aelon Prime. You really don't want to tick Mother off today."

Natalie shrugged.

"Good attitude," Alexis said as he lifted the newly loaded longsling back to his shoulder. "And good luck."

"Hey, I'm not looking to please everyone all the time like you are, A," Natalie said. "One of us has to not give a shaowshit."

"We're telling Mother you said that," a little girl said as she hurried into the shooting gallery followed by a little boy that looked exactly like her.

"You aren't supposed to say that," the little boy said.

"And you two aren't supposed to run away from me!" a nurse snapped as she hurried in after the Teirmont twins. "This room is dangerous!"

"How'd they get the door open?" Alexis asked as he lowered his longsling. "It's locked so no one can accidentally get shot by running in here!"

"My apologies, my lord," the nurse said. "They seem to know the code to the lock."

"It's easy," the boy, Harry, shrugged.

"Three, three, five, five, one, one," the girl, Claudia, said. "Stupid code."

"And they're only six," Natalie laughed. "We are so screwed."

"You're not supposed to say screwed!" Claudia called out.

JAKE BIBLE

"Minoress Natalie," the nurse said. "Your mother, grandmother, and Lara are all looking for you."

"They must not be looking hard if they didn't think to look here first," Natalie said. She chugged the rest of her soda then burped loudly. "I better go before Daddy gets involved. I don't want him disappointed in me today. He promised me a dance at the celebration and if he's mad, then I won't get it."

"Hardly," Alexis chuckled as he held his longsling up so the twins couldn't get to it. Despite only being fifteen, the young minor pulled from his Teirmont heritage and was nearly as tall as his parents. Keeping the longsling up out of arms reach from the twins was not a problem. "Father would never risk making you sad on your Decade. He'd kill a million lowdeckers with his bare hands before he let that happen."

Natalie shrugged again and left, tossing the empty soda bottle in the trash as she exited the door.

"She's not supposed to do that," Harry said. "That goes in the recycling."

"How about you go chase her down and tell her?" Alexis said.

The twins instantly forgot the longsling and turned to chase after their sister. The nurse couldn't help but give the minor a dirty look as once again she was forced to take chase after the two little royals.

Alexis waited until the door had closed before he put the longsling to his shoulder and squeezed off twelve perfect shots.

*

The heat of the grand hall was almost too much for Alexis. He longed to be free from the noise and the constant motion of the dancers. It was all so dizzying. It didn't help that he had made the mistake of drinking each glassful of gelberry wine that was offered to him.

The music switched from a quick, up-tempo jig to a more slow and somber waltz. Alexis could see several young noblewomen eyeing him, waiting for him to approach them and ask for a dance. But Alexis had no desire for making a fool out of himself. He was known for his skill with blades and a longsling, but no one in court had any illusions as to his prowess on the dance floor.

Before one of the young women could muster up the courage to take the initiative, Alexis excused himself from the side of Steward Neggle, one of the members of Mistress Alexis's elite Order of Jex, and made his way to the wide hallway just outside the grand hall. He took several deep breaths as he quickly made his way to the nearest door that led outside.

Alexis rushed through the door and was only a few yards into the open, shielded courtyard before his stomach rebelled and all the appetizers, cake, and gelberry wine reappeared at his feet. Even after he emptied his stomach, Alexis stayed hunched over, his hands resting on his thighs. His queasiness had subsided, but there was still a deep unease inside him.

The sound of boots scraping on stone made him straighten instantly. He whirled about, but he saw no one.

"Who's there?" he called out. "Show yourself."

No response.

Alexis peered into the dark corner of the courtyard and swore he saw a shadow waiting there, watching him. Wiping his mouth with the back of his left hand, Alexis drew the short blade from his belt. It was a blade he only ever wore during important occasions, and was supposed to be ornamental, but he was his mother's son, so he always made sure it had a true and sharp edge before he strapped it on.

The blade glinted in the muted light of the courtyard as Alexis held it out in front of himself. He approached the spot by the courtyard wall where he saw the shadow, his steps deliberate and cautious. His belly grumbled and he was afraid he would throw up once more, but he stifled the feeling and kept his focus, determined to root out the lurker.

"Hiding from a royal and ignoring a minor's orders is grounds for severe punishment!" Alexis snapped. "Unless you are willing to hang or be beheaded, I would advise you show yourself!"

Another scuffle of boots and the shadow detached itself. But try as Alexis might, he could not make heads nor tails of what he was seeing. It was if the person was made of Vape smoke and not flesh and blood.

"*Follow*," the voice of the shadow whispered.

"Excuse me?" Alexis laughed. "I think not. Come into the light more or I will call for the Royal Guard. If I don't cut you down right now then you will be quickly cut down by them. You no longer have a choice in the matter."

"*Follow*," the voice whispered again and then was lost around the corner of the wall.

The unease still gripped Alexis, but the nausea left as his adrenaline began to pump. He was not used to being defied and the royal privilege in him began to turn to royal anger.

"You will stop this instant!" Alexis yelled. "Do you hear me? I said to stop!"

There was the sound of a door opening and then footsteps on marble. Alexis hurried around the corner to find a set of courtyard doors open onto a side hallway. It was a hallway Alexis knew well as it was a shortcut he used often to get from the grand hall to the training wing of Castle Aelon.

Alexis caught sight of the shadow again, but only just barely. The minor rushed back inside the castle and looked down the hallway, but saw only empty space. With his short blade gripped tightly, he took chase after the shadow, careful not to let his dress boots slip out from under him on the recently polished floor.

Each side passage that Alexis came to was empty and it was with slowly dawning dread that Alexis realized the illusive shadow was not leading him to the training wing, but directly to the royal wing. Alexis also realized that he had let no one know where he was going. He highly doubted that his parents even knew he'd left the grand hall since they were so wrapped up with Natalie's Decade celebration and the dozens and dozens of dignitaries that clambered for their attention.

"I demand that you stop!" Alexis roared as he caught a brief glimpse of the shadow turning onto the hallway that housed the royal quarters. "Dammit! Stop!"

Alexis, the unease in him no longer down deep, but right at the surface of his consciousness, sprinted around the corner to see the shadow disappear through the doors of his younger siblings' nursery. He nearly dropped his blade as his mouth hung open in disbelief. He attempted to rationalize what he saw as a product of the gelberry wine, but when a scream came from inside the nursery, he knew deep down that it was no mere alcoholic hallucination.

"Grandmother?" Alexis called out as he rushed to the doors and threw them open.

"Alexis! Look out!"

Before he'd taken more than a couple steps inside, his head erupted in pain and he stumbled a few feet forward before collapsing to his knees. He was able to turn himself as the next blow came and his shoulder took the brunt of it, causing him to drop his short blade. His fight training took over and he kicked out with his right leg, knocking the attacker off balance with a solid hit to the knee. He rolled away and then came up, his fists ready for the fight.

"Grandmother? What is this?" Alexis asked as he saw the twins' nurse standing before him, a heavy lamp in one hand and a bloody blade in the other. A split second thought rushed through his mind about how lucky he was he had been hit by the lamp and not the blade. "What's happening?"

Wedged in a corner of the nursery's sitting room was Bella, the four year old Minor Richard clutched in her arms. Alexis could see there was blood, but he didn't know whose it was, his brother's or his grandmother's. Or both. There was certainly something wrong with his grandmother's face.

"Alexis, run!" Bella shouted. "Save yourself and get out!"

"What have you done?" Alexis spat at the nurse, his eyes studying her body language, watching for the next attack.

The woman did not reply. She took a step towards him and lifted up the blade. Alexis could see her hand shaking and knew she was not a trained assassin, but someone who had either lost her mind or had been paid to harm his family.

"Answer me!" Alexis roared at the woman.

He saw her flinch at his anger and he took his opportunity. He lunged at her, moving for the blade. She lashed out as he knew she would and he was able to spin to the side and bring his elbow down on her wrist, sending the blade clattering to the floor. The lamp came at him fast, but he ducked under the swing and landed a hard punch to the woman's belly, forcing her to lose her grip on the lamp as well.

"Grandmother! Go! Get Richard out of here!" Alexis yelled as he grabbed the nurse's skirts and threw her aside. "Now!"

Alexis didn't see his grandmother flee with his brother as suddenly his feet went out from under him. He was able to get his arm out before his face impacted with the floor, but he didn't have time to scramble away as the nurse climbed onto his back and grabbed him by the hair. She lifted his head up and was about to slam his face into the floor when his hand found his short blade. He twisted and lashed back blindly.

There was a cry of pain and the weight on his back eased up as the nurse moved off of him. Alexis rolled over and thrust with his short blade, sending it deep into the nurse's belly. The woman cried out and scuttled back, her hands going to the weapon. She pulled it free and let it fall away then pushed herself to her feet. Blood trickled between her fingers as she swayed there for a second, her eyes moving back and forth between Alexis and the open nursery doors.

Before Alexis could stop her, the nurse ran from the nursery, yanking the doors closed behind her. The minor stared at the bloody handprints on the door handles for a couple of seconds and wondered why she had closed the doors. Then reality snapped back into place and two faces came rushing into his head.

"The twins," he gasped as he got to his feet and spun about, looking for them in the sitting room of the nursery.

They were nowhere to be seen so he hurried to a set of doors and shoved them open. His eyes instantly found the drops of blood that trailed down the private hallway that led to his siblings' bedchambers. He followed the blood without thought and found himself with the twins' bedchamber door in front of him. He didn't even bother to try the door, just kicked it as hard as he could and rushed inside.

The minor's mind wanted to retreat from what he saw. There was just so much blood. The furniture was coated with it, the walls, the ceiling, it was everywhere. But most of the blood was pooled in the center of the bedchamber. And in that pool were the small bodies of Minor Harry and Minoress Claudia.

"No," Alexis said as he collapsed next to them, his hands hovering over their still forms. "No, no, no. I'll get you out of here. I'll get you to the physicians."

Alexis scooped his brother into his right arm and his sister into his left then pushed upright with his legs. They were heavy in his arms and he knew he couldn't carry them for long, but he refused to give up as he turned and stumbled out of the room.

He made it down the private hallway and back into the nursery's sitting room before the dead weight of his siblings overwhelmed him and he collapsed to the floor. Their bodies lay heavy in his lap and he cradled them both, his eyes going from one to the other.

"Wake up," he whispered. "The woman is gone. You can wake up now."

He gently shook them, praying to Helios that they would open their eyes and smile up at him. But they were already so cold. Even through his thick dress clothes he could feel the lack of heat in the children who had always been full of so much energy. They were each no more than kindling; heavy deadwood in his lap.

Alexis leaned down and nuzzled his face to their necks, kissing them back and forth as shock and grief slammed against his soul. When the doors to the nursery opened, he forced strength back into his legs and stood, his shaking arms gripping his dead siblings with all of their might.

There was screaming and then he was enveloped in his mother's embrace as she rushed at him. She took the twins' corpses into her own arms with such force that Alexis stumbled and fell back to the floor. More voices, more screaming, so much blood.

It would be the blood that Alexis remembered for the rest of his life. Not the wails of agony from his parents, not the shouts from the stewards and the guards, not his sister Natalie's voice as she came upon the scene, not even the frantic search for his grandmother and brother Richard.

It was the blood he remembered when he closed his eyes at night. The blood and a shadow that led him from a celebration of life into a nightmare of death.

*

The minor sat upon the stone bench in the main courtyard of Castle Quent, his eyes cast upwards to the shimmering light of the shield that protected the Surface from open space. The night sky was full of stars, as it always was, yet they didn't seem nearly as bright to him as they had in times past.

"There you are," Mistress Alexis said from behind him. "I have been hunting the entire castle for you. I almost called the Order together to put out a search party."

"I've been here," Alexis said, smiling weakly at his mother. "Sorry if I alarmed you or anyone else in the castle."

"I wasn't alarmed," Mistress Alexis replied, but not very convincingly.

"The night doesn't hold peace anymore," Alexis said as his mother sat down next to him.

"No? And why is that?" Mistress Alexis asked, taking her son's hand in hers. "Do you see something that I do not?"

"Grandmother once told me a story when I was little about how all the stars in the night sky were the souls of children that died before their time," Alexis said. "That they looked down on us all, looked down on the families they left behind, the parents, the grandparents, the sisters, the brothers. They looked down and kept watch over us."

"Oh," Mistress Alexis said quietly. "I think she may have told me that as well when I was little."

"I can't look up there anymore without thinking of Harry and Claudia," Alexis said.

"Knowing that your lost siblings are looking down on you, protecting you, doesn't bring you any peace?" Mistress Alexis asked.

"No, because they aren't up there," Alexis replied. "I have counted the stars and there are not two new ones. And if there are not two new ones, then that means that Harry and Claudia were not taken before their time, but exactly at the time Helios meant them to be taken."

"You have counted all the stars?" Mistress Alexis asked. Alexis turned and gave her a stern and serious look. "You must stop this, Alexis. You will drive yourself mad with thoughts like that."

"But it doesn't bring me madness, Mother," Alexis replied. "Nor peace. What it brings me is determination."

"Determination?" Mistress Alexis asked. "And what determination does it bring, my sweet boy?"

"A determination to kill the people that butchered my brother and sister," Alexis said. "A determination to bring them to their knees, to force them to look me in the eye, and to make them beg for their lives."

"Alexis—"

"But they can beg all they want, Mother," Alexis continued. "It will do them no good. I will slit their throats, one by one, and let their blood feed the land. There will not be any joy in the act, but there will be satisfaction."

Mistress Alexis sat there a moment, her hand gripped so hard around her son's that she was surprised he did not protest.

"The Order is preparing for war," Mistress Alexis said finally.

"I know," Alexis responded.

"We are to strike Thraen Prime by the end of the month," Mistress Alexis stated.

"I know," Alexis responded again.

"I want you and your sister by my side. It is your place," Mistress Alexis said. "Your father is not happy about it, so he has insisted he be down on the prime with us. Your grandmother will rule as regent up here on the station, and watch over Richard, until I return. Until we return."

"Yes, I know," Alexis said.

"How do you know?" Mistress Alexis asked.

"Because it is our fate, Mother," Alexis said, looking the mistress directly in the eye. "Isn't that what you have always said?"

"I suppose it is," Mistress Alexis responded, wrapping her arm about her son's shoulders and pulling him close. She leaned in and kissed the top of his head, although it wasn't as easy as it had been when he was younger, smaller, vulnerable.

"Are we insane, Mother?" Alexis asked, reveling in the warmth of his mother's embrace. "Are we completely insane to attack Thraen Prime?"

"No, Son, we are not," Mistress Alexis said. "As you said, it is our fate."

"Then perhaps our fate is insanity," Alexis said quietly.

Mistress Alexis did not have a response for that, so she just kissed the top of his head again and turned her face up to the stars. After a while she said, "Did you really count all the stars?"

"Yes," Alexis said. "I really did."

"That's my boy," Mistress Alexis sighed. "That's my sweet, determined boy."

CHAPTER TWO

Vape gas.

It covered the entirety of Planet Helios.

Clouds of Vape occluded the sky, keeping the lands below—the primes—in a perpetual grey light. The only break from the never-ending gloom was the sky above The Way Prime, the only clear portal on or off the planet. Those that tried to penetrate the oppressive Vape cover quickly found themselves obliterated as their shuttles ignited the clouds around them.

But the Vape gas that drifted across the boiling gas seas and prime lands was a wild Vape, unusable, unable to be harnessed for fuel and energy. It was the Vape that dwelled under the ground, deep in the Vape mines, that could be harnessed, contained in canisters for use on the primes and up on the Six Stations. Each of the primes had some Vape, whether it was Aelon, Flaen, Ploerv, Klaerv, Haelm, or Thraen.

Yet Thraen Prime had more mineable Vape than all of the other primes put together. It was those riches that kept Station Thraen one of the most powerful of all the monarchies in the System.

Which made the war for the land that much more sweeter for the Aelish crown. Not only could Mistress Alexis fight for her birthright, since she was the direct heir, via her mother, to Thraen's late Master Paul the Fourth, but she could also fight for a resource that would make Station Aelon the undisputedly dominant Station of System Helios.

It was those thoughts, coupled with a bloodlust that ran hot in the Teirmont veins, that drove the mistress on as she sent her men after the retreating Thraenish soldiers that ran for the safety of an abandoned Vape mine.

"Mistress!" Steward Fleurtine shouted, his voice crackly and harsh over the com in Mistress Alexis's environmental suit helmet. A member of the Order of Jex, Steward Fleurtine, led a flanking troop of Aelish soldiers and longslingers that boxed in the Thraenish troops and forced them to flee into the mine. "Mistress! We have the day!"

"Not yet, steward," Mistress Alexis replied as she hacked a Thraen soldier in half with her long blade.

The man's body fell to the ground in two pieces and began to bubble and smolder as his fluids burned from exposure to the ambient Vape gas. Mistress Alexis didn't give the man's burning and liquifying corpse a second thought as she turned her attention on her next target, driving her long blade through another unfortunate Thraenish soldier's belly.

"Mistress!" Steward Fleurtine insisted. "We can withdraw and regroup while the cowards flee! They have no place to go but the mine! We will cover the entrance and let time and the loss of oxygen take care of the rest!"

"If I wanted to fight a war of attrition, Fleurtine, I would wait out this war on one of my royal cutters by the coast," Mistress Alexis replied, dispatching a third, then a fourth Thraenish soldier. "Does waiting on the sea sound like how I conduct a war?"

"No, Mistress, it does not." Steward Fleurtine laughed in spite of himself. "But may I suggest that you let the Order finish this job while you fall back to the base of operations?"

"I have no intention of leaving the battlefield and returning to the BOP," Mistress Alexis said, ducking a pitifully weak blade swing by an obviously poorly trained Thraen. She almost let the man live, since he was not even close to her match. Almost.

"Mother? Fall back and let me take a band of longslingers into the mine," Alexis's voice called over the com. "They are ready to go to work."

The mistress killed four more soldiers before she stopped and turned to see where her son and heir stood. She squinted into the gloom and found him easily since he wore a distinctively black environmental suit which covered his black polybreen armor. While the minor had stopped wearing his mourning clothes a year after the twins were murdered, he insisted on honoring them with his black armor. Mistress Alexis did not agree with the decision, but she understood why he did so.

And he did strike an imposing figure when wearing the armor. That she did understand.

A band of two dozen longslingers from Station Aelon's Middle Deck Twenty stood behind the Dark Minor, as he had begun to be called by the men due to his armor choice. Born and bred to handle longslings, and the deadly particle barbs the weapons shot, the longslingers were some of the most loyal of Mistress Alexis's forces. They had proven themselves to be unrelenting in their attacks and deadly accurate with their shots.

"You think you can take those Thraens? They are boxed in like animals in a dark hole, Son," Mistress Alexis said, pointing her long blade at the mouth of the Vape mine. "It is not the open battlefield, A. There are traps and pitfalls in there that could kill you before you fire a single shot. Not to mention a boxed in animal is the most dangerous of animals."

"We can take them, Mother," Alexis replied. "I have no doubt in my men."

Having been waging war on Thraen Prime for five years, Mistress Alexis had noticed her son turning more and more to the longslingers. Instead of leading platoons of bladesmen and battle skids, as most in the Order preferred, Minor Alexis had begun to entrench himself within the ranks of longslingers, fighting side by side with the men of Middle Deck Twenty, not as their minor, but as their equal.

Not that Mistress Alexis thought his choice put the minor in any more danger than she faced herself. She knew each and every one of those longslingers would die for her son in the blink of an eye. She had no worry there. What did worry her was the moving away from traditional battle tactics. The longslingers did not conduct themselves by the rules of combat that had allowed Aelon to prevail time and time again over the centuries. Yes, she had witnessed their triumph when putting down the Lower Decks, but Thraen Prime was not the Lower Decks of Station Aelon.

Thraen Prime was true war.

And unless she could find a way to end the war swiftly, Mistress Alexis feared it was a war her son would inherit. So she hesitated in allowing her son to change things too quickly. Change was a danger her son couldn't be protected from, no matter how many longslingers he surrounded himself with.

"Mother?" Alexis called. "Do I have the go ahead to attack? Or should I take my men into the swamps to shoot bog toads?"

"Cheeky shit," Steward Fleurtine laughed.

"You have the go ahead, Son," Mistress Alexis said. "Take them in, kill them all, and watch your back."

"I'll be too busy watching Thraens die to watch my back," Alexis grinned, hooking a thumb over his shoulder. "That's what I have these lunks for."

"Who ya calling a lunk?" one of the longslingers shouted.

"All of you," Alexis laughed then pointed at the mine. "No mercy, gentlemen."

"No mercy!" the longslingers shouted then followed their minor into the mouth of the mine.

*

The grand hall was full of men enjoying more than their fare share of drink and song. Groups huddled around tables that overflowed with plates pilled with food and pitchers of every manner of drink known to the primes.

Soldiers from all regiments clasped hands and draped arms over shoulders as they swayed back and forth, singing along to the song being performed by a disheveled looking young man at the front of the hall. He had a mass of curly red hair and deep, deep brown eyes, making it seem like he stared at the world through shadows. In his hands was a stringed instrument of his own making, long and sleek, which responded to the touch of his fingers like it was born into the world with him.

"*To the prime he came, tall and dark, a leader of all the men,*" the young man sang. "*He walked across those bloody fields, a black figure so grand. The Dark Minor! The Dark Minor! The Dark Minor of all the lands!*"

"*The Dark Minor! The Dark Minor! The Dark Minor of all the lands!*" the soldiers sang along.

Alexis sat with his head in his hands, his face looking down at the table, his eyes refusing to look up at the spectacle and revelry that surrounded him.

"Come on, Alexis," Steward Vast laughed as he clapped the minor on the shoulder. "Enjoy yourself! This is all to celebrate your victories of this year! To think it all started with your assault on that mine and now has ended with you taking the Thraen's primary Vape refinery. You should be holding your head up high!"

"The Dark Minor?" Alexis asked as he looked up at the man. "Do they have to call me that?"

"Your great grandfather was called Longshanks," Vast said. "He hated that as well, I hear tell. You don't want to know what your grandfather was called."

"A flip," Alexis responded. "That is not a secret in my family. They never came up with a name for Mother."

"Well, not one that any person would dare say aloud," Vast chuckled. "Not if they want to keep their privates intact."

The grand hall erupted into even louder singing and despite his reticence, Alexis looked over his shoulder at the musician. As soon as he saw that the man was heading in his direction, Alexis tried to stand and escape, but Steward Vast clamped a hand on his shoulder and shoved him back in his seat.

"No, you don't, my lord," the steward laughed. "You aren't getting away from this."

The musician stopped right next to the minor and continued his song. Soon everyone in the room had surrounded the one table, completely closing ranks around Alexis. Except for the musician, the singing was nothing but drunken shouting, but no one cared; they were all having the time of their lives.

When the song was done, the musician bowed to the minor and started to make his way through the crowd and back to the front of the hall.

"You, bard, stop," Alexis ordered. He slapped his hand on the table. "Sit and drink with me."

"I have more songs to sing, my lord," the musician replied. "I am being paid by—"

"I will double your pay if you stop that singing for a spell and have a drink with me," Alexis said and looked to Steward Vast. "Pour this talented man a drink, Vast. He deserves it."

The steward eyed Alexis carefully then poured a tall glass of liquor and slid it across the table. The musician hesitated for a brief second then nodded and sat down. He looked about for a place to set his instrument, but every inch of the table was covered in spilled drink and bits of food.

"I, uh. . . ." the musician stuttered.

Steward Vast whistled loudly and an attendant appeared at his side almost instantly.

"Secure this man's instrument," Vast ordered. "Put it with my weapons and make sure it meets the same care."

"Yes, my lord," the attendant said and gently took the instrument from the musician's hands.

"What's your name?" Alexis asked as he picked up his glass and nodded for the musician to do the same.

"Clerke, sire," the musician replied. "Petro Clerke."

"Did you write that song yourself, Clerke?" Alexis asked. "That song about the Dark Minor?"

"I did, sire," Clerke nodded as he drank half his glass in one swallow.

The minor and the steward exchanged impressed looks as Clerke did not cough or sputter from the strong drink.

"I see you are used to your liquor," Alexis smiled.

"I am a musician, sire," Clerke grinned then finished off his glass. "I tend to spend my time in places of drink and merriment."

"Bars and whorehouses, he means," Vast said.

"Yes, I am familiar with where musicians perform, Vast," Alexis responded, rolling his eyes. "I am a minor and do spend my whole life around these sorry louts."

There were several shouts of feigned insult from the men close enough to overhear the Minor. Alexis responded with two middle fingers and the hall erupted into cheers and applause.

"More drink then?" Alexis asked as he held a pitcher over Clerke's empty glass.

"As much as you are willing to pour, sire," Clerke smiled. "Although, I warn you I have yet to find my fill."

"Is that so?" Alexis laughed. "Now I have a reason to be here."

"Sire?" Clerke frowned as he lifted the refilled glass. "This celebration is in your honor. Is that not reason enough?"

"The minor doesn't like to be fussed over," Vast said as he leaned back and kicked his boots up onto the table. "He is a modest royal."

"I have heard of those, just never seen one in the wild," Clerke said, draining his second glass and taking the liberty of refilling it himself. "If I may ask, sire, what is your new reason for being here?"

"The challenge of drinking you under the table, Bard Clerke," Alexis smiled, drained his glass, refilled it, and drained it again. "That seems reason enough."

"I'll drink to that," Clerke said, drained his glass, refilled it.

"Yes, you will," Alexis nodded, drained his glass, refilled it.

"Helios," Vast frowned. "This could get ugly."

"Isn't that the point?" Clerke asked, drained his glass, refilled it.

*

"So I say, I'd rather eat a grendt's rotten shit vent than put my cock back in you!" Clerke slurred, his arm draped across Alexis's shoulders. "That's what I told her!"

"So, you left?" Alexis asked, spilling more liquor onto the table than he got into his glass.

"Left? Fuck no!" Clerke yelled. "I tossed her back on the bed, flipped her over, and then put it right up her—"

The doors to the grand hall flew open and in walked five figures, all covered in blood and dirt.

Only a couple of heads were lifted at the noise as most of the soldiers that remained in the hall were passed out on tables and the floor, many half clothed from the second half of the celebration when the professional women arrived. Those heads that were lifted took quick glances at the bloody figures then fell back down into their drunken slumber.

"Well, fuck, looks like we missed the party," Natalie said, the lead figure of the group. She walked by a table and slapped a man's naked ass as hard as she could, but he didn't stir. "And what a party it looks like it was."

"Nats!" Alexis shouted and waved his sister over to his table. "You're alive!"

"Just barely," Natalie said as she shoved a man out of a chair and took it for herself. The man awoke and started to protest then saw who he was protesting against and chose to pass back out right on the floor. "We were ambushed."

"Helios, are you injured?" Alexis asked, an edge in his voice that countered his drunkenness. "Your men?"

"She looks in good form," Clerke said, pouring several glasses of drink and shoving them towards Natalie and the four men that stole seats from other unconscious men. "More than good form, if you ask me."

"Watch yourself, Clerke," Alexis said, wagging a finger at the bard. "We may have bonded tonight, but you are talking about my sister and a minoress of Station Aelon. Show some respect." Alexis leaned close to Natalie. "He's a musician, be careful."

"I know, Brother," Natalie said as she killed her glass and held it out for Clerke to refill. "Petro Clerke, the Maestro of the Lower Decks."

"At your service, my lady," Clerke said.

"The Lower Decks?" Alexis asked, looking at Clerke. "Is this so?"

"Don't judge me for my heritage, sire," Clerke said then rolled up his left trouser leg and knocked on the metal leg that appeared. "And I won't judge you for yours."

Alexis looked at the prosthetic and frowned. "Why would you judge me for that?"

"He lost his leg when Mother put down Jaeg," Natalie said. "Seriously, Brother, read something other than just battle plans and prime maps."

"Was it a royal guard that did that?" Alexis asked.

"It was a stray particle barb," Clerke shrugged and pulled his trouser leg back down. "Safe to say it was from the Royal Guard, but I hold no ill will towards the crown."

"Good to know," Alexis said. "My apologies for your loss."

"You did not fire the barb, sire, so no apology needed," Clerke said. "I am the one who should apologize for not showing proper courtesy." He refilled Natalie's glass then took a short bow. "It is my honor to be in the presence of such a beautiful young woman."

"Young is the operative word, Clerke," Alexis said. "She is only fifteen."

"I'm almost seventeen, A," Natalie corrected. "Learn to keep track."

"Almost seventeen?" Alexis asked. "Then that makes me what? Twenty-two?"

"It does at that," Natalie said, her eyes locked on to Clerke. "Since we are sharing, Petro, how old are you?"

"Please call me Clerke," Clerke said. "I've never liked the name Petro."

"I'll call you what I choose," Natalie smirked. "Clerke."

"Of course," Clerke smirked back. "And to answer you, my lady, I have recently turned twenty."

"Recently?" Alexis asked.

"Yes, as of two hours ago," Clerke said. "Today is my birthday."

"Well, happy birthday!" Alexis called out. "We should sing for you!"

"So accomplished for someone so young," Natalie interrupted before Alexis could begin to sing.

"I could say the same for you," Clerke responded. "What is this about an ambush?"

"My lady?" one of Natalie's men interrupted, his eyes locked onto a naked and still very conscious woman that was waving to him from across the hall. "I believe the boys and I will retire for the night to get cleaned up and tend to our wounds."

"Make sure she tends to more than your wounds, Buck," Natalie laughed. "And find one for each of you. Do not share a whore. That's disgusting."

"Aye, my lady," Buck smiled as he stood up and bowed to Alexis. "Dark Minor, it has been an honor."

"The honor is mine, Buck," Alexis nodded then looked at the other three men. "Lang, Jay, Baise, I wish you a good night. Do everything I would do and more."

"We aim to, my lord," Baise chuckled as he looked about for a woman of his own.

"I recommend the brunette in the far corner," Clerke suggested. "She seemed to have paced herself this evening."

"Thank you," Baise nodded. "I appreciate the heads-up."

"If I can't serve on the battlefield then I can at least serve in the drinking hall," Clerke said, smacking his hand against his metal leg. He waited until the men were gone then looked at the minoress. "So, what is this about an ambush?"

"Oh, nothing," Natalie said, waving him off. "My team and I were hunting down some guerilla fighters made up of Vape miners and commoners. What we found was a troop of Thraenish soldiers, ready with their blades out. They thought they could take us."

"And how many of these Thraenish soldiers were there?" Clerke asked.

"Why does it matter?" Natalie asked. "They're dead now."

"I like to hear tales of the war," Clerke replied. "The better the tale, the better the song I can write."

Natalie leaned across the table. "And you would like to write of how I cut down thirty men with my longsling? Will that make for a better song?"

"Thirty men?" Clerke laughed. "That's how many you and your men killed? Just the five of you?"

"That's how many men I killed," Natalie said, taking the pitcher from Clerke's hand and filling her glass. "Buck killed just as many. The others were a little slow and only killed around twenty each."

Clerke looked to Alexis, disbelief on his face. Alexis only shrugged.

"If she says she killed thirty men by herself, then she killed thirty men by herself," Alexis smiled. "I've seen her kill more; I've seen her kill less."

"Then the stories are true," Clerke said, taking the pitcher back from Natalie. "Astounding. I've always hesitated in writing a song about you, my lady. I was afraid the crowds wouldn't believe, even with my reputation for aggrandizement."

"The stories are more than true," Natalie said. "All of them."

"All of them?" Clerke grinned.

"All of them," Natalie said again.

"All of them? What does that mean?" Alexis asked. "What other stories are there?"

"I couldn't comment on that, sire," Clerke said, his eyes locked onto Natalie. "It wouldn't be appropriate."

"It wouldn't?" Alexis said then looked at Natalie who was busy locking eyes with Clerke as well. "Nats? What stories?"

"You don't want to know, Brother," Natalie said. "It would break your image of me and shatter that innocent brain of yours."

"Oh, sweet Helios," Alexis sighed. "Say no more." Then he turned and smacked Clerke in the chest. "And you look no more! She is too young for you!"

"Please," Natalie said. "I've had much older."

Alexis coughed and sputtered, spewing liquor across the table. "Nats!"

"I'm a Teirmont, Brother," Natalie said. "We're good at two things: fighting and fucking."

"Dear Parent...." Alexis sighed. "I need more to drink."

"I need to get showered," Natalie said as she stood up and started lifting pitchers from the table until she found one that was full. Her eyes went to Clerke once again. "Care to help get the blood from my hard to reach places?"

"That is quite possibly the most disgusting and erotic come on I have ever heard," Clerke smiled as he stood. "It would be my honor."

"It will be your death if you take one step out of this hall with my sister!" Alexis cried. "Too far, bard! Too far!"

"Oh, he hasn't even begun to go too far," Natalie said and walked off. She stopped a few feet from the grand hall doors and looked over her shoulder. "Coming, Clerke?"

Clerke looked at Alexis then at Natalie. "We are never more alive than when we stare directly into the face of death."

"Oh, fuck off and go," Alexis said. "Like I can stop my sister from anything."

"Now you're learning, A," Natalie laughed as she waited for Clerke to catch up.

The two left the grand hall and the minor realized he was the only man still conscious in the whole room. Natalie's men had already left with their companion choices and all of the Aelish soldiers were busy snoring into their spilled drink or into the naked laps of passed out whores.

"Well, shit," Alexis said. "I guess I am the party now." He raised his glass. "To the party of one!"

"My lord?" a voice asked from behind him. "May I join the party of one? Or is alone your true intent?"

Alexis spun about in his chair and found himself looking at a woman of immense beauty. She was tall and lithe with almost white hair and striking green eyes. Dressed in a slight skirt and an even slighter blouse, the woman smiled at Alexis, a pitcher of drink in one hand and a glass in her other.

"I don't remember seeing you earlier?" Alexis said.

"I did not make myself available earlier," the woman said. "I was waiting."

"Waiting?" Alexis asked.

The woman moved and sat down next to Alexis, topped off his glass then filled her own. She clinked her rim to his then drained her glass and set it gracefully down on the table.

"Waiting for you, my lord," the woman said.

"I didn't know whores were allowed to wait," Alexis replied then his eyes went wide and he held out his hands. "I apologize, miss. How rude of me to say. I automatically assumed when I had no reason to."

"I didn't know royals apologized to whores," the woman laughed. "I guess we have both learned something new."

Alexis smiled at the woman and took her hand in his. "What is your name?"

"Breen," the woman replied.

"Breen? Like the crop?" Alexis chuckled.

"It is what my parents named me," Breen shrugged. "We don't get to pick our names."

"Tell me about it," Alexis sighed. "I certainly wouldn't have picked mine."

"Alexis? It is such a powerful name," Breen said.

"No, no, I mean the Dark Minor," Alexis replied.

"Oh, well, that is even more powerful," Breen said as her free hand slid under the table and between Alexis's legs. "But that is not all that is powerful with you."

Alexis laughed long and hard at those words and Breen drew back.

"You mock me?" Breen asked then stood up. "I have made a mistake. I should not have waited. It was silly of me to—"

"No, please, sit," Alexis said. "Hold on. Don't sit."

"Oh, well then," Breen glared. "I will take my leave."

"That's not what I mean," Alexis said as he stood up and moved close to her. He leaned in and kissed her softly on the lips. "I mean that there's no need to sit when we are leaving this hall for more private quarters."

"Are we, my lord?" Breen asked, still unsure.

"We are," Alexis said. "We most certainly are."

*

The salty taste of sweat, the heat of flesh on flesh, the groans and cries of effort and longing.

The two rolled across the floor, clothes long since discarded, drink long since finished, their bodies on, around, in each other. Hands found legs, ran up to buttocks then backs, gripped muscle, pressed and pushed. Hips thrust and pounded, moving fast then slow, fast then slow, joined, never parting.

Mouth found mouth, found neck, found breast and nipple. Mouth opened wide, gasped, close to screaming. Mouth found mouth once again.

A hand on a belly. A hand tracing muscle and scars.

A hand on a belly. A hand tracing muscle and lotioned, scented skin.

Hands moving lower, feeling the strength of muscle, feeling the strength of where the bodies were joined.

Bodies rolling, a body riding. A body lifted, a body shaking, shaking, releasing. A body relaxing, falling forward, lying gently onto the other.

"That...." Breen gasped. "Did you...?"

"Not yet," Alexis said.

"Let me," Breen said as she slowly, carefully lifted and fell, lifted and fell.

"I shouldn't," Alexis said.

"You should," Breen said, lifting and falling faster then faster until the body under her shuddered and Alexis gasped with that pleasurable pain all men wait for. "You did."

"Shit," Alexis laughed. "I guess I did."

The two lay there on the floor, the sweat cooling on their bodies as they drifted into sleep. Just before his conscious mind left him, Alexis reached out and found a stray blanket, covering them both, content and happy.

*

"When are you going to find someone?" Natalie asked, her hands resting on the railing of the royal cutter's stern. The protective dome shield shimmered before her and she ignored it as she focused her attention on the roiling waves of the gas sea the ship cut through. "You have the pick of the System. And considering Mother plucked Father from the ranks of the Burdened, it's not like you are required to wed royalty or nobility."

"It's not so easy, Nats," Alexis said.

"Sure it is," Natalie laughed. "I found my mate. Found him and claimed him. Haven't let him leave since."

"Clerke is different," Alexis said. "He's a romantic. He doesn't see you as a minoress or as a warrior. He sees you as a woman of legend. You're his muse."

"You may have that backwards," Natalie sighed. "I sometimes think he's mine."

"Is that a bad thing?" Alexis asked. "He's an artist. What more is there to fight for than art and love?"

"Whoa, whoa, whoa, who said anything about love?" Natalie responded.

"Nats, it's been what? Three years since you met?" Alexis laughed. "Even after Mother tried to forbid your relationship, you still stuck with him, fought for him, refused to give in."

"Yeah, because she was wrong," Natalie said. "What does she have against musicians?"

"I think it was more the content of the songs he creates than the fact he creates them," Alexis said. "Did he really have to compare her to an unstoppable Vape storm? That wasn't very nice."

"I thought it fit her perfectly," Natalie laughed. "And I came up with that second verse."

"I know," Alexis said. "It was pretty obvious. You sure don't make it easy for any of us."

"Not my job to make it easy, Brother," Natalie said. "It's my job to kill Thraens in the name of Station Aelon. I'm a twenty-year-old minoress who has blood perpetually crusted under her fingernails. I've been fighting a war for most of my life. If a man accepts me for who I am and also writes songs about me, then I'm a fool to let him get away."

"But you don't love him?" Alexis asked.

"I probably do. I don't know," Natalie said and cast her eyes up to the Vape clouds above. "Mother and Father have such a certain love, destined by fate. How do I compare what I have with Clerke to that?"

"Now you see my dilemma," Alexis said, looking up as well. "Vape storm might be brewing."

"Might be," Natalie said. "And don't change the subject."

"Why are we on this subject anyway?" Alexis asked. "This is our time of glory, Nats. Two days at the BOP then we push on across Thraen Prime to their Castle Thraen. We take that and the conflict is over. We take what is ours by birth."

"I know," Nats said. "Then what? You want to know why I'm asking about love, A? Because when we take that castle, then we are unemployed. Our parents will expect us to settle down. Diplomacy will be our new vocation, not butchery."

"You call what we do butchery?" Alexis asked.

"What else would I call it?" Natalie shrugged. "Show no mercy, right?"

"I suppose so," Alexis said. "Unemployed? You can't think that. Our men will still need leaders. Our forces will always need to be at the ready. The conflict will be far from done."

"That's what the Order of Jex is for," Natalie said. "They'll oversee everything once this is over. We move on to our marriage and baby-making days."

"Helios, Nats, what a thought," Alexis laughed. "Baby-making days? Are we to go from being warriors to breeders?"

"I sometimes wonder if I'm not the older sibling," Natalie said. "Your innocence is confounding."

"So, you'd make babies with Clerke?" Alexis chuckled. "Those children wouldn't know whether to sing or fight."

"They'll probably do both," Natalie said. "Why limit them? And I never said Clerke would be the father."

"You torture that man to no end," Alexis said.

The two siblings stood there for a minute, silent with the thoughts of the future and their roles in the royal hierarchy.

"You haven't ever had someone you wanted almost more than life itself?" Natalie asked.

"You have it so bad for Clerke, just admit it," Alexis smiled.

"Stop turning this onto me. I'm asking about you," Natalie said. "And shut the fuck up about Clerke."

"There may have been someone," Alexis shrugged. "But I haven't seen her in years. We had a week together and then she was gone."

"A week together?" Natalie asked. "When was that?"

"The same time you and Clerke met," Alexis said. "You were so wrapped up with him that you didn't even notice I wasn't around."

"Helios, those first days," Natalie sighed. "We were a lot more than wrapped up. I do have to say that Clerke has been good for my flexibility."

"No, Nats, just no," Alexis grimaced. "I do not need to hear about your sexual calisthenics with the bard."

"Whatever," Natalie said. "So, tell me about this woman? Who was she? A noble's daughter? A commoner perhaps? Was she a miner's daughter? Clerke has written a hundred ballads about miners' daughters and their failed attempts at love."

"I guess he knows a lot about miners' daughters then," Alexis said and quickly stepped away as Natalie took a swing at him. "I'm kidding, I'm kidding! He would never stray from you! The man values his privates too much!"

"Damn right he does," Natalie said. "And stop deflecting. Tell me about her."

"No," Alexis said. "It was a long time ago. I haven't seen her since."

"Did you look for her?" Natalie asked.

"I tried, but it wasn't easy considering. . . ." Alexis frowned.

"Considering? Considering what?" Natalie asked.

Alexis hesitated. "Considering her profession."

"Her profession? Why would that...? Oh. She was a professional woman," Natalie smiled. "Good for you, A. I didn't think you had a character low enough to go for a slice of prime trash."

"She wasn't trash," Alexis said. "And this is why I haven't ever talked about her. You asked if I ever cared for someone and when I tell you who it is you mock me and belittle her station in life."

"Calm your quivering ass cheeks, A," Natalie said. "I'm not mocking you. I was actually complimenting you. You were born on a pedestal, Brother. It's good for you to willingly step down once in a while. Trust me, I live down here. The view is not so bad."

"Ha!" Alexis laughed. "You don't think you're on a pedestal as well? Every man under our command would die for you. They already kill for you. And your team? If Clerke wasn't so Clerke, I am pretty sure Buck, Jay, Baise and Lang would have slit his throat by now so they could have a shot with you."

"That song has been written, as Clerke likes to remind me," Natalie said. "Mother and Father are the tale of the warrior minoress and her soldier love. But get back to your lady that got away. What if you could find her? What would you do?"

"Nothing," Alexis replied. "She's moved on by now. I was just another client to her, I'm sure."

"Did you pay her?" Natalie asked.

"Well. . .no," Alexis admitted.

"Did you give her any gifts of value? Did you make her any promises?" Natalie pressed.

"No and no," Alexis said.

"And she left after a week and hasn't contacted you since? No asking for money or threatening to blackmail you with your indiscretion?" Natalie asked.

"Was it an indiscretion?" Alexis asked.

"You are the Dark Minor, heir to the crown of Station Aelon and its Prime," Natalie said, shaking her head. "The meeting of stewards would see it as a scandalous indiscretion, even if you tried to justify it as a soldier's prerogative during times of war on the primes. You know how conservative those grouchy bastards are."

"Well, that doesn't matter because she never tried to use our time together against me," Alexis said. "She just left."

"Maybe she left for the station," Natalie said. 'That could be why you never found her down here."

"Maybe," Alexis sighed. "Doesn't really matter now."

"Damn, A, she broke your fucking heart," Natalie said. "You really should have confided in me. I'm kind of hurt you didn't."

"You were busy with Clerke and your team," Alexis said. "And I was busy helping Mother wage war. Still am. Both of us." Alexis clapped his hands and turned away from the bow. "Come on, time to suit up. We'll be at the Thraen Prime coast in a couple of minutes. I want our time at the BOP as short as possible so we can get our men to that castle."

"Now you're talking about something we both agree on," Natalie grinned. "Time to kill some more fucking Thraens! Helios, I love this job!"

*

"It is your job and duty as a minor of Station Aelon to be wed to another royal in order to strengthen ties and keep the peace in the System," High Guardian Victor the Eighth snapped, his eyes locked onto the visibly upset Alexis who paced back and forth at the far end of The Way's reception room. "Stop moving, for Helios's sake! You are making me nauseous! And why are you still wearing your armor, boy? Do you expect an attack within The Way?"

"A? Please calm yourself and sit," Mistress Alexis said, her voice filled with the same regret that was on her husband Kel's face. "This has been decided and there is no stopping it."

"And why would you want to, boy?" Master Lionel of Station Thraen, but no longer it's prime, asked. "Is my Rebecca not the picture of beauty and grace? All the available men in the System would sell their souls to have her."

"Careful, master," Victor growled. "I will not tolerate blasphemy today."

"Yet you tolerate this marriage to go forth. It is blasphemy of love," Kel mumbled. Mistress Alexis reached out and gripped his hand. "Sorry."

"The joining of the bloodlines of Station Aelon with Station Thraen is the only solution I can see to ending this conflict once and for all. With this marriage, the minor and minoress will reside here on Helios and oversee their primes as royal regents. Many lives will be saved with this union, Master Kel," Victor responded, spitting out Kel's title with barely contained contempt. "But, I do not expect a man who does not know his own parentage to understand the complexities involved."

"You should be careful what you say to my husband, Victor," Mistress Alexis snapped. "I have proven that even the Burdened cannot stop me."

"That has been years," Victor replied. "and while the Burdened were under my predecessor's administration. I can assure you that the Burdened you see now are superior soldiers and guards to that lot. You can thank your own actions for that."

"Only way to know is to have them try," Mistress Alexis said and started to stand up, her hand on the hilt of the short blade on her belt.

"Mother, stop," Alexis said. He quit his pacing and walked over to the four royals seated before the High Guardian. His eyes found the young Minoress Rebecca of Station Thraen. "Walk with me, please. Let us discuss this between us before my Mother slits a throat, whether it is the High Guardian's or your father's."

The Minoress Rebecca turned in her seat and looked at her father for silent permission. She was a woman that had all the dark features of the Thraenish royals. Except for her golden eyes, which blinked repeatedly in a nervous tick as she waited for her father to give his consent.

"You may walk with the boy," Lionel said. "But our guards will follow them closely."

"I would prefer we speak in private," Alexis said. "No harm will come to her, I guarantee that. She is safe by my side."

"Oh, is she?" Lionel scoffed. "You wear battle armor within the walls of The Way and expect me to believe that my daughter will be safe with you? Do you find me to be a fool, boy?"

"Call him boy one more time and you will find yourself gutted and begging for mercy," Mistress Alexis growled. "My son is a *man* of honor and integrity. Something that a Thraen like you could never understand."

"I will be fine, Father," Rebecca said. "Let me walk with him. We should talk in private if we are to be wed."

"Fine," Lionel barked. "Go and talk with the...minor. Get to know each other." He pointed a finger at his daughter then at Alexis. "But know that this marriage will happen. Do not conspire otherwise."

"Of course, Father," Rebecca said as she stood then turned to her future husband. "I believe we both know what our duties are in life. Isn't that right, Dark Minor?"

"Do not call him that!" Lionel barked. "You are his equal in standing and superior in breeding!"

"That does it," Mistress Alexis snapped as she stood and drew her short blade.

"Son! Go!" Kel said as he jumped up and grabbed his wife's arm. "Take Minoress Rebecca for that walk. Take as long as you need to in order to discuss your future. I'll keep your mother from killing this Thraen."

"Come," Alexis said and held out his hand to Rebecca. She took it willingly and he led her to the door. He leaned in close and whispered, "We'll get through this. Marrying you will be a welcome rest from the horrors I have witnessed. Please know that."

Rebecca gave him a small, polite smile, but did not reply.

*

The Way's main cathedral was packed with dignitaries, nobles, and royals from all of the Six Stations and their primes. Not a single seat was open and the Burdened had to stand shoulder to shoulder at the cathedral's entrance in order to keep space open for Minoress Rebecca, on her father's arm, to make her way down the aisle to her waiting groom.

"All stand!" a Gatekeeper announced and the massive room was filled with the shuffling of feet and rustling of stiff suits and gowns brought out only for the highest of occasions. "Let the Mistress Rebecca of Station Thraen be seen as she presents herself to the Minor Alexis of Station Aelon! Oh, holiest of occasions! Oh, holiest of unions! Praise be to Helios the Dear Parent!"

"*Praise be to Helios!*" the attendees all called out.

Alexis, dressed in his own formal attire—which threatened to choke him and cut off circulation to all of his extremities—stood at the front of the cathedral and waited patiently as his bride walked to him, taking six careful steps at a time, then pausing to honor the System that Helios created. He tried desperately to catch Rebecca's eye, but she kept her gaze unfocused and neutral, waiting until the very last few feet to finally connect.

"Who gives this most holy ordained woman to this most holy ordained man?" the High Guardian Victor the Eighth asked in a bellowing voice for all to hear. "Is it you, Master Lionel of Station Thraen?"

"It is I, High Guardian," Lionel replied and reluctantly let go of his daughter. He gave a quick glare to Alexis then turned crisply and walked to his seat.

"Then let it be known that the most holy ordained woman before me has been given freely by her father," Victor announced. "Before Helios the Dear Parent, you all bear witness to this act of courage, duty, and piety. Let it be said now that the Minoress Rebecca is standing before us under her own power until she gives that power and will to her husband. Praise be to Helios!"

"*Praise be to Helios!*" the attendees parroted.

"Please join hands," Victor said to the minor and minoress. "I shall begin the litany of vows passed down through the millennia from the first monarchs of the Six Stations. Listen, one and all, as we remember why these most holy ordained royals are before us. Listen well!"

The High Guardian droned on for close to an hour, but Alexis never let his attention wander from the words the man said. He listened closely to each and every vow that had come before him, taking in the history of marriages between minors and minoresses, hoping to gleam some insight into his own soon to be completed marriage. He listened as words of love and duty swirled around each other, sometimes intertwined, sometimes completely separate.

Staring into the golden eyes of his bride, Alexis honestly couldn't tell what meaning his words would have when it came to his turn to add his vows to the litany. Would they be only duty or would there also be love in there? How would he be remembered when his vows were repeated to future royals that found themselves standing where he stood? Would the fear that threatened to knock his legs out from under him be evident? Or would the strength he fought to find in his soul be what the future betrothed heard?

"Minor Alexis?" Victor asked. "Will you now say your most holy words to the witnesses that are seated before us today? Will you now say your most holy words before Helios and all the Dear Parent represents?"

"I will," Alexis replied and cleared his throat. He wanted more than ever to look over at his family, to see the faces of his mother, father, sister, and brother. But he restrained himself and kept his focus on the woman before him, the woman whose hands he held firmly, but gently.

Alexis had prepared for days the words he would speak, spending hours memorizing every single line, every single nuance and cadence. But as he opened his mouth he realized all that preparation had left him. Not a word remained in his conscious mind. Panic started to rise, but he stamped it down and took a deep breath.

"Minoress Rebecca, you honor me more than you can ever know," Alexis said, his voice thick with emotion. "What you do today takes courage that is rarely seen, it takes courage that only the most battle hardened understand. So I say these words, all to honor the person that you are and the standing you come from. I swear before Helios the Dear Parent, that as long as I live I will fight for your safety, for your honor, and for your love. I have proven myself on the battlefield, but now I must prove myself in your heart. I give my own heart to you as proof of my sincerity. It no longer resides in my chest, but in your hands. It is yours forever."

The cathedral was silent for several seconds before the High Guardian leaned in close to the betrothed. "Is that all?" Victor asked. "Do you not have at least another dozen paragraphs to recite?"

"Is there more that needs to be said?" Alexis asked.

"No," Rebecca replied, a tear threatening to spill from one of her golden eyes. "May I say my vows now, High Guardian?"

Many attendees gasped at the minoress's breaking of the marriage customs and protocols. None of those from Station Aelon gasped, though. Instead they smiled as they realized they were receiving a minoress that might fit in perfectly with their unconventional, and often scoffed at, ways.

"Please, Minoress Rebecca, say your own vows," Victor frowned. "I trust they are more suited to tradition than the minor's."

Rebecca began to recite the written vows she had memorized. She said every line with a flat intonation, no different than if she had been reciting a recipe for gelberry tarts, or reading aloud instructions on assembling a piece of furniture.

Until she came to the end.

"Minor Alexis, your legend is known throughout the System," Rebecca stated. "There are tales and songs about the Dark Minor and his many triumphs on the battlefield. Not a steward, sector warden, deck boss, or common soldier on any of the stations or primes would dispute the warrior that you are. This, despite your honest humility, is something I am sure you know. But what you do not know is what the women of this System say. It is not your skill with your famed longsling or your skill as a bladesman that we have cared about, but the stories of your kindness, your capacity for fairness, and most of all, as you proved with your own vows to me this day, it is your open heart that has been the late night dreams of every woman, from royal to passenger, that is the true legend. As I hold your hands in mine, and feel their strength, I know in my very soul that it is that legend that I marry today, not the one of blood and triumph, but the one of courage and compassion."

The sounds of blown noses and stifled sniffles filled the cathedral as the minoress's words echoed through the chamber.

"Thank you, Rebecca," Alexis smiled and bowed his head. "I will strive to live up to the legend you speak of. It will be my true vow from this moment on."

The High Guardian cleared his throat and launched into the final portion of the ceremony. After another hour had passed he raised his staff and rapped it on the floor six times before declaring, "Let it be said under the authority of The Way and Helios the Dear Parent that these two persons are now married! Let them proceed from this cathedral as man and wife!"

Alexis and Rebecca turned and faced the attendees, all of whom had stood and begun to cheer. The newlyweds stepped from the dais and walked down the aisle, their hands gripping each other's, both hoping to find the courage they needed for their life ahead.

CHAPTER THREE

The two royals sat on the skid, their environmental suits keeping the Vape gas that drifted here and there across the breen fields from igniting oxygen in their blood and liquifying their bodies. Life on the primes was harsh and brutal, whether a person was of royal or common blood. Vape did not care one way or the other.

Minoress Rebecca worried at the collar that clasped her helmet to the body of her suit and Alexis had to reach out for the tenth or eleventh time to get her to stop.

"You do not want to accidentally undo that, dear," Alexis said. "We are far enough away from Castle Aelon that if something were to happen, I do not know if even I could drive us back in time."

"Which is why I did not want to come out today, Alexis," Rebecca replied. "You know I do not enjoy being out in the open. I prefer the safety of the shields back at the castle. Why did you insist on bringing me out here?"

"Look about you, dear," Alexis said and swept his hand across the landscape. "Look at them work. This is the apex of the breen harvest. All of these workers cutting, sifting, sorting. Isn't it amazing to think that the very material your environmental suit is made from started with all of this."

Alexis smiled as he gazed upon the hundreds of commoners who were busy harvesting the almost infinite breen that stood tall in the wind and Vape gas. Sharp blades whooshed one way then the other, taking down large swathes of the crop in a couple of strokes. A few heads turned to study the royals, but most stayed on task, knowing they had quotas to fill in order to get enough credits to keep up the meager existence they were used to.

"Switch your com channel to open, dear," Alexis said. "You can hear them talking to each other, coordinating their work to achieve the most efficiency. It all has such a rhythm compared to the Thraenish industry of Vape mining."

"I wouldn't watch that either," Rebecca said. "Can we please go back to the castle?"

"We have lived on the primes for a year now," Alexis sighed. "Yet you know nothing of the land."

"I do not need to, Alexis," Rebecca replied. "We have managers for that. Just as we have managers for the Vape mines on Thraen Prime. Your love of the prime is not regal behavior."

"It's not Tharenish behavior, you mean," Alexis said. "We Aelish have always been connected with our prime. As our children should be."

"That is not fair," Rebecca whispered. "Not fair at all, Alexis. Do not be cruel."

"Oh, my dear, it was not my intention to be cruel," Alexis said as he wrapped his arm about his wife's suited shoulder. "I was only suggesting we try again."

"We have our duty, I know," Rebecca said.

"It is not just that," Alexis said. "I miss your bed."

Rebecca was silent for a while.

"You could always take a lover," she said finally. "It is traditional with Thraenish monarchs. Helios knows that many have had more than their fair share of women on the side."

"That is not my way, Rebecca, and you know it," Alexis said softly.

"No, it is not," Rebecca said. "I will make you a deal, Alexis."

"A deal?" Alexis asked. "What sort of deal?"

"My bed will be your bed again," Rebecca said. "But no more forced trips out into the wilds of the primes. We travel only because we have to move from prime castle to prime castle as required by the treaty signed by our parents."

"If that was all it would take for me to get back into your bed, I never would have dragged you out here!" Alexis laughed.

"No, it wouldn't have made a difference," Rebecca said. "I wasn't ready until now. Not after losing. . . ."

"Hush, do not speak of it if it pains you," Alexis said.

"Did you ever tell your mother?" Rebecca asked.

"No, I just couldn't," Alexis replied. "If she knew of the miscarriage she'd have every physician in the system down here. Plus, royal courts are hardly places where secrets stay put. The news would have reached your father eventually and neither of us need him plotting and planning if he thinks there will not be a legitimate heir to the Aelish crown."

"My father does not plot and plan," Rebecca responded. "He has a retinue of advisors that plot and plan for him."

"Yes, I am sure he does," Alexis laughed. He fired up the hover skid's drive engine. "Now, how about we head back to the castle so I can make sure your bed is as soft as I remember it to be."

"Alexis, it's not even noon yet!" Rebecca exclaimed. "We both still have duties and appointments today."

"Appointments will be canceled," Alexis said, swinging the skid around and gunning it back towards Castle Aelon. "As for duties, there is only one on my mind at this moment."

*

Sweat dappled Rebecca's exposed skin and she shivered as the fan above the bed slowly turned.

"I'll fetch a blanket," Alexis said as he shifted and sat up. "I believe they all fell off the foot of the bed."

"No, don't," Rebecca said, her hand clutching his arm. "Just warm me with your heat. You Teirmonts burn hot."

"That we do," Alexis smiled as he pulled his wife close and enveloped her in his arms. "And being my wife, my heat is your heat."

Rebecca kissed his chest and sighed, nuzzling her face against him. "You have the temperament of a philosopher, Alexis, not of a warrior and killer."

"I hope my killer days are done," Alexis said. "I have lost my appetite for it."

"What about your sister? Do you miss being by her side in battle?" Rebecca asked.

"I don't think the subject of my sister by my side is appropriate when I am lying naked with my wife, having just made love," Alexis chuckled "But, to answer your question, yes, I do miss her sometimes. Now she has her own life, though, traveling the System with Clerke while he entertains the royal courts and nobles' estate houses with his songs."

"Travel, travel, travel," Rebecca said. "You Teirmonts need to learn to stay put. I'd rather just be here in the castle."

"I'd rather just be here in bed with you," Alexis said. He pulled his wife on top of him and kissed her hard.

"Alexis," she giggled. "Again?"

"We Teirmonts burn hot," Alexis laughed.

"Yes, I can feel that," Rebecca said.

There was a quiet knock at their bedchamber door.

"Ignore it," Alexis whispered. "It can't be more important than this."

The knock came again, but more insistent.

"They aren't going away," Rebecca said.

The knock grew louder and faster.

"What?" Alexis shouted.

The door opened slightly and the face of one of Alexis's attendants appeared. "My lord, there is urgent news from Station Aelon. You are being summoned to the communications room at once."

"Summoned?" Rebecca asked. "By whom?"

"Mistress Alexis," the attendant replied. "She is waiting, my lord, and you must hurry before the planet's rotation cuts off the signal."

"Helios," Alexis said as he gently shifted out from under his wife. "This can't be good. Where are my damn trousers?"

"On that chair," Rebecca said then looked at the attendant. "Have you seen enough, young man? Would you like me to stand and parade about for you?"

"My apologies, my lady!" the attendant exclaimed and shut the door quickly.

"I'll see what it is and be right back," Alexis said as he buttoned his trousers.

"You need a shirt, dear," Rebecca said.

"No time," Alexis replied as he hurried to the door. "Wait right there. If it's nothing then I want to continue exactly where we left off."

"And if it is something?" Rebecca asked.

"Then your body might prove the perfect distraction for a troubled mind," Alexis smiled and left.

*

"Nats! Nats, over here!" Alexis shouted across the great hall as his sister entered, Clerke on her arm. "Nats!"

Natalie smiled and rushed over to her brother. The two royals embraced fiercely as Clerke stood awkwardly off to the side. They held each other in their arms for several minutes, causing many in the great hall to grow uncomfortable at the public display of emotion. When they finally drew back, they both had tears streaming down their faces.

"Have you spoken to Mother yet?" Natalie asked, wiping at her eyes. "I just got off the shuttle from Klaerv and haven't even had a chance to go to the royal quarters."

"She's handling it," Alexis smiled weakly. "Father is there for her."

"I can't believe Grandmother is gone," Natalie said. "I honestly thought that woman would outlive us all, even Mother."

Alexis frowned and studied his sister. "She didn't tell you, did she?" he asked. "You didn't know?"

"Tell me what, A?" Natalie asked, holding her hand out to Clerke. The bard moved quickly and took it then wrapped himself about the minoress. "What didn't Mother tell me?"

"Grandmother has been sick for months," Alexis said. "She kept it from Mother, but it got so bad there was no hiding it anymore."

"Sick? Sick with what?" Natalie asked.

"The physicians aren't sure," Alexis said. "Mother says fate finally caught up to Grandmother. That it stole her last years just as she stole Grandfather's last years by allying with Beumont."

"Helios, that's cold," Natalie sighed. "I know Mother and Grandmother had their issues over the years, but even Mother can't believe that."

"I doubt she does," Alexis said. "Grief can cloud judgment and make many say things they never truly mean."

"Or it makes many say things they've never had a chance to say before," Clerke interjected.

"Mother has never been shy in saying what she means, especially when it comes to Grandmother," Natalie smirked. "So I don't think it's that."

"She's only being Mother and going straight for the most overdramatic reaction she can," Alexis said. "She'll come to some understanding with fate and everything will be alright again, as usual. She just has to work it all out. That Teirmont fire."

"Yes, the Teirmont fire," Clerke smirked. "I have become intimately familiar with it."

Natalie rolled her eyes. "I believe my lover here was expecting a silent groupie who would hang on his every note and just wait backstage while he entertained the undergarments off the crying throngs of teen girls who have become his most ardent fans."

"You actually expected that?" Alexis chuckled. "This is the minoress of the Slaughter of the Storm. Ten thousand Thraens were butchered by our longslingers while she stood by my side on that castle wall."

"Yes, I am well aware of that," Clerke said. "Which is why I can't get a booking on Station Thraen or its prime. Apparently, the Thraens aren't too happy with my choice of companion."

"You can't even get a booking on the prime?" Alexis asked. "Why didn't you contact me? I'm the minor of Thraen Prime. One word from me and you have your choice of venue."

"It doesn't matter what venue I have," Clerke replied. "If there are no fans to fill it then there's no point in booking it. The Thraens want nothing to do with me as long as Natalie is on my arm."

"I believe you are on my arm, love," Natalie said. "I'm the royal here, not you."

"Depends on which station we're on," Clerke grinned.

"And we are on Station Aelon, so I own your ass," Natalie said and kissed him quickly. "Isn't he adorable when he tries to assert his manhood?"

"He's something, that's for sure," Alexis chuckled briefly before his eyes caught sight of the latest group to enter the great hall. All mirth was wiped from his face instantly. "Speaking of Thraens."

Natalie and Clerke turned around just as the delegation from Station Thraen was announced to the hall. A group of Thraenish nobles were led by a striking young man and young woman, both dressed in the very latest fashion of bright, vibrant colors; he in striped trousers with a layered, shaow leather doublet; she in an ornately patterned gown that ran from just under her chin all the way to the floor.

"Prancers," Natalie scoffed. "Look at them. This is a funeral, not a fashion show."

"I'm surprised Thraen even sent anyone," Alexis said.

"Grandmother was a minoress of Station Thraen," Natalie said. "Although I think she had more blood in common with Clerke than these impostors."

"You really can't stand Thraen, can you?" Clerke said, turning to Alexis. "That must be rough on your marriage."

"My wife and I feel slightly used and abandoned by both our stations," Alexis admitted. "It has brought us together."

"Oh, please, now who's being overdramatic?" Natalie laughed. "Abandoned, my ass. Oh, shit, here they come."

"Cousins!" the young Thraen called as he and the rest of the Thraens made their way through the milling groups of nobles and emissaries. "Minor Alexis! Minoress Natalie! How good to see you!"

"Is it?" Natalie snapped. "Our grandmother has died."

"My brother meant no offense, minoress," the young woman said. "George is always forgetful of others' feelings at these sorts of things." She turned her eyes on Clerke and appraised him up and down. "And who is this handsome fellow? He looks strangely familiar."

"Petro Clerke," Alexis said. "May I introduce you to my brother-in-law and sister-in-law, the twins, Minor George and Minoress Georgia of station Thraen."

"And its prime," George sneered.

"I don't believe that is true," Alexis said.

"Petro Clerke? The famous bard?" Georgia laughed delightedly. She clapped her hands together then grabbed onto her brother's arm. "Georgie, this is the man taking the stations by storm."

"Better to take by storm than slaughter by storm," George said as he held out his hand. "A pleasure to make your acquaintance. I purchased one of your discs for my sister for Last Meal, I believe."

"I hope you enjoyed it," Clerke said as he shook the minor's hand. "My music isn't always to everyone's taste."

George looked down at the bard's hand and laughed. "The custom is to kiss the rings, bard. You do not shake a royal's hand like you are making a deal on some Middle Deck market."

"My apologies," Clerke said.

"Don't apologize, love," Natalie said. "You are used to royals slightly more approachable than the Thraens. They'd make you kiss their assholes if they could get away with it."

"Nats," Alexis warned. "Let us not start a fight on this day."

"Will you be performing?" Georgia asked Clerke. "For the service? Have you written a song specifically to honor the daughter of Thraen? The Minoress Bella Herlect Teirmont Beumont deserves nothing less."

"I was not asked to prepare a song," Clerke said, looking to Natalie. "Was I supposed to?"

"No, you were not," Natalie said. "You are here for me and my family, not to perform like a trained grendt."

"Oh, we have the most wonderful troop of trained grendts on Station Thraen," George laughed. "Their owner can have the hens lay eggs on command and the cocks will fight to the death right before your eyes. It makes a horrible mess, but what a delight to watch!"

"Sounds wonderful," Alexis said.

"So, Alexis, where is our sister?" Georgia asked. "Did she not come up to the station with you?"

"She did not," Alexis said. "She was not feeling well and is not a fan of traveling, as you know."

"Do we?" Georgia asked. "Our older sister has always been so quiet and boring that I really don't know much about her personal tastes."

"She's very un-Thraenish," George added. "Demure and polite. Never rocking the cutter. But, I guess that's why Father married her off to you. She certainly wasn't any good at court."

"No, she was not," Georgia laughed.

Clerke stepped between the royals instantly as everyone present saw Alexis's face turn red with anger.

"You never said whether you enjoyed my music, my lord," Clerke said to George. "The disc you purchased for your sister. Did you like it?"

"How would I know?" George replied, his eyes locked onto Alexis and not the bard standing before him. "I didn't buy the disc for me; I bought it for my sister. The sister that actually enjoys life. You should ask her about music. My tastes run more towards fine drink and fine girls."

"George," Georgia exclaimed with mock shock. "I thought I was the only woman in your life."

"I said fine girls, dearest sister," George said. "You are a woman. One of singular radiance and grace."

"Oh, you flatter," Georgia smiled. "He flatters."

"I can see that," Clerke said.

An awkward silence settled amongst the royals and they all stood there, staring at each other until a bell chimed and an attendant at the doors to the great hall made an announcement.

"The ceremony for the remembrance of Minoress Bella Herlect Teirmont Beumont will begin shortly," the attendant called out. "Please proceed to the main chapel where Gatekeeper Donner will perform the service. Refreshments will be served back here immediately after."

"How quaint," Georgia said. "They have to provide instructions for the lessers that don't understand how these things work." She smiled at Natalie. "Did you catch all of that, dear? Or should I have one of my ladies repeat it for you?"

Natalie instantly reached for her belt, but realized too late she did not have her blades strapped on.

"Just like the butcher of the prime to leap to violence," George said. "Come along, dear sister. Let us find our seat. I do hope it is in the front row since we are relations."

The Thraens turned and sauntered off casually, as if they were the royals of the station.

"Murdering cunt," someone in the Thraen group muttered.

"What did you say?" Alexis barked as he grabbed one of the Thraens by the arm. "Did you just call the Minoress of Station Aelon a murdering cunt?"

The man, a Thraen with an ugly scar across his nose and chin, whirled about on Alexis and spat in his face.

"I did! And you are one as well!" the Thraen shouted then pulled a short blade from inside his doublet and lashed out at Alexis.

Alexis jumped back and nearly lost his footing, but Clerke caught him and held him steady. Natalie rushed in at the attacker and slammed her fist into the man's throat then grabbed his wrist and twisted until the short blade clattered to the floor.

"Murderers! Butchers!" the man garbled. "Thraen will never forget the Slaughter of the Storm!"

"You will if your brains are spread all over the floor," Natalie said, sweeping the man's legs out from under him while still holding his wrist.

The back of the Thraen's skull was the first part of him to impact with the great hall's floor and there was a thickening thud as his skull fractured on contact. All in attendance went silent as the sound of violence echoed

REIGN OF FOUR: BOOK IV

through the hall. For a split second no one made a move then the sound of blades being drawn was almost overwhelming.

Those not of Aelish or Thraenish blood quickly retreated to the far walls of the great hall, their mouths open in shock, their eyes wide with fear of what would happen.

The members of the Order of Jex converged on Alexis and Natalie, their long blades drawn and pointed at the Thraens, who in turn all had short blades out and ready for the fight.

"Sire, make your escape out the back way," Steward Kinsmon said. "We will handle these scrim vipers."

"No one will handle anything!" Mistress Alexis roared from the doors of the great hall. She held a long blade in each hand and she pointed them at the Thraens. "Bringing weapons on board this station when all guests were specifically asked not to is an act of war. I would be within my rights to execute each and every one of you without worry of any repercussions from The Way."

"The High Guardian would never allow it!" George shouted. "He would excommunicate all of Station Aelon!"

"Would you care to find out, Minor George?" Mistress Alexis asked. "Oh, wait, how would you find out when you would be dead? Dead just like my mother, whom this day is supposed to be about. Drop your blades and I will show mercy. Keep them in your hands for one second more, and this mistress will not be held accountable for what happens next. After all, I am grief stricken and quite out of my head."

"Drop the blades, George," Georgia whispered. "The mad woman will kill us."

"I can hear you, dear," Mistress Alexis said. "The acoustics in this hall are surprisingly good."

Blades clattered to the floor and the Thraens all held their hands up by their shoulders.

"Are we to be escorted to your famed Third Spire now, mistress?" George asked. "Will we be prisoners of the Aelish crown?"

"I wouldn't dirty those cells with the likes of you," Mistress Alexis said. "Just get off my station. You may skip the memorial service and take the next shuttle back to Station Thraen." No one moved. "NOW!"

The Thraenish delegation jumped then hurried to pick up their fallen comrade. They rushed past the onlookers, around the enraged mistress who refused to move, and out into the hallway beyond. Once gone from sight, there was a collective sigh of relief.

"Are those the Thraens?" Master Kel asked as he walked into the great hall. "What happened to their man?" All eyes turned on Kel and he frowned. "Helios, what did I miss?"

"I will fill you in, sire," Clerke said as he came forward and shook Kel's hand. "I believe the Teirmonts will need to talk."

"My Love? What did you do?" Kel asked Mistress Alexis.

"Why must you always think I did something?" Mistress Alexis responded. Kel gave her a look. "Well, this time I stopped something, instead of starting it. Ask Petro while you two walk to the chapel; he'll tell you. I'm going to speak with our children."

"Very well," Kel sighed then embraced his son then daughter. "Hello, children."

"Hey, Daddy," Natalie smiled. "I missed you."

"I missed you as well," Kel said. "Talk to your mother while I walk with your man. We will meet later."

Kel and Clerke left quickly, as well as the rest of the attendees, leaving only Mistress Alexis with her son and daughter.

"Where's Richard?" Alexis asked, once they were alone. "I haven't seen him since I arrived on the station."

"Richard is off being Richard," Mistress Alexis said. "Losing his grandmother has nearly broken the boy. They were so very close, especially after what happened with the twins."

"Yes, they were close," Natalie said. "And he is not a boy, he is a young man."

"I wish that were so," Mistress Alexis said. "Your brother is, to say the least, a troubled soul. It is probably best he not attend the service."

"What is it you would like to speak to us about?" Alexis asked. "Something other than the passing of Grandmother weighs on you, I can see it."

"I am not sure now is the best time, but considering what I just witnessed, I believe we no longer have the luxury of waiting."

"Excuse me, Your Highness," an attendant said quietly from the doorway. "There is an urgent communication for the Minor Alexis."

"It will have to wait," Mistress Alexis snapped.

"It concerns the Minoress Rebecca," the attendant said. "It is from one of her physicians."

"I have to take this," Alexis said and quickly kissed his mother. "Our talk will have to wait."

He hurried from the great hall, following on the heels of the attendant, leaving Mistress Alexis and Natalie alone.

"You can still talk with me, Mother," Natalie said.

"No, no, Alexis is right," Mistress Alexis said, taking her daughter by the arm. "Our talk will have to wait."

"Are you sure? It seemed urgent," Natalie replied.

"Yes, I am sure," Mistress Alexis smiled. "I am probably rushing things, like I do. Let's forget about the talk and go say goodbye to my mother."

"Alright," Natalie said. "But you know you can always be open with me, right?"

"Of course, dearest," Mistress Alexis said and kissed her daughter's cheek. "We Teirmonts are always open. Secrets fight fate and we would never want to fight fate."

*

"How the Helios was she allowed to travel across the seas to Thraen Prime in her condition?" Alexis roared as he towered over the group of royal physicians that quivered before him. "You all know her history!"

"We are sorry, my lord," one of the physicians said. "But we did not learn of her pregnancy until she arrived here at Castle Thraen. Otherwise I can assure you, we would have stopped her immediately."

"Did not know? You did not know?" Alexis shouted. "It is your job to know! You are not paid to deal with sniffles and sore throats, but to make sure my wife is healthy and can bring an heir to term!"

"The minoress did not inform us she had missed her cycle, my lord," another physician said. "It is not like we can force her to alert us when her—"

"You can ask her attendants, you morons!" Alexis yelled, his fists balled up with anger boiling close to rage. "Her ladies know everything about her! Did none of you think to have them inform you?"

"That would...that would be a severe breach of propriety, my lord," a third physician said. He was on the floor and grasping at his bloody nose before the last sound of the last word of his sentence finished echoing through the room.

"The next piece of shaowshit that utters one more excuse will be tossed out the airlock and into the Vape gas," Alexis growled low. "Do not test me, gentlemen. I may not have the Teirmont anger that my mother is known for, but I have enough to make sure your skins boil off your bodies at the next moment of your stupidity."

The physicians helped their colleague to their feet and cowered before the enraged royal.

"Get out," Alexis hissed. "I wish to be with my wife alone. I will call you if you are needed."

"My lord, she is still in a delicate way," the first physician said. "It would be wise if one of us remained." He held up his hand to ward off any possible blow coming his way. "I say this not as an excuse, but as an honest medical caution. You can inquire with a midwife for confirmation if you do not believe me. Continual bleeding from the miscarriage is still a risk."

"Then one of you stays," Alexis said. "Over there. In that corner. On the floor. Do not speak to anyone, do not look at anyone. You are a piece of furniture and nothing more. If someone cares to sit on you then you will let them. Am I understood?"

"Yes, my lord," the first physician replied and looked at his colleagues. "I will volunteer."

The others bowed low and quickly left the royal quarters.

"Your corner," Alexis snarled as he pointed to the far side of the room.

He did not wait to see if the physician obeyed, just turned on his heel and stomped to the door of the royal bedchamber. He paused as his hand gripped the handle, took a slow, deep breath, then opened the door and stuck his head inside the room.

"Rebecca?" he whispered. "Are you awake?"

"Alexis? What are you doing here?" Rebecca asked from the shadowed bed. "You are supposed to be up on Station Aelon for your grandmother's funeral service."

"Well, apparently my wife decided to take a trip across the seas," Alexis said as he stepped into the room. He noticed several of Rebecca's attendants sitting off to the side. "Out. Please."

The women quickly got up and made their way around the minor and closed the door securely behind them.

"So, that was you yelling out there?" Rebecca asked. "I'm so tired that I thought it was all a dream."

"Why didn't you tell me you were with child?" Alexis asked as he sat down on the bed. "I would never have gone up to the station."

"Which is why I did not tell you," Rebecca replied. "Your duty was to be by your family's side, not down here on this Helios forsaken land with me."

"My duty is to be with my wife when she is in need," Alexis countered. "And you were obviously in need since you went mad and decided to come to Castle Thraen four months before our scheduled transition time. What were you thinking, Rebecca?"

"I wasn't thinking," Rebecca sighed. "I just wanted to be somewhere familiar. I wanted to be with my people for a change instead of under the constant watch of resentful Aelons. I may be their minoress, but I am not *theirs*. They hate me, Alexis. I feel it every single day I walk those halls of that castle."

"I am sorry you feel that way," Alexis said, not even trying to argue, knowing full well how the Aelish felt about the minoress. "But you cannot go traipsing around the planet at your whim. Not when you are pregnant, and not with your history."

"My failing, you mean," Rebecca whispered then started to sob. "There is something broken with me, Alexis. I know it. The physicians say I am wrong, but I have always known that my insides are not right. Even back on Station Thraen I knew it. I fear. . . ."

Alexis waited for her to continue and when she didn't he asked, "You fear what, my dear? What do you fear?"

"I fear that my father had learned of my issues from one of my attendants on the station," Rebecca admitted. "I believe he knew I would have trouble bringing a child into this world and that is why he agreed to have me wed you. He doesn't want your bloodline to continue. He did this on purpose."

"Helios," Alexis said. "Would he really do that?" Alexis thought about his father-in-law and snarled. "Yes, of course he would. That fucking bastard."

"My father has always been insecure about his claim to the Thraenish crown," Rebecca said. "He would never admit it, but he knows that your mother, as well as all of you Teirmonts, have more Thraenish royal blood in your ring fingers than he does in his whole body. He keeps power by the skin of his teeth."

Alexis held his breath as those words raced around his brain.

"How do you mean?" he finally asked. "Who would take the crown from him?"

"There are those that believe your mother's claim has merit," Rebecca said. "Not many, but enough of the Thraen court to put my father's rule in jeopardy. She is the daughter of Bella Herlect and the direct Herlect line is nearly worshipped on my station."

"Interesting," Alexis said then caught himself. "But let us not talk of stupid politics while you are recovering. Put all talk of claims behind us. You need your rest and you need to recover so one day we can try again."

"Oh, Alexis, I don't think—"

"Hush, hush," Alexis said. "You will get better, I will find physicians that are infinitely more competent than those boggy toads out there, and we will have children. Many, many beautiful and wonderful children."

"Alexis, I don't know. . . ." Rebecca whispered. "Do not put that pressure on me."

"No pressure, dear," Alexis soothed. "No pressure at all. It is fate that we produce heirs. Fate for Station Aelon as well as Station Thraen."

"Yes...you are right," Rebecca mumbled. "I am so tired, Alexis. Just lie here and hold me, please. Will you do that?"

"Yes, my dear, I will," Alexis said as he crawled up next to her and took her in his arms, careful of her condition.

*

"I shouldn't be gone," Alexis said as he sat in the courtyard with his father, his eyes cast up to Station Aelon's shield. The light from Helios was bright, but Alexis knew it would only be an hour or so before that light was gone and the millions of stars shone down on them all. "I promised Rebecca not to leave her side this time."

"This was business that could not be conducted over the communication system, Son," Kel said, patting Alexis on the knee. "If the conversation was intercepted then Station Thraen would move against us in a heartbeat. The announcement of your taking the crown must be handled with care. We do not want Station Aelon to look weak for even a moment."

"She's serious then?" Alexis asked. "She no longer wants the crown?"

"You know your mother," Kel smiled. "She will always want the crown, she can't help that. But she no longer wants the uncertainty of your reign weighing on her. She is getting on in age, as am I, and we'd both like to live to see what you will do as the Master of Station Aelon. That is not something any other monarch has had the privilege of seeing, how their child rules after them."

"I still do not believe that the High Guardian will accept this," Alexis said. "And even if he does, the other stations may balk at it. If they do not recognize me as the rightful ruler of Station Aelon and its Primes then we will have no standing when it comes to trade or diplomatic issues. We could end up isolated and ignored, Father. This decision could undo everything we have fought for over the years."

Alexis watched as the manufactured clouds of moisture worked their way across the sky. They were wispy, not like the thick Vape clouds down on Helios. For a brief second, Alexis felt like he was one of those wispy clouds, ephemeral, manufactured, unreal.

"What about Natalie?" Alexis asked.

"What about her?" Kel replied.

"How do you think she will feel about this? She will no longer be a minoress with a mistress for a mother, but a minoress with a master for a brother," Alexis said. "It will change her position on the station. Not necessarily for the better. With Mother still reigning, she was a legitimate heir, but now that Rebecca's health looks good, and I may have an heir of my own soon, Helios willing, Nats will only be a royal relative, not the possible heir."

"I think your sister will be fine with it," Kel laughed. "I do not believe she has ever cared about the crown. She loves to defend it, whether in combat or in argument, but being the mistress is not her destiny."

"How do you know?" Alexis asked. "There is no way for you to know that."

"It's not about knowing, Son," Kel sighed. "It is about fate. You have to trust me on this. I have had more than my fair share of dealings when it comes to fate. You cannot overthink it. You cannot try to push it. What happens will happen and there is nothing you can do to stop it."

"Yes, I know," Alexis said. "You and Mother have been more than forthright when teaching us about fate." He sighed and stretched. "You really think Nats will be fine with this?"

"I really do," Kel replied. "She is having fun with her bard. Clerke is good for her. He keeps her moving, keeps her active. He worships her as I worship your mother. She gets to see things in a way none of us get to. If she became mistress she'd be locked to Station Aelon and its Primes. Her days of wandering the System would be over. I think that would kill her. Plus, I've always had a feeling her fate would be out there, not here. She has a destiny off this station."

"But my destiny is on it," Alexis said, then laughed. "Yet, as always, we forget Richard." He looked about the courtyard, as if the minor would suddenly appear. "Where is my little brother?"

"That is always the question," Kel said and Alexis picked up on his tone instantly.

"What? Is something wrong with Richard that I don't know about?" Alexis asked.

"Wrong? No, not so much wrong as, well. . .off," Kel answered. "The day the twins were murdered placed a black spot on his soul."

"It placed a black spot on all of our souls," Alexis said. "Black enough for me to wear armor to match."

"But you had that outlet, as did your sister," Kel said. "You dealt with your demons on the battlefield. Richard did not have that chance. As the third heir he was required to stay here on the station. He had to be safe, in case you or your sister fell in the war."

"He ruled as regent well, didn't he?" Alexis asked. "I did not hear of any issues with him and the meeting of stewards nor the meeting of passengers. The Lower Decks didn't try for another uprising and the station remained stable."

"That was more your grandmother's doing, I think," Kel said. "Bella steered him in the right directions. With her gone, and your mother and me looking to move down onto the primes, I fear that, when the time comes for him to be regent again, he will not be as effective."

"Why? What could be so off with my brother to make you say that?" Alexis asked.

Kel looked about and double-checked they were not being observed.

"Your brother. . .talks to those that are not there," Kel said.

Alexis stared at his father for a second then burst out laughing. "Is that all? Mother has been talking to her dead father for as long as I have been alive. Even longer from the stories. I even spoke with the late master a few times myself when I was little. I can remember those conversations clear as the portal through the Vape clouds above the The Way Prime."

"Yes, I know," Kel said. "But Richard is different. He does not act like your mother would, nor as you did when you were little. There was a strength, a confidence that you two had, and your mother still has, when speaking to whatever you were speaking to. Richard has none of that strength."

"He's always been. . .delicate," Alexis said.

"No, it's not that," Kel said, shaking his head. "The few times I've walked in on him talking to no one, it's as if he wasn't himself. He'd turn and look at me and there was nothing in his eyes. It would take him a moment to recognize who I was. His eyes would be blank, A. Empty. If you ever see those eyes, you will know what I mean."

"Like battle-shocked veterans," Alexis replied. "Yes, I know that look."

"No, you do not," Kel said. "It isn't like that at all. His eyes were not the eyes of someone remembering past horrors, but someone lost in a void. And they are not the eyes of someone communing with fate. Have you ever stared into a Vape storm, A? When the clouds swirl so fast and grow so dark that you think a slice of deep space has landed on Helios?"

"I have seen that more than I like, Father," Alexis bristled. "I am the minor of the primes."

"Yes, well, sorry about that," Kel nodded. "But that is what I am talking about. He has the depth of destruction in those eyes, but no comprehension to go with it."

"Helios," Alexis said. "I had no idea it had gotten so bad."

"No reason you should. Like you said, you are the Minor of the Primes," Kel said. "But if you are to be Master of Station Aelon and its Primes then you will need to know who you can trust. I am not sure your brother can be trusted."

"And Mother? What does she think?" Alexis asked.

"We are of the same mind on this, but she refuses to openly admit it," Kel said. "Richard is her baby boy. He is mine as well, but there is a blindness with mothers when it comes to their sons."

"Is there now?" Alexis smiled.

"There is," Kel said. "Luckily, you have nothing she can be blind about."

"Oh, I don't know, Father," Alexis said. "We all have our secrets and our troubles that no one knows about but ourselves."

*

The cathedral of Castle Aelon went silent as the last of the six bells rang out and the coronation of Master Alexis the Fourth of Station Aelon and its Primes was completed. High Guardian Victor the Eighth stood before the assembled royals, nobles, and persons of power and wealth, and raised his staff. The staff itself was made of intricately woven breen stalks, so tightly put together that it rivaled some of the strongest metals. It was a true work of art and he lifted it into the air, then brought it down six times onto the dais. Due to his advanced age, he struggled to raise it as high as was expected, but those assembled pretended not to notice the lack of force when the tip struck stone.

"Let it be known that Station Aelon and its Primes has a new master!" Victor announced. "Let all acknowledge Helios's will! Let all acknowledge Helios's wish! Let all acknowledge Master Alexis!"

"Master Alexis!" everyone echoed.

The High Guardian leaned in close to Alexis and whispered in his ear, "It is all yours now, boy. Be careful what you do with it. Your mistakes will be multiplied a million-fold as master."

"Yes, thank you, High Guardian," Alexis replied out of the corner of his mouth. "Those are wise and welcome words."

"You say that now," Victor smirked. "See how welcome they are if you even live a year."

Alexis had to restrain himself from whirling on the pontiff. The man's words were too close to a threat to be coincidence.

Holding his head high, Alexis stepped down from the dais and over to where Rebecca sat in the first row, waiting for her husband to fetch her.

"Mistress Rebecca," Alexis smiled at his wife.

"Master Alexis," Rebecca smiled back. Two of her attendants rushed to her side and helped her stand up as her belly was so swollen with child that she threatened to topple over with just a slight breeze.

"I can take it from here," Alexis said to the attendants. "I promise not to let her fall."

The two women looked to their mistress and Rebecca nodded. They hurried off, headed for the great hall to prepare the mistress's seat at the head of what would become an almost endless receiving line of well wishers, both true and feigned.

"How are my wife and heir feeling today?" Alexis asked as the two royals walked down the center of the cathedral, nodding and smiling as those gathered stood and applauded. "I hope you are well."

"I am," Rebecca replied. "And your heir is doing fine, too. In fact, the little one just punched me in the ribs so hard I thought I would pass out from the pain. I feel he is a fighter, just like his father."

"I am not so much a fighter as just really good at war," Alexis said. "Now, my sister, she is a fighter. Born ready for battle, just like my mother. It is the Teirmont women you truly have to watch out for."

"However you name it, it is foreign to me, Alexis," Rebecca said. "I could no more go to war than I could breathe Vape."

"I don't know about that," Alexis smiled. "You have a lot more fight in you than you think."

Rebecca winced and stumbled slightly, but Alexis held her firm and kept her from tripping.

"Are you alright?" he asked, not even trying to hide the worry in his voice.

"Fine, dear husband," Rebecca sighed. "Just tired from all of this. I'm so very tired, Alexis."

"It will all be over soon, my dear," Alexis said as they finally reached the doors of the cathedral and were led into the hall by the Order of Jex. "Then you will be able to rest as long as you'd like."

*

The bedchamber was dark as night with all the shades pulled tight from the dreary light of Aelon Prime. Attendants had tried to come in and light lamps or burn candles, but Alexis had sent them running in fear as he roared at them from his bed.

His stillborn daughter's corpse had been taken from the room by his father, but a day had passed before Alexis would let anyone touch his deceased wife. She had lasted through the first night, her will all that held her soul in her body. Alexis had whispered to her the entire time, telling her all the secrets he hadn't told her before, confiding in her all his deep seated fears that no one knew but him. He'd gone on and on, unburdening himself while she slowly, pitifully slipped from life.

Then that last breath left her and he knew all he held was quickly cooling flesh and still bones. Rebecca had not been a wife of his choosing, but she had surprised him as being a match he could only have hoped for. She was cautious while he was easily emotional. He could see the beauty and promise of the primes, while she saw only the strength of the stations. She knew which nobles to keep close and which to keep at arm's length, and he knew who was plotting and who was scheming.

They complimented each other in ways neither expected from the arranged marriage. Alexis was almost willing to say fate had a hand.

But as he sat there, three days having passed since he traded a wife and child for a crown, which was how he saw it, Alexis couldn't help but wonder if his parents weren't completely wrong when it came to fate. He wondered if it wasn't fate that guided them all, but fate that listened closely to their needs and changed course to fit their wills.

At that moment, still in the blood soaked sheets his wife had died in while giving birth to their already dead daughter, Alexis found himself believing not that fate was an outside entity, but perhaps dwelled inside him the whole time. He firmly believed that fate was as much a part of him as his hand or leg or ear. All he had to do was learn to flex it and it would respond like the fists he held clenched in his lap.

"Do you really think that, boy?" the voice asked from the corner of the room. "Do you really think you are fate? That you are so mighty and powerful you can control all of destiny?"

"Go away, old man," Alexis said. "You are not my vision. You belong to my mother. You belong to my brother."

"Your brother? Richard?" the voice laughed. "That man wouldn't know me if I sat on his face with my trousers down and forced my privates up his nose."

"I could do without the vulgarity, if you please," Alexis responded.

"Life is vulgar, boy!" the voice shouted, making Alexis jump. "Don't you get it? Life is supposed to be messy with blood and shit, piss and cum. There is evil and desire, jealousy and anger. Life is filled with sins and vices so that when we meet Helios after we die, we will appreciate the beauty of the afterlife. Without vulgarity, there is no peace."

"Shaowshit," Alexis spat. "You are only my mind trying to drive me mad. But I have news for you, old man: I am already mad."

"Yes, but are you angry?" the voice laughed.

"What does that even mean?" Alexis sighed, leaning his head back into the piles of soiled pillows at his back. "I most certainly am angry. I am angry at Helios for allowing my wife and child to die. I am angry that I now have the crown of Station Aelon, but no one to share it with. I am angry that my reign will be marked by death and failure. I am angry that—"

"Blah, blah, blah, blah, blah," the voice mocked. "That's not anger, that's self-pity. No, boy, I am talking about true anger. I am talking about the fire of the Teirmonts that smolders deep in your soul. That's the anger I mean. Not this boo hoo hoo crap that you are whining about."

"Whining? My wife and child are dead, you imaginary fuck!" Alexis roared. "Leave me alone!"

"That," the voice said. "That is what I mean. Use that. Harness that. Direct that."

Alexis sat there for a second, silent as the last few words played about in his mind.

"Direct it at what?" Alexis finally asked. He waited, but there was no answer. "Have you left, old man?"

"No, I am still here, I'm afraid," the voice replied. "I fear I will always be here, never to know peace, always to be tethered to this monarchy like a dingleberry on a shoaw's ass."

"Cute," Alexis said. "So, if you are to always be here then answer my question. Direct my anger at what?"

"Oh, I think you know the answer to that, boy," the Vocie replied.

"Stop calling me boy," Alexis snapped. "I am thirty-three years old and Master of Station Aelon and its Primes."

"Is that all?" the voice asked. "Just the one station?"

"Yes, of course," Alexis said. "But I have two primes, which no other master has ever had."

"Yes, but what is a prime without its station?" the voice asked. "It is nothing, I say. It is a piece of land that sits in limbo. It is a lonely continent adrift without direction. A prime without a station is not a prime at all."

Alexis thought that through and something deep inside him began to grow and burn, like a slow moving fire.

"Are you saying I should take Station Thraen?" Alexis asked.

"I am saying that a man fights for what is his, no matter the cost," the voice replied. "You can no longer fight for your wife and child, but you can fight for what is yours by birthright. If that is Station Thraen, then so be it."

"It would be madness," Alexis said. "No master has ever tried to take another station, let alone kept it and ruled over it while still ruler of another. The logistics alone are insurmountable."

"And the glory is immeasurable," the voice responded. "Such a fine line between insurmountable and immeasurable, don't you think?"

"That makes no sense," Alexis said.

"No, I suppose it does not," the voice laughed. "But that's part of my privilege of being a dead man talking. I can make as little sense as I want. Your privilege is you get to sort through my sense and see what rings true."

The voice moved from the shadows of the room and Alexis drew back as he stared at the apparition of his dead ancestor. But it was not the ancestor he expected.

"So, tell me, Master Alexis," the ghost of Master Alexis the First, known as Longshanks in life, said. "What rings true to you? That your destiny is to sit in this dark room in the filth of your dead wife? Or to pick yourself up and do what Teirmonts are born to do and go kill every last one of those motherfucking Thraens before they decide they want to kill you? Because that is what I think you should do. Kill them. Kill them all!"

ACT II

THE DARK MASTER

"The Dark Master rose from grief and pain. It was a state of mind many monarchs had dealt with, but only Alexis the Fourth acted upon it, changing the System forever."
    —Dr. D. Reven, Eighty-Third Archivist of The Way

"To touch another's heart is to touch Helios. To break another's heart is to break Helios. To ignore one's own heart is to ignore Helios."
    —Book of Times 43:11, The Ledger

"I fear I have lost my brother. I fear I have lost myself. I fear everything that is about to happen. Ah, fuck this self-pity shoawshit, let's kill some Thraens!"
    —From the Lost Journals of Natalie Teirmont, Minoress of Station Aelon and its Primes

CHAPTER FOUR

The shuttle, a perfect cylinder four hundred yards long by one hundred yards wide, moved quickly through space, propelled by Vape jets. It approached the station, its pilot hailing the landing dock, readying the airlock crew for what should have been a routine boarding.

But the passengers aboard the shuttle were far from routine.

*

"This is cutting it way too close, A," Natalie said, seated next to her brother in the cargo bay of their shuttle. She glanced around at the four hundred longslingers that were packed into the bay with them. "In order for this to work, all shuttles will have to dock at the same time."

"And they will," Alexis said, his hands gripped around his own longsling like it was a life preserver and the only thing to keep him from drowning. "We have coordinated this to the millisecond, Nats. The Order know their jobs. They understand that timing is the key to success. They'll have their shuttles dock precisely when ours do."

"And the Thraens won't think it's funny that five shuttles are all coming in to dock at the same time?" Natalie asked, knowing the answer but refusing to let her brother off the hook.

"It's the biggest time of year for trade," Alexis said. "It's funny, but not unheard of. Having five shuttles come in at once will keep the docks from communicating with each other. They'll all be too busy doing their jobs to even think twice about the other docks' jobs. It'll work."

*

The station rotated slowly and the pilot set the Vape thrusters on the side of the shuttle to synchronize with the same rotation speed as the station. In seconds, the shuttle was no longer moving only forward, but in a slow spiral that would take it straight into the open dock port. The dock crew hailed the shuttle's pilot, giving him reassurances that his trajectory was on point. They also asked for docking control, but the pilot balked and refused to give up his helm to the dock crew.

Tense words were spoken, but the dock crew relented in the end, letting the shuttle pilot keep control of his ship's approach.

*

"I don't like that we can't com with the rest of the Order," Natalie said. "One second off and we won't know."

"No coms," Alexis said. "Helios, Nats, we've been over this! If the station even catches a hint of communications that are not standard from a trade shuttle, then they'll lock those docks down faster than a cutter gets swallowed in a Vape storm."

"If one of us docks too early, and they figure out the ruse, then the rest of our shuttles will be blasted out of space by Vape cannons," Natalie said.

"Like Thraens can shoot straight," one of the longslingers laughed. "They probably miss and blow up Helios."

The rest of the longslingers laughed hard at the joke then stopped quickly as they received a hard glare from Natalie.

"My apologies, minoress," the longslinger said.

"No apology needed, 'slinger," Alexis responded, cutting his sister off before she could lay into the man. "My sister could do with some humor right now."

"You could do with some reality, A," Natalie muttered.

*

The dock was a wide hole, just barely large enough to encompass the shuttle as it carefully made its way inside the station. Despite the boring routine of the back and forth flights from one station to another, shuttle pilots were not a breed of men and women who caved under pressure. As everyone knew, no matter how many successful flights a pilot had, it only took one botched docking to end it all.

The pilot concentrated on the dock opening, listening to readings called out by his copilot and navigator. He adjusted slightly when needed, then let the shuttle coast inside the station. Once it was inside, the dock doors closed behind it and the pilot double checked that the locking mechanism was set to receive the grapplers and airlock that slowly extended towards the ship.

"Docking complete," the pilot said. "Please let our passengers know that they can disembark in just a couple of minutes."

*

"Everyone up!" Natalie yelled as she unhooked her travel harness from the side of the cargo bay. She let the straps and clips fall to the floor and, if her shouting hadn't gotten the longslingers' attention, then the clatter of metal did. "You all know the drill! I will go in first with Master Alexis! It will confuse the holy fuck out of the dock crew and station guards. By the time they figure out they are under attack, then it will be too late! You do not use your coms until we have all exited the shuttle and made it through the last of the airlocks! Once we have done that, then we will have open com and the mission is a full go! Am I understood?"

"Yes, minoress!" the longslingers shouted.

"Good speech, Nats," Baise said as he stood up and double checked his longsling.

"Yeah, Nats, you really put the fear of Helios into them," Lang smirked.

"I think I need to go pee pee," Jay said.

Natalie looked at Buck and raised her eyebrows. "Got something to add to these smartasses' shaowshit?"

"Nope," Buck smiled as he put his longsling to his shoulder and eyed down the barrel to the sight. "Saving my energy for killing Thraens."

"Feel good to have your team back?" Alexis smiled at his sister.

"Only reason I agreed to do this shit," Natalie said.

"Right, because you didn't miss combat at all while you were traipsing across the System with your bard boy," Alexis replied.

"Oh, she missed us," Lang laughed. "She missed us hard."

"Ain't no bard gonna replace the feel of putting a particle barb up the ass of some idiot Thraen," Jay said.

"That's a little graphic, don't you think?" Baise responded.

"These gilly slits are about to find out what graphic really is," Buck said. He nodded to the master and minoress. "After you, my liege and lady."

"You solid, Nats?" Alexis asked.

"Like a motherfucking asteroid," Natalie replied. "Let's fuck some shit up."

*

The airlock doors opened and the royals stepped onto the station proper.

"What's this?" Master Lionel asked as he saw Minor Richard standing before him. He looked about the airlock hallway and frowned. "Are you to be my reception?"

"Where is Master Alexis?" Minor George asked, looking around his father's shoulder at Richard and the royal guards behind the man. "Where are any of the nobles?"

"This is not how you treat Thraens," Minoress Georgia snapped. "This slight will not be tolerated."

"I have to apologize for my brother's absence," Richard said, his voice wavering slightly. He swallowed hard, then cleared his throat before continuing. "Alexis's grief is still almost too much for him to bear. He was afraid that if he saw the minoress here, she would remind him of his late wife. He did not want his greeting to become an emotional breakdown. I hope you understand."

"Remind him of his late wife?" George barked. "My sister looks nothing like our Rebecca. They are of two different molds completely."

"Yes, well, uh, there are similarities enough to make it painful," Richard replied. "Again, my most humble apolo—"

"Oh, shut up, you minor worm of a royal," George said. "Just show us to our quarters so we may freshen up before the reception." He chuckled and turned to his sister. "Oh, did you hear that? I called him a minor worm when he is actually a minor. How clever of me."

"Yes, Brother, how very clever," Georgia laughed, then let the mirth fall from her face as she turned a withering glare onto Richard. "Well? Did you not hear my brother? Show us to our quarters, worm!"

"Yes, minoress, of course," Richard said and bowed low.

Master Lionel smacked the minor on the top of the head. Several of the Aelish royal guards took steps forward at the physical slight, but Richard held out his hand to stop them.

"Our cousin was only playing," Richard said as he straightened and tugged at his doublet. "Isn't that so, Master Lionel?"

"If by playing you mean giving you a whack to hurry your incompetent ass, then yes," Lionel replied. "Now, please, let us move along. I am here to attend my late daughter's funeral service, not stand in an airlock hallway until I die of old age."

"Right this way, master," Richard said as he turned and led the Thraenish royals down the hallway. "We have the perfect accommodations for you."

*

"Manifest papers," the Thraen guard said as Alexis and Natalie stepped into the shuttle dock's airlock. The man didn't even look up at the royals, keeping his head down, studying a tablet that showed what cargo the shuttle was supposed to hold. "Come on, hurry it up."

"I believe we do not have papers," Alexis said.

The guard looked up and his eyes went wide as recognition seeped into his brain. "Master Alexis?"

"Yes," Alexis nodded. "I'm surprised Master Lionel is not here to greet me."

"Uh, Master Lionel?" the guard asked.

"Yes, your lord and liege. You have heard of him?" Alexis said.

"Of course, but he is with the minor and minoress on their way to Station Aelon," the guard said. "For your wife's funeral, my lord."

"Station Aelon? No, the funeral was to be here!" Alexis barked and pointed back at the shuttle airlock. "I have my wife's body with me right now!"

The guard just stood there.

"Have you nothing to say, man?" Alexis yelled. "Speak up or I will slit your—"

"Alexis, brother, calm yourself," Natalie said as she moved forward and put her hand on the guard's shoulder. "Take us into the control room so we may use the com there. We'll have to get this straightened out immediately."

"Right, yes, of course, this way," the guard said. He turned and led the two royals into the dock's control room and pointed at a console at the far end of the room. "You can use that com there."

"Perfect," Natalie said. Alexis turned and left the control room quickly. "Now, where is he getting off to?"

The guard and the control room crew all stared at the minoress as she stood there with her hands on her hips and a sly smile on her face.

"Hey, why are you wearing battle armor?" one of the control crew asked.

Realization dawned on the guard's face just as Alexis stepped back into the control room, his longsling at his shoulder. The weapon barked several times quickly and the control crew, as well as the guard, were vaporized almost instantly.

"Where's mine?" Natalie asked.

Alexis reached out of the room's door and grabbed the longsling he had set against the wall. He tossed the weapon to Natalie, then hurried over to the control consoles and picked up a set of earphones. He listened closely and smiled.

"All the other shuttles have docked," Alexis said. "The control rooms are going offline one by one as we speak."

"Then let's do less speaking and more killing," Natalie said. She put her fingers to her mouth and let loose with a high-pitched whistle. "Team! On me!"

Alexis and Natalie stepped back out of the control room and smiled as their men began to pour from the shuttle airlock.

"Lead the way, Master Alexis of Station Aelon," Natalie said. "Soon to be Master Alexis of Station Thraen as well."

*

"The royal guest quarters are down that hall there, not this hall," Lionel snapped at Richard. "I have been on this station enough, and in Castle Quent more times than I'd like, to know which way to go, you little toad."

"I really wouldn't keep insulting me," Richard said. "I am a minor of Station Aelon and its primes."

"You are a minor minor and I will always be closer to Helios than you," Lionel growled. They all stopped at a set of doors and the master frowned. "What is this? Where are we?"

"My brother has done some renovations to the castle," Richard said as he unlocked the doors and threw them wide to reveal a set of stairs that wound up into the dark. "We call this the Third Spire."

"The Third Spire?" George laughed. "Why would your brother renovate your royal prison?"

"To make it harder for prisoners to get out and harder for soldiers to get in," Richard said.

The Aelish Royal Guard all drew their long blades. The Thraenish royal guards were too slow to react and had their throats slit, bellies gutted, and limbs hacked off before they could utter a word of warning.

Richard had his own blade drawn and he pointed it at Lionel. "Master? Would you like to see your room now? I trust you can climb these steps on your own? Or should I have my men pick you up and carry you to your new home?"

"How dare you!" George shouted and started towards Richard, but Lionel held his hand out and stopped his son. "Father? We cannot stand for this! The little whelp has obviously lost his mind! This must be a coup!"

"It is not a coup," Lionel said, a disgusted sneer on his face. "Richard is not overthrowing his brother. No, we are the ones being overthrown."

"Father? What are you talking about?" Georgia asked. "They cannot overthrow us. We are Thraens and this is Station Aelon!"

"Yes, Daughter, I know what I am and where I am," Lionel said. "I also know where Master Alexis is at this moment." He took one step towards Richard and a dozen long blades were instantly pointed at his chest. Lionel held his hands up, but kept his eyes on the minor. "Your brother is not on Station Aelon, is he?"

"No, he is not," Richard smiled.

"And I am guessing that neither is your sister. Am I right there as well?" Lionel asked.

"You are right there as well," Richard said.

"When did they dock with Station Thraen?" Lionel asked.

"If it all timed our correctly they would have docked there the same time you docked here," Richard said. "Timing was crucial."

"Yes, I suppose it would have to be," Lionel sighed then nodded in the direction of the stairs. "George? Georgia? Follow the minor to our new home."

"Father!" the twins shrieked.

"*Do it now!*" Lionel roared. "Unless you want our intestines strapped to weights and ejected from the airlocks of this station!"

"Oh, that form of execution was banned from Aelon years ago," Richard said.

"I was not talking about you doing it, fool. I was talking about me doing it," Lionel said. "I abhor children who talk back to their elders. You would be wise to keep that in mind."

"I shall, Master Lionel," Richard said and bowed low. He straightened and licked his lips. "Now, follow me, please. You'll be pleasantly surprised with the upgrades to the cells. My brother is not without his kindnesses."

*

"Slaughter all that refuse to comply!" Alexis yelled back to his men as he and Natalie stepped from the lift and out onto the Surface of station Thraen. They found themselves right in the main market area of the Thraen court and were met with nothing but disbelief. Thraenish nobles and stewards, vendors and servants, stared in horror as four dozen longslingers poured from the cargo lift and out into the sunlight that filtered in through the station's shield.

"People of Station Thraen!" Alexis shouted into the stunned silence. "I am Master Alexis Teirmont of Station Aelon and its Primes! I have come to take my birthright and the crown of Thraen! Those who do not fight, and step aside, will be met with mercy and courtesy! Those that choose to fight will be butchered here on the spot!"

No one said a word. The Thraens just gaped at the impossible spectacle before them. Then someone coughed and suddenly all were in motion, screaming, running, fleeing the invaders who had appeared out of nowhere.

"Leave no guard or soldier alive!" Alexis ordered as several Thraenish guards began to run at him and his sister. "Then secure all lifts, skids, and buildings! I want the court taken by sundown!"

Two more cargo lifts opened and dozens upon dozens of Aelish longslingers hurried onto the Surface, their longslings sending particle barbs into the oncoming soldiers and guards. Thraenish flesh was torn asunder, obliterated before the nobles' and passengers' eyes. The Thraens who were not trained in combat, but patriotic enough to challenge the longslingers, met with deaths just as awful as the Thraenish fighters who refused to lay down their weapons and surrender.

"Steward Vast has called in and his men have the eastern quadrant of the Surface under their control already," Natalie cried out to Alexis as she shot a guard point blank in the face, turning his head into a barely perceivable mist. She grinned and flipped her longsling about, slammed the butt into another guard's throat, whipped it over her head and brought it down on a third's skull, then put it back to her shoulder and shot a fourth in mid-blade swing. "We'll have the Surface from these cowards by today, Brother!"

"Do not get overconfident!" Alexis warned as he dropped his empty longsling, pulled his long blade, and slashed his way through two market stalls, cutting down Thraenish guards with a fury that caused more than a couple to drop their blades, turn tail, and run. "They may be cowards, but cowards can be very dangerous!"

"Down!" Buck yelled and Alexis responded with a diving roll as the man fired over his head into a throng of Thraen guards coming at them from the left. "Clear!"

Alexis jumped up and nodded to the warrior. "Excellent work, Buck. I'll have to give you a medal for that."

"I don't need a medal," Buck said. "but you could clear my bar tabs down in the Middle Decks when we get home. That would be appreciated."

"A medal would be easier," Alexis said as he sheathed his long blade and took the newly loaded longsling that was tossed to him. "A medal doesn't involve accountants."

"Breen counters, man," Buck laughed. "They always get in the way of fun."

"Learn to manage your funds better," Alexis said, taking aim as a wave of new soldiers entered the marketplace. He fired until empty again, dropping two thirds of the new attackers.

"I never expected to live long enough to need to manage my funds," Buck said. "No soldier ever does."

Buck opened fire as Alexis reloaded his own longsling then, once Buck was empty, Alexis started firing, allowing Buck to reload. Natalie, Jay, Baise, and Lang joined them and they took turns reloading and the firing, as they pushed forward through the marketplace and into the castle itself.

"What the Helios is the name of this castle?" Jay asked as they stepped into the main atrium and entryway.

The warriors and royals looked at each other then all shrugged.

"Helios, I have no clue," Natalie said. "I don't think I have ever been told."

"Wait, I know it," Alexis said. "Rebecca talked about it all the time. It's Castle Herlect. They name their castles after themselves on this station."

"Is Master Lionel a Herlect?" Lang asked. "I thought he was such a distant cousin that he no longer had that name."

"He took the name when he took the crown," Baise said. "Helios, pay attention. This is basic stuff."

They moved through the main entryway and came to two wide passageways. The sounds of battle drifted in to them from outside, but as for the castle itself they could have heard a pin drop.

"Did they all flee?" Lang asked.

"Not likely," Buck said.

"Steward Maglion has reported success in his quadrant," Natalie reported. "And now Steward Fleurtine has also. The Order are doing their jobs brilliantly."

"Not bad for a bunch of old fighters," Buck said.

The sound of their boots echoed through the passageway as they decided to go left, half of them turning and covering their backs. A door slammed from somewhere far in the castle, but there was no other sound to be heard.

"You don't think they have the castle rigged to blow, do you?" Baise asked.

"They don't have the courage to do that," Alexis said.

Two doors opened in front of them and soldiers rushed out with blades drawn. Alexis was shoved out of the way by Baise as a blade came at his head. The warrior countered the attack by blocking the blade with his longsling, pulling a short blade from his belt, and slicing through the soldier's polybreen armor, sending steaming intestines spilling out into the passageway.

"You alright, sire?" Baise asked.

"Fine, Baise," Alexis said. "Down!"

Baise had barely lowered his head before Alexis fired, the particle barb flying just over the warrior's right shoulder and into the chest of an attacking Thraen. The man screamed for half a second before his lungs were atomized, leaving him standing there with his mouth open until the particle barb finished its work and the rest of the man was torn apart, molecule by molecule.

"Thanks," Baise said.

"It's my job," Alexis said. "We are all equal in battle."

More Thraens came at the group, but they were taken apart easily as the warriors and royals worked seamlessly. It would have taken a finely tuned troop of Thraenish soldiers to stop the battle-tested veterans of the prime war. And the men that came at them were far from finely tuned.

More doors opened and more soldiers came at the Aelons, but they all met the same fate. Blood and guts filled the passageway, the smell of bodily fluids and spent particle barbs almost overpowering.

"We need to get to the communications room," Alexis said as they pushed forward. "We take that and we can control communications with and between all the decks. If we isolate the Middle Decks then the next phase will be much easier."

"Ya think?" Natalie said as she yanked her blade from the eye socket of a brave, but stupid, Thraen. "We all know the plan, A. My team doesn't forget details."

"Just saying it out loud," Alexis replied. "This is the first time I've fought this closely with you and your men. Usually I'm standing next to a few hundred longslingers."

"You need to go back outside?" Buck grinned. "They might need you out there."

"Kiss my ass," Alexis smirked. "I want to be the first person that walks into this castle's great hall. I expect to plant my ass at the head of that hall and smile for days."

"If you are planting your ass then how can I kiss it?" Buck asked.

"Oh, I'll make time for that, don't worry," Alexis said. "Now, which way to the com room?"

"Two passages up and one over," Natalie said. "It'll be heavily guarded by now, though. We'll have to go in hot and fast and never let up."

"Because we were going to just going walk up to them and ask nicely?" Lang said. "Now it's you that's forgetting we know how to do our jobs."

"Zip it, craphole," Natalie said. "Let's move."

*

"My lord?" an attendant said stepping to Richard as the regent sat at the head of the long table in Castle Quent's great hall. "Word is reaching us that Master Alexis and Minoress Natalie have secured Castle Herlect on Station Thraen. They are coordinating across the Surface with the Order of Jex to push the campaign below into the Middle Decks."

"Thank you," Richard smiled. "Please keep me informed when they begin the fight for those decks."

"Yes, my lord." The attendant bowed then turned crisply and left the great hall.

"Gentlemen," Richard smiled, looking down the table at the hastily assembled meeting of stewards. "My brother and sister are accomplishing what many here never believed would be possible. In days, if not perhaps hours, Station Thraen will be under Aelish control, as it should be by birthright."

"Many of us are not pleased the meeting was not informed of this action," a steward called out as he stood from his seat halfway down the table. "The crown is required to get the meeting's approval for all military campaigns. A vote was not taken to fund this endeavor and I fear that if one were to be called for now, Master Alexis would find himself in arrears when it comes time to pay his precious longslingers."

"My brother has already thought of that, Steward Neem," Richard replied. "All longslingers, as well as my sister's team, have volunteered. If the meeting sees fit to award them bonuses for their heroics when they return, then I am sure that would be appreciated. But most of the men expect to profit from the spoils of Station Thraen, so even your withholding of possible bonuses does not bother them."

"The High Guardian will not stand for this!" another steward cried as he stood and pounded his fist on the table. "The Way will punish Station

Aelon and restrict our access to Helios and the primes! How will we get our breen shipments out to the other stations? Or utilize our Vape holdings?"

"You have answered your own question, Steward Oweyn," Richard said. "The Vape."

Steward Oweyn waited, but when Richard did not elaborate he looked about at his colleagues. "Did I miss something? That is not an answer, Minor Richard."

"You will refer to me as Regent Richard," Richard replied. "And if you use your brain, steward, then you will see the answer is before you. We control the Vape mines of Thraen Prime. If The Way wants Vape at prices that will not bankrupt them, then they will stay neutral in this conflict. After all, my brother is the great grandson of Master Paul the Fourth of Station Thraen. His blood, the same blood that flows through my veins, is directly tied to the Thraenish crown. More so than the impostor Master Lionel."

"None of us dispute the claim, Richard," Steward Neem said then cleared his throat. "Forgive me, I mean *Regent* Richard. None of us dispute that claim, but Master Alexis is required to inform us if he takes this type of action against another station."

"And what are we to do with Master Lionel and his heirs?" Steward Kispee asked, adding his voice to the outrage. "Are they to be prisoners here indefinitely?"

"Of course not," Richard laughed. "They will be set free once my brother feels they are not a threat to his claim. The choice of freedom is in their hands, not in ours."

"The choice *is* in our hands, my lord," Steward Kispee insisted. "Holding another master prisoner returns us to a more primitive time that the System has fought hard to get away from. It has been a thousand years since anything like this has been done. We may be able to hold back The Way, but their neutrality will make no difference if other stations protest and refuse to conduct trade with us."

Angry voices were raised by the other stewards in agreement and Richard tried not to look rattled as the mood of the meeting became close to mutinous.

"Gentlemen! Gentlemen!" Richard shouted. "Please, calm yourselves! My brother will address all of your concerns when he communicates with us! We must be patient until he has taken Station Thraen! All will be well when that happens!"

No matter how loudly Richard called out, control of the meeting was lost and he had to grip the armrests of his chair to keep from bolting out of the great hall and fleeing to his quarters.

*

"The Surface is secure, Your Highness," Steward Neggle said over the com. "Most of the estates gave up without a fight when they saw the longslingers. Those that resisted were put down easily. The forces on the Surface are negligible. Taking the Middle Decks will not be so easy. That is where the bulk of their military resides."

"I am well aware of that, Neggle," Alexis replied, holding the earphones to his head tightly as skirmishes still raged within the castle's walls. "But keeping control of the Surface is key. Many of the sector wardens and deck bosses, or whatever they call them here on Station Thraen, will fall in line when their stewards order them to. These are naturally self-serving people; they'll see the logic in complying to avoid the blade."

"So we stand and hold for now?" Steward Kinsmon asked from his quadrant of the station. "Just keep the nobles in line?"

"Feed your men and rest," Alexis said. "I need to assess the situation from here before we plunge into the depths of the station. Coming from the shuttle docks up was easy, but going back down will be considerably more tricky, as Neggle has voiced."

"Can we appeal to their lowdeckers?" Steward Vast asked. "Incentivize them to rise up and attack the Middle Decks with us? We could offer them the same autonomy that our own Lower Decks have."

"No, that won't work," Alexis replied. "The Thraens think as one. They are spineless, mindless people that will roll over once they see their struggle will be hard and bloody. These are a people that prefer to eat, drink, and fuck than to conquer and rule. Let's not put ideas in their heads."

"Very well, sire," Neggle said. "We will hold, regroup, and rest up for the next phase."

"Good," Alexis said. "I will keep you posted."

*

"It has been six days since the strike!" Steward Neem shouted as the meeting of stewards glared at the regent seated before them. "We are already feeling the diplomatic, and economic, repercussions from other stations. While the High Guardian has not outright condemned the action, he has chosen strategic, and hurtful, words in his few statements. Alexis must take that station in the next few days or none of this will matter!"

"My brother is more than capable of winning this campaign," Richard said, his skin pale and drawn. He looked not to have slept for days, which he had not, and deep, dark bags were under his eyes, making him look more like a ghoul than a person.

"System opinion is against us!" Steward Oweyn yelled. "The bloodlines of the royal families of the Six Stations are so intertwined that several masters have stated they fear this will lead to a Systemwide campaign by Master Alexis and not stop at Station Thraen alone!"

"Are they saying that?" Richard asked, shocked. "Really? That's...that's absurd! We Teirmonts have no blood claim to any of the other stations. Alexis would not dream of going after Klaerv or Flaen. We only fight for Thraen because we are direct descendants of Master—"

"Master Paul the Fourth," Steward Kispee interrupted. "Yes, we are very aware of this, Regent. In fact, the reason we are so very aware of this is because it is the only justification you bring to the table. As far as I can tell, no one here in this meeting has been given any economic, diplomatic, political, or even spiritual reason to wage war against one of the most powerful stations in the System. Logic would dictate at least one, perhaps two, of those categories would be satisfied before we committed ourselves to such an undertaking."

"I have a spiritual reason," Richard stated. "Fate. It is the Teirmont fate to rule over Station Thraen!"

He gave the meeting a smug smile, but it quickly vanished as he saw the looks of disgust and disdain aimed at him.

"Fate?" Kispee asked. "Fate is how your mother ruled, Regent. Everyone let her make that statement because no matter what she said, her actions always brought results. She was a successful monarch, with a proven record of triumph. She was also a novelty and the entire station, not to mention the System, was watching her closely to see how she would fail. But she did not. Your brother, our Master Alexis, does not have the luxury of that novelty to fall back on. He will be held to the same standards as the male Teirmont rulers that came before him. Do you honestly think he can live up to the legend of Longshanks?"

"I. . .I do," Richard nodded.

"You do? Why would our Alexis be more like Alexis the First than Alexis the Second?" Neem asked.

"Yes, why are we to think Master Alexis the Fourth will not turn out like that sad flip of a ruler?" Oweyn asked. "You speak of bloodlines and birthrights, but you forget that the Teirmonts are not as pure and noble as you would like to believe. There are flaws in those veins. As we can all see right now."

There were several laughs of derision aimed at Richard, but he chose to ignore them and focus on the attendant that was hurrying into the great hall.

"Here, see!" Richard announced as he was handed a piece of paper. "It is from my brother! News of his. . . ."

Richard trailed off as he read the note. He tried to smile, but he could not keep up the facade.

More derisive laughs filled Station Aelon's great hall.

*

"They are holding steady by the rotational drive!" Fleurtine shouted. "We cannot use our longslings in there or we risk destroying the entire station! With us on it!"

"Then we go in with blades!" Natalie shouted back, her eyes studying the narrow passageway that led into the main rotational drive area. "These Thraens are weak of heart and will fall easily!"

"Yes, but they are also desperate, Nats," Alexis said. "Desperate men do desperate things. While we would like to keep the station intact they may not feel the same way. If they are to die anyway then why not take us all out at the same time? We have fought hard from the Surface, through the Middle decks, and down to these Lower Decks. It may well be time to put the blades aside and use words."

"If we'd wanted to use words then we could have done that from back on Aelon," Natalie spat. "We came here to kill Thraens and take what is ours."

"We came here to assert our claim to our birthright," Alexis countered. "And there is no claim if there is no station."

"Then what do you propose?" Fleurtine asked. "We've come too far to walk away. And that is what they want. They want us to walk away and return their master to this station. All will be for naught if we comply."

"Maybe we should consider their demands," Alexis smiled. "Maybe they have the solution to holding this station that we never thought of."

"A? What are you proposing? That we give up?" Natalie asked.

"Never," Alexis said. "But if they want their master back then I think that is exactly what they should have."

"You've lost your Helios damned mind," Natalie sighed.

*

"So he just sits there and negotiates while our trade agreements shrivel up like unharvested breen?" Steward Oweyn sneered, his eyes filled with venom and hatred for the regent that sat hunched over at the end of the table. "First all Master Alexis wants is war and now he proposes peace instead? This is not what your mother would have done. At least when she committed to a campaign she saw it all the way to the end."

"And where is the former mistress?" Steward Kispee asked. "Why has she not added her voice to this crisis?"

"Because she does not feel it is a crisis," Richard said. "She has all the faith in the System in her son. She is letting the Master of Station Aelon conduct his rule with all the power and privilege that Helios has bestowed upon the monarchy. She will not intervene, even with words of support, because it is now my brother's fate that steers this station, not hers."

"So she is afraid he will fail and does not want to be locked to the losing side then?" Steward Neem chuckled. "She is hedging her bets. If Alexis fails, and dies, then minoress Natalie takes the crown since no heir has been produced."

"No living heir," Kispee muttered.

"What was that?" Richard shouted, jumping from his seat. He reached for his belt, but he had forgotten to strap on his blade. Instead he adjusted his doublet and then slammed his palm down on the table. "You dare desecrate the memory of my stillborn niece! I should order you to be placed in the Third Spire with Master Lionel and his children!"

"My apologies, Regent," Kispee responded. "I spoke out of turn and stepped over the line."

"Your apologies will mean nothing if your head is no longer attached to your body, steward," Richard spat.

"Now, hold on!" Steward Oweyn yelled as he jumped to his feet. "You do not have the authority to order, or threaten, the execution of any member of the meeting of stewards!"

The majority of the table cheered in agreement which spurred Oweyn on.

"You may be regent, appointed by your brother, but a regent is only allowed to administrate, not magistrate. You cannot conduct royal trials, which is what you would have to do to authorize the execution of a steward. Be careful what you say, Richard, or you will find it is you that is on the end of the executioner's blade!"

"How dare you!" Richard yelled. "Guards! Seize this man for threatening a member of the royal family!"

The stewards all leapt to Oweyn's defense verbally, but none moved to protect the man when the royal guards converged on the steward and took him in their grasp.

"Place him in the Third Spire!" Richard yelled. "He will remain there until my brother returns!"

The meeting quickly quieted down as the realization that Steward Oweyn was actually being dragged away from the table hit them. They all saw themselves in the stunned steward's face and none wanted to meet his same fate. Not that many of them believed in fate. They left that for the former mistress.

"Now," Richard smiled once Oweyn was gone from the great hall. "I expect the rest of you to conduct yourselves properly. Any more threats against Family Teirmont will result in the same punishment. And while the Third Spire has been refurbished, it hardly meets the standards of living you men are used to in your quarters here at court."

*

The room was nothing but tension and the ever present threat of instant violence as the two men stared across the table at each other.

"You would return our master to us?" a thick man asked, his eyes locked onto Alexis's. "You would let our Lionel come back to his place here on Thraen as if none of this had happened?"

"No. Too much blood has been spilled for us to ever forget this has happened," Alexis replied, making sure his eyes never left the thick man's. "And I have no intention of letting anyone ever forget. What I will do is I will let Master Lionel return and oversee this station, administering as he sees fit, but under my rule. He will swear fealty to Station Aelon, and Family Teirmont, as the true claimants to the Thraenish crown. I get my birthright and you get your master."

"We get a cuckold," the thick man said as he leaned back.

Muscular and covered in scars from the heavy and hard work of maintaining the rotational drive, Steffen Grove had been appointed by the other Thraenish lowdeckers to speak for them. He was more than rough around the edges, and possessed not an ounce of diplomatic skill, but he was also unimpressed with the royal that sat across from him. As far as he was concerned, he was just dealing with another noble that wanted to take and take without ever having to give.

"Your offer is worthless," Grove said finally. "You give us nothing. We might as well return the favor and destroy the rotational drive, putting all of us Thraens out of our misery."

"Is that the route you want to take, Steffen?" Alexis asked. "Suicide? Not only will you shame Station Thraen for all of history, but you will damn the souls of every living being on this station. You may defeat me, but you will instill the wrath of Helios for all eternity. Is that what you feel will be best for your fellow Thraens?"

"It would be better than giving in to Aelish aggression," Grove replied.

"What would get you to change your mind, Steffen?" Alexis asked.

"A, we are wasting time," Natalie said from directly behind her brother. "He is not going to agree with you."

"Then I need to agree with him," Alexis said. "Tell me, Steffen Grove, what do I need to do to get you to approve of my plan and bring your master home?"

"Die," Grove chuckled, joined quickly by the men that stood behind him. "Die horribly."

"Very well," Alexis said and stood. He slid his long blade from its sheath and set it on the table. Slowly, he pushed it across to Grove. "Then I die. But it must be your hand that takes my life. Lift that blade and cut me down right here and right now. Once you do that then the agreement will be in place and signed by my spilt blood. Kill me here, kill me now, and you agree to all of my terms. That is the deal you just proposed is it not?"

Grove's eyes went from the offered blade to the master, back and forth, again and again.

"What is the catch?" Grove asked, his hand easing towards the blade.

Natalie and the Order of Jex all reached for their blades, but Alexis held his hands out.

"Stay yourselves," he commanded. "I offer my blade willingly."

"No one offers to die willingly," Grove said. "There is a catch."

"No one offers their lives willingly?" Alexis asked. "But didn't you just say only moments ago, that you would destroy this station to keep me from taking it? Are you not offering to die willingly? Or is it perhaps the hundreds of thousands of Thraenish lives you will murder with your decision that are the ones that are not going to die willingly? Is that what you mean with your statement?"

Alexis looked at the men who stood behind Grove.

"Are you all offering to die willingly? Are your wives? Your mothers, sisters, brothers? Are your children all offering to die willingly? Does this man who sits here speak for every single soul on this station? When he picks up that blade and cuts me down, can all of you say that Station Thraen is of one mind and prepared to commit suicide and be judged by Helios? If so, then I applaud your courage."

Grove jumped up and grabbed the blade. He started to strike, but stopped in mid-thrust. His mouth opened to speak, but only blood came trickling out. The blade fell from his hand as he collapsed to the table then slid to the floor, a short blade imbedded in his back.

"He does not speak for all of us," a thin man said as he stepped forward, shoved Grove's corpse out of the way, and took the empty seat at the table. "I am Xander Grove. Steffen was my nephew. I do not kill him lightly, Master Alexis, so the next words out of your mouth had better be to the benefit of this station and all Thraens."

Alexis nodded to the man and took his seat. "I believe they will be, Mr. Grove," Alexis replied.

*

"Is that so?" Master Lionel asked as he listened to the voice complain from the cell across the staircase from his. "The master did not seek the approval of his nobles for this campaign? How rude of him. That is a mistake I would never make."

"Yes, well, the Teirmonts have not been known for listening to others," Steward Oweyn's voice echoed. "Their blood is nothing but fire and violence. They have never had the coolness of reason that is required for true leadership. Not like you, my lord."

"Oh, you flatter me, steward," Lionel replied, rolling his eyes with disdain. "If only this station was run by someone such as you. Your temperament would be of considerable benefit to the people of Station Aelon. If it was my decision, I'd remove every last Teirmont and give you and your lineage the crown. You know as well as I that the Teirmonts are a family destined for ruin and disgrace, not glory and triumph."

Lionel waited patiently as his words made it through his cell door, across the staircase of the Third Spire, and into the cell, and mind, of Steward Oweyn.

"Yes, well, as true as that might be," Oweyn replied after several long seconds of silence. "The Teirmonts have the crown and they will never give it up. Especially not to a distant bloodline like mine."

"Oh, do you not know my story, steward?" Lionel asked. "I may be a Herlect by name, after taking it myself to ensure peace and stability on my station, but my heredity is quite a few branches away from the true Herlect line. Yet, once the Herlect line died out, I was the next choice for the monarchy. Do not let distance from the current family deter you, because all families must fade away at some point."

More silence.

"You make an interesting point," Oweyn finally replied. "You give me a lot to think on, Master Lionel." Then the steward laughed nervously. "But, of course, this is only harmless conjecture amongst wronged men. I could never actually act on it. That would be treason."

"Of course, steward," Lionel laughed. "We are just two gentlemen prattling on to pass the time. Our words are in jest to help lighten the load from our shoulders as we sit here with such uncertain, serious futures."

"Master Lionel!" a guard called as he stomped up the stairs. "Present your hands for shackling through the slot in the door!"

"I will present nothing!" Lionel yelled. "Unless Master Alexis is here to speak to me himself, I do not intend to leave this cell!"

"You're getting the next best thing," the guard replied. "I am to escort you to the communications room where you will confer with Master Alexis. The scuttle is, he is going to give you your station back."

Stunned by that news, Lionel barely noticed as the slot in the door opened before him.

"Your hands, Your Highness?" the guard asked. "You can't leave the cell without your shackles. Unless you don't want to speak with Master Alexis. Then, I'll pass that message along and leave you here to rot."

"No, I do want to speak to him," Lionel said as he slowly slid his hands through the door.

His wrists were shackled and he withdrew his hands so the cell door could be unlocked and opened. The guard grabbed him by the chain that connected his wrists and began to pull him down the stairs.

"Steward Oweyn?" Lionel called out as he passed the man's cell. "I would advise thinking long and hard about our conversation. It may not have been words of jest after all."

*

"You're sure about this, Alexis?" Mistress Alexis asked." Do you really trust Lionel to keep his word? Because I certainly do not."

Alexis smiled at the face of his mother on the small video screen set before him. "I am sure, Mother," he replied. "And, no, I do not trust Lionel at all. That is why Natalie will stay behind on Station Thraen to make sure the master does not try to exceed the terms of our agreement. If there is even a hint of rebellion then she will take her team, and the regiment of Aelish longslingers I will be leaving, and she will cut down every Thraenish noble she can find."

"So, you expect the nobles to keep Lionel in line then?" Mistress Alexis asked. "It is the pressure from their boot heels he will feel on his neck?"

"That is my hope," Alexis said and sighed. "Listen, Mother, I cannot see any other way to maintain my claim on Station Thraen. History has shown that without a stable monarchy, a station will devolve into chaos and brutality. And we both know I cannot run two stations at once. I need Lionel to rule over Thraen so I can rule over him. As long as his fealty remains intact, then Station Thraen is mine."

"Until that fealty is no longer intact, A," Mistress Alexis said. "But that is another battle for another day."

"Yes, it is," Alexis agreed then changed the subject. "How is Father? How is life back on the primes? I do miss it somewhat, although I believe the dark memories of the place will haunt me if I return."

"The primes are fine, Son," Mistress Alexis smiled. "And your father is fine as well. In fact, we are planning a trip to Thraen Prime tomorrow to see a demonstration of a new Vape mining technique. Apparently some engineer has figured out how to capture and contain the Vape gas straight from the rock instead of releasing it first and then compressing it. If it actually works, it will save us millions of credits a year in productivity."

"That sounds promising," Alexis smiled. There was a knock at his door. "Mother, I have to go. I need to meet with Natalie and the Order to finalize the transition plans. My tomorrow is filled with greeting and welcoming Master Lionel back on his station."

"Good luck, A," Mistress Alexis said. "Always remember you have fate on your side."

"Thank you, Mother, I will remember that," Alexis said. "Goodbye."

He switched off the screen and stood up as a second knock echoed through his quarters. He looked about at the foreign fashions and furnishings of the Thraenish room. He could not wait to be done with the whole business and return to his place on Station Aelon.

CHAPTER FIVE

The room was filled with bureaucratic chatter as delegates and diplomats worked through the details of what Master Alexis would assume and Master Lionel would keep. The most contentious part was not about duties or privileges, but about the exact title of Master Lionel.

"He is Master of Station Thraen," a Thraenish diplomat insisted. "He will be addressed as such."

"But that is no longer the case," an Aelish diplomat countered. "He may keep the title of master, but Station Thraen is now part of Master Alexis's holdings and he will be addressed as Master of Stations Aelon and Thraen as well as their primes. There is no room for discussion on this."

"The High Guardian has stated—" the Thraenish diplomat began.

"The High Guardian has already deferred all authority in these negotiations," the Aelish diplomat interrupted. "Master Lionel will simply be called that: Master Lionel. He may, of course, add his surname to his title, if he so chooses. But as of the signing of the treaty this morning, he has no claim to Station Thraen except as its appointed regent."

"This is ridiculous!" the Thraenish diplomat shouted. "We will not tolerate such abuse and discourtesy! His title is as his title has always been! If you do not agree then I declare these proceedings illegitimate!"

"Your mother is illegitimate!" the Aelish diplomat yelled.

"Wha-wha-what?" the Thraenish diplomat stuttered. "What did you say to me?"

"Gentlemen, shut up," Natalie said as she sat at the head of the conference table. She sighed and rubbed at her temples. "Let him be called Master Lionel, Regent of Station Thraen."

"But, my lady—" the Aelish diplomat said.

"Did I not say to shut up?" Natalie barked. "Didn't I? Pretty sure I did! You can agree with my version of the title or go take a long walk out a fucking airlock. Those are your choices. Now, let's move on. What's next on the list?"

"Such language," a Thraen muttered.

"That language will be the last thing you hear if you open your mouth again," Natalie growled. "Now, move on. I asked what was next."

"Pensions for the Thraenish soldiers forced to retire in order to comply with the mandatory draw down of forces," the first Thraenish diplomat said. "The honorable thing to do would be full salaries and benefits."

"Full salaries? That is not what any retired soldier receives, even before the claim," the Aelish diplomat replied. "They can have half-salaries or nothing."

"Half? You must be joking!" the Thraenish diplomat cried. "They will starve.

"How about this?" Natalie smiled. "They get half-salaries and any that want more can fight me for it. Every nick on my body is another five percent. Of course, when I chop their fucking heads off, they'll get nothing, so it'll probably work out in Station Aelon's favor. Or did you not understand my language? Want me to demonstrate on you for all to see? I don't mind."

All of the diplomats, Thraenish and Aelish, stared at the minoress. No one replied to her suggestions since none in the room was quite sure whether she was joking or not.

"Hey, Nats?" Buck asked from the doorway. "Got a second?"

"No," Natalie replied. "But I'll give you one anyway." She stood and eyed the men in the room. "When I return I want half this list accomplished, otherwise all of you will be walking out of an airlock. Am I understood?"

There was only silence in response. Natalie just shook her head as she turned and followed Buck out of the room.

"What is it?" she asked, rubbing her temples again.

"We have a situation down on Middle Deck Thirty-Six," Buck said. "A woman claims she was violated by three of our soldiers."

"And what do the soldiers say?" Natalie asked.

"They deny it, of course," Buck replied. "But that's expected."

"Yes, it is," Natalie said. "And the physicians? Was she examined?"

"I had her examined the second the report came across my desk," Buck said then rolled his eyes. "Helios, I can't believe I have a desk."

"I cannot believe it myself," Natalie frowned. "What did the physicians say?"

"They say there was evidence she had sexual intercourse, but couldn't say if she had been violated," Buck said.

"Did you interview her?" Natalie asked.

"I did," Buck nodded.

"And...?" Natalie asked as voices began to rise from the conference room. "Hey! Don't make me come in there!"

The voices quieted instantly.

"She was raped," Buck said. "I have no doubt. I've been in this game a long time and know when a whore is trying to make some credits. This woman isn't a whore and she isn't trying to make any credits. When I talked to the men they could barely keep the smirks off their faces."

"Then what's the fucking problem, Buck?" Natalie asked. "Throw the rapist assholes in cells and let them rot for their entire tour on this stupid fucking station! Helios, I hate this place!"

"The problem is the woman's deck wants blood and the rest of the men in our soldiers' troop are willing to kill to keep their guys free," Buck said. "Oh, and one of the men is the son of a steward. If it wasn't such a mess then I would have handled it myself."

"Shit fucking shit," Natalie muttered. "Just what I need today. Take me to the men. I'll have a nice chat with them then we'll go talk to the deck boss so he can get his people under control. Maybe Mr. Son Of A Steward can have daddy make a large donation to Middle Deck Thirty-Seven for some clinic or something."

"Middle Deck Thirty-Six," Buck corrected.

"I don't fucking care!" Natalie roared.

*

"So, your father is a steward, is he?" Natalie asked as she sat across from the smirking young man.

"He is," Case Oweyn replied. "He's pretty important in the meeting."

"Yeah, not so much anymore," Natalie grinned. "Your daddy is in the Third Spire. Didn't your mother tell you?"

"That's shaowshit," Case responded. "Someone would have sent word."

JAKE BIBLE

"Not your mother?" Natalie asked.

"My mother is dead," Case said.

"No siblings?" Natalie asked as she opened a file in front of her. She looked it over then closed it and shoved it aside. "Helios, I hate paperwork. How about you just lay it all out on the table? Admit you raped the Thraenish woman, do your time, then you can go home to daddy. By then, he'll probably be out of the Third Spire. My brother Alexis is reversing a few decisions that my brother Richard made while acting as regent."

"I'm not admitting to anything," Case said. "The whore took my money, took my friends' money, then started crying rape as soon as we left. This is a shakedown."

"I'd agree with you, if you weren't so obviously lying through your asshole," Natalie said. "I've been around grendt vents like you my whole life. Privileged, whiny scions of powerful families that think their shit doesn't stink and they can do whatever they want and get away with it. Which, to be honest, on Station Aelon, brats like you can. News like this would never reach my ears. I'd have no clue you even existed."

"We met once when I was younger," Case said.

"Great, how wonderful for you," Natalie responded. "Doesn't change the fact that we aren't on Station Aelon, we're on Station Thraen. This is enemy territory, Case Oweyn, steward's son. Every tiny, little mistake you stupid idiots make is amplified by a million and I have to be the one to deal with it! Me! Shit can't be swept under the rug because all the shit that happens here gets swept over to me and I don't have a fucking rug!"

"You have a nasty mouth, though," Case smirked.

"Next person that says that to me gets theirs sliced open," Natalie snarled. "You got anything else you want to say, smartass?"

Case sat there, his arms crossed, silent and grinning. The minoress stood up and grabbed his file from the table.

"Last chance," Natalie said. "Play this my way or I hand you over to the Thraens."

"You what?" Case shouted. "You can't do that! They'll kill me!"

"Yeah, they will," Natalie said. "They'll not just kill you, they'll cut your nuts off and feed them to you before they slit your throat. If you're lucky, that's all they'll do."

"Even if he is in the Third Spire, my father will not let this stand!" Case said. "He'll have you all killed for this!"

- 297 -

Natalie was stepping towards the door of the small room, but stopped in her tracks.

"What did you say?" she asked, crossing back around the table. She leaned down and got right in Case's face. "Did you just threaten the royal family?"

"No," Case said. "How can I threaten the royal family? I'm just a steward's son stuck on a whole other station."

"Kid, you had better watch what you say around me," Natalie said. She flicked the end of the young man's nose. "I don't play anywhere near as nice as the Thraens."

"What does it matter?" Case sneered. "The Thraens are going to kill me anyway."

"Helios, you are a moron," Natalie said. "You actually think I'm going to let them kill one of my soldiers? I do that and Station Aelon will be calling for blood. Not that the Thraens won't get theirs."

"What does that mean?" Case asked.

"It means I am giving you this last chance to confess to raping that woman," Natalie said. "You confess and you get to spend the next couple of years in a holding cell. Then I transfer you and your buddies back to Station Aelon. They aren't sons of a steward, but simple middledeckers. They'll do more time on Aelon and you will get to go home to daddy under estate arrest."

Natalie poked him in the chest.

"Keep acting like an idiot and I hand you over to the Thraens. They flog the shit out of you and then you spend the rest of your tour in a holding cell here on Station Thraen. And surprise! You re-up for another tour and get to spend that one in the same holding cell! By the time you get out you'll be too old to have kids of your own and that Oweyn line dies off, because no self-respecting noblewoman wants an old, wrinkled, rapist piece of shit for a husband. You'll be lucky if you can get a lowdecker to suck your cock when you get home."

Case glared at the minoress and shook his head. "I. Didn't. Do. It."

"Alright," Natalie said. "You didn't do it. You can scream that when the whip splits your back wide open."

*

"We want a piece of them," the Middle Deck Thirty-Six Deck Boss said to Natalie as the last of the three soldiers was done being flogged. Thirty-six lashes apiece directly from the deck boss, then thirty-six more apiece from the woman they raped. "My people will not be satisfied unless something is taken from each of them, just like something was taken from Madleeda."

"You've pretty much stripped the flesh from their backs, Wellot," Natalie stated. "Now they are mine. I'll take it from here."

"We want a piece of them," Deck Boss Wellot insisted. "There will not be satisfaction unless they leave pieces of themselves on this deck. We will cast the pieces in metal and place them in the atrium for all to see."

"Helios, that's pretty sick," Buck said from Natalie's side. "Look at the guys. If we don't get them to a physician soon, at least one of them is going to bleed to death. No way you're cutting more off."

"Then we do not have satisfaction," Wellot said. "No soldier will be safe on my deck."

"The Helios they won't," Natalie growled. She stepped up to the man and looked him right in the eye, which was possible because of her Teirmont height. "This ends now, Wellot. This was the deal. Now, we are taking these soldiers to be treated by a physician and then they will spend a very long time in very small cells. Step back, do not try to stop me, and I'll forget this insult. Don't step back, do try to stop me, and I'll have my longslingers open fire on this crowd until all are obliterated."

Wellot looked around and noticed the men standing off in the shadows of the atrium for the first time. Natalie couldn't help but smile at his surprise.

"Yeah, you're dealing with Aelons now, Wellot," Natalie said. "We like to fight. We especially like to fight when our opponents don't see us coming."

"Your opponents," Wellot scoffed. "Yes, that is how you see us." He waved his hand at the three bleeding Aelons strapped to posts in the middle of the atrium. "Take them. Get that Aelish trash off my deck. And do not come back."

"Oh, I'll fucking come back if I want to come back!" Natalie shouted.

"Nats, calm," Buck said as he took the minoress by the arm. "Everyone is watching. Let's not make it worse."

Natalie looked around at the Tharenish eyes that were focused on her. She spat a wad of phlegm at Wellot's feet then turned and stormed from the atrium. By the time she reached the lift, all she could see was red.

"I want every commander to meet with me first thing in the morning," Natalie growled as she stepped onto the lift with Buck. "This shit does not happen again. Not while I'm on this station. Are we understood, Buck?"

"Loud and clear, Nats," Buck said. "Loud and clear."

*

"It looks like we both have our Oweyn problems," Alexis said as he sat in front of the video monitor. "Nats? Can you hear me? The signal is breaking up."

"Yeah, I can hear you, A," Natalie replied, her face a grainy, wavy mess on the monitor. "The tech is saying there is interference from Helios."

"The Dear Parent is breaking up video coms now?" Alexis laughed. "He must truly be bored."

"Funny," Natalie said. "No, it's spots or something. Doesn't matter. What do you want me to do about Case Oweyn?"

"What do you mean?" Alexis asked. "Keep him locked up for the term of his sentence."

"Is that a good idea?" Natalie asked. "I've been talking with my boys and the Order and they are somewhat in agreement that by locking up Steward Oweyn on Station Aelon while also locking up Case Oweyn on Station Thraen may look suspicious."

"That's what your boys and the Order said?" Alexis asked, leaning closer to the monitor. "That doesn't sound like them at all. Who have you really been talking to, Nats?"

"No one," Natalie replied.

"And you call me a shit liar," Alexis laughed. "Who have you been talking to?"

Natalie took a deep breath then let it out slowly. "Father. I've been talking with Father. It's his opinion—which I do not agree with a hundred percent, by the way—that we let Steward Oweyn go and use the incarceration of his son to keep him in line."

"If I let that man go, he will stir up dissent within the meeting," Alexis said.

"Then remove him from the meeting," Natalie suggested.

"Nats, I can't do that," Alexis replied. "Every steward has a right to sit at the table. It is in the basic charter of Station Aelon that all stewards are part of the meeting. The basic foundation of the monarchy rests on the fact that the nobility get a voice."

"Then change the charter," Natalie said. "Our great-grandfather did it when he created the meeting of passengers. Those passengers have to be appointed to their meeting by their stewards. Make it so *you* appoint the stewards to their meeting. Those bastards will all step in line once they realize their positions on the station depend on your whim."

"Are you listening to yourself, Nats?" Alexis frowned. "You can't honestly believe that. I think the Thraens are getting inside your head."

"This whole place is getting inside my head, A!" Natalie shouted. "I'm not meant to be an administrator! If you can even call me that! I'm more like a glorified nanny for Master Lionel!"

"How is the man?" Alexis asked. "I haven't spoken to him in a week or so."

"Do not change the subject," Natalie growled. "His Royal Assholeness is just fine. Or I think he is. He doesn't grant me much time."

"He does not have to grant you anything, Nats," Alexis said. "You tell him when you will meet. He has to listen to you or he is in violation of the treaty. One violation and I have the right to toss him out an airlock. You negotiated all of those terms beautifully, now use them."

"If I toss him out of an airlock I'll have the right to kiss my ass goodbye, A," Natalie replied. "Occupying a foreign station is not an easy thing."

"I am aware of that, Nats, I have—"

"Shut up and listen to me," Natalie snapped. "You aren't aware of anything. This isn't the primes, A. This isn't a wild, wide open piece of land where we can send battle skids and regiments of soldiers in to take care of a commoner riot or a miner uprising. This is a station with hundreds of thousands of people on it. Hundreds of thousands of angry people who would love to catch me in a dark passageway and shove particle barbs up my twat. You do not know Helios all about this situation because you are on Station Aelon playing Master of the System!"

Alexis sat there for a couple of seconds then nodded.

"You are correct, Nats," Alexis finally admitted. "I don't know shit about what you are dealing with despite, all the reports I receive from you and the Order. I apologize. I have put you in a dangerous and chaotic situation. You deserve more respect."

"Damn right I do," Natalie said. "And it doesn't help that I haven't gotten laid in a really fucking long time."

"I didn't need to hear that," Alexis grinned. "But, speaking of, Clerke is waiting outside the door to talk to you. I'll go get him."

"Clerke is there?" Natalie cried. "I thought he was performing on Station Flaen all month?"

"Some contract dispute," Alexis said. "I'll let him explain."

"Yeah, go get his ass," Natalie said. "I'm done talking to your ugly face."

"Love you too, Sis," Alexis grinned.

"And tell him to lock the door when he comes in," Natalie said. "We need some private time."

"Didn't need to hear that either," Alexis said as he went to the com room's door. "I'll call you later in the week, Nats. Be safe."

"You too, A," Natalie said. "Now go get my man!"

*

The meal was cleared from the table and Alexis waited as two glasses of gelberry wine were poured before he started a conversation he did not want to have.

"I hate to bring this up," Alexis said. "Especially since it's been such a nice lunch and you've only been back on the station for a couple days, but I have a favor to ask you."

Clerke took a sip of his wine and smirked. "Oh, you do? I would never have guessed. You always bring out the best vintages when we have lunch."

"You noticed?" Alexis smiled.

"The point was for me to notice," Clerke said. "And I'm an artist. I know my wines."

"Fair enough," Alexis said. "Now, before I start, I want you to know that you can refuse my request without any worry of repercussions."

"Oh, I know," Clerke replied.

"You do?" Alexis asked.

"Sure," Clerke said as he took another sip. "Your sister would gut you if you let anything happen to me. She's handy like that."

"That is true," Alexis said. "But it's not just that, although that is a big part. It's also that I like you, Clerke. For all intents, you are my brother-in-law. Maybe not legally, or in the eyes of Helios, but you are the closest thing I have to a brother right now. Except for Richard, of course."

"You flatter me, sire," Clerke said. "And, yes, let us not forget Richard. He's a strange one, isn't he?"

"He has his quirks," Alexis replied. "But he handled himself well enough when I was off station taking Thraen. I'm not sure he has the stomach to be master, though."

"Few do," Clerke said, pouring more wine for both of them. "I certainly wouldn't want the job."

"There are days I don't want it either," Alexis laughed. "You aren't the most popular person on the station, or in the System, as a master. Which brings me to my favor."

"Yes?" Clerke asked, raising his eyebrows.

"I need someone that has access to other stations. Someone who people talk to that could perhaps relay information back to me," Alexis said, watching Clerke carefully. "Mainly so I know how I am perceived out in the System. I am so busy keeping my grip on Station Thraen, I do not have the energy to watch my back when it comes to the other stations."

"You need someone to give you a heads up if another station decides to pull an Alexis and lay claim to Station Aelon, is that it?" Clerke asked.

"That's exactly it," Alexis nodded.

"You know there's a word for a person like that, right?" Clerke smirked.

"Yes, well...." Alexis smirked back.

"A spy," Clerke laughed. "You want me to become a spy for Station Aelon."

"Not for Station Aelon," Alexis corrected. "For the Master of Station Aelon."

"What's the difference?" Clerke asked.

"You would only report to me, no one else," Alexis explained. "Not the meetings, not the Order, not even my mother and father. Me, and me alone."

"Hmm," Clerke mused. "Royal Spy, Petro Clerke. It does have a ring to it."

"It has no ring because you could never admit what you are doing," Alexis said. "You could tell no one. It would be bad for Family Teirmont and it would be bad for you. If you are caught."

"Caught? I'd never get caught," Clerke said. "You haven't caught me yet and I've been spying for Station Haelm for years." The look on Alexis's face changed instantly and Clerke rolled his eyes. "That was a joke."

"Stick to music, bard," Alexis replied. "Because your comedy needs work. Jokes like that could get you killed."

"Ha! You think threats like that scare me? Please," Clerke laughed. "You haven't performed in front of an atrium of Plaervian middledeckers before. You screw up one intonation on that station and it's the difference between saying you want to screw *some* ladies or screw *their* ladies."

"Will you do it?" Alexis asked, his eyes watching Clerke carefully.

"Do I have a choice?" Clerke shrugged.

"Of course you do," Alexis frowned. "I'm not some psychotic despot."

"I wouldn't say that in front of any Thraens," Clerke replied. He set his glass down and rested his arms on the table. "I'll do it. But I'm not doing it for you. I'm doing it for Nats. The more information I have, the safer she is. At least, that's how I like to see it. Makes me feel chivalrous."

"Except she can't know," Alexis said.

"Right, yeah, that is a problem," Clerke said. "Are you sure she can't know?"

"She can't know," Alexis insisted. "Not at all."

"Okay, I'll still do it," Clerke said. "But I get to write songs about it. I'll create a stage show around some new super spy persona. The ladies love that stuff, no matter what intonation I use."

"You are a strange creature, Petro Clerke," Alexis laughed.

"Which is why I fit in with you lot," Clerke laughed back. "Now, pour more wine, sire! We need to get thoroughly pissed to celebrate my new standing as secret agent to the Master of Station Aelon!"

*

"I trust my people have been treating you with respect, Master Lionel?" Alexis asked as he glanced at the video monitor that had been set up in Station Aelon's great hall. "My sister has told me that there have been some issues with some of the soldiers, but she is handling it."

"Do we need to use this blasted contraption?" Lionel snapped. "I have been told that these things will steal your soul right out of Helios's grasp. We never used these damned things before."

"The technology has improved considerably over the years," Alexis said. "A byproduct of our wars. Innovation is spurred when violence is about."

"I could do without either of those," Lionel sighed. "Can we get down to business, Alexis? I do have a station to run, despite your sister's constant hovering and unwanted suggestions. Say your piece so I may find my peace and turn this possessed machine off."

"Your people and my people have worked out all of the issues of our relationship except for one," Alexis said. He shuffled a couple stacks of papers that were in front of him on the long table until he found what he needed. "Ah, here. Proportionate taxes of competing goods and services."

"Proportionate...? What in Helios are you babbling about, man?" Lionel snapped. "You are already taxing my station enough to make us bleed. Anymore and we'll drop dead."

"I am babbling about goods and services that Station Thraen provides to the System that Station Aelon also provides," Alexis said. "I have been told that you are trying to undercut our prices and stifling my people's growth. I cannot have that."

"So, what? You will tax us out of the market? Is that your plan?" Lionel glared.

"No, not at all," Alexis said. "We will make sure pricing is even between the stations. I will catch flak from my people, but it is the fair thing to do."

"If my merchants and manufacturers decide to lower prices then I am not inclined to stop them," Lionel said. "Right now their sights are set on you and your sister. I agree to what you want and their sights will turn on me. It's suicide."

"No, no, no sights will turn on you, Lionel," Alexis said. "I propose a tariff on specific goods and services. If your people maintain an even and fair pricing structure then the tariff does not go into effect. But, if their pricing goes below Station Aelon pricing, a tariff is triggered and all of those proceeds go directly to the Aelish crown, bypassing Thraen altogether."

"My people would never willingly put money in your coffers," Lionel replied.

"Exactly," Alexis said. "That is their incentive to keep pricing fair. If they don't then they directly fund my monarchy. I think it's rather brilliant."

"I can see that on your face, even with this horrid signal," Lionel replied. He sat there for several seconds before continuing. "Fine. Put it in writing. I'll have my people read it over and I'll sign it. After that we are done. No more interference in Thraenish matters."

"Well, we aren't completely done," Alexis said. "We have the issue of you swearing public fealty. I have said from the beginning that, in order for you to return to Station Thraen, you would need to swear before the entire System that you and the Thraenish monarchy recognize my supremacy. That has not happened yet."

"I already swore before the High Guardian," Lionel growled.

"The treaty says 'System.'" Alexis smiled. "And as much as the High Guardian would like to believe he is the System, he is not."

"And how in Helios would you propose I do this? Tour every station like that bard of your sister's and perform my words? I am a master! I do not have time for this ridiculous request!" Lionel shouted.

"You wouldn't have to leave your station, Lionel," Alexis smiled. "You would be sitting right where you are now."

Lionel furrowed his brow and shook his head. "You make no sense, boy. Have you been sniffing...Oh, you mean for me to use this idiot box, don't you?"

"I do," Alexis nodded. "I'll have my techs coordinate with the other techs on the other stations. Once the technological arrangements have been made, I will contact you. I would advise you begin writing your speech now. I'll need to see it for approval beforehand, of course."

Lionel sputtered at the screen then stood and left. A second later a Thraenish tech leaned into the camera.

"I am sorry, Your Highness, but Master Lionel has left the communications room," the tech said. "But he did say to do whatever your techs need from us to make the arrangements happen."

"Good, good," Alexis said. "I'll have them get in touch with you directly. Goodbye."

An attendant hurried over to the monitor and switched it off then began wheeling it out of the great hall as another attendant spooled the wires and cables connected to the setup.

Alexis watched them go, then stared at the mountains of paperwork before him. He rubbed his temples and closed his eyes for a minute. Someone cleared his throat and Alexis reluctantly opened his eyes.

"What is it?" Alexis asked.

"Steward Oweyn is here to see you, sire," the attendant said. "He does not have an appointment, but still insists on speaking to you."

"Show him in," Alexis said then mumbled, "Helios, how I miss the days of battle and blood. This administrative crap is going to kill me."

"Your Highness?" Steward Oweyn asked as he was shown into the great hall. "Did you address me?"

"No, Oweyn, I did not," Alexis said. "I was just lamenting about simpler times."

"Aren't we all, Your Highness." Oweyn bowed then glanced at a chair close to the master. "May I sit?"

"You may," Alexis said, gesturing to the chair. "But please make this quick, Oweyn. I have more work to get to today than all the past reigns combined. What do you want?"

"I would like to speak to you about my son, sire," Oweyn said as he took his seat. "He is still being held on Station Thraen."

"Yes, I know," Alexis replied. "That was part of the agreement of your release. He stay incarcerated so that you do not resist the crown again."

"Yes, yes, of course, sire, I understand," Oweyn replied. "It is a wise strategy, but an unnecessary one, I feel. I have sworn my loyalty to you again and again. I have even given up my seat at the meeting to satisfy your trust in me. But. . . ."

"Yes, Oweyn? Continue," Alexis sighed. "Tell me what you need to tell me so I can get on with my day."

"Well, sire, his mother is very ill," Oweyn said. "She has been for some time. It is an affliction of the brain and I fear she will not hang on long enough to see the boy released."

"Yes, I can see why you have come to me," Alexis said. "But I cannot release him on those grounds. I have two stations to think about, not just one steward's son. If I let him go because of family issues then I'll be inundated with requests from every single prisoner in the cells on this station and Station Thraen." Alexis waved his hands at the paperwork before him. "Do you think I have that kind of time, man? If you do, then perhaps you have the brain affliction, not the boy's mother!"

"Right, yes, my apologies, sire," Oweyn said as he stood quickly. "I just thought I would try. Thank you for your time. I wish something could be done. If only he could see her face one last time, but the interest of the entire station must be thought of first. Thank you again, sire. I will take my leave now."

Oweyn bowed low and hurried away from the long table.

"Oweyn! Wait!" Alexis called out. "While I cannot set him completely free, I could be convinced to give him a brief leave. He could return to

Station Aelon for one day to see his mother, but he would have to go back on a shuttle the very same day and finish his sentence on Station Thraen. He will not be allowed to stay overnight on this station. Will that work?"

"You would allow that, sire?" Oweyn asked. "That would be most gracious of you!"

"Fine. Then it is settled," Alexis said. "Speak to the diplomatic corps. They will make the arrangements with Minoress Natalie and the Order of Jex. But, know this, Oweyn: if your son were to try anything, anything at all, I will have him cut down in front of his mother's eyes. Are we clear?"

"We are clear, sire," Oweyn nodded. "Thank you, sire!"

He hurried from the great hall, leaving Alexis alone with his mounds of papers once again.

Alexis held up a glass and it was refilled immediately by an attendant.

"Leave the pitcher," Alexis said. "And be sure to bring more. I will need half the wine cellar for today's tasks."

*

"Well, Oweyn, I am impressed," Minor George said as the steward stood before him. "I did not think you had it in you for such deception and planning."

"He's desperate, Brother," Minoress Georgia stated. "Look at the man. You can almost smell it on him."

"Is your wife really ill?" George asked.

"No, my lord, she passed away several years ago," Oweyn smiled. "The master was too busy playing war to have noticed or remembered. But my sister is ill, and that is who my son will see. If we are questioned, I will say there was some misunderstanding, is all. Master Alexis is drowning in mundane affairs of the station. I doubt he knows what day it is half the time."

"Lovely," George grinned. "Just lovely."

"How will this work exactly, Oweyn?" Georgia asked. "Tell us your brilliant plan for extracting us from this nightmarish Third Spire and returning us to our place by our father's side."

"It is simple," Oweyn said. "My son will be brought over from Station Thraen under heavy guard. He will proceed to my estate to see his aunt.

He will see her, there will be a tearful goodbye, then he will be brought back to the shuttle to return to Thraen. While the guards are focused on transporting him to and fro, I will arrange for your release from this cell. That will be the hardest part, but it can be done. You will be hidden aboard the shuttle and returned to Station Thraen with my son."

"They will search the shuttle before he boards," George said. "We will be found."

"You will not be aboard when they conduct the final search," Oweyn said. "My son will resist at the last second, causing a great commotion, and that is when we will sneak you aboard. The guards will be so focused on securing my son that they will not even notice you. The shuttle returns, you wait until my son and the guards have disembarked, then we sneak you out and hurry you to the royal castle and your father's arms."

"There is a lot of room for things to go wrong, Oweyn," Georgia said.

"No plan is perfect, my lady," Oweyn bowed. "I am risking my son's very life to secure your freedom. I do not take any step of this plan lightly."

"No, I expect you do not," George said then smiled at his sister. "I believe Helios is handing us our one and only chance, Sister. Do we take it?"

"Anything to get us out of here," Georgia replied. She leaned in and lightly kissed her brother's lips. "Not that the company hasn't been enjoyable."

Oweyn looked away in obvious discomfort.

"Well, is there anything else we should know?" George asked.

"No, my lord," Oweyn replied. "You need not be bothered with the specifics."

"Then leave us, steward," George said. "Go make your plans and begone."

"Yes, my lord," Oweyn bowed. "It has been an honor."

The steward quickly left the cell and hurried down the steps of the Third Spire. He had a million pieces to put into place before his plot could come to fruition.

*

"I believe you have used this video communications system more during your rule than all previous Aelish monarchs combined," Mistress Alexis laughed, her face surprisingly clear on the video monitor.

"Well, when you are the ruler of two stations and two primes, you have to find some way to efficiently coordinate all of the moving parts," Alexis replied from his seat in his royal sitting room. "The techs have made it considerably more portable, which adds to its convenience."

"Are you not worried that all of your broadcasts will be intercepted?" Kel asked, nudging his wife over so he could be seen as well. "Do not trade security for convenience."

"My techs have assured me that they have perfected a technique called 'scrambling.'" Alexis laughed. "Whatever that means. They tell me that the only way our communications can be intercepted is if the party on the other end has the proper codes. It has been done with audio for some time, but now works with video as well."

"What an amazing era we have entered," Mistress Alexis smiled. "My son not only rules two stations, but he rules the airwaves. Is that the proper term? Airwaves? The tech that set this new system up for us said it ran on airwaves."

"I believe he was referring to Vape gas, my love," Kel said. "It runs on Vape gas. Just like everything else in the System."

"No, love of my life, he did not mean that," Mistress Alexis said. "He said the signal was made of airwaves. That is how this all works. Airwaves that get sent out and airwaves that get picked up. Just like the com system, supposedly."

"Broadcast and received," Alexis said. "Those are the correct terms."

"Yes, well, now that we are all fairly educated on video communications systems," Kel said. "Can we speak of more important business?"

"I was hoping to avoid business today, Father," Alexis sighed. "All I deal with is business, business, business. Could we not just have a friendly, family chat?"

"That would be ideal, A," Kel said. "But you have appointed us to maintain the primes while you rule the stations. While we are both more than capable of handling the task—"

"The responsibility ultimately lies in the hands of the Master of Station Aelon," Mistress Alexis interrupted.

"I was about to say that, love," Kel said.

"I know, dearest heart," Mistress Alexis replied. "But you were taking too long."

"I was not taking too long, Lexi," Kel said. "I was taking as long as was needed."

"Mother, Father, please," Alexis sighed. "I do not have time to hear you two bicker."

"Oh, we aren't bickering, Son," Kel said. "We are just bored."

"Bored?" Alexis asked.

"Bored, love," Mistress Alexis said. "As much as we both love the primes, we are in need of a well...."

"Tell him," Kel said.

"I am!" Mistress Alexis snapped.

"In need of what?" Alexis asked. "Mother? Father? Just come out with it!"

"No need to take that tone," Mistress Alexis frowned. "I am still your mother and I will always be your better when it comes to a blade."

"Does it always have to come to that with you, Mother?" Alexis asked. "Just tell me what you need."

"A vacation, Son," Kel said. "We need a vacation. Off the planet, off Helios. Your sister's friend, Clerke, has invited us to one of his performances on Station Haelm. While neither of us are fans of the Haelmish people, we would be fools to pass up this opportunity."

"A vacation? Is work down there so hard?" Alexis asked.

"It is not the work, A," Mistress Alexis replied. "The work is simple and the managers handle most of the day to day operations. It is just that we need to see something other than the constant banks of Vape clouds."

"The Vape storms are hard on us, A," Kel said. "I swear to Helios I can barely bend my knees or roll my shoulders when a bad one comes in. We could use some station gravity to give these old joints a rest."

"I'll be honest," Alexis chuckled. "I never in my life would have expected those words to come out of your mouth. Mistress Alexis and Master Kel wanting off the planet? I'll need to mark the time and day of this occasion."

"Oh, stop being a shit," Mistress Alexis said. "Get us off the primes. Just for a couple of weeks."

"If you are going to Station Haelm then it will be more than a couple of weeks," Alexis said. "Between the portal schedules alone you'll need at least two months."

"No, no, not if we come to Station Aelon first," Mistress Alexis said. "Then we can take a direct shuttle to Station Haelm. It will cut off three weeks. We'll return to Station Aelon in time for the next rotation and return to Helios."

"Wow, you have thought this out, haven't you?" Alexis said. "Fine, if that is what my parents need then that is what my parents will have."

"It also means we will be on the station when Master Lionel gives his fealty speech," Kel said. "We would both like to be seated with you and Richard when that happens."

"If only Nats could be with us as well," Mistress Alexis frowned. "It has been so long since we've all been together."

"Unfortunately, Richard will not be here during that time either," Alexis said. "He is with a delegation leaving for Station Klaerv to discuss new breen weaving techniques and production."

"Oh, yes, that is right," Mistress Alexis said.

"We had forgotten," Kel added.

"You had forgotten? Why would you know in the first place?" Alexis asked. "This is a routine trade mission."

"Yes, of course it is," Kel nodded.

"Father, Mother, what are you two up to?" Alexis asked.

"Nothing, A," Mistress Alexis smiled. "We just keep up with the our children's lives, is all."

"I don't buy that for a second," Alexis said. "Out with it."

"Well. . . ." Kel started. "Should we say?"

"You are being ordered to say by the Master of Station Aelon, Station Thraen, and their primes," Alexis growled.

"You are so cute when you do that," Mistress Alexis smiled. "Go ahead and tell him, Kel."

"We have been speaking with Master Jeffon of Station Klaerv," Kel began. "And it turns out his oldest daughter is a widow. Her husband passed early last year and her mourning period is done."

"We believe she would be a great match for you, A," Mistress Alexis said. "It is almost as if fate wants two royals, both that have lost their mates, to come together."

"Mother, no," Alexis said. "I do not need more complications right now."

"Having a life partner helps ease the burden of complications," Kel said.

"You should at least wait to hear from your brother before you decide," Mistress Alexis said.

"No," Alexis stated. "And no more discussing it."

His parents stared out through the video screen and studied their son. Their shoulders slumped and they nodded at the same time.

"It was worth a try," Kel said.

"No point in sending Richard to Klaerv then," Mistress Alexis said. "He knows less about breen weaving than he does about how to handle the meeting of stewards. I love my youngest dearly, but the man was not born to rule. Not like you, A."

"I may agree with you there, but Richard is still going," Alexis said. "We need all the goodwill we can get with the other stations. Sending my only brother will help solidify relations with Station Klaerv."

"Which is why you are master," Mistress Alexis said. "You see the practical in all plans."

The video screen started to break up.

"A? About that vacation?" Kel smiled.

"Yes, yes, go ahead and make all the plans," Alexis nodded. "It will be nice to see both of you and to share in the occasion of that grendt Lionel having to eat shaowshit and swear his fealty to me."

"That will be the highlight of our trip," Mistress Alexis laughed as the screen wavered considerably. "We are losing you, A. We love you!"

"Love you too," Alexis said as the signal winked out. "And miss you more than you know."

*

"Well, this is quite the reception," Mistress Alexis said as she stepped from the shuttle dock airlock. "Are you expecting us to invade our own Station, Alexis?"

"Four guards is more than enough to keep watch over an airlock, Son," Kel chuckled. "I don't believe you need a dozen."

"We had some trouble last week with a prisoner trying to escape," Alexis said. "He caused enough chaos that the Order insisted we increase our manpower at all shuttle dock airlocks. At least until things cool off with Station Thraen."

"So this is permanent, then?" Kel grinned.

"Don't tease, love," Mistress Alexis said. "The Order is doing what the Order is supposed to do which is to support the crown at all times. If they feel more guards are needed then more guards are needed."

"Thank you, Mother," Alexis said as he kissed her on the cheek. "It is wonderful to see you both."

"You as well Son," Kel said as he embraced Alexis, clapping him on the back hard enough to make the guards nervous.

"Is the Order on board the station?" Mistress Alexis asked. "I thought they were still keeping watch on Station Thraen."

"Neggle, Kinsmon, and Vast have returned to Aelon," Alexis said. "Vast is expecting a granddaughter any day now and Neggle and Kinsmon needed some well deserved time away from the Thraens before they both snap and start a System incident."

"And Richard is still on Klaerv?" Mistress Alexis asked.

"He is," Alexis nodded. "And I have actually been receiving surprisingly good reports from him and the trade delegation. Our Richard may be blossoming into a statesman after all."

"One can only hope," Mistress Alexis said. "Now, lead us to our quarters. It has been too long since I've seen Castle Quent."

"We were just here during Last Meal, love," Kel said.

"Which is too long," Mistress Alexis replied.

"Come along, you two," Alexis said. "We'll take the new lift up the back way."

"New lift? I didn't know you were putting in a new lift," Mistress Alexis said.

"Another one of the changes the Order made," Alexis said. "They insisted on a more accessible escape route from the royal quarters in case of a siege."

"A siege? On the station?" Kel asked. "Do they have intel that we do not?"

"They are just being thorough, Father," Alexis said. "Which is fine by me since I have enough to worry about as it is."

"Show us the new lift, A," Mistress Alexis said. "Is it one of the faster ones?"

"It is," Alexis nodded, then looked about. "Mother? Where is Lara? Did she not come with you?"

"No, dear, Lara is not in the greatest of health," Mistress Alexis said. "I believe I spend more of my time attending to her than she attends to me."

"She has her own attendants, love," Kel said. "They are perfectly capable of keeping her comfortable."

"I will not pawn off her care to some silly young attendant girls," Mistress Alexis said. "It was Lara's fate to be included in this family and it is my fate to make sure her remaining days are filled with love and respect."

"You two have had this conversation before, it sounds like," Alexis stated. "No need to repeat it for my benefit."

"My sentiments exactly," Kel sighed. "Take us to the lift, Son, before your mother decides to rehash the skid incident from last month."

"I am not too old to drive skids at that speed!" Mistress Alexis snapped.

"See?" Kel grinned.

*

"I do not care about the extra burden placed on the Royal Guard because of the increase in men at the shuttle dock airlocks!" Alexis roared, sitting next to his mother and father at the end of the great hall as techs hurried about the room, setting up video equipment and several large monitors. "You do not lose prisoners from the Third Spire! And you do not first notice them missing a week after they have fled!"

"Sire, the men understand their mistakes," Steward Vast said. "I will have every one of them interviewed immediately to find out where the breakdown was."

"Vast, you need not bother with that," Mistress Alexis said. "Go attend to your brand new granddaughter. We will have Neggle or Kinsmon handle the investigation."

"With all due respect, my lady," Vast bowed. "I take this personally and will handle the investigation personally. I will also met out all punishment personally, if it is warranted."

"It is obviously warranted!" Alexis shouted. "The Thraen minor and minoress escaped! How in Helios's name could you not think punishment was warranted?"

"When was the last shuttle from here to Station Thraen?" Kel asked. "You will want to interrogate the crew as well."

"The last shuttle that left our station to Thraen during that time was the shuttle transporting Case Oweyn," Vast replied. "Which was quite possibly the most heavily guarded shuttle in quite some time. It would be near impossible for the minor and minoress to stow aboard that shuttle, my lord. They are more than likely being harbored by another of the stations having escaped on a different shuttle."

"Unless they had help," Mistress Alexis said.

"Son of a grendt," Alexis growled. "That double crossing, dirty, traitorous son of a grendt!"

Alexis stood and pointed at several royal guards that stood to the side of the great hall, all looking like they would much rather be anyplace else.

"You six men! Go and find Steward Oweyn this instant! I want his ass in front of me within the hour!" Alexis shouted.

"Son, that may not be wise," Kel said.

"Oh, it is more than wise," Alexis snarled. "That little gilly slit is going to pay for this if I find out he was involved."

"No, I mean sending the guards," Kel said quietly. "We do not know which ones we can trust. We could be sending the very men to fetch Oweyn that helped him with his plot."

"Out," Alexis hissed at the royal guards. "All of you! Out!"

"I should leave as well, sire," Vast said. "Until you are certain I was not involved."

"Do not be absurd, Vast," Mistress Alexis laughed. "You will remain here with us. Your loyalty to the crown is beyond reproach."

"I thank you for the kindness, mistress, but it is not wise to trust anyone at this time," Vast replied. "If it is not me then it could be one of the other members of the Order of Jex. It may not be any of us, but you cannot be certain until you investigate."

"I just told you not to be absurd, Vast," Mistress Alexis frowned. "Did I not?"

"You did, my lady," Vast nodded.

"Then shut your grendt vent, man," Mistress Alexis said. "Go find men you trust with your life and bring Steward Oweyn to us. Contact the rest of the Order as well and inform them what has happened. We will need to all put our heads together on how to handle this."

"Sire?" Vast asked Alexis. "Is this what you wish me to do?"

"Yes, steward, it is," Alexis said. "Go. Bring Oweyn directly here and then lock this hall down. We have the equipment already set up to conference with those of the Order that are not on station. This is dire indeed, Vast."

"I know, sire," Vast said. "I swear to you now that I will not let you down."

Vast turned on his heels and hurried from the great hall. Outside the main doors was a group of Aelish nobles and stewards waiting to be admitted to the hall in order to watch Master Lionel's official oath of fealty to the Aelish crown.

"What shall we do about them?" Kel asked. "They cannot stand out there forever."

"They can and will," Alexis grumbled. "Hearing Lionel speak is far from the most pressing business at this moment."

"They will have to be told something," Mistress Alexis said as she stood. "Let me speak to them. I will tell them that we have received word of Thraenish collaborators on board the station and they should all retire to their quarters immediately. I do not believe any of those cowards have seen a day of battle in their privileged lives. They'll scatter like grendts at the first word of any threat to their persons."

"Thank you, Mother," Alexis sighed.

"Sire?" a tech asked. "The signal is locked in from Station Thraen. Shall I turn on the monitors?" He looked about the empty hall. "Or shall I wait?"

"Turn them on," Alexis said. "We might as well see the Thraen prostrate himself before me, even if it is halfway across the System."

The monitors were all switched on and the symbol of Station Thraen was the first thing to come in.

"Asshole," Alexis snapped. "He was supposed to be showing the crest of Family Teirmont."

"Lionel will be considerably harder to deal with when he finds out we no longer hold his children," Kel said. "We should consider recalling Natalie at once. For her safety. Lionel cannot be trusted without his incentive to play along in place."

"Yes, father, I have already thought of that," Alexis said. "As soon as Lionel's oath is complete, we'll send word to Natalie that she is to return to Station Aelon. It leaves the man unattended, but I see no other choice. Nats's safety is more important."

The symbol of Station Thraen faded out as a quiet fanfare was played. Replacing the image was Master Lionel seated at the head of his great hall. On either side of him were his children, Minor George to his right and Minoress Georgia to his left.

"Greetings, System Helios and the Six Stations," Lionel said, his face nothing but one massive, smug grin. "This historic broadcast was to be about me swearing fealty to the usurper, Master Alexis the Fourth of Station Aelon and its primes. Unfortunately for him, that will not be what he hears tonight."

"I have calmed them sufficiently," Mistress Alexis said as she hurried back to her seat. Her eyes went wide as she saw the minor and minoress on the monitors. "Well, we know where the little brats have gotten to."

"Quiet, Mother," Alexis hissed.

Kel gave her a stern look before she could open her mouth and reprimand their son for the rudeness.

"Tonight will instead be a declaration of war on Station Aelon," Lionel continued. "From this moment forward, all Aelons present on Station Thraen are under arrest and will be held indefinitely until Master Alexis rescinds his claim on the Thraenish crown. As I speak, Aelish soldiers, dignitaries, nobles, and diplomats are being rounded up and imprisoned. I will execute one a day until Master Alexis complies with my most humble request. His claim on my crown is an affront to Helios and an affront to the way of life this System has lived for millennia."

Lionel leaned forward and glared into the camera.

"If you are watching this, Alexis, know that your sister is being hunted like a stray shaow. When I catch her she will be one of the first to be executed. You disrespected me by imprisoning my children, I will go one further by killing your sister. You brought this on yourself, and not a person in the System believes differently. Long live Station Thraen."

Master Lionel waved at someone offscreen and the monitors all turned to static.

"Alexis," Mistress Alexis said. "We cannot—"

"I know, Mother," Alexis said. "Believe me, I know."

CHAPTER SIX

The eight Aelish soldiers ran, their long blades barely clutched in their grips as they struggled to keep their feet, all of them wounded badly, bleeding from a dozen cuts, gashes and slices.

They fled down the passageway, doors shut to them, no chance of escaping into a room of safety, no chance of being given sanctuary by a kind soul.

The passageway ended at a T and the soldiers looked left, then looked right. Two of the soldiers collapsed to their knees, their blades clattering to the hammered metal floor. Those that still stood raised their weapons as Tharenish soldiers came at them from both sides.

Slowly, tauntingly, the Thraens approached the trapped Aelons, looks of pure disgust on their faces. The Aelons looked back, looks of resignation and despair upon theirs.

"We surrender," an Aelon gasped, his face scrunched in pain as the wound in his side poured out his lifeblood. "We give up and beg your mercy."

On came the Thraens, no mercy to be seen. They did not respond, they did not give any sign they heard the Aelons the rest of the trapped soldiers began to plead for their lives until the passageway was filled with cries for mercy.

"Helios will damn you all," an Aelon whispered as the Thraenish long blades were raised. "You will burn for eternity."

"He damned us the day he allowed Aelish trash like you on our hallowed station," a Thraen replied, the one and only to speak. "Now we cleanse our passageways of your stink, your filth, your blasphemy."

The long blades came down and the passageway's floor became slick with blood. The Aelish screamed as their limbs were cut from their bodies, hacked off like cuts of shaow. The Thraens not only did not show mercy, but they savored every cut and slice, every hack and slash. The Aelish soldiers wept as much as they screamed and the Thraens only laughed.

The laughter did not stop when the Aelons were finally silenced, their heads sent tumbling down the passageway. The Thraenish soldiers made sure to collect the severed heads, jokingly jabbing them at each other, manipulating the dead mouths to say foul, awful things about Station Aelon.

Into bags the heads went and soon the laughing Thraens left the passageway, ignoring the rest of the body parts, offal, and blood that covered the floor.

Once they were gone, the doors to passenger cabins began to open. Frightened, close to petrified at the sight before them, the Thraenish passengers had no choice but to leave the safety of their cabins and clean the mess left for them. Arms were bagged, legs were bagged, torsos, hands, feet, guts, all were bagged until finally all that littered the floor was the vast quantity of blood.

The adults hauled off the body parts, dragging the heaviest of the bags through the blood and down the passageway to the incinerator chute. That left the children to fetch mops and buckets, to prepare for a long night of cleaning, a long night with the stench of coppery blood, biting urine, and loosed feces close to overwhelming them.

The Thraenish passengers worked all through the night, making sure every inch of the passageway was cleaned, refusing to leave even a drop or smear of Aelish blood behind. They had no choice. For if they did not do it, who would?

*

The six Aelish guards couldn't have run if they wanted to. Yet none wanted to. They stood shoulder to shoulder, their hands bound before them with breen rope, their legs bound at the ankles, their heads held high as the executioner stood to the side of them.

"Do you understand the charges that have been read?" Alexis asked, walking back and forth, up and down the line. "Do you understand the sentence that has been passed?"

"Yes, sire."

"Yes, my liege."

"Yes, Your Highness."

"Yes, master."

"Yes."

"Yes."

Alexis stopped and nodded to the executioner. The masked man stepped up to the first guard and pressed him on the shoulder until the man fell to his knees then lowered his head to the long, bloodstained bench just in front of him. The guard turned his head and looked up at the executioner.

"Swift and sure, if you please," the guard requested.

The executioner nodded, lifted his blade, then brought it down in one fell swoop. The guard's head came away cleanly and tumbled from the bench. The headless body was removed by two of the executioner's attendants and the man with the bloody blade moved on to the second guard.

The same motion of pressing on the guard's shoulder, the same falling to the knees and presenting the neck on the bench, the same request of "swift and sure, if you please," the same death.

When the last head rolled and the body was removed, Alexis turned to look at his mother and father, at the three men of the Order of Jex, at the assembled nobles and stewards.

"I have said it many times since that night, and I will say it many times more until Oweyn is found," Alexis growled. "If I discover anyone that has even a slight connection to the minor's and minoress's escape, I will make sure they meet the same fate as these incompetent, greedy, traitorous guards who died here today. Mercy will only come when you admit what you know and help bring Steward Oweyn to justice."

No one said a word, they all watched the calmly enraged master.

"Get out of my sight," Alexis said then changed his mind before anyone could move. "No, stay. Stay and look upon the blood. Watch it until it dries. I will remove myself from your sight instead."

Alexis turned and walked to a doorway back into Castle Quent, his boots going from soft thuds upon the grassy courtyard to loud stomps upon the hammered metal of the castle floor.

"Alexis," Kel called as he followed and caught up to his son. "Alexis, hold up."

"I have work to do, Father," Alexis said. "Important work and I do not need a lecture from a man who has never been in my position."

Kel grabbed Alexis by the arm and spun the master about.

"How dare you!" Kel shouted, getting right in Alexis's face. "I have never been in your position? Well, Son, you have never been in my position! My daughter is still on Station Thraen and I do not know if she is alive or dead! At least you knew the outcome of your daughter's future the second she was born!"

"Kel!" Mistress Alexis gasped from behind the two men. "Take that back! You taunt fate and Helios by saying such a thing!"

"He taunts us all daily with his crusade to weed out Oweyn!" Kel snapped. "Our son believes he is the only one in pain, the only one hurt and betrayed, the only one who cannot trust any of the Aelish faces around him! Well, he is not the only one!"

Alexis looked down at his father's hand that still gripped his arm.

"You will unhand me, Father," Alexis said.

"Or what, A? What will you do? Have me executed? Fight me?" Kel laughed. "You think you can take me, boy? You may be the best shot with a longsling, but I will dice you into cubes when it comes to a blade!"

"I will dice you both to cubes if you do not stop this at once," Mistress Alexis hissed, yanking her husband's hand free of her son's arm. "I may be old, but I can take you both at the same time and do not even test me on that point!"

The three Teirmonts stared at each other until Alexis shook his head, turned and walked away.

"Alexis!" Kel yelled after him. "You have to stop this! Get ahold of yourself!"

"Nothing you say will change my mind, Father!" Alexis called back. "There will be more blood spilt, day after day until I find Oweyn and his collaborators!"

The two old royals watched their son turn a corner then they turned to each other.

"He is making it worse," Kel said.

"He is in agony," Mistress Alexis said.

"We all are," Kel replied.

"We cannot stop him," Mistress Alexis said. "I know that look. It is the Teirmont thirst for revenge that drives him now and only blood will quench it."

"But how much blood, Lexi?" Kel asked. "How much blood does he need before he sees reason?"

"I don't know, my love," Mistress Alexis said. "Only Alexis knows and he is not in his right mind now."

"There is only so much blood that can be spilt before the station turns on him," Kel said.

"I know, I know," Mistress Alexis said. "Let us hope he finds Oweyn soon or our dear Natalie comes home. I fear those are our only options to save our son from himself."

*

"Give me a count," Natalie whispered as she, Buck, Jay, and Lang sat in the Lower Decks storage room of Station Thraen. "I have three cartridges."

"Six," Buck replied.

"Six as well," Lang said.

"Ten," Jay said then shrugged as he got dirty looks from the others. "I've been placing careful shots, kiss my ass."

They each looked at the meager number of particle barb cartridges they held then one by one they turned their attention to the man that lay between them, covered in blood and barely breathing.

"This isn't right, Nats," Buck said. "I know you don't want to hear it, but we can't let Baise suffer like this. Look at him. No hands, half a right leg, more holes in his chest than a pincushion. I'll do it right now, Nats. I'll draw my blade and give him the end he deserves."

"No," Natalie said. "As long as he breathes, he still has a chance."

"But what life will he have, even if we can find a way off this fucking station?" Jay asked. "Did you not hear the no hands and half a leg part? He's only part of a man now. Baise wouldn't want to keep going. If he was awake he'd ask you to do it, and you know that."

"But he isn't awake, you fuck," Natalie snapped. "So he can't ask. It's our duty to protect him and keep him alive for as long as we can. We all swore an oath, and I swear to Helios I'll slice the throat of the first one of us that breaks that oath."

"He'll be the death of us," Lang said. "Don't you dare say you haven't already been thinking it, Nats."

"Oh, I fucking have, don't you worry," Natalie replied. "But know what else I have been thinking? That I am already the death of you. You all could have stolen a shuttle and gotten off this nightmare station. But you came and found me. Each of you died the instant you made that choice. That's what I am really thinking about."

She looked down at Baise and placed her hand on the man's cold forehead. She stroked it a couple of times then looked up at her team.

"I'll stay with him," she said. "You leave. Save yourselves. Find some way off this station without me."

"There is no way, Nats," Buck said. "Lionel sent all shuttles away and has forbid any from docking. There is nowhere to go. Eventually, that son of his will track us down. When he does, I want to die by your side, Nats, not running away like a coward."

"Same here," Lang said.

"I'm with them," Jay nodded. "And I'm with you. We're a team, Nats. We live as a team, we fight as a team, and we die as a team."

"You can all suck my dick as a team," Natalie sighed. "You stupid, suicidal fucks."

"Whip it out, girl," Buck said. "I'll take it like a man."

There was a noise from outside the storage room and they instantly went silent. Their eyes locked onto the door handle, they watched and waited for it to move. After several minutes, and no repeat of the noise, they relaxed slightly, their eyes going from the handle and back to Baise.

"Even if he doesn't die from his wounds, he's going to die of thirst," Buck said. "We're all dehydrated."

"Grab me that bucket over there," Natalie said, pointing to the corner. "I'll piss in it and you can all quench your thirsts."

"Are you fucking kidding?" Jay responded. "I'd rather die, if you don't mind."

"What?" Natalie smiled. "It's royal piss. Ordained by Helios. It'll probably give you visions or something."

"Yeah, you can fuck off with that," Buck said.

"Fine, stay thirsty," Natalie said as she got up and walked over to the bucket. She dropped her trousers and squatted.

"What the fuck, Nats?" Lang said. "We are not drinking your piss!"

"Yeah, I know, dumbshit," Natalie snapped. "Doesn't mean I still don't have to pee. Morons."

*

The man shook in his robes, his eyes cast to the floor as he stood before Minor George.

"You are saying you have no idea where the minoress could be?" George asked as he placed the tip of his short blade under the quivering man's robes. "You have been working with her for months and months now, side by side, whispering in each other's Aelish ears about how lucky we Thraens are to have you here, yet she never once spoke of a contingency plan should anything go wrong? I find that hard to believe."

"I was merely a scribe, my lord," the man said. "I took the minutes of meetings, logged them, and sent them to Station Aelon for Master Alexis to read."

The blade flicked back and forth so quickly that the scribe didn't notice at first. It wasn't until the blood began to flow down his neck and over his robes that he became alarmed. By then it was too late and he collapsed at George's feet, dead in less than a second.

"Brother, love, you have to stop doing that," Minoress Georgia said, seated across the great hall at the long table. "We are running out of Aelons to interrogate. Father will be cross if we do not learn the whereabouts of Minoress Natalie soon."

"Father gets cross when the form of his shit is not to his liking," George said, leaning down and wiping his blade on the dead man's robes. "My job is not to please Father, but to kill Aelons."

"You have that backwards, Brother," Georgia sighed. "Your job is to always please Father. That comes first. It just so happens that killing Aelons pleases him. The only problem is that finding Minoress Natalie would please him more. Always go for the more pleasing option, love."

"Pleasing, more pleasing," George said as he walked over and placed his hands on his sister's shoulders. "So much pleasing, it's hard to keep it all straight."

He leaned over and kissed her hair then placed his chin on the top of her head.

"Where is Father anyway?" George asked.

"He's with the Oweyn boy," Georgia said. "Squeezing him for all the information he can about the Aelish forces here on the station. Apparently, some of the soldiers took a liking to many of our lovelier Thraen women.

Case is helping Father find the little hidey holes where those men might be tucked away in. I pity the women that have done the tucking. You know how Father is with betrayal."

"Oh, those poor, stupid girls," Georgia said. "They'll be lucky if he kills them. The less fortunate will find their own hidey holes filled by so many soldiers they could stuff shuttles in them afterwards."

"Isn't that a funny thought," George chuckled.

"Yes, it is," Georgia replied. "We should get that cartoonist you like to draw that. A shuttle shoved up a stupid whore's gilly slit. I'd have it framed and put up on my bedroom wall."

"A delightful idea, love," George said. "We'll have him make two."

George kissed his sister's hair again then straightened and started walking to the hall's doors.

"Where are you going?" Georgia asked.

"To find the cartoonist," George said. "And find a whore. All this talk of shoving things up gillies has made me randy."

"Oh, you poop," Georgia pouted. "You make me jealous when you leave to screw whores."

"The cartoonist is handsome, should I send him your way once I am done speaking with him?" George asked.

"Ooh, yes!" Georgia said and clapped. "He has such talented fingers! What a lovely thought to have them drawing upon my skin!"

"I do not think it will be his fingers he will draw with, love," George laughed as he stepped out of the hall. "More like his ample pen! Careful you do not get stained by his ink! Last thing we need is an artist in the bloodline!"

*

"Where is he?" Alexis shouted. "Show me the fucking piece of shaowshit!"

"He is here, sire," Steward Neggle said as he stepped aside to show a badly beaten Steward Oweyn sitting against the wall of the interrogation room. "We found him on the last Middle Deck, about to escape into the Lower Decks. Kinsmon and Vast are still hunting for his accomplices. We know there are more than those we caught him with, but he refuses to say."

"Of course he does," Alexis nodded. "Why would he dare give up his collaborators when there is a slight chance they could come to his rescue?" Alexis walked across the room, leaned down, and grabbed Oweyn by the neck. "But you will talk to me, won't you, steward? You will tell me everything I need to know."

Oweyn tried to speak, but all that came out was a strangled, pained gurgle.

"Sire, you are killing him," Neggle said.

"Yes, I suppose I am, Neggle," Alexis replied. "Everyone out. Now. I need to be alone with the man."

The guards looked to Neggle and he nodded. They exited the room quickly. A man in the far corner, busy laying out various instruments of torture on a tray, glanced over his shoulder at the steward.

"You as well," Neggle sighed. "I believe the master would like to be completely alone with the steward."

"I would," Alexis said as he lifted Oweyn up by his neck and tossed him into a rickety metal chair. "And for no reason should I be disturbed."

"Please," Oweyn coughed, blood spilling out of his mouth. "Please. Neggle. You know me. Our fathers worked closely—"

"Shut your traitor mouth," Neggle spat. "You know me as well, Oweyn. Do you think I would give a grendt's shit about your hide now? After what you have done? I will pray for your soul, but that is all you will get from me."

The member of the Order of Jex glanced at Alexis, nodded, then left, closing and securing the door behind him. Alexis turned slowly to Oweyn and smiled.

"My sister is missing," Alexis said. "Minoress Natalie of Station Aelon, Station Thraen, and their primes, has not been heard from since the Thraen twins escaped and set foot back on their station. All communication has been cut off, Oweyn. We can only speak with Station Thraen when Master Lionel wants us to. I have heard nothing from any of my people. Not a word from any soldiers, diplomats, dignitaries. Not a word from the Aelish families vacationing on that station."

Oweyn's eyes went wide at that last revelation. Or one eye went wide, the other was horribly swollen and leaked a pink fluid from under the lid.

"Oh, you didn't think of that, did you?" Alexis said as he turned his attention to the tray of tools in the corner of the room. "All the innocents that were only trying to experience more of the System. For many it was their first trip off Station Aelon. With my taking of my birthright, the costs to travel there plummeted. So many Aelons, so many Aelish *children*, now trapped at the mercy of Master Lionel."

Alexis picked up a small pair of wire cutters. He opened them and closed them a few times before flipping them up in the air and catching them easily.

"Do you think Master Lionel is the merciful type?" Alexis asked. "Do you think he has shown our fellow Aelons the respect they deserve as innocents involved in a game not of their making? Do you, Oweyn? Do you think we'll ever see those people again?"

"Master...." Oweyn whispered.

"No, no, you do not get to call me that anymore," Alexis spat. "I am no longer your master. You gave that up when you started sucking Lionel's cock. You gave that up when you bent this station over and let that man ram us up the ass!"

Alexis stomped over to Oweyn and grabbed the man's right ear. He shoved the wire cutters up against the terrified man's scalp and began to cut. He kept cutting until he had a severed ear in his hand.

"Open your mouth," Alexis said as Oweyn whimpered and cried. "Open your mouth or I slice your lips off."

Oweyn reluctantly opened his mouth and Alexis shoved the severed ear inside then clamped the man's jaw shut with his hand.

"Now, chew," Alexis said. "Chew and chew and chew until you can swallow your own ear."

Oweyn began to gag and Alexis tossed the wire cutters aside so he could hold the man's jaw closed with both hands.

"No you don't, Oweyn," Alexis chuckled. "No throwing up. You puke and you'll have to swallow that as well. Now. *Chew!*"

Oweyn shivered and shook as he chewed and then swallowed his own ear. He was openly crying, his entire body heaving with sobs, once he was done.

"Let me see," Alexis ordered. "Let me make sure you don't have any stuck in your teeth." Oweyn painfully opened his mouth. "Oh, my, it doesn't look like you have many teeth left. Neggle sure let his men do a number on you."

Alexis looked about and saw a second chair in the corner by the room's door. He casually walked over, grabbed it, set it in front of Oweyn and sat down.

"I'll admit something, Oweyn," Alexis said as he took one of the steward's hands in his. "I don't really have the stomach for torture. I am not like my great-grandfather, his father, or his father's father. They knew how to torture. They knew how to cut a man for days, sometimes weeks, until that man told them everything they wanted, and did not want, to know. That is not me."

Alexis twisted Oweyn's thumb, pulled then tore it right off the man's hand. Oweyn screamed and found himself with his own thumb in his mouth.

"But, being a Teirmont, there is something inside me that has been there since birth," Alexis said, snapping his fingers. "Chew, man." Oweyn began to chew as he cried and cried. "My nature has always been one of compassion and understanding. My mother used to worry that it would be my weakness as a master one day." He leaned in. "Do you think it is my weakness, Oweyn?"

Oweyn kept chewing then swallowed, but didn't reply.

"I asked you a question, steward," Alexis said.

"No...sire...I...do not...think you...have a...weakness," Oweyn gasped, bits of thumb flesh and bone spilling out over his bottom lip and onto his chin.

"You got a little something there," Alexis said and wiped Oweyn's chin. "And, for the record, you are wrong, Oweyn. I do have a weakness. It is my family. That is something Master Lionel knows about me. That is something he is exploiting right now."

"I...am...sorry," Oweyn muttered.

"What was that, man? Speak up, for Helios's sake!" Alexis shouted. "Did you say you were sorry? Do you think any apology will save you now? There is absolutely nothing that will save you! Nothing!"

Alexis wiped his hands on his trousers and stood up. He paced for a couple of minutes then turned to Oweyn and grinned. It was a horrible grin, a predatory grin, a Teirmont grin.

"You and I have something in common, Oweyn," Alexis said finally. "Family. You did what you did because of your son, I understand that. I am doing what I am doing because of my sister. So let us come to an

REIGN OF FOUR: BOOK IV

agreement, shall we? You tell me the names of every last one of the men on this station that assisted you with your little plot and I will makes sure that every last one of your relatives is kept from harm. Your nieces, your nephews, your sister, your two brothers, your cousins and their families. All will be spared. Can we agree on that?"

Oweyn looked up at the master, his one eye almost rolling in his head.

"Look directly at me when I talk to you, man!" Alexis shouted and Oweyn's rolling eye snapped to attention. "Can we agree?"

Oweyn nodded once, spat some thumb out onto the floor, and nodded again.

"Good," Alexis said. "I swear you have my word that not a hair on your relatives' heads will be harmed. Just give me the names of your collaborators."

Oweyn nodded, bloody tears streaming from his one open eye.

"I'll probably need pen and paper, won't I?" Alexis asked.

Oweyn nodded again.

Alexis knocked on the door and it opened immediately. A guard looked in, deliberately averting his eyes from Steward Oweyn, and bowed his head at Alexis.

"Yes, sire?" the guard asked.

"Pen and paper," Alexis said. "The steward has decided to cooperate."

"Right away, sire," the guard said and closed the door.

Alexis turned and leaned against the wall by the door, crossing his arms as he smiled at Oweyn.

"It'll be just a minute," Alexis said. "You sit tight, alright?"

*

"We have one here, sir!" a Thraenish soldier shouted as he shoved open the storage room door. "Looks wounded!"

The soldier moved into the room, his long blade drawn and ready for an attack, but the storage room was empty except for Baise's body. The soldier knelt next to the Aelon and cautiously reached out and felt for a pulse on Baise's neck.

"Dead, sir!" the soldier called out as the doorway became crowded with more Thraens.

A tall man, battle scarred and looking as if he hadn't slept in days, shoved past the soldiers and into the storage room.

"Dead? Are you sure, soldier?" the man asked.

"Yes, Colonel, I am," the soldier nodded. "He looks familiar? Is this one of Minoress Natalie's men?"

"Move," the colonel snapped, shoving the soldier out of the way. "Can't get a proper look with you in the way and this corpse on its side." The colonel grabbed Baise's body by its shoulder and turned him over. "Get me Minor George on the com! I want to report this my—"

The explosion ripped the room apart and half the passageway outside it. Thraenish soldiers screamed as they were shredded by flying metal, their polybreen armor no match for the force of the shrapnel. The colonel was nothing but bloody mist, mixing in the air with the remains of Baise.

*

"Stay tight on me!" Natalie shouted as she and her team raced down the passageway, hoping they were headed for the rotational drive section of Station Thraen's Lower Decks. "We can't stop or slow down anymore! This is our one shot at getting off this fucking station!"

"They aren't going to let us leave, Nats!" Buck yelled, his longsling barely gripped in his right hand as a deep wound in his shoulder bled profusely. "Even if we threaten to blow the drive, they will not give in!"

"Then this whole station falls apart!" Natalie shouted. "And everyone dies with us!"

They skidded to a halt by a set of thick, double doors.

"Helios, Nats," Jay gasped as blood trickled from both of his ears. "We do this and hundreds of thousands of innocents die. Families, children, even our own people."

"We do this and we win," Natalie replied as she motioned towards the double doors. "Get us in there."

Jay and Buck looked at Lang, who was barely standing as he slumped against the wall.

"What?" Lang asked.

"You have the Vape torch," Buck said.

- 331 -

"Shit, right, sorry," Lang said as he unslung his pack and rummaged through it. "Here. You're going to have...to...do...."

He slid all the way to the floor as his eyes rolled up into his head.

"Shit!" Jay snapped. He knelt by Lang and checked his pulse. "Fuck. He's gone." Jay unsnapped Lang's polybreen armor and a massive amount of blood rushed out onto the floor. "Son of a grendt. He must have been hit a while ago and didn't say a fucking word."

"Give me that," Natalie said and held out her hand for the torch. "I'll cut us in."

She aimed the torch at one of the door handles and started to cut. The bright green flame sliced into the metal of the handle, melting it swiftly.

"We have company," Buck said as he turned around and lifted his longsling to his shoulder. He winced, but didn't let his wound stop him from keeping the weapon steady. "I can hear a lot of fucking boots, Nats. Get us in there."

"The torch is cutting as fast as it can," Natalie said as she nudged her longsling with her foot. "Take mine. Use it if needed."

Several Thraenish soldiers rounded the corner and Buck opened fire. Half a dozen soldiers were dropped instantly before his longsling clicked empty. He reached down and grabbed Natalie's longsling as Jay took his place and opened fire.

"Grab Lang's too!" Jay yelled as he sent everything he had at the Thraens.

Jay's longsling clicked empty and he tossed it aside, drew his long blade, and glanced back at Natalie.

"How we coming, minoress?" Jay asked.

"Cut the fucking minoress crap, asshole," Natalie said. "Fucking smart-ass."

Crouched on his knee, Buck brought up Lang's longsling and fired away. It was empty in less than a second. He got to his feet, drew his long blade, and stood shoulder to shoulder with Jay.

"Fuck this," Buck said. "Get in there and blow this place, Nats. We'll give you time."

Natalie turned her attention from the torch to the men behind her. They glanced over their shoulders and down at her.

"It has been an honor, gentlemen," she said.

"Who the fuck you talking to?" Jay grinned. "No gentlemen here, just a couple of idiot soldiers about to rip some Thraens apart."

"Then get to that," Natalie smiled.

Jay and Buck moved forward, their long blades held down at their sides, as they approached the oncoming Thraenish soldiers. Bodies and blood from those that fell to the particle barbs littered the passageway and the two Aelons stepped around the gore, their strides even and controlled.

The door handle fell away just as Thraens and Aelons met and Natalie only had a second to look back as her men went to work. She shoved the door open and rushed inside. She found herself on a walkway about fifty yards above the main rotational drive platform.

Down below, waiting for her, were close to fifty Thraenish soldiers.

And one Thraenish minor.

"Minoress! How lovely to see you!" Minor George shouted up at her. "I wasn't sure at first if you would choose this strategy, but my father was certain of it. Once again, that man shows his wisdom in matters such as this. Please, come down here and join us!"

"Suck my dick, Georgey-boy!" Natalie shouted.

She turned to go back the way she came, but she found her way blocked by several bloody Thraens. They held the heads of Buck and Jay in their hands. Natalie glared, then glanced past them and the glare turned to a smile as she saw how many soldiers her boys had cut down before being taken out.

"Better run, kids," Natalie said, drawing her long blade. "You're about to find out what it's like to fight a Teirmont."

She rushed the men, and more than a few took terrified steps backwards.

*

"Sire?" Steward Vast said quietly as he stepped into Alexis's bedchamber. "Sire? Are you awake?"

"Always," Alexis said from the bed. "Could you sleep at a time like this?"

"Apparently not, since I am in here with you at this late hour," Vast replied. "May I have a word?"

"Of course, Vast," Alexis said. "You never have to ask."

"We have rounded up all of Oweyn's relatives and they have signed the agreements," Vast said. "They shall be exiled to Aelon Prime where they will work for no less than five years. At which time they will be pardoned for any possible wrongdoing and free to travel to any station or prime they would like as long as none of them set foot on Station Aelon or its prime ever again."

"All of them signed?" Alexis asked. "There were no dissenters?"

Vast cleared his throat. "Not with the display of Steward Oweyn's corpse in front of them. I may not have agreed with your choice of motivation, but I cannot fault its effectiveness. Not a word was said by any of them as they signed."

"So they are on the shuttle to Helios now then," Alexis sighed. "Good. Let that business be done once and for all."

"I do worry that it may never be done, sire," Vast said. "These are all nobles. They hold grudges, as you know, and I am sure many will now see this as a fuel to start a blood feud."

"Fuel to start?" Alexis laughed. "The blood feud has already begun. If I were a simple steward, I would have butchered them all. But I am Master of Station Aelon and I cannot make the same mistakes that my ancestors did. Killing innocents is what led my mother's stepfather to rise up against my grandfather. I will let the people live and hope that the few fools that want a feud do not sway the others."

"That is quite a hope, sire," Vast said. "I would be lying if I thought it would come true."

"I would be lying to myself if I thought you were wrong," Alexis sighed. "But I cannot butcher more. Not now. I tried to be hard, Vast. I tried to be the killer that this station needed, but I am not that man. That part of me burned briefly and then sputtered out like a weak Vape flame."

"Which is why the Order follows you, sire," Vast bowed. "You have more heart than any other master before you. Even more than your mother did when she ruled."

"She had fate," Alexis chuckled. "And I have heart. What will the next master have, I wonder...."

"Speaking of the Order, sire," Vast said. "I have also come to ask if it may not be time to replenish its ranks. Half of the members were on Station Thraen and we have not heard from any of them. I would be surprised if they have survived."

"And you want to recruit new stewards into the fold, do you?" Alexis asked. "Bring our numbers back to full strength?"

"I do, sire," Vast said. "No matter how this business with Station Thraen ends, we will need our forces to be strong and ready. I do not believe Master Lionel will just sit back on his laurels and rest."

"No, I suppose he will not," Alexis said. He stood up from the bed and switched on a lamp. He couldn't help but smile when he saw the files Vast held in his hands. "You came prepared, I see."

"Like I said, sire, I cannot sleep at a time like this either," Vast smiled. "I have had plenty of opportunity to narrow the prospective field down."

"Then show me," Alexis said.

The two men moved to a small table and sat, Vast setting the files in front of the master.

"Tell me, Vast," Alexis said as he opened the first file. "The first members of the Order of Jex paid a heavy tithe to the crown. That tithe is what built Castle Aelon down on our prime. We will, of course, ask the same of the new stewards. But what shall the funds go towards this time?"

"That is for you to decide, sire," Vast said. "The Order will leave all financial issues to the crown, as it should be."

"Very well," Alexis nodded. He eyed the open file and was about to speak when the door to the bedchamber burst open.

"Richard?" Alexis cried, standing so fast he sent the files flying about. "What is it?"

"It's Natalie," Richard said, his skin white and eyes nearly popping from his head. "Come quick. Master Lionel is on the video com and waiting."

*

The monitors in the great hall flickered and popped from the bad reception, but even with the signal limitations, the Teirmonts could make out the figure of Master Lionel clearly, as well as the minor and minoress of Station Thraen as they stood next to their father. And, being held up by Thraenish soldiers, just behind the Herlects, was Natalie.

"My Helios, Kel," Mistress Alexis gasped. "Look what they have done to our girl."

"I know, Lexi," Kel nearly cried. "I can see."

Natalie's face was swollen almost beyond recognition. She had been stripped of her polybreen armor and stood only in a slight shift that was soaked through with blood. Deep, dark blood that continued to wet the undergarment.

"Master Alexis," Master Lionel said from the monitor. "Can you clearly see the state your sister is in?"

"I can," Alexis replied through gritted teeth. "And you will release her immediately."

"I plan to," Lionel smiled. "There is no question of that."

"Then what is there a question of?" Alexis asked.

"Your swearing fealty to me," Lionel said, his smile widening. "As it once was back when Station Aelon only held meager lease holdings on Thraen Prime. I insist you denounce your claim on Station Thraen and its prime and take a knee this second."

"You must be mad," Alexis snarled. "There is no way in Helios I will do any such thing!"

"Mad? Helios, no. I am far from mad," Lionel replied. "In fact, I believe I am being quite rational and reasonable. There has been so much pain and bloodshed over the years between our families, it is time we ended that. A truce will be called, and your sister will be released, if you just take a knee, swear fealty to me over your lease holdings, and we return to the glory of days past."

"And if I do not comply?" Alexis asked. "You will murder my sister before my eyes, is that it?"

"That is it precisely," Lionel nodded. "I do not want to, let me assure you of that. Minoress Natalie is a rare specimen in this System. Beautiful and brutal, able to lead men to their deaths willingly in battle. Smart, charming, driven. I almost believe she would have been better suited for the crown than you, Alexis. But that would be silly since Station Thraen has never believed in women ruling. That is an Aelish thing and that is Aelish folly."

"Alexis, you cannot give in," Mistress Alexis said from behind her son.

"Quiet, Mother," Alexis ordered. "Lionel? If I do as you say, I have your word my sister will be released?"

"You have my word," Lionel nodded. The minor and minoress next to him grinned and started to giggle. "Quiet." They stopped immediately.

"I give up my claim to Station Thraen, my claim to Thraen Prime, and we return to the agreement my great-grandfather made so many years ago," Alexis said. "That is the deal you put forth?"

"That is the deal I put forth, Alexis," Lionel said. "What say you?"

"May I have a moment to take counsel with my family?" Alexis asked.

"Of course, master," Lionel said. "I am not a savage. I would expect nothing less."

Mistress Alexis and Kel started to step forward, but Alexis held out his hand to stop them, his eyes locked onto the monitor.

"Nats? Nats, can you hear me?" Alexis asked.

"What is this?" Lionel frowned. "I assumed—"

"Shut up," Alexis barked. "You granted me a moment to take counsel with my family. My sister is part of my family. Are you withdrawing your consent, master?"

Lionel fumed for a moment then waved his hand for Minoress Natalie to be brought forward.

"I thank you, Lionel," Alexis said. "Nats? Can you hear me?"

Natalie raised her head, obviously using all of her strength to do so, and looked straight into the camera. Alexis had to use all of his strength not to smile as he saw the look in his sister's nearly swollen shut eyes.

"Nats? Now more than ever, I need your counsel," Alexis said. "I need you to tell me what to do. No matter what it is, I promise to obey. Tell me now, Nats."

Natalie mumbled several words, but her voice was not picked up by the com's microphone. The look on Lionel's face told Alexis exactly what he thought his sister would say.

"Move her closer, Lionel," Alexis demanded. "Let me hear my sister."

Lionel, his face red with anger, motioned for his soldiers to move the minoress. Once her face was taking up almost the entire screen, they stopped and Natalie swallowed hard before speaking again through broken teeth and shredded lips.

"Fuck...them...all," Natalie gasped.

"Then that is what I shall do," Alexis said.

Minoress Natalie was yanked back from the camera and before anyone could say a word, her throat was slit by Minor George's hand. The blood flowed like a river of pain and Natalie's body was tossed aside.

Mistress Alexis, Kel, and Richard screamed. But Alexis only stood there and stared at the monitor as Lionel moved in close.

"You have made a grave mistake, boy," Lionel hissed. "I will take everything from you."

"You already have," Alexis said. "See to it that her body is returned to Station Aelon. If it is not, or it is desecrated in anyway, I will make sure the High Guardian rescinds all travel privileges from Station Thraen. You and your people will be trapped on that station to rot, mark my words."

Alexis moved forward and yanked the cords from out of the back of the monitor and the screen went dead. He turned and looked at his family as they wept and wailed. Alexis did not go to them, but strode past and out of the great hall. The doors slammed closed behind him and the sound echoed through the massive room, mixing with the sounds of the Family Teirmont's grief and anguish.

ACT III

A SHADOWED REIGN

"As has been said and written before, the reign of Master Alexis the Fourth was one filled with triumphs and tragedies. His legacy is complicated and bloody, yet also filled with glory and hope. He did as much for the System as any monarch before him and some of the programs he built are still with us today."
—Dr. D. Reven, Eighty-Third Archivist of The Way

"When you look the other way, you look towards Helios. When you look towards Helios, do not look the other way."
—Book of Lines 1:2, The Ledger

"I will never forget. But I am so tired. So very tired."
—Journals of Alexis the Fourth, Master of Station Aelon and its prime

CHAPTER SEVEN

"You are weak," the voice said.

"Hardly," Alexis replied. "Now go away."

"They kill your sister and you just turn your head?" the voice scoffed. "That is pure weakness."

"It is not," Alexis said as he signed the papers before him and set them aside. He grabbed a second stack of files, sighed, and started signing those. "Natalie died because of Lionel's insanity, not because of my weakness." He looked up and glared at the shadowed figure in the corner of his study. "Although, if you keep talking to me, then I will have to consider myself almost as insane as Lionel. That would be true weakness."

"It is not my fault your soul seeks my council," the voice said. "I come when I am needed. It is the Teirmont way."

"Did the ghosts of your ancestors come when you needed them?" Alexis asked, shaking his pen as it started to run out of ink.

The voice gave a low chuckle. "I never needed them."

"Oh, how wonderful for you," Alexis chuckled as well. "Then this conversation must make you feel so superior."

"I am here to help, you little whelp," the voice snapped. "I will go away forever if that is what you want."

Alexis set the pen down and tilted his head. "Is that an option?"

"Of course it is an option," the voice growled. "You simply must ask."

"Good," Alexis said. "Then go and never return. I do not need you, I do not want you, and you are not welcome here."

"You will regret this," the voice said.

"I already do," Alexis replied. "Kill them all? Wasn't that your advice before? How did that work out? Oh, yes, they all died! Aelons as well as Thraens! War is your legacy, Great-grandfather. I refuse to let it be mine."

"If I leave now, you cannot summon me again," the voice warned.

"I will hold you to that," Alexis said. "Get out of my study, get out of my head, get out of my life. Now!"

There was nothing but silence for several seconds then a knock at the door.

"Sire?" an attendant asked as he walked into the study. He glanced around then frowned at Alexis. "Are you alone?"

"Do you see anyone else in here?" Alexis asked, not looking up from his paperwork.

"No, sire," the attendant replied.

"Then you have the answer to your own question, don't you," Alexis said. He finally looked at the attendant. "What is it?"

"You have a guest, sire," the attendant said. "I told him you were busy today, but he insists on seeing you."

"Does he also insist on being shot out of an airlock?" Alexis asked.

"Only if you get me good and drunk first," Clerke said, pushing past the attendant. "Speaking of, we'll need two glasses, please."

"There are glasses on the side table there," the attendant said.

"Then it looks like we don't need you," Clerke grinned "You can leave now."

The attendant looked at Alexis. "Sire?"

"Go," Alexis nodded. "I will be fine."

The attendant bowed low and quickly left the study, closing the door firmly after him.

"Top notch staff, you have," Clerke said as he set a bag down by a chair then fetched two glasses from the side table. "I almost came to blows with the first two before I was shown to that guy there. Not that I'd actually fight them. Wouldn't want to mess up these fingers."

"What do you want, Clerke?" Alexis asked. "I am busy."

"You are always busy," Clerke said.

"I am Master of Station Aelon and its Primes," Alexis replied. "I *should* always be busy."

"Too busy to answer any of my letters or respond to any of my communications?" Clerke said. "No one is that busy."

"You left," Alexis said. "My sister was butchered and you left. I figured it was you that did not want to speak with me."

"Want me to tear down the idiocy in that statement?" Clerke said as he pulled a bottle from his bag, uncorked it, and then filled both glasses with a generous pour of the brown liquid. "I'll gladly explain why you are a complete idiot. I have no problem with that. You need someone to tell you the truth about your idio—"

"Enough," Alexis sighed as he shoved his papers aside and nodded at the glasses. "You going to give me one of those or not?"

"Of course," Clerke said and handed a glass to Alexis then took his seat. "Cheers."

"Cheers," Alexis said as he sipped. His eyes widened and he looked at the glass before sipping again. "This isn't just Klaervian whiskey, is it?"

"No, it is not," Clerke smiled. "It is from the royal family's private reserves. The actual private reserves, not the other stuff they woo dignitaries with."

"And how did you come by such a rare treasure?" Alexis asked.

"Your brother," Clerke said. "I just spent the past three months as a guest of Richard and his wife. Lovely people, although a little off, as you know. To think the guy found a woman, a minoress of Klaerv, that's just as kooky as he is. What are the odds?"

"Amongst the royals of the System?" Alexis said as he leaned back in his chair. "They are fairly good odds. It's not even a bet the bookmakers would take."

"True, true," Clerke smiled. He waited for a minute then shook his head. "Aren't you going to ask why I was with your brother? Or why I am here now?"

"I assumed you were performing on Station Klaerv," Alexis said. "Now you are here to perform."

"Have you heard an announcement of me performing on Station Aelon?" Clerke asked.

"I have not," Alexis said then motioned to the rest of the room. "But I have been busy, as I said."

"Yes, I know," Clerke said. "Your mother has told me. Your father as well. In fact, every supporter and ally you have has reached out to me in some capacity over this last year to let me know how busy you are. Only a few of them know how much you talk to yourself, though."

Alexis frowned and set the glass down. "What do you want, Petro?"

"Ouch, first name time," Clerke laughed. "I've upset you."

"I haven't made that quite clear?" Alexis asked. "Just tell me what you want and then leave."

"First, I want you to stop being angry with me," Clerke said. "I left Station Aelon because I needed to. This place exudes Natalie. Every passageway, every deck, every time I saw a royal guard or a member of the Order of Jex. She was there. I needed time, Alexis. I had to lose myself in the System, get back to who I was when I was alone and just a wandering bard from the Lower Decks."

"How'd that work out for you?" Alexis responded. "Did you lose yourself? Did you escape the memory of my sister?"

"Far from it," Clerke said. "Every station I set foot on reminded me of her. That time on Station Ploerv when the minor insisted I play the same song again and again for like thirty times in a row and she just kept encouraging the man. On Station Haelm where the first row of seats collapsed because the stewards and their families sitting there were so overweight that the bleachers couldn't hold them. Or even on Station Thraen when we snuck into those Lower Decks and I gave an impromptu performance to a group of rotational drive mechanics. Damn, did we get drunk that night."

"You went to Station Thraen?" Alexi snarled. "You dared to set foot on that abomination and then come here and mock me with it?"

"Calm your shit down, A," Clerke said. "I didn't go to Thraen, I was just reminiscing."

"You will address me as Master Alexis, not as A," Alexis snapped. "You no longer have the right—"

"Oh, shut the fuck up!" Clerke shouted as he lunged to his feet and slammed his glass down on the desk. "Stop hoarding all the grief, you selfish bastard! We all miss her and we all still ache because of her death! You do not get to talk to me like I am some accessory to this family! Other than you, I knew Natalie the best!" He beat his chest with his fists. "I knew her, dammit! *I knew her!*"

The study doors opened and two attendants as well as two guards peered in, but were stopped by Alexis's raised hand.

"It's fine," Alexis said. "Do not disturb us again."

The attendants and guards paused then bowed and left, closing the doors behind them.

"It is not fine," Clerke said. "You have to admit that."

"I do," Alexis said. "Every day. I wake up and admit to myself I am not fine. I go to bed at night and admit to myself I am not fine. Nothing is fine, Clerke. Why do you think I stay so busy?"

"Well. . .it's good to hear you admit that, at least," Clerke said as he sat back down and poured more whiskey in his glass. "Shit. Such a waste to spill this stuff."

"What is this all about, really?" Alexis asked. "Get to the point, please."

"You know when you asked me to be your secret spy?" Clerke asked.

"Of course," Alexis replied. "Although I do not think I worded it quite like that."

"Doesn't matter how you worded it because I did it," Clerke said. "I was too late in figuring out what Oweyn and Lionel were up to, but I did have sources in place on all the other stations as well as The Way."

"Alright. And?" Alexis asked.

"And there are whispers," Clerke said. "They are small and isolated, but they sound serious."

"Tell me what the whispers are, Clerke," Alexis sighed. "I do not have the patience for melodramatic showmanship."

"The whispers are of Station Thraen taking back their prime," Clerke said. "Like I said, they are small and isolated, but the sources are sound. I just wanted you to know that they are out there. If I am hearing them then, well. . . ."

"Then they could easily be more than whispers," Alexis said. "This is good to know. Except that Lionel wouldn't dare. The High Guardian has strictly forbidden such an action. It is one reason my mother and father are staying on Aelon Prime and constantly meet with the man. High Guardian Victor would be risking all-out war against us. And considering how fresh the wound is from Natalie's death, that is a war The Way does not want. Not from Teirmonts."

"No, no, it is The Way I am hearing the most whispers from," Clerke said. "I think Victor is worried of the same thing. He does not want a war with the Teirmonts. No one does. Except for one person. Well, two people, to be precise, but I think of them as one."

Alexis set his glass down and leaned forward.

"The twins?" Alexis asked. "George and Georgia want to make a play for Thraen Prime? They would defy their father? That is a risky move that could end up with their heads on pikes. I doubt Lionel or the Thraenish stewards would want to risk another prime conflict."

Clerke tilted his head and then leaned back in his chair. "You don't know, do you?"

"Don't know what?" Alexis asked. "Stop being coy, Clerke. You are no good at it."

"Lionel's health is failing him," Clerke said. "He may have a few years left or he may kick it next week. His physicians are tight-lipped on the whole thing, so no one knows for sure."

"It could also be another Thraenish plot to stir up the System," Alexis said. "Gets the other stations to hurry up trade negotiations. No one wants to start from scratch with a new master."

"That could be, as well," Clerke nodded. "But I thought you should be informed."

"Well, now I am," Alexis replied. "Thank you for that." Alexis waited for a few seconds, his eyebrows raised. "That's not all, right? There is no way you'd come see me for just that."

"No, no, I actually have been thinking about something," Clerke said. "It's about Natalie's legacy."

"She, and her team, will be remembered forever," Alexis said. "We are having a memorial statue erected with their names engraved on Middle Deck Twenty. My longslingers were insistent that it be placed there and I could not argue with them."

"Yes, I know, I heard," Clerke smiled.

"You heard? How is that? I just finalized the plans a couple days ago," Alexis said.

"You wanted me to spy," Clerke shrugged. "Apparently I have gotten very good at it."

"Shaowshit," Alexis said. "Someone contacted you. Who was it?"

"Your father," Clerke replied. "He thought I should know, in case I wanted to attend the unveiling next year. Go ahead and block off some time in my schedule. He used your brother's personal communications line on Station Klaerv. By the way, why is Richard living on Klaerv with his wife and not here on Station Aelon? He wouldn't give me a straight answer."

"He wouldn't give you a straight answer because he doesn't quite understand the intricacies," Alexis said. "With Natalie dead, and a lack of my own heir, Richard is now next in line for the crown. We didn't want him down on Helios with Mother and Father, and we didn't want him here with me. It's for his safety and the security of the Aelish monarchy. His father-in-law will protect him with all the power of the Klaervian court, so we figured it was best he just stay there."

"Wait, why shouldn't he be down on Helios with your mother and father? They would be the most logical choice to keep him safe," Clerke said.

"Because, if something does happen to me and then Richard, before he has an heir, then Mother would assume the crown again," Alexis replied. "As long as she still lives, Helios willing."

"What if you all die?" Clerke asked.

"Then Station Aelon will be looking at its first battle for the crown in centuries," Alexis sighed. "Which we would all like to avoid, even the stewards that have an outside claim. Prosperity comes hand in hand with stability. We need the stability as much as we need the prosperity, at this time."

"Yes, speaking of prosperity," Clerke said. "I have been doing very well in the disc market, not to mention the revenues from my live performances. Which brings me back to Natalie's legacy."

"I'm not following you," Alexis said.

"I don't want her to just be remembered as the warrior minoress," Clerke said.

"But that is who she was," Alexis said.

"That is where you are wrong, A," Clerke said. "We spent a long time together, going from station to station while I performed. Being a bard means I meet many different people from all walks of life, no more so than artists from other disciplines. Natalie fell in love with the scene and we spoke at length about setting up our own artists' collective at some point."

"Like Helios you did," Alexis scoffed. "Nats was never into that artsy-fruity crap."

Clerke just stared.

"Well, she wasn't," Alexis insisted. Clerke's stare gave him pause. "Was she?"

"Your sister was quite the painter," Clerke said. "She was rough, but she had natural talent. A few more years of training and she would have been the one the stations called for, not me."

"Shaowshit," Alexis said.

"It isn't," Clerke said and stood up. "Follow me, I'll show you."

"Where?" Alexis said. "I have said I am awfully—"

"Busy, I know," Clerke said. "Helios, let that tired bit go. No one buys it, A. Just come with me."

"Not unless you tell me where?" Alexis insisted.

"To your sister's quarters," Clerke said. "I have it on good authority that you haven't set foot in there since Natalie died."

"Have you now? Who was the snitch this time? My mother?" Alexis asked.

"No, it was everyone," Clerke said. "Your attendants, the Order, your guards, the servants, stewards, everyone. It is well noted on Station Aelon that you refuse to go in those quarters and you have given explicit orders for them not to be disturbed. Sounds like you were building your own memorial."

"I have too much work to do to accompany you on some whim," Alexis said.

"It is not a whim, Helios dammit!" Clerke shouted. "Now get your Teirmont ass up and follow me to your late sister's quarters or I will start spreading rumors you copulate with grendts all day instead of doing any actual work!"

"You wouldn't," Alexis glared.

"Just try me, A," Clerke said. "I'm starting to get bored with being a bard. And getting on a bored musician's bad side is not a good idea. We tend to write nasty, salacious songs when we're bored."

*

"These. . .these aren't bad," Alexis said as he held a small painting up by the window in Natalie's personal study. The painting was of the view of the courtyard directly out the window and wasn't a perfect facsimile, but gave the obvious impression of the setting. "Why didn't she ever show me these? Or tell me she liked to paint?"

"Because to you she was your badass little sister," Clerke said. "She didn't want you to hesitate when you needed to call upon her fighting skills. And she didn't want the team to know."

"The team didn't know?" Alexis asked, setting that painting down and picking one up depicting an approaching Vape storm on Aelon Prime. "Well, I don't feel so bad now. If she didn't tell the team then she didn't really want anyone to know."

"Oh, she wanted you to know," Clerke said. "She was very proud of her work and it killed her she couldn't share it with you."

"I was starting to feel a little better, but that has wiped the good feeling away rather quickly, Clerke," Alexis frowned. "Thank you for that."

Alexis set the second painting down then reached for a third and stopped.

"Hold on. Why did you go see my brother on Station Klaerv?"

"Simple," Clerke smiled. "He is next in line for the crown. I didn't want all of my work to go to waste if you died and he took over the mastership. Before I decide to step away from the stage, I want to know that I am not doing so in vain."

Alexis walked away from the window and looked Clerke right in the eye.

"Are you having fun?" Alexis asked. "Giving me tidbits and morsels of information? You have me on the hook, Clerke, now reel me in."

"I want to start an artistic foundation in Natalie's name," Clerke said. "I would like it to be System-wide, but the odds are close to impossible to accomplish that. Too much red tape and bickering. So, for now, it would need to stay confined to Station Aelon. It would be a conservatory, a workshop, a museum, a retreat—all things up and coming, and even established artists, need."

"Just painting?" Alexis asked.

"No, of course not," Clerke replied. "All of the arts. Music, dance, sculpture, metal crafts, all of them."

"Hmm," Alexis mused. "It is an interesting thought. How much have you raised for it?"

"Yes, well, that's where you come in," Clerke said. "I know you have been interviewing new members for the Order of Jex, and part of them joining is to give a substantial tithe of credits. Your mother built Castle Aelon on the prime with tithes; you could build this foundation."

"That is an idea," Alexis said. "The Order does leave the use of the tithes to the crown."

"And Natalie was one of the bravest of warriors," Clerke said. "So those old fighters wouldn't have a problem with the credits going towards something she wanted."

"You are not wrong there," Alexis said. "I sometimes fear history will canonize her and just leave me as a footnote."

"I doubt that will be the case, sire," Clerke said, bowing low.

"Oh, fuck off," Alexis smiled, snacking the man on the head. "Stand up and let's go. I'm famished and we should talk more about this."

"So you are in agreement?" Clerke beamed.

"I am open to the idea and hungry," Alexis said. "You will have to do a lot more convincing for me to be in agreement."

"Oh, I'm very good at convincing," Clerke said. "That whiskey was only my opening. Wait until the main act!"

*

The veteran members of the Order of Jex—Stewards Vast, Neggle, and Kinsmon—all stood and bowed to Alexis, their faces filled with joy. Alexis, seated at the head of the long table in the great hall, bowed his head in acknowledgment and appreciation.

"It would be a fitting tribute to the minoress," Vast said. "She did not speak of her art to me personally, but I did catch glimpses of it on occasion. Why she took great pains to hide such beauty, I will not know."

"It is our honor to help provide funds for this foundation," Neggle added. "Not all Aelons can be fighters and warriors. And not all can be merchants or businessmen. I know my sister's boy is quite the artisan when it comes to working with patterns on breen." He withdrew a pair of gloves at his belt and held them up. "He placed our family crest upon my gloves for Last Meal."

"I say we make an official announcement of support," Kinsmon said. "If the station knows the Order is behind this endeavor then we should be able to raise even more funds from the Middle Decks. The passengers adored Minoress Natalie."

"I am sorry, Your Highness," a man said from way down the long table. "But, when I was asked to become a part of the Order of Jex, I was not aware my tithe would be given away to such a superfluous cause." The man, short and muscular, stood and nodded to the stewards that had just spoken. "No offense is meant. I admire everything the minoress stood for, but I am afraid that if we use her name to promote the arts we will lose a golden opportunity to use her name to promote the military needs of this station. Perhaps we should see that recruitment numbers increase first before we embark on supporting the bard's pet project."

"Thank you for your input, Steward Holsten," Alexis said. He turned and looked at Clerke, who was seated away from the long table, not being a member of the Order, and smiled broadly. "But the bard, as you call him, is an accomplished artist and a man I trust completely. This is far from his pet project and will only serve to strengthen and benefit Station Aelon for generations to come. The tithes given are to be used at my discretion. This is my discretion."

"Yes, sire, I understand that," Holsten replied. "And I am not disputing your right to use the tithes as you see fit. It is just that I feel it would have been good of you to let myself, and the other new members, know of your intentions before we had given them over so willingly."

"I see," Alexis said. He stood up and placed his hands on the table. "If I had mentioned my intentions, would it have changed your mind in regards to joining the Order? Would you have withdrawn your desire to become a part of the most honored of institutions on this station?"

"No, it would not have, sire," Holsten said. "I would have still proceeded with accepting your most gracious invitation."

"Then I do not see the problem," Alexis said. He turned his attention on the two other new members of the Order. "Steward Flain? Steward Triny? What say you on this subject?"

Steward Flain, the youngest of the men at the table, stood and bowed. He had slight, almost effeminate features, but when he spoke, a deep, rumbling bass of a voice came out.

"Master, I do not agree with my colleague," Steward Flain replied. "I believe it to be a most proper use of the funds. I look forward to seeing the results of this foundation and will pledge the resources and help of my sector if called upon."

Alexis looked surprised. "Well, that is very generous of you, Steward Flain. I thank you for the offer."

"Careful what you promise," Clerke said from his seat then held up his hands. "Sorry. I'll shut up."

"Steward Triny?" Alexis asked.

An older gentleman, Steward Triny was battle-hardened and the scars across his face proved it. A veteran of the prime conflicts and the taking of Station Thraen, Steward Triny was known throughout Station Aelon as a loyal supporter of the crown and strict disciplinarian within his sector holdings.

"Your Highness," Triny said, clearing his throat. "I know nothing about art, care nothing about art, see no purpose in art, and have no opinion on the subject. I leave it to you to make the decisions. It is your crown, sire, not mine."

"Well put, Triny," Alexis said. He focused again on Holsten. "Will this be a bone of contention between us, Holsten? I do not want there to be any issues or animosity within the Order. This is a brotherhood and we must trust each other implicitly or the Order does not work."

"No bone, sire," Holsten replied. "My beliefs are strictly personal and do not, nor will ever, influence my loyalty or behavior in regards to the Order." He smirked and shrugged. "I just may not be attending any of the foundation's functions, galas, or fundraising events, if that is acceptable."

"Understood, Holsten," Alexis said. He nodded to each of the members. "Then let it be known that the tithes you have all given are to be used to create the Natalie Teirmont Artistic Foundation. I am appointing Petro Clerke as the head of the institution. He will consult with me in all matters of importance, but at the end of the day his judgment will be final. Are we in agreement, gentlemen?"

"Aye," the table replied.

"Good," Alexis said. "Then let us adjourn. I have plenty more work than this to attend to. Until we meet again next week."

The members nodded and bowed then slowly made their way from the great hall, chatting amongst themselves about the meeting's topic as well as other matters of station. Once the great hall was empty, except for a handful of attendants, Alexis motioned for Clerke to join him at the table.

"Well?" Alexis asked once Clerke was seated and an attendant poured them both glasses of gelberry wine. "What are your thoughts? We have the Order's support, do you believe we can proceed or will we need the meeting as well as the passengers' support?"

"You are the Master of the Station," Clerke said. "I leave that for you to decide."

"I may be master, but I am not part of the art scene," Alexis said. "Aside from studies as a child, I have not participated in anything except for some bawdy singing while camped with my longslingers."

"Which is surprising," Clerke said. "Because you, of all the Teirmonts, have more of an artist's temperament than a warrior's. Even with your Dark Master's persona."

"My what?" Alexis asked. "Dark Master? I think you have that mixed up, Clerke. I was known as the Dark Minor."

"Then you became the Dark Master," Clerke frowned. "Has no one mentioned that before? Surely this cannot be the first time you have heard it said?"

"I am afraid it is," Alexis replied. "And I am not sure how I feel about it."

"No one meant any offense," Clerke said. "You were celebrated as the Dark Minor then you were crowned, lost you wife and child, and declared war on Station Thraen. It was a natural progression to Dark Master."

"Yet the name never reached my ears,'" Alexis sighed. "So I do not buy your assertion no offense was meant."

"Uh-oh, are you to begin holding executions now?" Clerke smiled. "Kill those that dare besmirch your name?"

"Shut up," Alexis said. "This subject bores me."

"Oh, well, we can't have that," Clerke laughed.

Clerke snapped his fingers and an attendant hurried over with several rolls of paper under his arm. The attendant set the rolls in front of Clerke and stepped back.

"Let's have a look at the first phase, shall we?" Clerke suggested. "It is a two step approach. We begin with a small space here on the station, build it up to something more significant then look to duplicate it upon Aelon Prime."

Alexis raised his eyebrows at the last part of Clerke's suggestion. "The prime? Why would we build there as well?"

"Because there are people there, A," Clerke said. "And where there are people there are potential artists. Creativity flourishes within miners and breen farmers too. If we establish a branch of the foundation on Aelon Prime then we will instantly elevate the culture down there. The frontier attitude of brutality will be softened and refinement of thought will begin. That will make managing the prime much easier and far less dangerous for all."

"How practical," Alexis said. "We shall soothe the savage beast of the prime with art."

"I truly hope so, A," Clerke said. "Because I am certainly tired of savage beasts."

"I as well, Clerke," Alexis sighed. "I as well."

*

"What we are trying to do here is create some type of space within each sector," Clerke said as he stood before the combined meetings of stewards and passengers. "We need to give as many passengers as possible the opportunity to express themselves and learn in an artistic environment."

The great hall was filled almost to capacity and it was obvious that more than a few members of the meetings were put out that they had to stand instead of being offered a seat at the long table. Alexis was seated at the head of the long table, with Clerke standing to his right, his eyes on the men that made up the groups that decided much of the fate of Station Aelon.

"Sectors Helble, Gwalter, Norbrighm, Kirke, Shem, Maelphy, Bueke, Gormand, and Trint have all agreed to host spaces," Clerke said. "But that is only a fraction of the sectors we need to establish this foundation properly. The requirements are meager, and any unused set of large storage rooms, offices, former factories, whatever you can spare would be greatly appreciated."

"I believe I have some space by my trash incinerator," a steward called out.

"As do I by the leaking sewage pipes on Middle Deck Forty-Eight," another steward said. "Most of art is shite anyway, so they could just toss it into the cesspool when done."

Alexis lunged to his feet and pounded his fists upon the table.

"Is this a joke to you?" he growled. "Is the idea of honoring my sister's memory with beauty instead of blood so repugnant that you would sit here and mock something that I believe in with my very being?"

No one replied.

"Master, let me address them, if you please," Clerke said. "You are here to observe, not intimidate."

All eyes watched Alexis closely as he sat back down and waved his hand at Clerke. "Yes, my apologies. Please continue."

"This is not mandatory, as you all know," Clerke said. "And I would not want it to be. Unwilling involvement does not make a conducive atmosphere for creativity. If you do not want to donate space to the foundation within your sector then I ask that you do not. I would prefer that the prestige of the cause be reserved for those that embrace the spirit for which it is intended. There will be much more favorable results from positive environs than from hostile ones."

"I'll donate space if you sing us a song, bard!" a deck boss called out. "Play that one about the Haelmish lass that kept her skirts up for six days straight! That is a classic!"

"I did not prepare myself to perform for you today, gentlemen," Clerke said. "It is not my purpose now to entertain, but to educate. There comes a point in every man's career when he must change. This is that point for me."

"Ah, come on!" a sector warden yelled. "Just one ballad! A gruesome tale for us all to hear!"

"As I have said, you do not have to participate in this foundation," Clerke said, ignoring the last request. "Allowing me to speak to all of you today was a courtesy granted by Master Alexis and it does not obligate any of you in any way. I thank you for listeni—"

"Just one tune!"

"Play for us, Clerke!"

"We came for a show!"

"Gentlemen! Please shut your traps and listen up!"

All heads turned to the doors of the great hall. Mistress Alexis strode inside and shoved her way through the crowd to the head of the table. Everyone quickly bowed their heads with respect.

"Mother?" Alexis said as he stood and kissed Mistress Alexis on the cheek. "This is unexpected."

"It shouldn't be," Mistress Alexis replied. "I have left word with your attendants for three days, trying to reach you."

"I apologize, Mother," Alexis said. "I have been so busy coordinating this event that—"

"Save it for later, Alexis," Mistress Alexis interrupted. "We have much to discuss beyond the arts."

She turned and faced the great hall, her back straight and her head held high.

"Gentlemen," she said. "I am surprised by you all. In my day the meetings would not have balked at supporting a request such as this. It costs you nearly nothing and requires zero work from any of you other than the occasional appearance at galas and fundraisers. Which, I assume, you all will attend anyway with your own selfish agendas."

"Mother, where are you going with this?" Alexis whispered.

"Hush, Son, and sit down," Mistress Alexis said. "Your mother is speaking now."

Alexis sighed and took his seat, knowing better than to argue with his mother. There were a few snickers from the crowd.

"Next man to snicker gets his lungs ripped out through his chest," Mistress Alexis barked. "That is a promise that I will execute myself. Are we understood?" All eyes were on her. "Good. Now that I have your full attention, I would like to explain why I have come here today."

She took a deep breath and placed a hand on Clerke's shoulder.

"This man is willing to devote the rest of his life to the memory of a woman he deeply loved. A woman that is indisputably the most cherished minoress to live on Station Aelon, which I do not say lightly since I was once a minoress myself." There were several smiles at those words. "Not only is Petro Clerke willing to work for my late daughter's memory, but he is willing to work for the betterment of all Aelons. And he is not even a native of the Surface or the Middle Decks, but a lowdecker! I am sorry that so many of you that are natives of the Surface feel that the arts are not worthy of your support. Perhaps only those on the Lower Decks can truly appreciate greatness."

Mistress Alexis moved from the head of the table and began to pace in front of the crowd.

"And I have to say that I understand completely. I am a woman that is more comfortable with two blades in hand than two paintbrushes or two pencils. My ears are tuned for the sounds of battle, not the sounds of choirs or orchestras. When I see the color red I think of blood, not of a flower blossom or a piece of stained glass. But that is me.

"I will admit I knew nothing of my daughter's secret pastime. Which is a shame since, now that I have seen her work, I know she had a great talent; a talent I would have loved to discuss with her, to encourage in her.

Perhaps if I had known sooner, if she had felt the willingness to confide in me, perhaps my daughter would be alive today. She may not have gone back to her warrior ways and held a brush the rest of her life instead of a longsling at the end."

Mistress Alexis raised her hand and pointed a finger at the crowd.

"How many of you have daughters and sons? How many of you know everything about their lives? How many of you would rather your children learn to express themselves with paint and charcoal instead of blood and gore? I know I would give anything to have my Natalie back."

She sneered and wagged her finger.

"Unfortunately, as it stands now, I could not say the same for any of you. I know there are some here that lost children in the war on Station Thraen. I know some of you lost children in the conflict of the primes. Yet, apparently, the cost of an unused storage room or empty warehouse is just too much to part with. So, I propose this: that whatever you donate will be named after those you lost. We will not let this foundation be only about my daughter, we will let it be about all daughters, and sons, who perished."

She lowered her hand and locked eyes with the younger members of the meetings.

"And for those of you who are fresh to this great hall, and perhaps are just starting or have yet to start their own families, I request that you look within yourselves. Ask yourselves if you would rather someday hold your living children in your arms, laughing at the paint smeared across their clothes, or would you prefer to grieve over your dead sons or daughters, while blood stains their uniforms? The choice is yours to make. We will always have plenty of Aelons with the courage to go to battle, that should never be up for debate. But how many Aelons will have the courage to express their very souls and lay them bare for us all to see? How many of you will have the courage to let them?"

Mistress Alexis bowed low and then turned to her son.

"I hope that helps," she said. "When you are finished, I will be in your study, waiting to speak to you."

The mistress quickly left the great hall, a path cleared for her instantly as men bowed before her.

Alexis and Clerke glanced at each other and rolled their eyes.

"You are a lucky man to have such a mother," Clerke said.

"That part is up for debate," Alexis chuckled then looked towards the crowd. "I think it is your turn to try again. They might be a tad more receptive this time."

*

"Father didn't come up to the station with you?" Alexis asked. "This is probably the first time you two have been apart for in I don't know how long."

"He is keeping an eye on the situation down on the primes," Mistress Alexis replied as the two royals sat next to each other in Alexis's study. "I want to make sure nothing slips by us."

"Why? What is happening?" Alexis asked. "Is Lionel making a move? I am told he is barely conscious."

"Lionel is not making a move, but George certainly is," Mistress Alexis replied. "Nothing overt or obvious. Most stations wouldn't see the signs, but your father and I know the ways of Helios well enough that even the slightest of ripples look like waves to us."

"Tell me what is happening," Alexis said. "Be specific."

"Ah, and that is the genius of the Thraen minor," Mistress Alexis chuckled. "There are no specifics to give. Just subtle shifts in supply deliveries, barge schedules, miner rotations, Vape deliveries. Small things that occur on a prime all the time. If you had them all in front of you on paper you wouldn't see a pattern."

"Then why are you here?" Alexis asked. "If there is no pattern, then how are any of these things significant."

"Because of their locations," Mistress Alexis said. "Come, I'll show you." She stood up and went to Alexis's desk. "Do you have maps of the prime battles?"

"Yes, of course," Alexis said. He went to a shelf and rummaged through a pile of rolls. "Here they are."

"Good," Mistress Alexis said as she unrolled the first map. "Perfect. This is excellent. Now, see how this location was where we routed the Thraens, pushing them from this Vape mine and out into the open?"

"Yes, I remember that day well," Alexis smiled. "That was the first day Natalie's team truly came together."

"Well, this is also where there is the highest turnover of Vape miners on the prime," Mistress Alexis said. "This mine here has had several accidents reported over the past few months, which makes the turnover understandable. No one wants to work where they will die within the week."

"Vape mining is dangerous," Alexis said. "So?"

"So, there are reports of accidents, but I have yet to find official reports of deaths," Mistress Alexis said. "With this many accidents there should be many dead Thraens. There aren't. Worker rotation, but not worker replacement."

"Those men were just lucky," Alexis said, not believing his own words.

"Could be," Mistress Alexis smiled. "Except for a couple of things. One is that Vape production in this mine is way down. Yes, training new miners can take time, but eventually you see the upswing in production. We are not seeing that upswing, A. Do you know why?"

"Because they are not miners in that mine, but Thraenish soldiers," Alexis replied. "Is that the why? If so, then I need proof to take to the High Guardian."

"I know that, A," Mistress Alexis said. "Which is why your father is still down on Aelon Prime. He is working to gather that proof."

"What else is happening?" Alexis asked.

His mother spread out a different map.

"See here and here? Supply barges used to disembark in these places regularly. They still do, except now they disembark here and here as well. Only once or twice a month. Do you see the significance of these locations?"

"They are where we cut off the Thraens' supply lines before," Alexis said. "They are creating caches, aren't they? Hoarding supplies and munitions?"

"Men are on their way to find out for sure," Mistress Alexis said. "But they must be careful. The primes are wild and men go missing all the time. If they tip off the Thraens that they are there to inspect the caches then we may never hear from them again. By the time we find out they have failed and we send out new men it could be too late. George is using the unpredictability of the prime against us."

"Which is what we did against Lionel during the conflict," Alexis said. "Just minus the subterfuge and subtlety."

"This is far from the worst part," Mistress Alexis said. "My sources tell me that station Thraen has increased deliveries of goods to other primes.

Not by much, not enough for anyone to take notice. The deliveries are well within a seasonal upswing in commerce. But when coupled with the other activities?"

"He's getting ready for war," Alexis said. "That fuck. His father isn't even dead yet and he is setting the pieces in place for another conflict."

"Do not kid yourself that this is only George," Mistress Alexis said. "Those twins are of a same mind. Georgia is as much involved with this as her brother is. She may not be able to rule as he will, but she will be wielding almost as much power. We are not fighting one royal, but two here, A. They are a deadly duo."

"Georgia is not a warrior," Alexis said. "She cannot hold a candle to what Natalie was."

"No, but she is an excellent strategist and administrator," Mistress Alexis said. "If George decides to lead his men in battle himself, Station Thraen will have a more than capable regent at its helm. This could possibly not just be about the prime."

"You don't think that the Thraens would attack Station Aelon, do you?" Alexis gasped. "They have no claim here! They could not justify any act of aggression!"

"Which was their argument against you, Son," Mistress Alexis said. "They could easily debate that The Way allowed you to take Station Thraen without the Thraenish crown recognizing your claim. Whether it is justifiable or not, they could do it and the rest of the stations will say it is what we deserve."

"Helios," Alexis said. "And here I am trying to develop the arts when I should be rallying my troops."

"It is not quite time to rally yet," Mistress Alexis said. "Lionel has to die first. And even then George will need the full support of his stewards and nobles. This will take time."

"Hopefully time enough for us to counter his plans," Alexis said. "We should start preparing now."

"We already have," Mistress Alexis smiled. "Do you think I would just come up here to deliver news? I'm also here to show you exactly what your father and I have been up to. I have never been one to let another station have all the fun. Fate is on our side, remember?"

The study doors opened and Clerke walked in with a huge grin on his face.

"If drunken pledges count then it is almost unanimous," he exclaimed as he semi-stumbled across the room. He gripped the back of a chair and steadied himself then took a deep breath. "Hopefully all the drunken pledges weren't just made by me."

His huge grin started to falter as he slowly focused on the royals before him.

"Uh-oh," he sighed then sat down in the chair he had steadied himself by. "Those are not happy Teirmont faces. Those are I-want-to-kill-kill-kill-Thraens Teirmont faces. What have I missed?"

"Would you leave us, Petro?" Mistress Alexis asked. "Now is not the time for artists."

"Oh," Clerke said as he tried to push himself up from the chair. "Say no more."

"Actually, we could use Clerke," Alexis said. "If George is using other primes then Clerke's sources may be useful."

"Fuck," Clerke grumbled. "We're going to war, aren't we?"

"You are doing nothing of the sort," Alexis said. "You are not technically a Teirmont and most certainly are not a soldier."

Clerke shifted his drunken gaze to Mistress Alexis.

"We're going to war, aren't we?" he asked the woman.

"Yes, Petro, we are going to war," she replied. "We just don't know when."

CHAPTER EIGHT

The Royal Guard made sure the Aelish delegation stayed together and no one strayed from sight.

"I'm surprised they allowed us to keep our blades," Steward Flain said as he walked with the rest of the Order of Jex down the Station Thraen passageway. "Considering the security here, I would have assumed they would have confiscated all weapons at the airlocks."

"Then everyone would be worried someone had smuggled in a weapon," Steward Vast replied. "All it would take is a paranoid royal or noble to set off a chain reaction of violence."

"But if everyone handed over their weapons then there wouldn't be any violence," Flain countered. "Maybe a couple of smuggled weapons, but the Burdened could handle those."

"You are assuming only a couple of weapons," Steward Kinsmon said. "When in reality every single one of us would have a weapon hidden on our person. This way the Burdened can see the weapons, our enemies can see the weapons, and everyone knows that stupidity will get you killed."

"If only that were true," Alexis said from directly in front of the men, walking side by side with Mistress Alexis and Master Kel. "But there is plenty enough stupidity here to worry about."

The group walked down the passageway until they came to the open doors of the Station Thraen great hall. An attendant bowed low and gestured for them to enter.

"Introducing Master Alexis and the most esteemed representatives of Station Aelon!" a porter announced.

The hall was filled with most of the royals and nobles of the Six Stations of the System. Heads turned at the announcement of the arrival of the Aelish delegation. Idle chatter was muted to deliberate whispers while hands holding glasses of wine paused. All eyes were on Master Alexis, then almost as one, the eyes turned to the newly crowned Master George who sat at the head of the great hall upon a massive, and ornately jeweled, dais.

"Alexis! Welcome!" George called out. "Please, please, come here so we may greet each other as equals!"

"Your bowel movements couldn't be considered equals," Mistress Alexis muttered. "Murdering son of a—"

"Civil, Lexi," Kel warned. "This is our chance to feel the man out on his true intentions with Thraen Prime. Don't start anything and spook him."

"My presence should spook the little cowardly shit," Mistress Alexis replied.

"Quiet, you two," Alexis said. "Let me handle this."

"Mother! Father!" Richard cried as he pulled himself away from the Klaervian delegation and struggled to get through the crowd to his family.

"Perfect timing," Mistress Alexis said as she patted Alexis on the shoulder. "You go talk to the smug murderer and your father and I will greet your brother. You can fill us in when we are seated."

"Be good," Alexis said.

"You as well," Kel replied. "Do not let him goad you into an argument. He is sure to push buttons and bring up Natalie. Do not take the bait."

"I've been master for a long while now, Father," Alexis said. "I know how to behave."

"I never assume when it comes to a Teirmont," Kel smiled and hugged his son. "Just be careful."

"I will," Alexis nodded then turned to the Order. "Go mingle. We came here for a reason. Do not waste this opportunity."

Each member of the Order of Jex gave Alexis a short bow then split off in different directions to talk to old friends and greet waving nobles.

"Oh, just you?" George asked as Alexis approached the dais and gave a quick bow. "The others did not want to give me any condolences or congratulations?"

"I would think they are almost one and the same," Alexis grinned.

"Yet not for you, Alexis," George replied. "You managed to get your crown and keep your mother. I envy you such a gift."

"Try having a former monarch as a parent and always second guessing your decisions," Alexis sighed. "It may not seem such a gift for long."

George leaned forward and pretended to whisper. "I have a twin sister, Alexis. I can almost relate exactly."

"What is this?" Georgia asked from her seat a step down and to the side of her brother. "Are you two talking about me? How very rude. Unless it's all flattery then please, gentlemen, carry on."

"It is nothing but flattery, love," George laughed. "To do otherwise would be to take my life in my hands."

"Oh, you, stop," Georgia laughed along. "I could never harm that beautiful face of yours, brother dear. It would be like splashing acid on a work of art."

"Speaking of art," George said. "Alexis, I hear you have begun to build quite the tribute to your sister. You and that musician friend of your late sister's. What's his name? Clergy or Klondike?"

"Clerke, love," Georgia said. "And you knew that. Stop being such a bog toad."

"I am afraid I have had more than my share of Klaervian whiskey today, Alexis," George said. "I'm in mourning, you know. Have you ever had good Klaervian whiskey?"

"I have," Alexis replied. "The best."

"Oh? The best? I hope you have some on you then," George said. "A man in mourning is a thirsty man indeed."

"Unfortunately, I have left my whiskey reserves back on Station Aelon," Alexis said. "But I do have this."

Alexis started to reach into his cloak and several Thraenish royal guards moved towards him. George held up his hands and they stopped, but the guards' own hands never left the hilts of their long blades.

"They are overly cautious, as you know," George said. "Our history and whatnot. But you wouldn't harm me here on my own station, would you Alexis? I should think not. Now, show me what you have there."

"It is a sculpture, Your Highness," Alexis said, pulling a small figure from his pocket. "One of the students in our new foundation made it from Thraen Prime clay. It is supposed to be in the likeness of your father, but I'm afraid it may need some work. It is a good thing our foundation has the funding to keep teaching these students."

"Oh, let me see! Let me see!" George exclaimed.

Alexis cautiously moved forward, very aware of the guards that watched his every move.

"It is nice you are allowed your own guards," Alexis said as he handed over the small statue. "Mine were forced to remain on our shuttle since the High Guardian insisted only the Burdened would handle security for the memorial service."

"Yes, well, I had to insist since it is my station," George replied, turning the statue over and over in his hands. "Plus, I absolutely abhor that armor those Burdened guards wear. All that blood red polybreen? Atrocious. They need to add some other colors into their styling. No one should be forced to stare at that one color all day. I do not know how the High Guardian does it."

"Speaking of, do you know where Victor is? I haven't seen him since I stepped on board," Alexis said.

"Oh, he is in his quarters," George said, still studying the statue. "He's old and frail. I'll have someone fetch him when it's his time to speak. For now we should just enjoy each other's company. It is so rare that royal Thraens and Aelons mingle these days. Not after what happened to your sister and all that unpleasantness."

George stopped studying the statue and started studying Alexis.

"The student did a passable job," George said. "While not perfect, this little trinket does have some resemblance to my father. It must be the way the head is held up high. In triumph. Like a true winner and man ordained by Helios to lead."

"I will tell the student you said so," Alexis replied as he struggled to keep his breathing even and his face neutral.

"Oh, you two," Georgia laughed. "Like a couple of shaow bulls facing off. All that unpleasantness my brother speaks of is in the past."

"Unpleasantness. Yes, you could call it that," Alexis said. He turned and looked about the great hall. "Is over there where it happened? Where Natalie died?"

Those nobles and stewards close enough to overhear the conversation stopped talking and looked from one master to the other, back and forth, waiting for the next move. Their attention rippled through the crowd and soon everyone, whether overt or not, was focused on the two men.

"I believe that is where she met her end," George replied. "Yes, I am almost certain of it."

Alexis looked back at George. "Met her end? You mean where you killed her?"

"I suppose I did kill her, didn't I?" George grinned. "Slit her throat right over there. Fairly sure the stain can still be seen. That Aelish blood is hard to get out."

"Presenting, the High Guardian!" the porter by the doors announced.

"Time to say goodbye to my father," George said. "But we should speak later, don't you think?"

"No, I do not," Alexis replied. He turned on his heels and shoved through the crowd, trying to get as much distance between himself and George before he ripped the man's throat out with his bare hands.

"Alexis!" Richard cried, stepping away from his parents to greet his brother. "Alexis? Where are you going?"

"Not now, Richard," Alexis growled, pushing his brother to the side. "We'll catch up later."

Alexis could hear his mother and father calling after him, and could see the High Guardian approaching him directly, but he had to shove all of that from his mind. He spotted a line of servants loaded with trays of food coming from a side door in the great hall's wall and he turned and bolted for it.

Once through he found himself in a large kitchen. Steam billowed from pots while smoke and flames rose up from the many stoves. Alexis wound in between the servants and cooks until he found another door. He shouldered it open and stepped out into a small courtyard, the night sky of Station Thraen filtering down through the station's shield above.

A group of startled servants froze in place.

"Leave," Alexis said and the servants didn't need to be told twice. They scurried through a far door and were gone before Alexis's words had stopped echoing in the courtyard.

Alexis stared up at the foreign constellations, so much different than what he was used to seeing on his station.

"Did you see those before you died, Nats?" he asked the night sky. "Did you even get that pleasure before they took your life?"

*

The Aelons stepped through the shuttle dock airlock, all grateful to be back on their station.

"I need a week of showers," Steward Vast said.

"That would hardly put a dent in the slime," Steward Triny replied.

"Alexis? Where are you going?" Mistress Alexis asked as her son hurried ahead of the exhausted group.

"Where do you think I am going?" Alexis asked. "To see the techs in the communications room. I want to know for sure our gift to George works."

"We will have plenty of time for that," Mistress Alexis responded. "You should clean up and rest first. All you'll do is start snapping at the techs and getting in their way."

"Like Triny said, cleaning up would hardly put a dent in the slime from being around that grendtshit George," Alexis said. "And as for rest, I need to know the device works first. My mind will not quiet until then."

"Very well, I am joining you," Mistress Alexis said.

"I shall too," Kel said.

"We might as well all go," Steward Kinsmon said. "Better to know now if dirtying our souls was worth the journey to that Helios forsaken station."

"Come along if you want," Alexis said. "But keep up. I want to get this over with."

*

"I can barely hear what they are saying," Alexis snapped at a tech.

"See?" Mistress Alexis said.

"Quiet, Mother," Alexis growled then leaned in close to the same tech he snapped at. "My apologies. Why is it so quiet?"

"It could have to do with the placement of the statue," the tech suggested. "It could be blocked by something or they could be across the room. It is also a very low frequency the device is transmitting on, meaning interference is possible from many sources."

"That seems like bad planning," Steward Neggle said.

Alexis glanced over his shoulder at all of the people crammed into the communications room.

"There was barely any planning," Alexis said. "It was a spur of the moment idea brought on by one of Clerke's star students. The young woman is a sculptor who is dating a stage tech. He adapted a com mic to fit into one of her statues and she showed it to Clerke. That's the extent of it."

"This arts foundation may have paid for itself right there," Steward Holsten said. "The meetings will be impressed."

"We say nothing," Mistress Alexis said. "Not until we have the information we need."

"Of course not," Holsten replied. "I can be dense, but I am far from stupid."

"Excuse me?" a woman said as she tried to squeeze through into the communications room. She was tall, with broad shoulders and chin length brown hair. Her eyes were a deep brown and several of the stewards turned their attention from the communications equipment to admire her. She ignored them and kept pushing into the room. "Excuse me, please."

"Young lady, this is a closed meeting," Mistress Alexis snapped. "It will do you well to—"

"Mother, stop," Alexis said. "This is Jen Webley. The station's Lead Com Tech. She is in charge of this operation."

"Webley? Why do I know that name?" Mistress Alexis asked.

"My great-grandfather was your grandfather's Lead Tech," Jen replied. "He was the one that rebuilt the broadcast system within the station."

"Webley! Of course!" Mistress Alexis said. She moved out of Jen's way immediately. "My apologies. Your family is part of station history. It is good to see you keeping the tradition alive."

"Thank you, my lady," Jen nodded. "I truly appreciate that." She smiled at the group. "Now get out. All of you. I need to coordinate with my techs and make sure we are getting the best signal possible. All data will be recorded to disc and I will deliver it personally as soon as we hear anything. I promise."

No one in the group moved.

"No, seriously, get out," Jen insisted. "With all due respect, of course."

The stewards grumbled and Kel had to grab Mistress Alexis by the arm to get her to leave. Alexis stood behind the first tech he had spoken with and focused on the quiet transmission coming in.

"Sire?" Jen said. "You as well."

"Me? I was hoping to stay here for a while and listen," Alexis replied.

"You make my people nervous, sire," Jen said. "And nervous techs miss important information. I will place the disc recordings in your hands as soon as we have everything dialed in and set."

"I...well...alright," Alexis responded. "I'll be in my study."

"It could be hours or even days before we have any significant information, sire," Jen smiled. "Go about your normal duties. I'll find you when warranted."

"Very well then," Alexis nodded. "Carry on, but keep me informed."

"Yes, I will," Jen said.

"The second you know anything," Alexis insisted.

"Of course," Jen replied.

"I'll be going now," Alexis said as he bowed. He straightened and frowned. "Not sure why I did that."

"Goodbye, sire." Jen waved. "I promise you will miss nothing."

Alexis nodded then left the communications room.

"I think the master likes you," the first tech said.

"I think you'll be looking for a new job if you say that again," Jen replied. "Now, what have we got?"

*

Clerke sat at the head of the small room, his eyes closed and head turned slightly as he listened to the young girl sing *a cappella*. It was a mournful song, filled with words of love and loss. The young girl finished and it was a full minute before Clerke opened his eyes.

"How old are you?" Clerke asked.

"She is nine, sir," a woman said from the back of the room. "She's been singing since—"

"I asked your daughter," Clerke snapped. "Grena is it?"

"Yes, sir," the young girl said and curtsied.

"How old are you, Grena?" Clerke asked again.

"Nine, sir," Grena replied. "I'll be ten next month."

"Well, Grena, then I have an early Decade present for you," Clerke smiled. "Your audition was nearly flawless and I would welcome you into the conservatory." He looked past Grena and to the girl's mother. "I take it you do not have the funds for any tuition?"

"No, sir," the mother replied. "It's why we applied to your school."

"Then a full scholarship will be arranged," Clerke said and clapped his hands together. "I will have my assistants go over all the damned paperwork with you. I hate that stuff, so I personally never deal with it myself. Once you have the forms filled out, then Grena can start. The new semester doesn't begin for three months, but we'll squeeze her in now. She has enough raw talent that she won't be far behind her peers."

"Oh, sir, thank you, sir," the mother nearly cried. "This is a dream come true."

"This is a lot of hard work without any promise of success, is what it is," Clerke said. "But you will learn that as she progresses through school."

He stood and offered his hand to Grena. The girl glanced back at her mother, received an enthusiastic nod, then shook Clerke's hand.

"Welcome, Grena," Clerke said. "Your life is about to change."

He watched the mother and daughter leave the small room then sat back down and slumped across his small desk.

"Bad time?" Alexis asked as he knocked at the door.

"Hey, A," Clerke sighed. "Thank you for coming down."

"My attendant said it sounded urgent," Alexis said as he entered the room and shut the door behind him. "But if it was so urgent then why didn't you come up to the castle?"

Clerke spread his hands across his desk, nearly knocking over several piles of files.

"Because, apparently, I will be listening to applicants until the day I die," Clerke said. "And because I'm not sure I actually have anything for you. I could be overreacting."

"I doubt that," Alexis said as he pulled up a chair to Clerke's desk and smirked at the stacks of files. "Welcome to my nightmare. Fun isn't it?"

"So much," Clerke said. He opened a drawer and pulled out a tall bottle and two short glasses. "Drink?"

"Stupid question?" Alexis replied. "Now, what do you have for me other than a new appreciation for administrative work."

"I have nothing," Clerke said as he handed Alexis a glass of liquor. "That's the problem. None of my sources are giving me any information."

"None of them?" Alexis asked, gladly taking the offered glass. "Not a single one?"

"Not a single one," Clerke said. "At first I thought it was because some of them were mad I was no longer touring, but when half tell me they haven't heard a word about Station Thraen and the other half won't respond at all, I start to get worried."

"With good reason," Alexis said. "It's not a matter of funds, is it? The crown will supply you with whatever you need to grease some palms here and there."

"No, everyone is well paid," Clerke said. "Or have been provided other favors. Which makes me think that other factors are in play."

"Such as a certain master using threats and intimidation to close the information leaks," Alexis frowned.

"Precisely," Clerke said. "I am sorry, A. I am of no use to you anymore."

"That's hardly true," Alexis said as he raised his glass. "You keep me in the good stuff."

"I try," Clerke smiled. "At least that connection is still strong."

There was a knock at the door and a woman peeked her head in. Her eyes went wide as she saw the master sitting in front of Clerke's desk.

"Yes, Blana?" Clerke asked.

"I, uh, don't mean to interrupt, Mr. Clerke, but there is a woman here to see you," Blana said. "I'll tell her you are busy."

"What is it about?" Clerke asked.

"It is Passengeress Webley, sir," Blana said. "She is returning the discs she borrowed."

"Passengeress Webley? Jen Webley?" Alexis asked, straightening up in his chair. "I don't mind the interruption."

Clerke shifted in his chair and nodded to Blana. "Show her in, please."

"Yes, sir," Blana said and opened the door all the way.

"Passengeress Webley, it's good to see you again," Alexis said as he stood and offered his hand. "I was meaning to come see you later today."

Jen was startled at the sight of the master, but recovered quickly.

"Your Highness," she said and curtsied. "It's an honor."

"All mine," Alexis said.

"I was just returning some discs to Petro that I borrowed," she said quickly and moved to set a stack of discs she held onto Clerke's desk. She saw the many piles of files and frowned then held out the stack directly to Clerke. "Uh, here, Petro. Thank you for loaning them to me."

"Petro?" Alexis asked, turning his attention on Clerke. "You hate being called Petro."

"No, I don't mind," Clerke said as he took the discs. "It doesn't bother me at all."

"Really," Alexis said as he sat back down and picked up his glass once again. "Good to know. . .Petro."

"Well, I need to get back to work," Jen said, curtseying again to the master. "An unexpected pleasure, sire."

"Still working hard on those transmissions?" Alexis asked, his eyes going from Clerke to Jen and back. "No new distractions that will get in the way of that work, I hope."

"It is my main duty every day, sire," Jen replied. She curtseyed once more, smiled at Clerke, then turned and left.

"Well, you scared her right off," Clerke said as he sat back down and set the discs on top of a dangerously askew pile of files.

"Not my intention, Petro," Alexis said, eyeing Clerke over the rim of his glass.

"Knock it off," Clerke said.

"Knock what off, Petro?" Alexis grinned.

"You know what," Clerke said. "She's just a friend."

"Is she?" Alexis asked. "Good, because I am familiar with Passengeress Webley and was considering asking her to dinner one night."

"You were?" Clerke coughed as he took a sip from his glass.

"That doesn't bother you, does it Petro?" Alexis asked.

"Doesn't bother me at all," Clerke said. "And don't call me Petro."

"But you don't mind being called Petro," Alexis grinned wider. "Petro, Petro, Petro, Petro."

"You are such an asshole," Clerke said. "And the answer is yes, by the way."

"I didn't ask anything," Alexis replied.

"Yes, you did," Clerke said. "I have been seeing her for a few weeks now. We have similar interests."

"Such as?" Alexis pressed.

"Such as she has the best sound system on this station," Clerke said. "And excellent taste in music."

"Does she now?" Alexis nodded. "Is sound system code for hot ass?"

"Damn, you Teirmonts are just crude, crude people," Clerke laughed. "To think it took a lowdecker like me to class you royals up."

Alexis finished his drink and tossed the glass to Clerke who caught it easily then flipped the master off.

"Cute," Clerke said.

"Let me know the second you do hear from one of your contacts," Alexis said. "Or if they still refuse to communicate."

"I'll give it another week," Clerke said. "If I don't hear anything from any of them then you may want to gives a heads up to the Order."

"Good idea," Alexis said as he walked to the door. "Petro."

"Fuck off!" Clerke yelled after the master as Alexis left.

Blana ducked her head into the room, her face pure white.

"Sir? Did you just tell the master to, uh. . .you know?" Blana asked, her voice shaky.

"I did," Clerke nodded. "He deserved it too."

*

"Well, good for him," Kel said. "Clerke is too nice a man to go to waste. Don't you think, Lexi?

"I do," Mistress Alexis replied. "We all know what a gentleman Petro is. He was very kind and loving to Nats and I am sure he will be to this Passengeress Webley as well."

"He hates being called Petro," Alexis smiled weakly as the servants served dinner to the three royals.

"I will call him Petro until I die," Mistress Alexis announced. "He doesn't mind it when I call him that."

"No, I'm sure he doesn't," Alexis nodded.

"Is everything alright, Son?" Kel asked.

"Fine, Father," Alexis replied quickly. "Now, let's eat."

"Hold on a second," Kel said. "What aren't you telling us? Are you bothered that Clerke is seeing this woman?"

"No, don't be ridiculous," Alexis replied.

"Oh, you are bothered," Mistress Alexis said. "That's your bothered voice. Now, Alexis, Natalie's passing has been hard for everyone, but even we must allow Petro to move on. We cannot expect the man to pine for Nats the rest of his life."

"I do not think that is it, love," Kel smiled. "I believe our son may have had an interest in Passengeress Webley himself."

Mistress Alexis was about to take a bite of food, but she stopped the fork in midair and looked to her son. "Is this true, A? Has Petro poached your love interest?"

"*Clerke*, has not poached anyone," Alexis said. "He is like a true brother to me and I wish him all the happiness in the world. I am sure he and Passengeress Webley will be good for each other."

"Oh, Alexis, I am so sorry," Mistress Alexis replied. "You did have an interest in her. Would you like a hug?"

"No, Mother, I am fine," Alexis said, rolling his eyes.

"Good, because I'm hungry and don't feel in the hugging mood," Mistress Alexis laughed. "Get over it, boy. You have the pick of the System when it comes to women. All you need do is say the word and you'll have gorgeous minoresses lining up at the airlock. I am constantly fielding correspondence from the other masters inquiring if you are to wed again."

"Yes, Son," Kel said as he cleared his voice. "It is one reason we asked to have dinner this evening. Your mother and I feel it may be time you consider a new partner. With Station Thraen acting suspiciously, it would do Aelon well to strengthen an alliance with one of the other stations."

"I have already been down that road, Father," Alexis frowned. "I do not need to go again."

"Sure you do, A," Mistress Alexis said. "It is not your fate to be alone forever. You need to find a woman that can help take some of the burden of running a station off of your shoulders."

"I'm not saying I do not want to find someone, Mother," Alexis replied. "I am saying I do not want to have my next marriage arranged like my first one. If I do wed again then it will be for love, not for duty. Doing it for duty is too painful and life is too short."

"That is true, Son," Kel nodded. "We will not bring it up again."

"We most certainly will bring it up again," Mistress Alexis snapped. "I want grandbabies, dammit. And it does not sound like I am getting any from Richard and his wife."

"Really? What's wrong?" Alexis asked, seizing the opportunity to move the conversation onto the subject of his younger brother. "Is the minoress unwell?"

"She is well enough to live and seem healthy," Mistress Alexis said. "But not well enough to conceive, apparently. This is not good, Alexis. If you do not have any more children, and Richard does not have even one heir, then this could be the end for the Teirmont line's hold on the crown. I do not want to see that."

"Maybe it wouldn't be such a bad thing," Alexis suggested. "Let one of the other families take a turn at it."

"Alexis!" Mistress Alexis snapped. "You take that back! You tempt fate when you say something like that! We have had enough tragedy in this family, we do not need you bringing more upon us!"

"Calm yourself, Lexi," Kel sighed. "Our son has a point. The Teirmonts have reigned for generations. Some good, some bad. But the crown has been in Teirmont hands longer than any other family in Station Aelon's history. It could be time for another bloodline to have a go."

"Blasphemy," Mistress Alexis growled.

"That you consider blasphemy?" Alexis laughed. "From a woman that I have heard curse Helios's name up and down for an hour straight? But the thought of me being the last Teirmont with the crown is blasphemous? I do love you, Mother."

"Oh, shut up," Mistress Alexis replied.

"Are you finished, sire?" a servant asked Alexis, struggling to ignore the mistress's less than delicate request of her son. "Shall dessert be served now?"

"I'm still eating, thank you," Alexis said then looked at his mother. "But I can be finished if you two are ready for dessert. I know how you like to go to bed early now that you are so old."

"You cheeky little shit," Mistress Alexis smiled. "I'll have you know that your father and I have a very romantic evening planned. I shall ravish him mercilessly as soon as we return to our quarters."

"Mother, that is enough," Alexis laughed. "You win. I do not need to hear any more of that, thank you."

"Oh, no, A, you brought it on yourself," Mistress Alexis said. "I shall now go into great detail of our amorous plans."

"Don't you dare!" Alexis cried. "Father, tell her to stop!"

Kel did not respond.

"Father, tell her," Alexis laughed some more as he turned to Kel. "She's being disgusting...Father?"

"Kel?" Mistress Alexis asked as she looked to her husband. "Kel? Are you feeling alright?"

Kel sat there, his skin pale, almost pure white, his jaw slack. A thin line of drool hung from his chin.

"Kel? Kel!" Mistress Alexis screamed as she jumped from her seat and raced to her husband's side. "*Kel!*"

"Call the physicians!" Alexis ordered, looking to the servants. *"Do it now!"*

*

Alexis closed the door to his mother's bedchamber and crossed to a high backed chair set close to a Vape fireplace in the royal sitting room. He adjusted the flames, making them burn brighter and higher, then sat down and closed his eyes.

"A? Are you in here?"

"Clerke?" Alexis asked as he sat up and turned to look over his shoulder. "Is that you?"

"It is," Clerke said as he crossed to a second chair. "May I? I don't want to disturb you."

"Please, sit," Alexis replied. "I could use the company."

Clerke sat and then looked back at the bedchamber door. "How is she?"

"For the first time in my life, she cursed fate," Alexis said. "I have never heard her do that before."

"I bet it was colorful," Clerke responded.

"It most certainly was," Alexis said. "She blames me, you know."

"What? She does? Why in Helios would she do that?" Clerke asked.

"Because I blasphemed fate at dinner the other night," Alexis said. "The night father had his first brain stroke."

"She doesn't mean it," Clerke said.

"I'm afraid she is so hurt that she might actually," Alexis said. He turned to look at the bedchamber door. "She is not one to use words in an idle manner. Oh. . .hello."

"Your Highness," Jen said from the doorway. "I am sorry. I was told Petro was here. I did not think you would. . .I mean, of course, you would, it's just that—"

"Stop, Jen," Clerke said. "Alexis will not bite. What is it you need?"

Jen started to step into the room then caught herself and curtsied. Alexis grinned and waved at her.

"Come in, Passengeress Webley," Alexis said. "Any friend of Clerke's is welcome here."

"Careful," Clerke laughed. "I am a musician, you know. Some of my friends I wouldn't let stain your toilet."

"I have these, Petro," Jen said. "And I need a second set of ears. There is something off about them."

"Something off about music?" Alexis asked.

"No, sire, these are discs of the recordings from Station Thraen," Jen replied. "I am finding a pattern. Too much of a pattern. I wanted Petro's trained ears to have a listen and tell me if I am right or wrong."

"Play them now," Alexis said. "There is a player against the wall there."

"No, sire, I couldn't," Jen said. "I should not have even come. This is something that can wait. Your father just passed...."

"And I am still Master of Station Aelon," Alexis responded. "My duty to the Aelish people does not stop because of the death of my father. Go ahead and play what you have for us."

"I, well...alright," Jen said then looked about the sitting room for the disc player.

"Right here," Clerke said as he got up and took the disc from her. "You sit, I'll play."

"Please," Alexis said and motioned to the chair that Clerke had just vacated. "Would you care for tea or anything to drink?"

"No, sire, thank you," Jen said, still standing.

"Passengeress Webley," Alexis smiled. "Please stop with the formalities. You were much less accommodating to me before you began seeing Clerke here. I would prefer to speak with that woman than the woman who keeps kowtowing to me. Bring the fire back, please. I am not one that is afraid of assertive women."

"You can say that again," Clerke said as he set a disc into the player and pressed play. "Otherwise you would have been eaten alive."

"It came close as it was," Alexis said as the sound of voices came from the disc player. "Is that Master George?"

"I believe so," Jen said, moving Clerke out of the way. "In fact, I am almost one hundred percent certain of it. But here is the strange part. Do you hear the conversation he is having?"

"He's speaking with one of his attendants, yes?" Alexis asked.

"Yes, that is what it sounds like," Jen said, then ejected the disc and put in a new one. "But listen to this." She cocked her head as the new disc began to play. She waited a minute then held up her hand. "There! Did you hear that?"

"He was talking to a steward, or some noble," Clerke said.

"True, but listen to this phrase," Jen said and replayed the last couple seconds of the disc. "Right there. It's the exact same phrase as when he was speaking with his attendant."

"So?" Alexis asked. "I use the same turns of phrase all the time. Masters can get into a conversational rut. It's a symptom of the monotony of holding the crown."

"No, I think I hear it," Clerke said. "Put the last disc back in."

Jen did and they listened to Master George speaking to his attendant.

"Shit," Clerke growled. "She's right. It isn't the same turn of phrase, it's the actual exact same phrase."

"I'm sorry, I don't understand the difference," Alexis said.

"You asked me to alert you the second I, or any of my techs, heard anything important," Jen said. "Yet we haven't come to you once. Why? Because there has been nothing important to report. Nothing at all. Isn't that strange, considering we have been listening to the conversations of a master for weeks? Wouldn't we at least hear some information, even if it doesn't pertain to Station Aelon?"

"I'm still not following," Alexis said.

"This is a recording, A," Clerke explained. "We are not actually hearing Master George's conversations, but spliced together, manufactured conversations created just for us."

"Son of a grendt," Alexis sighed. "He's been on to us this whole time."

"I believe so," Jen said. "I went back and listened to the very first conversations, and except for the first day or so, they all sound manu-factured."

"So our plan failed," Alexis said. "This is wonderful news. Just wonderful."

Jen's eyes went wide and she started to apologize, but Clerke placed a hand on her arm.

"Yes, Alexis, it is," Clerke said.

"I was being sarcastic, Clerke," Alexis responded.

"I know, but I was not," Clerke said. "This is wonderful because we now know that George is aware we are spying on him."

"I am not seeing the wonderfulness," Alexis said.

"We may not have gotten information, but we may have slowed his plans down," Clerke said. "I am willing to wager that he is paranoid enough to worry we have other devices, and perhaps actual spies, on Station Thraen. Think of it. If he was going to attack the primes, wouldn't he have done it already?"

REIGN OF FOUR: BOOK IV

Alexis thought for a moment then looked at Clerke and smiled.

"He had to scrap his original plans in case they had been compromised," Alexis said. "Our ploy did not yield useful intel, but it did slow him down."

"Precisely," Clerke said then saw the look on Jen's face. "What?"

"You know a lot about how this all works for a musician," Jen said.

"It's why we Teirmonts keep him around," Alexis said and stood up. "I need to speak with the Order about this right away."

"Good idea," Clerke said. "Should we come along?"

"No, no, you two have done enough," Alexis smiled. "Go be in love and let me worry about station matters." Alexis saw the looks on Clerke's and Jen's faces. "Oh, you two haven't said those words yet have you?" He looked at his mother's bedchamber door. "Well, don't wait until it is too late. Some of my father's last words were that life is too short."

*

The Order of Jex sat around the long table, every one of them lost in thought as they processed what Alexis told them.

"The unfortunate part of this news is that we still do not know exactly what George's plans are," Alexis said from the head of the table. "But couple this subterfuge with the fact that Clerke's sources have gone silent, I would wager that he will strike soon."

"We don't doubt that, sire," Steward Vast said from his seat. "But what do we do about it? I have already sent word to increase patrols on Thraen Prime's perimeters. We have been interrogating miners continuously and cannot find evidence that any are secretly Thraenish soldiers."

"I have received word from The Way that we are dangerously close to being in violation of the treaty if we continue harassing the mine workers," Steward Kinsmon said. "Part of our argument for taking Thraen Prime was that we would treat all Tharens on that land as equals to Aelons. Constantly stopping mining to haul out workers and get them to admit they are soldiers is not treating them equal."

"It is also not good for business," Steward Triny said. "The meeting of stewards is getting tired of complaints of delays on Vape gas deliveries because our investigations are harming quotas."

"To Helios with quotas," Alexis said. "We could be going to war any day now. We must do what we must to avoid that at all costs. It's not as if we can attack Thraen Prime. We hold Thraen Prime! It is us that must wait for the attack to happen!"

"Master George will be here next week, will he not?" Vast asked. "To attend your father's memorial service?"

"Yes, he will," Alexis replied. "I was surprised he accepted the invitation."

"It could be to throw us off," Vast said. "It will show the other stations, as well as The Way, that he is not being aggressive towards Aelon. If he keeps up the facade, then he can take more time to prepare, wait us out until the meeting pressures us to stop our investigations."

"I want us to triple our troop presence on Thraen Prime," Alexis said. "We need to prepare for the inevitable."

"We cannot triple our presence, sire," Steward Holsten said. "We can add twenty-five percent more soldiers to the land, but any more than that and we are in violation of the treaty as well."

"What?" Alexis asked. "How can that be?"

"It was a condition of the Treaty of the Primes that Aelish soldiers not outnumber the Thraenish miners," Steward Holsten said. "I know I am still one of the newer members of the Order of Jex, but I have read and reread the treaty in order to be absolute certain of where we stand. Twenty-five percent more is our limit."

"Why would my mother agree to such terms?" Alexis asked. "That hobbles us immediately."

"Your mother was a different ruler than you, sire," Steward Neggle said. "She trusted that fate would lead the station just as much as she led it. She also had a deep confidence in her military strength and believed Lionel to be weak and useless when it came to warfare. Which, to be fair, he was. His son is a different matter, and she underestimated George from the beginning."

"Plus, if we are being honest," Vast added. "I believe your mother was hoping we'd go back to war with Thraen. That woman does like to fight."

"Except it is now my fight," Alexis said. He narrowed his eyes and grinned. "Yes, it is my fight. Which means I should be down on Helios, on the primes, preparing for it."

"Your Highness, that is not wise," Vast said. "You are needed up here on the station."

"True, but the primes are currently without a planet-side regent," Alexis said. "My parents came back to the station to try to talk me into finding a new wife. They were scheduled to go see Richard next, then return to the primes as soon as possible. Mother is in no condition to travel at the moment, which means the primes are unattended. That is close to a treaty violation right there."

"Perhaps your brother, Richard, could go instead," Neggle suggested.

"No, that defeats the point," Alexis said. "If I go down to Helios then I will need the Royal Guard with me. The Royal Guard are not considered Aelish soldiers, but crown security. Their job is to protect the royal family."

The members of the Order all stared at Alexis, none of them catching his meaning.

"Let me spell it out," Alexis sighed. "We need more soldiers on Thraen Prime, but we cannot increase our numbers more than twenty-five percent, correct?"

"Correct," Holsten replied slowly.

"But the treaty only mentions Aelish soldiers directly, yes?" Alexis asked.

"Yes," Holsten said, his eyes widening with realization. "The Royal Guard are not soldiers. But, for you to travel to Thraen Prime, you will need the Royal Guard with you."

"Exactly," Alexis nodded. "What if we increase the Royal Guard's numbers? We induct as many soldiers as we can into the Royal Guard then have them accompany me to the primes. We'll have the numbers we need without breaking the treaty."

"The Way, and Master George, will see right through the ploy, sire," Vast said. "They'll know what you are doing."

"Good for them," Alexis replied. "Then maybe George will think twice about trying to retake Thraen Prime. We win no matter what. Either we have the numbers we need to fight George or the numbers we have keep George from fighting."

"We only win if we win, sire," Vast said. "Your idea may work to increase the amount of soldiers, er, *guards*, but those guards have to defeat George's troops. It is not foolproof."

"And what will we do about the station, Your Highness?" Kinsmon asked. "There will need to be a regent in place."

"My mother can do it," Alexis said.

"Your mother is grieving the death of her husband, your father," Neggle said. "Sire, you cannot expect her to be able to handle the administration of the station in her state."

"Oh, I think her state is the perfect time for her to administrate the station," Alexis said. "Like I said, gentlemen, my mother loves to fight. It is possibly the only thing she loves as much as her family. When I tell her she is needed to help keep Station Aelon stable while I defend the primes against Master George, she will no longer be grieving. She will just be very dangerous."

*

"You are sure of this, Alexis?" Mistress Alexis asked as she sat by the Vape fire in her royal sitting room, Alexis in the chair next to her. "This is very risky. You could lose the entire prime if the High Guardian decides Aelon has broken the treaty."

"We could lose the entire prime if George catches us unprepared," Alexis replied. "Without the increase in men, we won't stand a chance."

"*If* George is planning to attack," Mistress Alexis said. "We do not know for sure."

"We have to assume," Alexis said. "All signs point in that direction, Mother. If we sit on our hands and do nothing, then everything we fought for, everything good Aelons died for, will be for nothing. I could not hold onto Station Thraen, but I will be Helios damned if I do not do everything in my power to hold onto Thraen Prime."

"Well, I admire your spirit, Son," Mistress Alexis said. "As I know your father would as well. It is a shame he cannot be here to see this. He would love your creativity."

"We will honor him right today during the memorial service," Alexis said.

"Yes, well, I am afraid that the rest of the System is not honoring him as they should," Mistress Alexis frowned. "Sending only delegates and no royals. Not even Station Thraen has sent a member of their royal family. George has backed out. And after we attended his father's service. It is disrespectful and a disgrace. Kel was a master too, you know."

"In name, Mother," Alexis said. "Not in blood. I believe it could be that some of the stations are worried about relations with The Way. Father was once part of the Burdened, and only a commoner. If each station sent a royal, then they would be acknowledging Father had a claim to a bloodright that he did not."

"Still fucking disrespectful," Mistress Alexis snapped. "If I ever see any of these royals in person, I'll snap their necks like twigs."

"And the Order was worried you wouldn't be up to the task of being regent on the station while I am gone," Alexis laughed.

"They what?" Mistress Alexis cried, her cheeks burning red. "Which ones exactly? Give me names and I'll show them something to be worried about!"

There was a knock at the door and an attendant stepped in, holding the sitting room door wide open as Minor Richard entered. Alexis and his mother stood up instantly, both smiling broadly.

"Richard, my boy," Mistress Alexis said as she crossed to her son and kissed him on the cheek. "It is so wonderful seeing you here. It has been too long."

"It has, Mother," Richard nodded. "Far too long."

"Good to see you, Brother," Alexis said as he crossed and hugged his brother. "You are looking well. Where's your wife? I haven't seen Batonda in ages."

"Oh, unfortunately she could not attend," Richard said. "She was feeling under the weather."

"Under the weather?" Mistress Alexis asked. "Is it what I hope it is?"

"Do you hope my wife feels ill, Mother?" Richard frowned. "Because that would be rather rude of you if you did. I know Minoress Batonda is not exactly up to Teirmont standards, her being more delicate of character than the rest of us, but there is no need to wish ill of her."

"Shut up, Richard," Alexis said. "Mother is asking whether your wife is pregnant, is all. She would never wish ill of her."

"Oh, right, my apologies, Mother," Richard said then furrowed his brow. "But I do not know. If she is pregnant then she has not said a word of it to me."

"Is she sick in the morning or right after lunch?" Mistress Alexis asked. "Perhaps retaining water?"

"Retaining water?" Richard said. "How would I know if she is? What are the symptoms of retaining water?"

"Retaining water is a symptom," Alexis sighed. "She would look like she's gained weight. A little bloated."

"Oh, well, yes she has gained weight," Richard said. "But do not tell her I said that. She would be upset with me."

"Is she tired a lot? Having strange food cravings?" Mistress Alexis pushed.

"Oh, yes to all of that," Richard replied. "Hmmm. Do you think she is pregnant?"

"It sounds like it to me," Mistress Alexis said. "Oh what glorious news! Such a sad day is now made happy! Another Teirmont will join this family!"

"And an heir will be ready," Alexis said. "This is good news, Brother."

"Yes, I suppose it is," Richard replied, beaming. "I am going to be a father. How about that?"

"Are you fine with the idea?" Alexis asked as he crossed to a cart and poured three glasses of wine. "It changes your perspective on life instantly."

"Yes, it does, doesn't it?" Richard said. He took the glass offered him and drained it right away.

"Well, I was going to propose a toast," Alexis laughed. "But that was good enough. Cheers!"

"Cheers," Mistress Alexis said and drained her glass.

"I believe I would like to sit down," Richard said. "I'm not feeling so steady on my feet at the moment."

"Certainly, Brother," Alexis said as he took Richard's arm and steered him to one of the chairs by the fire. "We still have a couple hours before the service. Take some time and let it all sink in."

"Should I call Batonda?" Richard asked. "I should, shouldn't I? To confirm with her that this is all true."

"In due time, Richard," Alexis said. "It's early on Station Klaerv still. Let us get through Father's service and then I will take you to the communications room the second we have shaken the last dignitary's hand."

"Yes, yes, after the service I will call her," Richard said. "Oh, that reminds me." He reached into his jacket and pulled out a letter, handing it to Alexis. "This is for you from my father-in-law. Master Jeffon instructed me not to give it to you until after the memorial service, but I am afraid I'll forget in my haste to speak with my wife."

"Thank you," Alexis said and took the letter. He looked about the sitting room for a letter opener and then rolled his eyes when his mother offered him a short blade. "Seriously, Mother? You have a blade with you on the day of Father's service?"

"He would understand," Mistress Alexis said. "And expect nothing less."

Alexis took the blade and slit the envelope open. He handed the blade back to his mother, pulled out the letter and inspected it.

"There's no official royal seal on this," Alexis said, turning the paper over. "Jeffon's signature is here, but no seal." Alexis looked at his brother. "Richard? Are you sure this is actually from your father-in-law?"

Richard did not respond, just looked off into space.

"Richard!" Alexis snapped, making his brother jump. "I asked you a question."

"Oh, sorry, I was wandering," Richard said.

"I could see that," Alexis responded. "Are you sure this is from Master Jeffon?"

"It most certainly is," Richard replied. "He handed it to me himself. He said he wanted to make sure that you knew it was from him and he was sorry he could not tell you in person, but that circumstances were not in Station Klaerv's favor to do so."

Alexis stared at his brother for a brief second then turned his attention to the letter. As he read, his face darkened with anger and his hands began to wrinkle the paper around the edges.

"Alexis?" Mistress Alexis asked. "What is it? What is wrong?"

"We are wrong," Alexis said as he crumpled the letter up and threw it across the room. "We have been wrong from the start. I have to speak with the Order right now."

"Now? Whatever for?" Mistress Alexis asked.

"Is it bad news?" Richard asked. "I was hoping it wouldn't be bad news when he handed it to me."

"We are too late," Alexis said. "We may have already lost Thraen Prime."

"What? How?" Mistress Alexis asked. "Alexis, tell me what was in that letter!"

"Betrayal," Alexis said. "System-wide betrayal."

CHAPTER NINE

The mood in Castle Aelon's tactical operations room was far from jovial. Battle hardened men stood shoulder to shoulder with men that had not had the privilege of spilling enemy blood or of having their own blood spilt and living to tell the tale. Many wore their polybreen armor, while others only stood there in their uniforms, reluctant to don the protective garb, fearing it could be for the last time.

"The window is too tight, Alexis," Steward Vast said, his polybreen armor shining bright despite the many dents and gouges it held from battles past. "We will have almost no margin for error with this assault."

"Which is exactly what Master George wants," Steward Neggle added. "To narrow our advance across the open sea so we can only land at Scolari Beach. You remember Scolari Beach, do you not, sire?"

"I remember it," Alexis replied. "And do not speak to me as if I do not."

"You are acting as if you do not," Neggle said. "That beach is nothing but deep, soft sand that borders a fifteen foot ridge covered in thick scrim grass. And not your plains scrim grass, but scrim grass hardened and sharpened over time by the harsh sea winds. The blades of that grass rival the blades of our soldiers."

"I know what type of scrim grass is on that beach!" Alexis shouted. "I was there with everyone else when we landed to take Thraen Prime the first time! Do not speak to me like some noble that has bought a commission in order to impress his sector! I fought for, I bled for, and I won the last conflict!"

"Steward Neggle was not implying you did not do Station Aelon proud during those days," Vast said, giving Neggle a look of warning. "He was just saying that we made the mistake before of approaching via Scolari.

We cannot afford to make that mistake again." Vast rubbed at his temples. "With the other stations using their cutters to blockade access around Thraen Prime then we have no choice but to wait before we attack."

"If we attack," Steward Flain muttered.

"Dear Helios," Vast said under his breath.

"Do you have some insight you would like to share with the room, Flain?" Alexis asked. "Perhaps some amazing strategic advantage you have been holding back from the rest of us? Or a military maneuver you have come up with that none of us have thought to use?"

"No, sire," Flain replied. "My apologies."

"Oh, I do not want your apologies, Flain," Alexis snapped. "I want your undying loyalty. Is that too much to ask of you? A member of the Order of Jex who has sworn an oath to follow the Aelish crown to Helios and beyond? I'm not imposing on you by keeping you to that oath, am I?"

"Master, may I have a word in private?" Vast asked.

"No, you may not," Alexis replied.

"I'm afraid I must insist," Vast said. "Perhaps the others could see to their men and make sure all are prepared to make the trek across the sea while we speak?"

The rest of the Order, and the generals and military leaders that were present, quickly took the opportunity to leave the room. Alexis glared at them as they went then turned his full ire onto Vast once the room was empty.

"Talk fast, steward," Alexis said. "Every second wasted is a second we do not take back Thraen Prime."

"Sire, I am not convinced we can take back Thraen Prime," Vast said.

"Then why in Helios did you agree to come down here?" Alexis asked. "Your outlook was much more optimistic on the station."

"That is true," Vast said. "But none of us could see the entire situation from the station. Now that we are on Helios, and close enough to truly evaluate what we are up against, it is clear that Master George was fully prepared when he made his move and retook Thraen Prime."

"Stole, you mean," Alexis snarled. "He stole it from me. He stole it from the crown. He stole it from all of Aelon."

"Alexis, you must see reason," Vast said. "This is not like you. You are not a mad master who throws all caution to the wind and dives headlong into an unwinnable situation. Many masters before you, not just Aelish masters, have let their emotions rule them, sending thousands upon thousands of innocent men to their deaths. Do not be one of those masters. I beg of you, Alexis, see reason."

"Natalie fought to take this prime," Alexis said. "She fought to take Station Thraen. If I let George beat me now, then how will I face her when I die and go to meet Helios? How will I look her in the eye?"

"Those are thoughts for when you are much older and your time is close," Vast said. "And they are thoughts all men must face. There is not a soul in the System that does not have regrets that haunt them. But let me assure you, sire, that you need not have these thoughts. Your sister will never think less of you because you chose to walk away and live as opposed to rushing forward to die." Vast grinned. "In fact, knowing the minoress as I did, I would say she will have a hard wallop to the head waiting for you if you make the wrong choice."

Alexis watched the steward closely. "And you think that attacking is the wrong choice?"

"I do," Vast said. "As it stands now, it is a suicide mission. If we even had just a few more miles of room to maneuver, giving us the space to land either east or west of Scolari Beach, then I might be persuaded to change my mind. But we both know that the Thraenish bastard has promised too much to the other stations for that to happen. Splitting Vape mining profits? That may have been something we could have offered when we held the prime, but not now."

"I may have something to offer that is worth more than that," Alexis said. "At least to one of the stations."

"Sire?" Vast asked. "I do not catch your meaning."

"Never you mind, steward," Alexis said. "It is none of your concern. Yet."

Alexis turned to the battle plans laid out upon the table at the center of the room. He studied them for several minutes before nodding.

"Fine," he said. "We wait."

"For how long, sire?" Vast asked. "I do not foresee the situation changing."

"I do, Vast," Alexis said. "I see the situation changing considerably. All I need is to wait for a call from my brother."

"Your brother?" Vast asked, completely confused. "How does Richard play into this? No offense, Your Highness, but Richard is not a warrior and has no aptitude when it comes to military matters."

"I know that," Alexis said. "But what he does have is a wife with a child on the way. A royal child who could be heir to the Aelish crown one day. And that is something that could change the situation rather quickly."

*

"Are you sure your line is secure?" Alexis asked as he studied his brother's face on the video screen. "We cannot afford for this accord to leak. The only way this will work is if it is a surprise, Richard."

"The line is secure and the communications room here is empty," Richard replied. He squirmed before the camera and would not look Alexis directly in the eyes.

"What is it?" Alexis asked. "What is bothering you?"

"It is Batonda," Richard responded. "She is not happy with the deal I have brokered with her father. She feels we are using the life of our unborn child as a bargaining chip."

"That's exactly what we are doing," Alexis said. "Your child will be the heir to the crown of Station Aelon as well as a possible heir to the crown of Station Klaerv. This accord means that Master Jeffon could have his grandchild ruling both stations, if he so chooses."

"If the child remains here on Station Klaerv," Richard said. "Where I am to remain as well."

"That way you stay safe, Brother," Alexis said.

"I have been staying safe for years," Richard sighed. "I would like to come home, please."

"Not yet," Alexis said.

"Then when?" Richard almost cried. "I love Batonda, and I do enjoy the Klaervian people, but I want to return to Station Aelon. If something happens to you down there, Alexis, then I will be woefully unprepared as master. I do not know the political climate anymore, I do not know which stewards in the meeting to trust. I don't even know which labor groups or merchant coalitions are the ones to favor and the ones to shun. These are things a master should know, and a minor learns, when living on the station he is supposed to rule!"

"Mother will help you navigate all of that," Alexis replied. "She will guide you as she guided me in my early days."

"You were at war in your early days," Richard said. "I do not want to be at war in my early days, Alexis. I have no stomach for war."

"You will not be at war because I will win this conflict," Alexis said. "I promise you, Richard. I will win this conflict and I will live to continue my rule. You will be able to relax as father of the Aelish heir and all the privileges that go with that."

"What are Mother's thoughts on giving away the Aelish crown to Klaervian control?" Richard asked.

"I am not giving away the Aelish crown to Klaervian control," Alexis frowned. "Do not exaggerate the accord."

"However you want to define it, what does Mother think?" Richard asked.

"Mother does not know yet," Alexis replied. "And I expect you not to tell her."

"Helios, Alexis! Mother doesn't know? You have not informed her of your plans?" Richard cried. He shook his head back and forth, over and over. "Oh, this is not good. This is not good. She will kill you. She will kill us both. She will kill everyone. Oh, Alexis, there will be so much killing."

"Who do you think our mother is, Richard?" Alexis asked. "She will not kill me, she will not kill you, and she will not kill everyone. You are sounding very unstable right now. I advise you go take a rest and be with your wife. Comfort her and take care of her. That is your job now. You make sure that child of yours is born healthy and happy."

Richard continued to shake his head back and forth.

"Richard!" Alexis shouted. "Did you hear what I said?"

Richard stopped shaking his head, but his eyes looked wild.

"I heard, I heard," Richard said. "I'll go comfort my wife."

"And you will not tell Mother," Alexis said.

"Oh, no, I will not tell Mother," Richard replied with a manic cackle. "There is no way I am telling her this. No way."

He reached out and the video screen in front of Alexis went blank.

"Richard? Seriously?" Alexis sighed. "Helios, help Station Aelon if I pass before my time."

*

"I do not know what you promised Master Jeffon, but I have to hand it to you, Alexis, whatever it was it has made all the difference," Vast said as he and Alexis stared out of the shield dome covering the royal cutter as it made its way across the roiling, gas covered sea toward Thraen Prime. "There isn't a Klaervian cutter in sight, just as you said there would not be."

"We have the space we need to adjust our landing zone," Alexis said. "The Thraens will think we are still aiming for Scolari Beach, but we will come at them from the east instead. The day will be ours, Vast. Fate is on our side."

"I pray you are right, sire," Vast said. "For if not then we will be butchered and I do not want to leave this life at the hands of a dirty Thraen."

"Nor do I, steward," Alexis laughed, clapping the man on the shoulder. "Nor do I."

"We are getting close," Neggle said as he came up behind the two. "Would you care to say some words to the men, sire? We can broadcast to all the cutters at once."

"Yes, that would be perfect, Neggle. Thank you," Alexis said. "Bring me a handset. I am not ready to don my helmet yet."

"I have one ready here, Your Highness," Neggle said, offering a bulky handset to Alexis. "It is dialed to the correct frequency already, just press the button and speak."

Alexis took the handset and cleared his throat. He glanced back out the dome at the Vape gasses that floated above the choppy waves. Then he pressed the button and spoke.

"Fellow Aelons, I do not speak to you now as Master of Station Aelon, but as Alexis Teirmont, your comrade in arms. I have fought with many of your before, led you to victories on Station Thraen and on the very prime we are approaching. I have also suffered the indignity with you of losing control of Station Thraen and now the prime.

"But, let me assure you, I intend to reverse those indignities. While we may not be able to retake Station Thraen, we most certainly can retake the prime. This land before us is my birthright by blood, and since my blood is Aelish blood, then this prime belongs to all Aelons, all that have the truly righteous blood of a chosen station flowing through them.

"When we land on this beach, we will not be fighting just for dirt and scrim grass, for territory and Vape mines, we will be fighting for our very souls and for the honor of all Aelons. Far above us, through the thick Vape clouds and waiting in the cold of space, is Station Aelon. That is our home and that is our spirit. It is for those who live up there, who rely on our strength, our determination, our refusal to accept defeat, it is for those people that we fight.

"Many of us will lose our lives today, I would be a liar to say otherwise. Even I may fall at the hands of a wicked Thraen. But even if I do fall, I want every single one of you to know what an honor it is to fall for such a cause and what an honor it will be to die next to the greatest people that populate this System.

"To die an Aelon is no death at all! To die an Aelon is a gift! And if today, fate chooses to hand me that gift, then I take it willingly! I take it with open arms! So join me, Aelons, and raise those arms! Raise them up high and shout to Helios that we cannot be broken, we cannot be beaten, we cannot be destroyed!

"*For we are Aelons!*"

Alexis let the echoes of his words fade before giving back the handset.

"Not bad," Vast smiled. "Makes me want to die for you."

"Good," Alexis replied. "Because it appears we are here. Are you ready, steward?"

"I am, sire," Vast said. "It has been a privilege serving you, Alexis."

"The privilege has been mine, Vast," Alexis said. "And I look forward to serving you for years to come. Today is not our day to die, Vast. Today is our day to solidify our glory for Station Aelon."

Vast smiled as he put on his environmental suit's helmet and secured the clasps. Alexis hesitated for a few seconds then did the same.

The view before the men changed from nothing but wild sea to one of a great landscape, increasing in size with every second that the royal cutter raced towards it.

*

"We have to fall back!" Neggle shouted over the com. "They knew we were coming!"

"It cannot be!" Alexis yelled. "Richard assured me the Klaervians would not engage!"

"They have not, sire," Steward Holsten replied. "But they may have let the Thraens know of our plans!"

"We will not retreat!" Alexis bellowed. "We will push forward and take the hill to our right! Order the men to skirt the beach and go for the break in the land there! We regroup when we crest the hill!"

"Sire, we do not know what is on the other side!" Neggle responded.

"Kinsmon is down!" Triny screamed. "Dear Helios, he was ripped in—"

"Triny? Triny!" Neggle called. "Dammit, Alexis, we are being torn apart! Their numbers are too great!"

"Their numbers are nothing against our will!" Alexis shouted as he slashed open a Thraen soldier's environmental suit, exposing the man to the deadly Vape gas. "We shall overcome everything they send at us! Now, all of you, on me!"

Alexis shoved the Thraen soldier aside as the man's body began to smoke and dissolve. The master ducked the swipe of a blade then dove and rolled out of the way as a Vape grenade exploded to his left. He heard screams cut short as many of his men did not get out of the way in time. Alexis pushed the thoughts of the screams from his mind and kept moving, his eyes locked onto the hill ahead.

Thraenish soldiers poured onto the beach, their long blades raised over their heads. Wave after wave met the Aelish forces and collided in an avalanche of bloodlust and violence. Alexis kept running, urging his men to follow, to flank the oncoming Thraens. But most of his soldiers could not get free from the Thraenish assault and in seconds Alexis found himself alone as he crested the ridge and gazed out on the expanse of Thraen Prime.

"No," he whispered. "How?"

To his left, thousands of Tharenish soldiers moved towards the beach while directly in front of him, stood a dozen regiments of longslingers. Thraenish longslingers.

"Sire!" Neggle yelled as he came up behind Alexis. "Sire! I must insist...that...Longslingers?"

"They are using our tactics against us, Neggle," Alexis said. "They have developed their own—"

But Alexis didn't finish as he saw the muzzles of the Thraens' longslings bark with Vape fire. He flattened himself on the ground and covered his head while the com system in his helmet was filled with Steward Neggle's screams.

"Neggle? Neggle, answer me!" Alexis ordered.

He felt something hit his back and he shoved it away, rolling over to see most of Steward Neggle's body consumed by something that had once been singularly Aelish.

"Particle barbs?" Alexis gasped. "They have particle barbs?"

He scrambled to switch his com to an open channel.

"Vast? Vast, do you hear me?" Alexis called out.

"Yes, sire! Where are you?" Vast replied over the com.

"Retreat! Retreat now! The Thraens have particle barbs! They have longslings with particle barbs!"

"Dear Helios," Vast replied then Alexis heard him calling to all commanders and members of the Order of Jex to retreat immediately.

Alexis felt a burning on his right calf and looked down to see his environmental suit torn open and his polybreen armor ripped to shreds. Vape gas seeped in and he could feel his skin start to bubble and melt. Alexis frantically tried to find his patch kit, but all he had on him was his long blades. Even his longsling had been lost somewhere on the beach.

Despite the intense pain that was growing in his leg, Alexis forced himself to his feet. He gripped his long blades and looked out at the longslingers in front of him.

"I know you," he whispered. "I do not know the men that wield you, but I know *you*. If this is how the man once known as the Dark Minor must die then so be it. I would not want it any other way. Bring me my death, longslings."

He lifted his arms out to the side and stood before the Thraens.

"*I am Alexis Tiermont the Fourth! Master of Station Aelon and its Primes! And today, I live forever!*"

The longslings all fired at once and Alexis welcomed them with open arms.

*

Mistress Alexis sat at the head of the long table in Station Aelon's great hall. The select stewards from the meeting that made up the royal council sat close to her, their eyes locked not on the aged monarch, but on the nearly broken member of the Order of Jex who stood before them all, still in his bloody polybreen armor.

"All of them?" Mistress Alexis asked. "The entire Order?"

"I am the last, Your Highness," Vast replied, his head held high. "I was coordinating the rear assault when Master Alexis gave the order to retreat. I was able to get a quarter of our men back onto the cutters before the Thraenish longslingers attacked the beach. We escaped only seconds before pure annihilation."

"And you could not save the others? Could not go back for them at all?" Steward Neem asked.

"There was no one to go back to, Steward Neem," Vast glared. "Do you know what a particle barb does to a man? A direct hit means nothing is left. The man is broken down to his molecules and all that remains is vapor and a stain."

"How did these Thraens get particle barbs?" Steward Kispee asked. "The longsling design is not a secret, but only Aelish manufacturers know how to make particle barbs."

"I will leave that investigation to this council," Vast said. "I am only here to report on our defeat. How the Thraens obtained the plans for particle barbs, or how they were able to train so many men to be longslingers without us knowing is not my job. That will have to be something that you accomplish, Steward Kispee. And I wish you all the greatest of luck with that."

"And what does that mean?" Kispee snapped.

"It means that someone here on the station assisted the Thraens with obtaining the knowledge and expertise needed to create their own regiments of longslingers," Vast replied. "That is a matter of espionage, not of military tactics. The meeting of stewards will have to flush out the traitor. I am going to go see my wife and children and retire to my estate house."

"You are quitting?" Neem asked, looking at the rest of the council. "Can we allow that? We will need someone to lead the counterassault on Thraen Prime."

"Counterassault?" Vast laughed. "There is no counterassault! Our main assault failed and we lost more men in one day than we have lost in the last few wars combined! Thraen Prime is gone, gentlemen. It is gone from our grasp forever. Or at least it is gone from my lifetime."

"Steward Vast, you have sworn an oath to defend and protect—" Neem started.

"That is enough," Mistress Alexis said. "Thank you, Vast. I will sign the papers for your retirement commission as soon as they reach me. Station Aelon thanks you for your years of service and for the many sacrifices you have made in that service. At some point I will like to visit and speak with you, but for now, please tend to yourself and your family. Be at peace on your estate, Vast. You deserve that peace."

"Thank you, Your Highness," Vast bowed. He glared at the council. "Gentlemen."

No one said a word as the old warrior left the great hall, the sound of the doors closing behind him a sad coda to a life of great honor and dedication.

"Let me make this clear," Mistress Alexis said. "We are done with Thraen Prime. We mined enough Vape from that land to hold us over until we can negotiate our lease holdings back, but at no time will Station Aelon engage in warfare to retake the entire prime. Am I clear?"

"Is that not something Master Richard should decide?" one of the other members of the council, Steward Gheort, asked. "We can table the discussion and decision until then."

"There is no discussion or decision to be tabled," Mistress Alexis replied. "I have made my decision and it is final."

"Mistress, please," Neem said. "We all respect your power as regent of Station Aelon, but with Master Alexis's death, the power now shifts to your only living child. Richard will be crowned master when he returns for his brother's funeral service. The choice of whether or not he avenges his brother's death is up to him."

"I think not, gentlemen," Mistress Alexis said. "Because Richard is not returning to Station Aelon. He is to remain where he is, on Station Klaerv, until I know the exact circumstances that led to our defeat on Helios."

The council stared at her, many with their mouths hanging open in shock and surprise.

"Mistress, what are you saying?" Kispee asked. "Do you suspect Minor Richard, your own son, of betraying Station Aelon? Do you think he is how the plans for the particle barb were relayed to Station Thraen?"

"Do I believe my son willingly betrayed Station Aelon? Helios no!" Mistress Alexis snapped. "But we all know that Richard is easily influenced and not always the most stable of personalities. I want all of the facts in front of me before I allow him to return. I must know that Station Aelon is safe for my son."

"Safe?" Neem asked. "How so?"

"Even in grief, I am forced to do all of the thinking," Mistress Alexis sighed. "Richard is more valuable to Station Klaerv alive than dead. With him in their clutches then he will be protected, for they will have the heir to the Aelish crown right where they want him. If he is to return here, and there are those amongst us that helped orchestrate the betrayal that has occurred, then Richard will become a liability. The betrayers will want Richard dead so he cannot point me in their direction."

"Can he not point you in their direction from Station Klaerv?" Gheort asked. "A simple communication can alert us to the traitors, if there be any aboard the station."

"I do not think my son even knows what he has done, if he is involved," Mistress Alexis said. "My gut is telling me he lives on, oblivious to any wrongdoing. He could not name names if he wanted to. He is safer on Klaerv."

"So is he to be crowned on Klaerv, then?" Neem asked. "How would that look to the System if we cannot bring our own master home?"

"He will not be crowned on Station Klaerv because he will not be crowned at all," Mistress Alexis said. "At least not until I die."

"Your Highness, you cannot hold the role of regent indefinitely," Gheort said. "At some point, for the stability of the station, you will have to step aside and allow your son to take his proper role."

"I will not be ruling as regent, steward," Mistress Alexis said as she stood up. "I will be ruling as Mistress of Station Aelon. As of this moment, I revoke my abdication. I am now the true monarch of Aelon, with all rights and privileges."

"Mistress!" Kispee shouted. "That cannot be done! It has never been done!"

"Look at me, Steward Kispee," Mistress Alexis frowned. "I am the embodiment of what has never been done. I am the first minoress in the System to be crowned. I am also the first living monarch to abdicate and hand the crown to an heir. Now I will be the first to retake the crown and watch over Station Aelon during this time of crisis. If I find that my son is ready to rule, then the crown will become his. If I do not feel he is up to the task, or he is under outside influences that could harm Station Aelon, then I will remain the mistress and monarch of this station until I die. It is that simple."

"It is far from that simple," Neem said. "This will have to be brought before The Way and the High Guardian. It will take his approval for your claim to be valid."

"No, it will not," Mistress Alexis said. "My son has died without an heir. The crown is to go to the next closest living relative. Traditionally, that would mean a younger sibling, but in this case, if you look at family structure, I am the next closest living relative. Believe me, gentlemen, I do not take this action in haste. I have already researched the issue thoroughly. Contact The Way, and contact the High Guardian, but it is well established that parents are closer than siblings. Just look at the land and title laws that grant you all your stewardships. You will see that I am right."

"We will look into this, mistress," Kispee said. "This issue is not settled."

"Nor would I expect it to be," Mistress Alexis said. "You would be remiss in your duties if you did not give it the council's full attention. In the meantime, I will return to my quarters and prepare the memorial service and funeral for my son. I will keep it humble and simple, for that is what my Alexis would have wanted. Good afternoon, gentlemen."

The council all rose as the mistress walked confidently around the long table and out of the great hall. But, once in the passageway, that confidence was lost instantly and Mistress Alexis had to will her feet to move in order to get her to her quarters and away from the ever present eyes of the station.

*

The knock at the door was quiet, but loud enough to wake Clerke from his light slumber in the chair by the Vape fire.

"Come," Clerke called out.

"I hope it is not too late," Mistress Alexis asked as she stepped into the parlor. "I would have sent word I was coming, but I did not want others to know where I was."

"No, no, please come in," Clerke said as he scrambled to reattach his prosthetic leg. "Forgive my appearance."

"I always forget you have that," Mistress Alexis smiled. "Even though I should not, since it is the result of my actions."

"Hardly, Your Highness," Clerke said "It was the result of men wanting more than what they could achieve. To say you did not warn them would be a gross misrepresentation of history."

"That is kind of you, Petro," Mistress Alexis replied. "Too kind for someone that has been shown nothing but heartbreak from this family." She nodded towards a second chair. "May I sit?"

"Yes, yes, of course," Clerke said, glancing at a clock on the wall. "Would you care for some tea? The servants have retired by now, but I am a man who knows how to make his own tea. I will gladly—"

"Stay where you are, Petro," Mistress Alexis said. "I do not need tea or any other refreshment. I just need the company of the only person on this station that knows the Teirmonts as they were."

"You and Richard still live, Your Highness," Clerke said. "There is no were; there is only are."

"Well, I hope that is true," Mistress Alexis smiled. "And call me Alexis, Petro. We are family."

"Your Highness, I would never presume to call—"

Mistress Alexis held up her hand. "I insist. I will make it an official decree, with deck criers announcing it in all the atriums, if I must."

"That will not be needed, Alexis," Clerke replied, bowing his head. "Thank you for the honor."

Mistress Alexis turned her attention to the Vape flames in the hearth before them. She stayed silent for several minutes, watching as they flicked and danced.

"What happened, Petro?" she finally asked, returning her attention to Clerke. "In the last days of my son's life, I know he confided in you. What happened that sent him down to Thraen Prime?"

"I think only Alexis knows the answer to that," Clerke replied. "His mind was all over the place. But, if I were to venture a guess, the main reason he went to fight again is because taking Thraen Prime was all that was left of his legacy. He had no heir, he had no wife, and Station Thraen was already lost. I believe he felt all of history pushing at his back and only a void ahead."

"So it was me," Mistress Alexis said. "I drove him to it."

"What? No, of course not," Clerke replied. "Why would you say that?"

"I was the first mistress crowned," Mistress Alexis shrugged. "I was a warrior from a long line of Teirmont warriors. He had to live up to that."

"No, he had to live up to himself," Clerke countered. "Alexis was a gentle soul. His core being was one of compassion. He fought for Station Aelon again and again, taking Thraen Prime, taking Station Thraen, but neither of those things were for him. The prime was while serving you and the station was out of intense grief for his dead wife and daughter."

Clerke stood up and walked to a side table.

"I am pouring a drink," he said. "Would you like one?"

"Well, since you are already going to the trouble," Mistress Alexis replied. "And you might as well bring the bottle."

"That is my intention," Clerke said as he returned with the drinks. "Here you go."

"Thank you," Mistress Alexis said.

"To continue," Clerke said, holding his drink in both hands, rolling the glass the back and forth in his palms. "My belief is that Alexis will be remembered for the foundation he created in Natalie's name. He hid it behind her memory, but of all his accomplishments, that is the one that most closely reflects who he was inside. In another life he would have been a great artist. He had that type of charisma that could hold the attention of so many."

"A bard like you, perhaps?" Mistress Alexis asked.

"I assume that is a joke," Clerke laughed. "Because the man could not sing."

"No, he could not," Mistress Alexis smiled. "Perhaps a painter, like his sister."

"Perhaps," Clerke nodded. "But I see him with something more solid. A metalsmith of sorts. His connection to the longsling tells me he understood that craft on a cellular level."

"That could be," Mistress Alexis said. "That would have been nice to see. Maybe one day a master, or mistress, will feel free enough to express themselves that way. The foundation is flourishing, so perhaps there will be a time when artistry and leadership can be excepted as going hand in hand."

"It would be a dream come true," Clerke said. He studied the mistress for a second. "Are you going to tell me why you are really here, Alexis? I know you need someone to speak with about your pain, and about Alexis's motivations, but I have known you a very long time and your face is telling me you have a very specific agenda. What is it?"

"You have heard I am taking back the crown, yes?" she asked.

"Hard not to hear news such as that," Clerke said. "Will you be making an official announcement?"

"I will, but not until after Alexis's service," Mistress Alexis replied. "I want the focus on him and not me."

"Not an easy task," Clerke chuckled. "You tend to take the focus whether you want to or not."

"More times it is not," Mistress Alexis replied. "Yet I constantly betray myself and go against my own wishes."

"I completely understand," Clerke said. "My performing days are over, but I cannot help but crave the attention whenever I stand in front of a group of people."

"Yes, well, it is those performing days I want to speak to you about," Mistress Alexis said. "There was a time, back when you first met my daughter, that I believe my son found someone he could love. Do you know of which time I am speaking of?"

"How close to when Natalie and I first met?" Clerke asked. "Those days were a whirlwind of passion and excitement for me, so I am afraid the details might be a bit hazier than I would like to admit."

"The very first night you performed for Alexis," Mistress Alexis explained. "That was the first night Natalie took you as hers."

"Yes, that is an excellent way of putting it," Clerke said. He finished his drink and refilled the glass, topping off Mistress Alexis's as well. "It was quite a role reversal for me. You seem to know a good deal about this time in my life?"

"I was mistress," Mistress Alexis grinned. "I knew a great deal about everyone in my children's lives."

"Of course," Clerke chuckled.

"Now, if I remember correctly, my sources said Alexis disappeared for close to a week after that night," Mistress Alexis said. "There were many rumors floating about the station and the prime afterwards, but the one that kept reaching my ears was that he had found a woman. The story is either she left him or he came to his senses and realized that perhaps her role, or profession, was not one the station would accept."

"Ah, yes, I know exactly the woman you are speaking of," Clerke said. "And the decision to leave was hers, not his, I believe. It close to killed him when she disappeared. He tried to find her, but being in the profession she was, as you say, she had enough connections in the darker areas of Aelish life to keep even the master's eyes from finding her."

"Or she left the prime altogether," Mistress Alexis said. "That could be."

"Yes, perhaps," Clerke said. "Alexis investigated every avenue he could and found no evidence of her on the prime. But he also did not find evidence of her leaving Helios. But, like I said, she lived in the darker areas of life. Being from the Lower Decks, I know there are ways to stay hidden, even with a master looking for you."

"Why would a woman such as that leave at all?" Mistress Alexis asked. "She had my son by the balls, literally, and yet she throws that all away and goes into hiding. It makes no sense."

"Love rarely does," Clerke replied. "And that could be the simplest answer. She may have started out trying to trap Alexis, but after meeting him and being with him, she found, just like we all did, that he was very real. If she had feelings for him then she could have left to save him any embarrassment or scandal. The truth is, that Alexis could never have married a whore, but he would have fought tooth and nail to try. Maybe even have given up his title for her."

"Maybe," Mistress Alexis said. "Which would not have benefited either of them."

"No, it would not have," Clerke said. He stifled a yawn and shook his head. "My apologies, Alexis. I think I may need to make that tea after all."

"No, Petro, do not bother," Mistress Alexis said as she stood up. "I will go now. You need your rest."

"As do you," Clerke said. "You have some very big days ahead of you."

"That is true," Mistress Alexis replied. "Are your choirs ready to perform at the service?"

"They are," Clerke nodded, standing as well. He walked her to the door and smiled. "I have picked out some of Alexis's favorite songs for them to sing."

"Wonderful, Petro, thank you," Mistress Alexis said. She leaned in and hugged him then stepped back quickly. "I had better go before I start to cry. I've held it well enough, but I am afraid even my strength is not large enough to keep the tears at bay."

"Understood," Clerke said.

"Oh, and Petro?" she asked. "I expect you to sit next to me at the service."

"That is quite the honor, Alexis, but I will be helping coordinate the choirs and other presentations from the foundation," Clerke replied.

"Delegate, Petro, delegate," Mistress Alexis said. "Because I am not taking no for an answer." She turned and walked out the door then stopped and looked back at Clerke. "One last thing, I promise."

"Anything," Clerke replied.

"You wouldn't happen to be able to recollect that woman's name, would you?" she asked. "Alexis's woman that could have been?"

"That I certainly can do," Clerke laughed. "It was a name no Aelon could forget. Breen. He said her name was Breen."

"Breen," Mistress Alexis smiled. "Of course it was. Good night, Petro."

"Good night, Alexis," Clerke said and closed the door behind her.

He walked back to his chair and sat down. He removed his prosthetic leg and sighed as he set it in the other chair. His eyes focused on the Vape flames.

"Now, where were we?" he whispered as his eyes slowly closed.

In seconds he was snoring quietly, memories of days long since past rising from his subconscious to both warm and haunt him.

*

"Breen! Darling, it is so wonderful to see you!" the woman cried as she approached the market stall. The woman's hand went to the first rack and she quickly started browsing the assortment of skirts and blouses that hung there. "You are quite lucky to get such a great spot in the atrium today!"

"The deck boss contacted me and said it was my turn to move to the first row," Breen replied. "It was about time since I have been a part of this market for nearly two decades now."

"Yet you haven't aged a day," the woman said. "I swear that you turn the heads of men half your age every time you set up your stall. Those long legs and those bright green eyes of yours. You make an old woman jealous."

"Well, that is kind of you, Zonna," Breen replied. "But I think you exaggerate. If any heads are turning this way, they are young and female and they are looking at my boy."

"Where is your son today?" Zonna asked, looking around the other racks and into the back of the stall. "He shouldn't leave his mother to work here all by herself."

"He's off fetching inventory from our cabin," Breen replied. "I have quite a few new trousers made and a few tunics and doublets."

"Doublets? Oh, my husband detests those things," Zona laughed. "But the fashion is what the fashion is."

"And is there any particular fashion you are looking for today, Zonna?" Breen asked. "Or are you just browsing?"

"Browsing, I'm afraid," Zonna responded. "Kimmel doesn't get paid until the end of the month."

"That is what I am hearing from everyone," Breen sighed. "I may have finally landed a perfect location, but it means nothing if passengers don't have credits to spend."

"So very true," Zonna said then pulled a large blouse from one of the racks. "Is there any way I could convince you to hold this for me until payday?"

"I would love to, Zonna, but that is a popular pattern," Breen replied. "If I do make a sale today it will probably be that blouse."

"You cheeky little conniver," Zonna laughed, fishing out a couple of credits from her purse. "Is this enough to hold it then?"

"That is enough to hold that blouse and perhaps the skirt that matches," Breen grinned. "You wouldn't want a blouse without its skirt, would you?"

"You know your business, alright," Zonna responded, taking the matching skirt off the rack as well. "Hold these both and I'll be back with the rest of the credits next week."

Breen took the two garments and folded them carefully then set them aside. "They are yours and I will let no one touch them."

"You are such a dear," Zonna said then waved at someone across the market. "Oh, I better go. My sister is buying lunch today and I am not going to miss that."

"Eat well, Zonna," Breen called after the woman. "See you next week."

Breen set about switching out inventory from the racks, moving the flashier items to the front to catch the eyes of passersby. She nodded hello to many that walked by, but realized quickly that it was not to be a day of great sales. After an hour or so she went to the back of the stall and sat down, letting out a long sigh.

"Business that good?" a man asked as he walked into the stall.

"Steward Wexxon, what a surprise," Breen said as she instantly got back to her feet. "I was just having a sit down between the rushes."

"Were you then?" Steward Wexxon laughed. "Had a bunch of sales during these rushes, did you? I'm amazed you still have inventory left."

"Don't tease," Breen smirked. "It is hard enough being a single woman struggling to make ends meet. I do not need a noble of your stature mocking me."

"I would never mock a woman of your beauty, Passengeress Breen," Wexxon said. "And a single woman such as you would not need to struggle if she was no longer single. Why haven't you been snatched up yet?"

"I do not have the time for men, steward," Breen replied. "I work long hours here at the stall and even longer hours sewing at night. Plus, I have had a son to raise on my own. The idea of men will have to wait until my boy is out of the cabin."

"Well, hopefully your new location in the atrium market will increase sales enough for you to hire an assistant," Wexxon said. "Then you will have the time for men. At least, that was my intention."

"Your intention?" Breen asked. "How do you mean?"

"Do you think Deck Boss Gleever just gave you this spot out of the kindness of his heart?" Wexxon laughed. "He may administrate this deck for me beautifully, but I am keenly aware that the man may not actually possess a heart."

"You did this?" Breen asked, her eyes narrowing. "Why would you do that for me?"

"Passengeress Breen, are my intentions not obvious?" Wexxon replied. "I come by your stall every chance I get."

"Yet you never purchase anything for yourself," Breen said. "A couple of things for your nieces before Last Meal, but nothing for you. I just assumed you liked to speak to all the atrium merchants."

"I never purchase anything because I never want you to feel obligated," Wexxon replied. "I do not want you to believe I am buying your affections."

"This new location says the opposite of that," Breen said, irritated.

"You earned this location, Passengeress Breen," Wexxon said sharply. "And do not let anyone tell you otherwise. Your garments are amongst the finest in my sectors. Your talent and business acumen is why you have this location."

"Well...thank you then," Breen replied. "I apologize for sounding harsh."

"I expect nothing less," Wexxon said. "A woman of your character should always stand up for herself and her talents."

"That is very appreciated, steward...Wait, did you say sectors?" Breen asked.

"I did," Wexxon smiled. "I hoped you would catch that. With Mistress Alexis taking the crown again, she has cleaned out the royal council and appointed new members. I am lucky enough to be counted amongst those new appointees and with that privilege comes the addition of a new sector. I believe it belonged to the late Steward Holsten, Helios rest the patriot's soul."

"Well, congratulations, Steward Wexxon," Breen said and curtsied. "Now your presence is even more of an honor."

"Mother? Are you being bothered by this man?"

"There he is," Steward Wexxon laughed, extending his hand. "I was afraid you'd abandoned your mother today."

The young man, in his early twenties, unbelievably tall with golden blond hair and shining blue eyes, walked over to the steward and shook eagerly.

"Steward Wexxon, it is an honor, as always," the young man replied.

"My Helios, have you stopped growing yet?" Wexxon laughed as he looked up at the young man that towered over him. "You have your mother's height, that's for sure."

"He has his father's as well," Breen said. "Helios rest his soul."

"Ah, yes, a shame he passed before he could meet his son," Wexxon frowned. He clapped his hands together. "My what a dreary note to end a meeting on, but end it must. I have to attend to business in Middle Deck Twenty-Six. Their atrium market does not have quite the organization as this one. Apparently the deck boss can't pull his head out of the gelberry wine barrels and I may be in need of a replacement." He leaned in and winked. "But that is between you and me."

"Of course," Breen smiled. "Lips are sealed."

"Then good day to you, Passengeress Breen," Steward Wexxon bowed. "I would like to continue our discussion at a later date. Perhaps in three days? I will be back on this deck then. Set aside some time for me?"

Breen blushed fully and pursed her lips. "If I am not occupied with customers," she replied.

"No, I wouldn't want to interrupt business," Wexxon smiled then nodded to the young man. "A pleasure to see you again, Alexis."

"And you as well, steward." The young man, Alexis, bowed. "I hope your business on Deck Twenty-Six is not too tedious.

"Helios, I hope that as well," Wexxon chuckled as he walked off.

Breen watched the man go then turned to see her son smiling down at her.

"What?" she asked.

"He is completely infatuated with you," Alexis grinned. "You should consider it."

"Consider what?" Breen asked, pretending to busy herself with looking through the crates of trousers Alexis had just brought to the stall. "There is nothing to consider."

"Mother, he is a widower without children," Alexis said. "You are a single woman with a grown son."

"And a widow I shall remain," Breen said. "There was one man for me and that was your father."

"Who left before I was born," Alexis insisted. "I am grown now and you should relax and enjoy life."

He leaned down and took his mother's hands away from her invented task.

"You must listen to me," Alexis said. "Life is too short. I am old enough to watch the stall. You should seriously consider taking Steward Wexxon up on his overtures. He is a good man, Mother. He will give you a good life. A life you deserve after slaving away to raise me."

"Oh, and how do you know it will be such a good life?" Breen asked. "You never truly know a person's future, Alexis. Believe me."

"That is true," Alexis nodded as he leaned down and kissed the top of his mother's head. "But I believe your future is for more than this stall. Call it a hunch. Call it a feeling."

He hugged her tight and looked out at the hustle and bustle of the atrium market.

"You could even call it fate."

ABOUT THE AUTHOR

Jake Bible, novelist, short story writer, independent screenwriter, podcaster, and inventor of the Drabble Novel, has entertained thousands with his horror and sci/fi tales. He reaches audiences of all ages with his uncanny ability to write a wide range of characters and genres.

Jake is the author of the bestselling Z-Burbia series set in Asheville, NC, the Apex Trilogy (*DEAD MECH*, *The Americans*, *Metal and Ash*) and the Mega series for Severed Press, as well as the YA zombie novel, *Little Dead Man* and the Teen horror novel, *Intentional Haunting*, the ScareScapes series, and the Reign of Four series for Permuted Press.

Find Jake at jakebible.com. Join him on Twitter @jakebible and find him on Facebook.